FAMILY JEWELS

THE BOYARS

Family Jewels

By Petru Dumitriu

Translated from the French

BY EDWARD HYAMS

in consultation with

Princess Anne-Marie Callimachi

PANTHEON BOOKS

TRANSLATOR'S NOTE

Since the Eastern European historical and political background is largely unfamiliar to the Western reader, a few words of explanation seem to be called for.

The country known today as Rumania, originally a Roman province and later abandoned to Germanic and Eastern tribes (Goths, Huns, and Tartars), remained for long one of the main battlefields of Europe. In the fifteenth century, the two principalities known today as Rumania—Moldavia and Wallachia—fell under the Turkish yoke and had to refer to the Sultan for validation of the nationally elected princes.

By the middle of the nineteenth century, the grip of Turkey on the European vassals slackened, as a result of constant harassing interference from Russia. On May 22, 1858, after many preliminary parleys, Rumania was given her first modern constitution at the Conference of Paris, under the name of "The United Principalities of Moldavia and Wallachia."

The Rumanians chose as their prince a practically unknown man of about forty: Colonel Alexander Ion Couza. He took the name of Alexander Ion I and settled in Bucharest, chosen as the capital. Although Couza had liberal leanings, a right-wing majority in the newly formed Parliament forced upon him the premiership of the Conservative leader, Barbu Catargiu, a great boyar, a remarkable orator, but also a bitter reactionary (in fact, the Vogoride of this novel, whose fate he shared). Later, the Rumanians invited a Hohenzollern prince to become their constitutional king, an honor which he accepted, taking the name of Carol I.

Apart from a few princely families, the Rumanian boyars bore no titles of nobility, for the Turkish conquest prevented the development of feudalism along European lines. The upper class spoke

Greek among themselves; later, like the Russian upper class, French. But Rumanian was coming in among them at the time of Dumitriu's story, and Rumanian was, of course, the language of the ordinary people. The Rumanian Domnul, Doamna, Domnisoara may be taken to mean roughly Lord, Lady, Little Lady—rather like Monsieur, Madame, Mademoiselle in French; but in the same way as in French, these words lost much of their ring of nobility and became commonly used terms of address like Mr., Mrs., and Miss. They were then applied by courtesy to everyone, and not only to the persons entitled to them by rank. They have here been translated by their French equivalents, because whereas the French nobility were in fact so addressed (a countess could be Madame de —), Mr., Mrs., and Miss are exclusively bourgeois.

CONTENTS

PART ONE

Davida

I

The Coziano family was first recorded in the cadastral registers in the time of Prince Constantine Brancovan. The name Coziano has no connection with the monastery of Cozia, that famous cloister on the banks of the River Olt at the foot of the mountains, but derives from a vast estate, then belonging to the Cozianos, situated in the hill country between Bucharest and Tîrgoviste. Deeds dating from that time refer to a certain Davida and Grecea Coziano; then to others, their issue, successive lords of Cozia, who enlarged this estate by the purchase of adjacent domains, Gîrla, Slobozia Veche, Dîrdori, and other properties. In addition, their descendants bought land in the plain, particularly at Tataru, where they settled families of Bulgarian peasants.

All that took place much later, however, at the time when the rescripts of the reigning princes Mavrocordato and Callimachi were couched in the consecrated form: *"We . . . Voivode by the grace of God, Hospodar of Wallachia . . ."* and concluded with *"This is what the Master has written."* Under the seal of the Hospodar were affixed the signatures of all the high dignitaries. Among these names, written in a markedly angular hand, numerous documents bear those of Sherban Coziano, the *serdar,* or cavalry commander, and of Alexander Coziano, the *logothete,* or Chancellor of the Principality, as well as that of Lascarake Coziano, who was also *logothete* in his day. From a very tender age, all Cozianos were princely *mumbachirs,* or pages at court. One of them took holy orders and became Bishop Neofit of Rîmnic and Noul Severin. As for the daughters of the Coziano family, they were married to scions of noble houses—the sons of the Villaras or younger brothers in the Pîrscoveano and Vacaresco families. Eventually, by the reign of Prince Soutzo, the Cozianos emerge as second and third cousins of the Gradisteanos, Grecianos, and Florescos.

In 1848, fleeing from the revolution, the *paharnic,* or Grand Cupbearer, Manolake Coziano, took refuge at Brasov with his eldest son, Alexander, his daughter-in-law, Sophia, and their young children. Later he returned and continued to manage his estates, but lived in constant fear of revolution and the distribution of his land among the peasants. At his death, Manolake Coziano left behind him a reputation for unprecedented avarice. But he also left Cozia and Gîrla the richer by three thousand acres each, Dîrdori by eight thousand, and the remaining lands proportionately enlarged. Such was the extent of the accumulated property, in fact, that in 1850 his son Alexander saw fit to have his house in Culmea Veche Street pulled down and the old chestnut trees in the courtyard felled, in order to build a new mansion in keeping with his immense fortune, which was well known to English importers who had agencies in Danubian ports.

This mansion, still standing to this day, stood at the far end of a paved courtyard enclosed by tall iron railings with gilded spikes. On either side of the two wrought-iron gates were ornate lampposts decorated with wrought-iron flowers and foliage. Carriages drove in at one gate and out at the other; they stopped at the foot of a curved flight of steps which led up to the main entrance to this two-storied mansion. Beyond the hall, a few steps led into the large drawing room whose diamond-paned French windows reached almost the full height of the room and were surmounted by arches in the French style. Two smaller drawing rooms opened off on one side, and on the other, a dining room and a library—for Alexander Coziano prided himself on his taste for belles-lettres. Having studied in Paris, he had acquired, mostly as a result of book learning, a vanity commensurate with his father's avarice. It was this vanity which had driven him to cover the walls of his house with a series of apocryphal portraits representing the *serdars, logothetes,* and bishops of his family, painted by Theodor Aman.

This same vanity had led him to fill the large drawing room with sofas and armchairs with curved legs and upholstery of Aubusson tapestry, the carved wood frames being covered with a layer of gold obtained by melting down louis d'or and ducats. Again, his vanity had persuaded him to crowd the room with rosewood cabinets inlaid with rare materials in floral and other fanciful designs; to hang three gigantic crystal chandeliers from the ceiling; and to place in one corner of the huge room a harp and a strangely shaped piano—a sort of chest with legs in the form of an X—a model which had been discontinued after this isolated attempt by its maker, whose name, *Gaveau: Fournisseur de S.M. l'Empereur,* was engraved on the keyboard cover. The walls of the drawing room were hung with flowered silks and those of the smaller drawing rooms with velvet; the library walls were lined with books and those of the dining room paneled in oak. The kitchen was placed beyond the courtyard, near the servants' quarters and alongside the stables and coach house; it consisted of whitewashed sheds with irregularly shingled roofs, the last vestiges of the original house.

One evening in the early spring of 1862 a number of carriages were waiting on the far side of Culmea Veche Street. The horses snorted and fidgeted; their coachmen were drinking mulled wine in the kitchen; the house's tall windows glittered. The sky was red on the horizon, but deep blue overhead; a few stars were already visible. A keen wind was blowing through the dry branches of the trees bordering the street. But inside the house, in the drawing rooms, the heat from the stoves shimmered and the ladies were wearing *décolleté* dresses.

That evening most of Sophia Coziano's visitors happened to be women. M. Coziano spent a quarter of an hour with the ladies and then, taking M. Lascar Lascari by the arm, led him out of the brilliantly illuminated drawing room without a word. Lascari was a deputy for a constituency down in the plain. The two men walked through one of the small drawing rooms, lit only by a single taper, and passed into the other, the last room on that side of the house. It was in total darkness, except for a rectangle of yellow light cast on the floor and one wall by the open doorway, which transmitted the brilliance of the main drawing room from beyond the adjoining room. In that rectangle of light a large dark-green armchair was discernible, and beside it a table of varnished wood decorated at the four corners with garlands of roses and cupids in gilded bronze. Beyond was the faint reflection of a gilded Louis Seize chair. As they entered the room, both men perceived a slight movement.

"Who is there?" Coziano asked.

"It's me, Florica, your lordship," a rather hoarse feminine voice hastened to reply. "I kiss your lordship's hands."

"So you've been asleep in here? Come, light the lamp."

Coziano halted on the threshold, still holding Lascari by the arm, and waited. A tiny woman emerged from the shadows and went swiftly past them, head bent and hands crossed on her chest. Her head was covered by a black kerchief and she wore a skirt gathered in at the waist and made of some gleaming, dark-blue material. Lascari tried—unsuccessfully—to see her face. After a few moments the woman returned carrying a candle, and knelt to insert the flame under the shade of a lamp. Her face emerged suddenly from the darkness. Florica was still young. Beneath heavy eyelids, her half-closed eyes appeared sea-green. Her cheeks were smooth and rather sallow. Her mouth was smiling, revealing several teeth and the gaps of those she had lost. The half-closed green eyes, the smile, the decayed teeth, all combined to give Florica a look of animal cunning.

The gypsy rose in a single lithe movement, and went away with lowered head, avoiding the two men's eyes. Lascari put out his hand and pinched her bottom as she passed. Florica continued on her way, saying nothing.

"What did you say her name was?" Lascari asked.

"Florica."

"Not bad."

The comment was in French. Coziano ignored it. He opened
out the table with the cupids to display its green baize card-top,
pulled open a drawer, and took out a pack of cards. Lascari put
an arm around his shoulders. The display of friendship toward
his host and the almost affectionate familiarity with which he addressed him had about them something at once oily and cloying.
His smile disclosed dirty teeth, and the pallid face with its thick
brown side whiskers, the thinning, unkempt hair through which
gleamed patches of incipient baldness—everything about the man
suggested a piece of white cheese which had sprouted hair. Nobody
would have been surprised had Lascar Lascari smelled of cheese;
but his creased frock coat, badly tied silk cravat, dirty shirt, and
dandruff-powdered shoulders merely smelled strongly of coffee and
good Turkish tobacco. Lascar Lascari had a large fortune; for all
his unwashed, unbrushed appearance, he was forever jingling the
gold coins which he carried in his pockets but which nobody ever
saw.

He smiled affectionately, showing all his dirty teeth. "My dear
Alexander, why not confide in me as in a brother?" Then he
added, lowering his eyes and with an air of exaggerated casualness,
"They tell me you've been making hay among the peasant girls
of Cozia. . . ."

Coziano shrugged. He was a thickset, heavily built man, round-
shouldered, with a face the color of clay, dull eyes, and a slack
mouth. In his young days in Paris an astrologer had told him that
he had been born under the evil influence of Saturn. Coziano
suffered with his liver, but that did not stop him from being a
glutton and a heavy drinker. As a result, he was invariably morose,
discontented with humanity in general and himself in particular.
Beneath his taciturnity, he was forever brooding on his own barely
controlled, chronic rage. His melancholy only yielded a little when
he was in the country and could spend the whole day walking over
the fields with his gun and his dog.

He turned toward Lascari and demanded sharply, "What of it?
I really see no connection——"

"Now don't get angry," Lascari murmured, lifting the skirts of his frock coat to avoid sitting on them. "I've told you, as a friend, what people are saying, to put you on your guard."

Coziano followed the other's example and sat down at the card table. He began to shuffle the pack.

"Florica's a filthy beast," he said, "a whore and a poisoner. Take a card, Lascar."

"Who's she poisoned? I've drawn a queen."

"I had a coachman, in the country; she let him do what he liked with her. . . . A ten. Your deal, Lascar. . . . He cheated her with some other gypsy. Then one day he died, writhing in agony with his belly on fire and roaring with pain. People said Florica had poisoned him. You've only to look at her to feel convinced of it. But you can't know. Sophia protects her—she brought her to town so that her rival wouldn't kill her. The fact is, Sophia's too easy with her women."

He fell silent, and thenceforth gave all his attention to the cards. From the drawing room came the sound of laughter; at times a man's ringing, metallic voice rose above the rest.

"Hear our orator?" Lascari said, laughing. He played a seven. Coziano did not even smile; with a bitter, spiteful look he covered the seven with an eight. He had won the hand. Lascar was already regretting the louis he was about to lose. He stole a sly glance at Coziano—the tormented, sickly face set in that expression of chronic fury peculiar to the liverish. Lascar was well aware that he had it in his power to strike at the most sensitive spot and inflict cruel pain, but it was not enough that he had it in his power: he felt the need to exact vengeance for the gold coin he was about to lose. When the metallic voice rang out in the drawing room, Lascar muttered, as if he were thinking aloud, "Yes, indeed; Madame Coziano is certainly very kind. . . ."

Then, without any apparent connection, he observed noncommittally, "You're very friendly with Sherban, aren't you? Isn't that his voice?"

"Yes, he's here all right," Coziano said, without raising his eyes from the cards.

"You are old friends?" Lascar asked, as if the question were of no importance and he was simply asking it for the sake of saying something. He played a card: a seven. This time Coziano covered it with a ten.

"He and Sophia are cousins."

"Oh! I see," Lascar said, laughing. "So he's really a relative of your wife's."

He placed a card on the table. What he had just said was quite silly, but he had said it deliberately. What meaning could be attached to the words "Oh! I see" and "So he's really a relative of your wife's"? They could have any meaning one cared to give them—or none. For a moment Coziano, cards in hand, seemed struck dumb. Then he played a card ill-advisedly. Lascar slapped a ten on his opponent's seven. Coziano's game began to deteriorate. A little later Lascar said, "He's been coming here quite a lot lately, hasn't he?"

"Yes," Coziano said, curtly, icily; again he played the wrong card. A few minutes later Lascar had won the game and pocketed with obvious satisfaction the louis d'or which Coziano threw onto the green baize. For a moment Coziano stood grasping the edges of the table with both hands, frowning, with the concentration of a man who suddenly feels a sharp, unexpected pain.

"One more hand?" Lascar suggested.

"No."

"Oh, come, you must have a return game, my dear fellow!" There was a chance that he might take another couple of louis off Coziano.

"No," Coziano said, "I give up. I don't feel well. I think I shall go and lie down for a while."

"Are you ill?" Lascar was all anxiety, all solicitude. He tried to draw nearer to Coziano, to touch him, run his hands over him, but Coziano gently warded him off.

"It's nothing. I shall go and lie down for a little. Go and keep the ladies company, Lascar."

"I'm staying here with you, my dear Alexander. I'm not going to let you brood all alone," Lascar said with feigned kindness.

"No, no, just leave me, I'll be better alone," Coziano insisted, almost beside himself with distress.

"All right, all right, I'm going. Would you like me to send someone to you? Do you need anything?"

"Nothing. I need nothing and nobody," Coziano said abruptly, blowing out the lamp. He groped his way in the dark toward a divan covered with a bearskin, lay down, snatched furiously at his cravat to bare his throat, and remained there in the darkness, sweating with anger.

Meanwhile Lascar Lascari had left the gloomy little room, walked with deliberation across the second small drawing room, and jingling the money in his pocket, to which a new gold piece had just been added, entered the great drawing room. His first glance was for Sophia Coziano, who was sitting in an armchair beside the stove; in the same look he was able to take in Sherban Vogoride standing beside her, his back to the tiled stove which was decorated with little flowers in the Viennese fashion of about 1830. Vogoride was talking loudly, very sure of himself, and with that dominating presence which made him so formidable at political meetings. Sophia Coziano sat looking up at him with a tranquil rapture which Lascari considered expressive of something more than the satisfaction of a friend.

Sophia Coziano was in her late thirties and beginning to put on weight. She had a white skin, well-marked eyebrows, black eyes with a gentle expression, and a pink-and-white complexion. Her mauve taffeta dress, its sleeves and low neckline embellished with lace, flared out over her hips in the style made fashionable in Europe by the Empress Eugénie; the bright folds of her crinoline covered the whole of the huge armchair, and her plump, well-rounded arms, softly curved shoulders, and statuesque neck rose from the corsage of her dress like a flower from its calyx. Her hair fell about her temples and the nape of her neck in soft curls that were also reminiscent of Eugénie de Montijo. Sophia moved indolently, and her languid gestures were in perfect harmony with the full roundedness of her whole plump, ripely attractive person.

Sherban Vogoride affected to be quite insensible to the perpetual invitation of her bearing, but Lascari knew him too well not to conclude, from his very indifference, that he was already her lover. Sherban was a man of insatiable desires and made no effort to hide them, except as a means to their more certain and better satisfaction.

Sherban was the nephew of Nicolai Vogoride, the *caïmacam*, Regent of the Principality. The *caïmacam's* wife, Coca Konaki (daughter of the *logothete* Konaki, the poet), had settled abroad after her husband's death. Around 1860 Sherban was therefore the last of the Vogorides to be living in the principality, where he owned vast estates inherited from his father, the Regent's brother. He was about forty-five, tall, broad-shouldered, and beginning to run to fat, but he was still a fine figure of a man in his well-cut frock coat and white waistcoat, which concealed a corset. He had placed his silk hat on the floor beside him and carelessly thrown his gloves into it. He bore himself very erect, and his head was held high by a starched collar and black cravat. He wore his hair rather short and brushed forward in a sort of windswept effect copied from Chateaubriand, whom he had seen in Paris in his youth. But he bore little resemblance to that romantic poet-statesman. His face was big and fleshy, with a powerful nose, thick eyebrows, red lips, and piercing, light-blue eyes. He played constantly with a monocle attached to his buttonhole by a ribbon, occasionally screwing it into his eye to cast a colorless and contemptuous glance at anyone who happened to displease him: it was a look which could wither.

"How did you answer them, Sherban?" Sophia Coziano asked.

He gave a slight shrug and said, laughing, "No point in repeating it—I'm no orator except when those scoundrels make me angry. And I can assure you I was furious!"

The ladies all burst into laughter.

"Come now, tell us about it," the old Princess Sturza said in a wheedling tone. She was the wife of the *vornic,* the Minister of the Interior. Now she clasped both hands on the ivory knob of her stick, and added, "What happened exactly? The whole town is talking of nothing else."

Vogoride let them cajole him a little, laughingly resisting their pleas, but without hypocrisy; he was too proud to be vain. Lascar Lascari came and stood beside him.

"Tell them, my dear fellow. If you don't I will, and the story will lose all its flavor."

"Very well then," Vogoride said. "When I saw them howling like a pack of mad dogs against the boyars, I was on my feet in a flash. But I didn't go up to the tribune; I spoke from my place on the Government front bench. I turned to the left and shouted at them: 'Gentlemen! God told the prophet Jonah that if there was but one just man in the city, He would grant His forgiveness. But you cannot forgive the boyars even when you find men worthy of esteem among them. Of course, you are not gods—only men. And what men!' "

He had spoken in that thundering, metallic voice which filled every corner of the Chamber of Deputies, and his final words— "And what men!"—had been uttered with such joyful and deadly insolence that all the ladies began clapping and giving little cries of admiration, exactly as the Conservative deputies had done during the afternoon session of the Chamber.

Lascar, raising his voice, exclaimed, "What could they say, the scum! Your intervention was perfectly in accord with parliamentary usage. It was only your manner that wasn't!"

As he spoke he had cast a look around the circle of faces, all radiant with pleasure, his eyes lingering on Sophia Coziano's expression of devotion and the tender smile with which she responded to Sherban Vogoride's loud shout of laughter. He, all good nature, was enjoying the witticism as if it had been another's. In a corner, Sophia's daughter Davida sat leaning on the piano. She was a girl of seventeen, slight, even thin, with jet-black hair. There was a strange intensity in the way she was staring at Sherban Vogoride; it was almost as if she were looking at a creature of some unknown species, fantastic and incomprehensible. Lascar Lascari crossed the room to her, while in the circle of chairs about the stove conversation was resumed, still dominated by Vogoride's laughter and by the masculine voice of the *vornic* Sturza's aged wife, who was saying, "Well done, Sherban, my dear boy! We could do with more men like you. You were wonderful—come here, I must give you a kiss!"

Lascari idly turned over the music which lay untidily on the piano, while he watched the girl out of the corner of his eye. Davida was so absorbed in her contemplation of Vogoride that she did not even notice him. Her nose was slightly aquiline, her full mouth rather pale; her black eyes were darkened by the shadow of long, curved lashes, and her hair, gathered into a large chignon, had a bluish sheen. Davida still retained the wildness of the awkward age. Quite motionless, she held aloof from her mother's guests, staring at Sherban Vogoride. With his usual familiarity, Lascari drew her toward him, which enabled him to stroke her still childishly thin arm. Involuntarily, his hand closed on it. Davida did not even notice.

"Well, what do you think of it all?" Lascar asked her.

The girl started and looked at him fiercely, almost hostilely. "Think of what?"

"Why, of our good friend Sherban," Lascar replied, with a little sniggering laugh which exposed his greenish teeth. The girl turned her head away, her eyes still fixed on the circle of guests, and said, "He is our greatest statesman."

She spoke with such intensity that she had the air of enunciating life's supreme truth. Lascar Lascari grimaced amusedly.

"I am delighted to find you so interested in politics."

The girl raised her head with a movement of regal pride. "Papa says it is the duty of every girl of good family."

Lascari laughed and tried to take her arm again. "Why, in that case, we must have a little talk, eh? Thrash out certain topics . . ."

Davida firmly disengaged her arm and said solemnly, "If that's what you want, you can talk to me as if I were a man."

Lascari burst out laughing; her simplicity, her untamed adolescence, aroused his desire. He put his arm around the girl's shoulders in an ostensibly fatherly gesture, and drew her to him. "You'll have to marry a politician," he said. Davida turned pale and murmured through dry lips, "I shall."

Lascari was disturbed; he went on, only half joking now: "You had better not say so in front of politicians, or one of us will be asking your hand in marriage before you can turn around."

He seized the girl's hand, but at that moment Sherban Vogoride's deep voice called from across the room, "Come over here, my dear Lascari. Tell these ladies what the scoundrels want of us. Come along, come along!" And drawing him into the circle of ladies, Vogoride called him to witness: "They want to steal our land, give nothing in exchange, and divide it among the peasants. Then, when the peasants need capital, the scoundrels will get their hands on the land themselves by lending money through their banks. That's what they want! And they seem to imagine we shall allow ourselves to be stripped!"

"If it weren't for you," Lascari said, "I really don't see who would stop them. The Prince is all for reform and so is Kogalniceano; Rosetti, Ionesco, Bratiano, all the small fry have taken it into their heads to despoil us. . . ."

The phrases spouted forth spontaneously; he had said the same things thousands of times, at the club, in fashionable drawing rooms, in newspaper offices, and in the Chamber of Deputies. Out of the corner of his eye he was watching Davida, who still stood staring at them from the far end of the room, near the piano. It was Vogoride she was looking at, of course, not Lascari; and the latter resented it. For the moment he could have wished Sherban a thousand miles away, or dead, instead of sitting there, talking so loudly, so sure of himself, the center of attention, listened to, questioned, and admired wherever he went. *Devil take the fellow!* Lascari thought, aware that though he himself was not yet forty he was ugly and not very bright, so that he had to be satisfied with loose women, singers at the Café de l'Union, girls who required of him nothing but a share—far too large in his opinion—of the gold he was forever jingling in his pocket. *The man's intolerable,* his train of thought continued. *Devil take the beast and his monocle! What can they all see in him?* The fact was that "they" were all in fear and trembling for their land. They knew themselves

powerless in the face of the danger threatening them; they had no
men of spirit in their ranks, no fighters, no orators to be compared
with their adversaries. Even His Highness Mitica Ghica, son of the
former reigning prince, listened to Vogoride and followed his advice as if it were gospel. They were all at his feet; they all called
him their "savior." And the shopkeepers and small urban businessmen, the journalists and merchants, Kogalniceano, Rosetti, Prince
Couza himself, all knew that Vogoride was the only man they
had to fear.

Lascar Lascari said nothing more that evening, but confined
himself to casting occasional furtive glances at the Cozianos' daughter who, motionless and silent, did not take her eyes off Vogoride.
Lascar was tormented by an exasperation even more painful than
the feeling which had afflicted him at the moment when he looked
like losing during the card game with Coziano, losing. . . . But
that was done with, he would play no more. What was the point
of losing money? In future, too, he would stop thinking about
women also. Mlle Fanny, the actress, was good enough for a man
like him. A man like him? Yet he was more intelligent than
Vogoride, younger, more avid for pleasure (he was not thinking of
those facile and far from brilliant conquests which he was sick of).
So why "a man like him"? *Am I not a man like Vogoride?* Lascar asked himself. And he chewed on the bitterness of the hatred
which had been devouring him ever since Vogoride had begun
to put him in the shade. He knew that Sherban was perfectly at
home in this house. But on this particular evening he could no
longer bear the sight of the man being the life and soul of the
party. He must leave as soon as he could, get away from all these
people. Lascari consoled himself with the thought that Sherban
and Sophia would stay with Coziano, who had certainly understood that allusion during their game of écarté; and it was with a
kind of satisfaction that he thought, *They'll be no more at peace
than I am this evening.*

When he saw the wife of the *vornic* Sturza rise, groaning and
leaning on her stick, and noticed that the other ladies were like-

wise getting ready to leave, Lascari hastened to offer the old Princess his arm and make his bow to Sophia Coziano. When he came to Vogoride he shook his hand and kissed him on both cheeks.

"Until tomorrow, in the Chamber."

Vogoride tried to turn his face away, but failed to avoid Lascari's wet kisses and greasy whiskers. He did not like such close contact with any man, and particularly when the man in question was this livid, flabby, hirsute creature. He remained alone in the drawing room with Sophia Coziano, quivering with disgust and twirling his monocle on the end of its ribbon. From outside came the stamp and clatter of horses' hoofs on the paved road, and the rumble of carriages driving away. Davida had not left her place against the piano. Sherban Vogoride, stooping over her mother, smiled and murmured in French, "You are as lovely as the dawn."

Sophia, about to acknowledge this comparison of her beauty with the light of the sun, checked herself when she suddenly realized that they were not alone; she turned toward Davida.

"Were you there all the time? What's the matter with you, moping all alone like an owl?"

Vogoride stood upright again. In a tone almost too natural he said, "Of course she's here. Didn't you see her? She's been there all evening without uttering a word."

"Come over here and talk to us," Sophia said, mastering her resentment with effort. She had a rare moment of freedom, and the silly child had to come and spoil it. What did she want, anyway?

Davida, not suspecting that her mother really desired to be rid of her as soon as possible, crossed the room to them. Vogoride looked at the girl with genuine pleasure. He stroked her hair as if she were a child.

"How this girl has grown! We shall have to be thinking of a husband for her one of these days. . . ."

"Don't say such things, Sherban. I don't want to feel I'm getting old. . . ."

"My dear, you'll be enchanting even at eighty—and whoever has loved you in your youth will love you still." Vogoride bowed politely, as if he were paying her a commonplace compliment. But from his way of looking at her Sophia realized that he had meant it, and she blushed with pleasure. Vogoride's hand was still resting on Davida's head and the girl closed her eyes for a moment. Then Vogoride gently touched her face and said, "You must think of me tomorrow. I shall be fighting a hard battle in the Chamber."

"You will win it!" Davida exclaimed with a passionate fervor which made the other two laugh.

"She has even more faith in you than I have," Sophia said. "Nobody in this house can say a word against you, or she's on them like a tigress."

Davida smiled timidly.

"If only the honorable members of our Conservative Party had some of this child's enthusiasm," Vogoride said. "The Prince and Kogalniceano wouldn't find it quite so easy to do as they please with the country, despite all their shopkeepers and peasants. . . ."

A woman in a black dress appeared at the far end of the room. It was not until she stood beneath the first of the three crystal chandeliers hanging from the ceiling that it became apparent that she was about forty, fair, with light eyebrows and pale-green eyes. Her mouth, closed in a thin line, added to the coldness of her naturally severe face. Her plain black silk dress was relieved only by a narrow white collar and white cuffs. The woman acknowledged Vogoride with a slight inclination of the head; he responded with a bow of marked reserve, as if he found himself in company with a perfect stranger; then he put his monocle to his eye and examined her with an expression of cool indifference.

"I was looking for Davida." The newcomer spoke in French, and turning to the girl, added, "Come, mademoiselle, it is bedtime."

"It is not. I don't want to," Davida said angrily.

"Of course you must go to bed. Mademoiselle Marchand is quite right," her mother said, only too pleased to get rid of her, and in a burst of benevolence toward Mlle Marchand whose arrival on the scene was so opportune, she turned to Sherban, saying, "You have not yet met Mademoiselle Marchand, have you? She has charge of this child's education. Mademoiselle," she added in French, "come and be introduced to His Excellency Sherban Vogoride."

The Frenchwoman came forward with a pale smile, ready to offer her hand. But suddenly she withdrew it; her smile froze and slowly disappeared. Sherban had thrust his hands into his pockets and was staring into space above the woman's head, as if she were nothing but air. He did not even seem to hear what Sophia Coziano was saying to him.

"Sherban, this is Mademoiselle Marchand, Davida's governess."

For a moment Sophia Coziano was petrified with astonishment. A heavy silence descended upon the whole vast room, empty now except for the corner where they stood. Sophia Coziano flushed and, speaking French, said to the governess, "Thank you, mademoiselle, you may take Davida to her room. To bed, Davida."

Mlle Marchand bowed with downcast eyes. "*Bonsoir,* madame. *Bonsoir,* monsieur." She went out, taking Davida with her, Vogoride again stroking the girl's hair as she passed him.

As they went out, Sophia Coziano turned to Vogoride and said, "Now, really, Sherban, what on earth came over you, insulting the poor woman like that?"

He laughed, but his expression was grim. "You are much too good-hearted, my dear. One of these days you'll be introducing me to your serving-women or your little gypsy girls! Now let me ask *you* a question: what on earth possessed you to try and introduce me to a person to whom you pay wages? Who is Mademoiselle Marchand? I don't know her. She doesn't interest me, and consequently she doesn't exist. It is weaknesses and kindnesses like yours that make the common people forget the respect they owe us. That's the sort of thing that makes it necessary for me to be always shouting myself hoarse in the Chamber, trying to keep rebels and demagogues in order."

"But this Frenchwoman has nothing—I mean there's no comparison——" Sophia began, but he interrupted her with a curt laugh.

"Scum is scum, French or Rumanian, it's all the same to me.

Besides, they're the ones who export all these revolutionary ideas. It's France we have to blame for stuffing our intellectuals' heads with all that rubbish. First it was Balcesco, and now it's his friends, Ion Ionesco, Rosetti, and all the lot of them. Well, let's forget it, or you'll have me making a speech. And," he added, lowering his voice and smiling, "we have a great many other things to say to each other."

"If that's how you feel, I've nothing more to say," Sophia replied delightedly. "All the same, I'm terribly upset. Poor Herminie! She's such a respectable woman, Sherban!" And, suddenly amused, she went on, "You can't imagine how virtuous she is, too! Last winter the poor thing was taken ill. She had a high fever and became delirious. Do you know what she said? No, you'll never guess——"

"Indecencies, probably," Vogoride said with a coarse chuckle.

"You've an evil mind! On the contrary, my dear, she kept shouting, 'Send for a doctor to certify that I am a virgin!' "

"Poor creature!" Vogoride gasped, tears of laughter running down his cheeks. "I'm sorry for her. Do you mean to tell me, my dear, that there was not a man in all Rumania to take pity on her fate and rescue her from that calamity?"

They were still laughing when Coziano appeared in the doorway. He stood there, his face waxen, his cravat in disorder, his clothes creased.

"What are you laughing at?" he asked sullenly. Then, casting a look around the room, he went on, with an expression of exaggerated surprise and in a surly voice, "Has everybody gone?"

"What's the matter with you?" Sophia asked. "Are you ill?"

"Yes—my liver's troubling me again," Coziano muttered, and collapsed into an armchair. Sherban Vogoride and Sophia exchanged a quick, furtive glance. Sherban lingered a few minutes longer, talking generalities, then rose to take his leave. "Why are you leaving us so early?" Coziano inquired indifferently. He made it obvious, however, that he preferred to be alone. Sherban made his farewells and left them. Coziano walked over to the window and stood there awhile, until he heard the clatter of horses' hoofs

and saw the carriage lamps pass in front of him in the courtyard
and out by one of the gateways. Then he spun around and advanced on his wife, livid, and controlling his rage with great
difficulty.

"My dear Sophia, I've got to talk to you. I have always acceded
to your every wish. When you wanted us to sleep in separate
rooms, I agreed. I have allowed you to lead your own life, travel
by yourself. I have never touched any of your fortune. Your cousin
Sherban is a great man, I grant you, but for all that, I am not
willing to become a laughingstock because of you and him. I am
still the master here, I fancy. And for your own good, I'm going
to put an end to this nonsense. In your own interest, mind! One
of these fine days people will be pointing the finger of scorn at you,
and you'll be forced to go and live abroad because nobody will
want to set foot in this house. Well, I've said enough. All I need
add, therefore, is that we are leaving for Cozia tomorrow morning."

"What! Tomorrow?"

"By eight o'clock tomorrow morning we shall be on our way.
Have you any objections?"

Madame Coziano bit her lip. She forced herself to collect her
wits and to concentrate. She was frightened, but she did her best
to smile.

"My dear," she said, "you're not well. That's what makes you
take such a gloomy view of things. Wherever did you pick up all
this nonsense about Sherban, and people refusing to set foot in this
house?"

"What does it matter where I picked it up? You'll kindly take
my word for it," Coziano shouted; he was shaking with rage. "I've
been given to understand—and only too clearly—that there's no
secret about what's going on. People aren't such fools as you seem
to think." He turned sharply as a woman entered the room, and
demanded, "What do you want?"

"I came to tell madam that dinner is served."

It was Florica, the gypsy who had lit the lamp when Coziano
had gone into the small drawing room to play cards with Lascari.

"Very well. Get out."

"You may go, Florica," Madame Coziano said calmly. "You can all go to bed. We shall not want dinner tonight."

She waited until the door was shut and then said, "People? My dear Alexander, what does it matter what they say? Let them. As the song has it, 'Everyone says what he likes. . . .' We'll set out now, at once, if you like. But do you really want us to quarrel with Sherban? What is he going to think of us? That we've suddenly gone mad? Or that we've something—heaven knows what! —against him? Do you think it's in our interests to be on bad terms with him?"

"I don't care!" Coziano roared. He began to stride up and down the room, then halted suddenly.

"Understand, madam, that it does not suit me at all to be made a fool of by him. Do you hear me? Or do you want me to be forced to fight a duel with him? Because that is otherwise what it will come to."

"This is the last straw," Sophia Coziano said, turning pale. "So now you want to kill him!"

"It may be that he will kill me. That possibility hasn't occurred to you, has it?" Coziano replied, with a bitter laugh.

"I simply meant you're a better shot than he is, that's all," Sophia explained. "You spend half your time out shooting. And if anything did happen, I suppose you realize what the consequences would be? Would you take his place in the Chamber? Would you be the one to stand up to Kogalniceano and restrain the Prince? I can just see you doing it!" she said contemptuously, and went on, "Do we really want to have a scandal just at this moment?"

Coziano seemed taken aback. Sophia, the mild and feeble Sophia, summoned all her strength of mind, all her audacity.

"Supposing, for argument's sake," she began, "that he has some —some feeling for me——"

"Do me the kindness not to treat me as a fool on top of all the rest," her husband interrupted her, with a sneer compounded of indignation and distress. But Sophia continued: "Supposing he has such a feeling and I leave here without a word of explanation: if his feeling is genuine, the result will be that he'll be good for nothing. What sort of account will he give of himself in the Chamber, and at Cabinet meetings? I tell you, he'll be useless. I know him. He's capable of throwing up everything to follow me—you can imagine the scandal, his political career ruined! . . . Or he's liable to resign and go abroad, or retire to his country house, or even to kill himself. . . ."

Sophia did not really consider any of these eventualities at all likely, but she was talking with the courage of despair. Seeing her husband shaken, it was with still more resolution that she continued, "And if he goes, Couza and Kogalniceano will have nobody to oppose them among the Conservatives. Compared with him, the others don't exist."

"With or without him, they'll confiscate our lands," Coziano said, frowning gloomily. "We're done for in any case. No one man can stop this torrent——"

"Are you really sure of that? So sure that you'll take responsibility for what must follow?"

Coziano was silent. He started pacing the room again. After some time he muttered, "We'll talk about it again tomorrow."

He walked out of the room without another word. Sophia Coziano passed her hands over her face and sighed deeply. She whispered to herself, "You can have no idea, Sherban, no idea . . ."

She went to bed very late. The candles in the great chandeliers burned all night long. By dawn they began to gutter and go out, giving off an acrid smoke.

Meanwhile Davida was sleeping like a child, breathing softly and easily. Mlle Marchand lay in bed, rigid and cold, with her eyes wide open, thinking hard.

When she had shepherded Davida into the room which they shared she had gone behind the screen and undressed in silence. Seated on her bed, Davida talked to her.

"Don't you think he's like Lord Byron? Or no, perhaps more like Chateaubriand. Oh, mademoiselle, what a pity you weren't there when he was describing how he answered the Liberals in the

Chamber! It was unforgettable! He's unique, a man who'll go
down in history. He has all the pride and diabolical genius of
Manfred, or Lara, or—mademoiselle, do you know what it made
me think of? Papa read me something in Sallust which I shall
remember till I die: *'Contemptor animus atque superbia, consueta
mala nobilitas!*—Pride and a contemptuous spirit are the usual vices
of nobility.' But Papa says that they aren't vices; on the contrary,
they're indicative of a noble mind, the signs of a high and generous
soul. *'Contemptor animus atque superbia, ipsa nobilitas!*—Pride
and a contemptuous spirit are nobility itself.' "

The room was square, its walls covered with a flowered paper;
it was furnished with two large brass bedsteads and two commodes,
on one of which stood a china basin and ewer—Mlle Marchand's.
Davida's basin and ewer were of silver, with a spiral groove forming a pattern all around them. Mlle Marchand came from behind
the screen, blew out the candle, and got into bed. She had not
uttered a word. Davida sat daydreaming for a while and then, with
unusual submissiveness, she said, "Mademoiselle, may I do a bit
more mathematics preparation?"

Mlle Marchand made no answer. Davida hurried to the commode,
ferreted in one of its drawers, took out a notebook, lit a candle,
and began to write at the pedestal table, the wax from her candle
falling from the candlestick onto its marble top. Her notebook was
a small exercise book with a black cover. At the top of the page
she wrote the date and then:

> Today he spoke to me again. I had more than ever the feeling
> that he looks like Manfred, although there is something of Lara
> about him, too. I was listening to him when all of a sudden he
> called me and began talking to me. He said he needed me; he
> asked me to think of him tomorrow when he will be face to
> face with his enemies. I shall think of you and you will be
> victorious, oh, my beloved!

She paused, sucked the end of her pen, and then began to write
again:

How I wish I had been a man, to help him and fight side by side with him. Papa does not understand him and Mama even less. Mama is nothing but a goose, the best proof being that she thinks I am still a child. She is wrong! She ought to have a heroic heart, and then he would love her. He can only love a character as brave as his own.

Another pause, another nibble at her pen, and then:

L. L. told me today that I ought to marry a politician. He is a repulsive little creature but not lacking in insight. How well I know it—that I should marry a politician! But not just—any politician. There is only one.

She underlined the words "only one" with two lines, and went on writing:

His wife, his beloved, his slave!
How I wish I could give my life for him!

She closed the little exercise book and looked at Mlle Marchand out of the corner of her eye. She was perfectly still under the bedclothes. Speaking low, Davida said, "Are you asleep?"

The governess did not answer. Evidently she was asleep. Davida hid the notebook, undressed quickly, and got into bed. She began trying to imagine romantic scenes in which Sherban and she played the leading parts. But little by little the mental images became confused, ran together, melted away. And soon Davida fell asleep, her black hair spread across the pillow and one hand under her cheek.

Mlle Marchand, however, was not asleep. She had not answered because she was choking, her throat dry; because she was suffocating; because she could not permit herself to express her thoughts. She lay in her bed, her body cold, her teeth clenched; she could not even cry. All her thoughts tended toward one end. And in this attitude she remained all night long. At dawn she rose, washed her face in cold water, and dressed. She sat down in an armchair, a book in her hand; but she did not read. Davida, when she opened her eyes, smiled like a little girl and asked her if she was up already. "What a silly question. You can see I am. Why do you ask?" She was calm and severe as usual.

Davida sighed, stretched, and wanted to linger in bed, but Mlle Marchand briskly pulled away the bedclothes. The sound of voices rose from the courtyard and the clatter of hoofs on cobbles. Davida jumped out of bed and ran barefoot to the window. The carriage which was used for long journeys was drawn up at the front door.

"What's happened? Who's going away? Are we going on a journey?" she asked.

"I have no idea," Mlle Marchand replied. "The sooner you're dressed, the sooner you'll know what is happening. Come, hurry now. With that long white nightgown and your black hair tumbling over your shoulders you look like a savage, *une vraie sauvage!*"

2

Just at that moment the heavy red velvet curtains across Sophia Coziano's window parted ever so slightly, then swiftly fell back into place. Behind the drawn curtains, in the room where the little flame of a taper flickered below the faint gleam of silver icons, a determined Sophia Coziano settled herself in an armchair and waited. If Alexander should come in and request her to take her place in the carriage, she would refuse categorically. She felt nervous. Her satin mule quivered on the toes of her small white foot. Her silk dressing gown had suddenly ceased to keep her warm, and she gathered it across her breasts. Outside, the horses stamped, and she could hear the voices of stableboys and of Dumitru, the coachman. Sophia was waiting for the knock on her door, when she would rise to her feet to declare: "I refuse to accompany you!"

When she was dressed, Davida had left her room, escorted by Mlle Marchand, who that morning was paler than ever. She came face to face with her father, who had flung a heavy overcoat over his shoulders and was wearing the cap he used when out shooting, and greenish-gray suède gloves. Having stooped to enable his daughter to kiss him respectfully on both cheeks, he turned to Mlle Marchand, drew her to one side, and said in French: "I have to leave for the country. It is possible that I shall be away for some months. Be good enough to keep me informed of Davida's conduct and progress. I must ask you, above all, to be firm, and even strict with her. Be severe. Her mother, at any rate, is hardly likely to interfere with your management of Davida's education," he added, with a smile which Mlle Marchand received without raising an eyebrow.

"Be with her constantly. Keep an eye on her reading, her games, everything. I will have no frivolous distractions. Mathematics, history, Latin. Keep her at work from morning till night. And do not neglect music, nor deportment, which is most important. She must become a person outstanding in every way. I am counting on you."

"I know my duty, monsieur," Mlle Marchand said, with so much firmness that M. Coziano's bitterness gave way for a moment to a kind of dull satisfaction.

"Very well, mademoiselle. Au revoir," Coziano said, dismissing her with a nod.

"Au revoir, monsieur."

Mlle Marchand bowed stiffly, then returned to her place, straight as a ramrod. Coziano caressed Davida's cheek as he passed her, put on his hunting cap, signaled to Hector, his French valet, to follow him, and got into the carriage. Davida, standing at the top of the steps, wanted to wave her handkerchief and call out something. Mlle Marchand did not even turn her eyes toward the girl, but merely murmured between her thin lips, "Really, Davida! A display of sentiment before the servants!"

Davida started; she thanked her mentor politely and the pair went back into the house. At that moment the carriage passed through the gateway.

At the sound of wheels Mme Coziano ran back to the window and saw the heavy coach swing out of the courtyard. She could hardly believe her eyes. She forced herself to appear calm, to make the servants believe that she knew all about her husband's departure. But she could not prevent herself from knocking on the door before going into Coziano's room, which smelled of stale cigar smoke. Alexander was not there. He was nowhere in the house. He was actually gone. She had no means of knowing where, or for how long. He was probably making for one of his estates—Cozia or Gîrla. He had gone in order to avoid seeing her; he had been ashamed, ashamed of himself. "The coward!" Sophia whispered with a contemptuous smile.

From then on Sherban Vogoride came more and more frequently to the house on Culmea Veche Street, as did all the rest of the Cozianos' friends, who had never been attracted by Alexander Coziano's sullen disposition and bitterness, but rather by the natural grace and charm of his wife. And now that Sophia could blossom, she was gay and witty without spitefulness; she did not even arouse jealousy in other women, because they sensed that her attention was centered. During this period, the political strife and the virulent exchanges in the Chamber had the effect of making the Cozianos' house a meeting place for all the most influential figures of the Conservative Party, if for no other reason than that they were sure of finding Sherban Vogoride there, and they looked upon him as their last chance. To judge from the Liberal press, his opponents were very well aware of the fact. They had slyly begun to slip into their articles vague threats against Vogoride, who laughed them off every evening, leaning against the drawing-room stove in the house on Culmea Veche Street.

Davida continued to live in those heroic and passionate dreams which marked the end of her adolescence. Her head was stuffed with Tacitus and geometry, and she was dogged from morning till night, rising, eating, retiring, everywhere and always, by the unwearying watchfulness, calm voice, and icy criticism of Mlle Marchand. Davida saw the people around her only superficially; she concentrated on herself, was utterly indifferent to what others might be thinking. She contrived ruses to enable her to write in her black exercise book from time to time, and to keep that compromising document concealed from Mlle Marchand's vigilant eye.

One day Sherban Vogoride came to lunch, as he had been in the habit of doing for some time. Sophia Coziano, in a spring dress, laughing and light-hearted, presided over the long table. Lascar Lascari was there, and so was one of Sophia's brothers, the deputy for a constituency in Moldavia—a man with long side whiskers, sullen and quite remarkably stupid. There were also two poor relations, Sophia's aunts, faded and silent ladies who ate greedily, their eyes on their plates; Mlle Marchand, who answered nothing beyond "yes" or "no" to questions addressed to her; and lastly Davida, listening with delight to Vogoride's fiery words. ". . . Prince Couza is determined to carry out the agrarian reform program. He's another of your theorists bent on progress." Vogoride uttered the last word with crushing contempt. "The Liberals are only backing him in order to get into office themselves —in fact, to replace us all! There's just one obstacle—not one of us is going to let himself be despoiled of a fortune built up through the labor of his ancestors by allowing Messieurs Rosetti and Bratiano to form a government."

Davida was forgetting to eat. Mlle Marchand, speaking low, said, "Why aren't you eating, Davida?" And as Davida did not seem to have heard her: "I am asking you why you're not eating."

"I beg your pardon. Did you say something?"

"Why are you not eating?"

Davida remained silent for a moment, as if she had just been roused from a deep sleep; then, gathering her wits, she replied, "I'm not hungry." And she turned back toward Vogoride.

Mlle Marchand said nothing and went on with her lunch, eating moderately, in small mouthfuls. Her throat felt constricted, and only a constant effort of will enabled her to keep her face impassive.

After the meal the men stayed with their hostess for coffee and brandy; the two aunts withdrew to their room, whose windows looked out on the inner courtyard and the servants' quarters. Davida would have liked to remain in the drawing room, but her mother would not allow it.

"Run along, child. Back to your books."

Davida rose, showing her annoyance. Lascar Lascari took her part laughingly. "Come now, my dear Sophia, let her stay for a little while. She understands politics better than any of us."

"Certainly not. She's a child. She has to study, my dear Lascar. Alexander has tremendous plans for her. Run along, Davida. You must go and work."

The girl looked toward Vogoride, hoping that he would come to her aid. But Vogoride's mind was on other matters; he was warming his brandy glass between his palms and probably thinking of the next day's session in the Chamber. Head down, and looking furious, Davida left the room, preceded by Mlle Marchand.

In her own room a wide band of light in which danced golden motes of dust shone through the gap between the half-drawn curtains, illuminating a large rectangle of the red carpet. Davida crossed this bar of light, opened her desk of yellow wood, and sat down, but without picking up a book.

"They take me for a child," she muttered, scowling. "How little they know me. . . ."

Mlle Marchand went behind the screen and emerged with an exercise book in her hand. Approaching Davida, she held it out to her. "Perhaps you will be good enough to explain this, mademoiselle," she commanded in a quivering voice.

Davida started to her feet, deathly pale. It was her black notebook. She made a swift movement to snatch it from her governess. "Where did you get that? How did you find it? Give it back to me! You've no right to read it!"

Mlle Marchand held the notebook out of reach. Davida stood confronting her, with only a single pace between them, and the two women glared defiantly at each other. Both were trembling, the one with indignation, the other with a terrible anger, held in check so far, but obviously about to burst out at any moment.

"You have no right to pry into my things! You spy!" Davida almost hissed the words.

"No right? On the contrary, it is my duty. I am entrusted with your education, and I must know how your mind wanders, you scatterbrained little fool!" Mlle Marchand spoke passionately. "I am responsible to your father for your conduct. What do you think he will say when he sees what you have written here?"

"You have no right to tell him. It would be treachery, infamous treachery!"

"Infamous? *My* behavior infamous? It is your idol who is infamous! So Mademoiselle has seen proper to worship nobility and generosity in him, has she? And the little idiot even contrives to be in love with him! Really, you make me laugh!" And Mlle Marchand gave a forced laugh.

"What did you say? You dare to say that, dare to judge him?" Davida raised her hand to slap the woman's face, but Mlle Marchand caught hold of her arm and pushed her away.

"Beast!" Davida said between clenched teeth. "I'll have you thrown out of this house."

"Throw me out, will you? Ah, you're right, I should be out of this indeed! What am I doing here? What can anyone who still has a sense of honor expect in this house? Yes, I'll go, and go gladly, because I cannot bear to stay and watch what's going on here. The only man worthy of respect in this household is your father, yet I see him dishonored, flouted, and because of my position I can mention neither what I think nor what I see. Oh, yes, I'll go. I leave you to your idiotic admiration of your mother's lover!"

Davida turned paler than ever. After a moment's silence she stammered, "What did you say?"

Mlle Marchand pulled a large suitcase from under the bed, opened her wardrobe, and began taking out her dresses and throwing them into the case with feverish haste. Davida rushed at her, seized her by the shoulders, and shook her. "What did you say? Are you mad?"

"I am not in the least mad," Mlle Marchand replied, without interrupting her packing. She was shaking all over and spoke in a low, rapid voice. "No, I'm not mad. I inherited common sense and self-respect from my parents, and I have been very much at fault in remaining here so long to endure humiliation. Why should I bear it? I am a more honorable person than your mother and her lover! My parents worked hard for their small pittance. They had the best hotel in Nogent. It was the envy and wickedness of others that ruined them. And then the railroad was built, and there were no more coaches to stop at our hotel. We faced up to that misfortune as bravely as we could, but then the tyrant Louis-Napoleon Bonaparte seized power and my father, whose republican opinions were well known, was deported. And I'm proud of him! He was a man of integrity whom people respected, not a depraved, corrupt aristocrat dishonoring his best friend's marriage bed—like your idol! I'm not afraid of work. I'd rather work with my hands than stay in this house. I'll leave this accursed land of savages. I'd rather die than lose my self-respect."

Davida tugged at Mlle Marchand's arm and made her sit down on the bed. Unresisting, the governess submitted.

"What you said just now. It's not—it can't be true?"

Davida's voice expressed doubt. Her tone begged for reassurance, for confirmation that all this was a bad dream and that her governess had been talking wildly and at random.

"Yes, it's true," Mlle Marchand replied firmly.

"You're lying," Davida cried, jumping up. "You're lying! You're a liar and a troublemaker!"

Mlle Marchand smiled wanly. "It is hard to be a servant—especially to masters of slaves."

Davida spoke low. "Forgive me, mademoiselle, please forgive me. I was out of my mind. I didn't know what I was saying. But you must realize what all this means to me! I beg you to forget the way I spoke to you. Please, please, mademoiselle, don't go away, don't leave me, I beg of you, don't leave me alone like this. . . ."

She let herself slip from the bed to the floor, sank to her knees, and putting both arms around the governess's slender waist, looked up into her face with terror.

"Don't leave me. I've nobody to talk to, nobody in all the world! Stay here and help me learn the truth. I must know everything. I can't believe that what you have just said is true!"

Mlle Marchand smiled coldly and answered firmly, "Very well. You shall find out for yourself."

Anyone who had taken the trouble to observe Davida's behavior from that moment onward could hardly have failed to notice that she became more silent and reserved than ever and that she kept hostile watch over Sherban Vogoride and her mother. But no one thought of observing Davida, except Lascar Lascari; and if he did so, it was simply because he was on the lookout for chances of getting close to her, of touching her arm and putting his own around her waist while he whispered a compliment. When he succeeded, Davida, quivering with disgust, answered him curtly and made her escape as quickly as she could.

One afternoon Davida was again sent to her room. She was sitting on her bed, quite still, dreaming. Outside the sun was shining and a breath of wind stirred the curtains at an open window. Mlle Marchand came into the room; she had opened the door very softly so that it should make no sound, and she moved noiselessly. Her green eyes were very bright, and a contemptuous smile tightened her thin lips. Davida rose, hypnotized. The governess beckoned, and she followed. In the dark corridor which separated the suite of reception rooms from the bedrooms they halted for a moment. Through a glass door could be seen two potted palms at the far end of the big drawing room, and between them another glass door opening into the anteroom. Beyond, the gilded spikes of the iron railings were visible, the chestnut trees lining the street, and the old houses opposite. Mlle Marchand took Davida's arm and led her to the far end of the corridor. There she pushed open a door, already ajar, which led into Mme Coziano's dressing room; there was a smell of lavender, dressing gowns had been thrown carelessly on a chair, and slippers were scattered about the floor.

The governess drew Davida quietly into the dressing room, and standing back, pointed to the door that led to Sophia Coziano's bedroom. Then she withdrew discreetly and returned to Davida's room, where she sat down in an armchair and picked up a book which she placed on her knees. Outside in the courtyard sparrows twittered. A woman in the kitchen quarters was shouting, "Stan! Stan!"

Some time later, when Mlle Marchand could bear the tension of waiting no longer and was on the point of rising to go in search of Davida, the door was pushed open. Davida came in. The governess rose, startled. Davida faltered. She had grown suddenly ugly, and her hair had come down and was tumbled about her shoulders. She walked past Mlle Marchand, sat down on the bed and remained there for a moment, then suddenly hid her face in the pillows and began to cry. From time to time, still weeping, she moaned, "It's so ignoble—oh, how vile, how vile!"

Mlle Marchand tried to draw the girl to her and caress her, but Davida started wildly and pushed her frantically away.

"Leave me alone. Go away. I want to be by myself."

"Very well," Mlle Marchand replied with dignity, and left the room.

That night Davida did not come down to dinner, sending a message to say she did not feel well. When her mother came up to see her, Davida turned away her head and asked her to go, and Sophia, who had guests waiting for her in the drawing room, shrugged her shoulders and went. It would be time enough to-morrow to see if it was necessary to send for a doctor. But when tomorrow came Davida was as calm as if nothing untoward had happened. She never mentioned that afternoon to Mlle Marchand, nor the black exercise book, nor Vogoride. The governess did not dare ask questions, but without knowing exactly why, she began to feel very uneasy.

A few days later, when they were all at table, Sophia Coziano said, "I don't know what can be the matter with Davida. She is not herself. So silent and sullen . . ."

She spoke in Davida's presence as if the girl were still a mere child. Vogoride laughed, screwed in his monocle, and surveyed Davida with a sort of fatherly benevolence.

"Is it the spring? A disappointment in love? Tell us what the trouble is, Davida."

Davida turned pale and did not answer. Sophia and Sherban Vogoride smiled at each other and said no more. But after the meal Sophia took the governess on one side and asked her what was the matter with Davida. Could it possibly be . . . ?

"Certainly not," Mlle Marchand replied coldly. "She is never out of my sight. Girls of her age have these moods sometimes."

The governess was very much afraid that Davida might sooner or later lose control of herself and make a scene. The source of her information would inevitably be traced, in which event she, Mlle Marchand . . . It would obviously be better if no questions were asked about Davida's ill-humor. Perceiving that Mme Coziano did not seem altogether convinced, Mlle Marchand smiled discreetly and added, "It may be nothing but a physical indisposition. . . . At her age that sometimes upsets them, you know."

"Oh, of course. I had not thought of that," Sophia said, reassured.

Two or three days later, when Sophia, Vogoride, Davida, and Mlle Marchand were alone at table, Vogoride, after a glance at Davida, interrupted the conversation to ask, "What is the matter with our little girl?" speaking with that friendliness which now made Davida flinch with disgust.

Davida did not utter a word. But Sophia gave a little laugh and, speaking in Rumanian so that the governess should not understand, replied in terms which, though she seemed unaware of it, bore witness to an excessive intimacy: "The curse of Eve . . . She may be only a child still, but Mother Nature will have her say!"

She had expressed herself with a kind of bucolic good nature, as befitted a woman whose childhood had been spent in the country on her parents' estates and who had often heard the servants calling a spade a spade, even in the presence of the gentry. Vogoride, who had likewise spent his childhood in the country and was, in any case, well informed about women and the curse of Eve, laughed easily and changed the subject. Davida did not flinch, but as soon as the meal was over she withdrew to her room and locked the door. The governess, finding herself locked out, knocked timidly.

"Who is it?" Davida inquired in a hostile voice.

"It is I, Davida. Please open the door."

"I locked the door by mistake," Davida said, opening it. Mlle Marchand stopped short on the threshold: her china basin was on the floor, in pieces; the ewer lay in the midst, cracked from top to bottom, its handle smashed. Davida's silver basin and ewer had vanished; but the panes of the window that opened onto the courtyard had been shattered, indicating the route which those utensils had followed. Davida, awaiting questions, gazed fixedly at her governess; but her face wore such an expression of disgust and fury that Mlle Marchand judged it best to say nothing and simply summon Sultana, the gypsy girl who acted as their maid. By means of her few words of Rumanian, but principally by gestures, Mlle Marchand made the gypsy understand that she was to fetch a glazier. She bought a new basin and ewer at her own expense. As for the silver ones, dented and twisted as they were, they resumed their places on Davida's commode. The events of that day were never referred to again.

Thereafter Herminie Marchand lived in a constant state of anxiety. Normally she did not know the meaning of fear; but she now felt herself caught as if in a vise between forces capable of crushing her. There were times when she regretted having unleashed them by telling her charge what was happening between Sophia and Sherban Vogoride. But to quell that regret she had only to recall her satisfaction in seeing Davida broken and Sherban Vogoride cast down from his pedestal. Nevertheless, her fears persisted. In her present state Davida was capable of anything: she might, for example, proclaim her opinion of Vogoride at the top of her voice in a drawing room full of her mother's guests.

In such an event, Mlle Marchand would be ignominiously dismissed on the spot—for she certainly did not expect Davida to defend her. What would happen to her then? Sherban Vogoride, the all-powerful Minister, would have her deported within twenty-four hours. And then? It would mean returning to her native town with its gray slate roofs. In Nogent, on the Place de l'Hôtel de Ville, was the old Hôtel des Voyageurs, now belonging to M. Hébrard, her father's old enemy and business rival. And she—she would be nothing but "old Marchand's daughter," that is, the daughter of a bankrupt tradesman, a deported republican. The contempt and coarseness of these Wallachian magnates were surely easier to bear than the deadly charity of her Nogent relations. It would soon be known that she had been driven out of Wallachia, and the gossips would talk of it for years. "There goes Herminie Marchand. We were at school together. Such a quiet girl she was, too; whoever would have thought she'd have done such a thing?" "What was it she did, exactly?" "She was a housemaid with some Russian prince or other, or he may have been Polish, nobody knows exactly, but it seems she was his mistress, or else she poisoned someone—anyway, she was a fugitive from justice, and the French ambassador smuggled her out under a false name."

At Nogent the green waters of the tranquil Seine flow between banks planted with elms and willows. At Nogent Herminie Marchand would not make old bones; one night she would walk out of the town and along the river to a certain lonely spot she knew of. . . .

3

One spring morning Davida asked for the victoria. Nicolai, the coachman, put on his long, velvet-caped coat and harnessed the two high-stepping dapple-grays. Vasili, the footman, opened the door and lowered the step. Davida, followed by Mlle Marchand, tripped down the stone stairs, holding up her skirts with her fingertips. Vasili helped the two ladies in and closed the door,

then swung himself into position on the step fixed at the back of
the carriage. Nicolai cracked his whip and the carriage and pair
passed out between the tall gateposts to the rhythmic beat of hoofs,
the grays stepping high and tossing their heads. The air was still
damp, and a chill breeze brought the scents of rain, wet earth, and
young foliage. Mlle Marchand was wrapped up in a cashmere shawl
which Mme Coziano had given her; only her thin, colorless face was
visible. Davida had gathered her black plaits into a low chignon
at the nape of her neck. She wore a small green hat with a pearl-
gray veil which streamed in the wind, slapping the face of Vasili,
who blinked but remained motionless, gripping the brass handles
fixed behind the victoria.

Nicolai kept his whip cracking. People in the street, in caftans
or short jackets, scurried out of the way; shopkeepers, standing
on the thresholds of their shops, watched the carriage pass, their
eyes narrowed under the peaks of their tall, Leipzig-style caps.
Peasants, leading the horses harnessed to their country carts, tried
to drag them to the side and leave the road clear. Gentlemen in
frock coats raised their silk hats politely as the victoria went spanking past them, covering the ground at a fine pace so that it had
soon passed St. George's Church, driven the length of Prince
Soutzo's palace, swung down the street beside the Sarindar Church,
and rumbled along the Mogosoaïa Bridge* between noblemen's
town houses, each surrounded by its trees and gardens. It clattered
past old churches with leaning belfries, and past huddles of low,
open-fronted shops where Lyons silks and Shiraz carpets were
piled in the half-darkness beside Siberian furs, English guns, and
Meissen porcelain. Davida greeted with a curt nod such gentlemen
as rose from their chairs on café terraces, and vouchsafed a cold
smile to Grigoritza Sturza who was out riding for the first time
since falling backward downstairs and breaking both legs.

At the point where the four rows of linden trees lining the
principal avenue ended and the small coppices of willows which

* Until the end of the last century the principal streets of Rumanian
towns were composed of wooden beams set transversely, and were therefore called "bridges."

extended as far as the lakes at Floresca and Herestrau began, the
boyars' carriages turned and, at a spanking trot, were driven back
toward the center of the city. The pedestrians, on the other hand,
in dense and noisy groups made for the Chaussée Kisselev. The
victoria, however, kept on at an increasing speed against a stream
of carriages coming the other way, whose occupants frequently
waved to Davida. She would not, however, give the order to turn
back. Nicolai was a cool customer, well used to boyar whims: he
had been told to keep going; he therefore kept going for as long
as he could. The victoria was almost at the end of the avenue; to
the right there was a dilapidated posting house, its roof caved in.
A few years ago it had been the departure point for the stage-
coaches for Tîrgoviste and Brasov, but their terminus was now the
square in front of the Metropolitan Church. The posting house
was therefore abandoned, and the inn adjoining it was also falling
into decay. The area was usually deserted; but on this occasion it
was filled by a noisy crowd. There were many townsmen in round
hats and black and brown jackets; but for the most part there
were peasants—perhaps three thousand of them in their rough
homespun suits, black felt shoes, and long dark capes; all were
either shouting angrily, or laughing and exchanging jokes with
the townsmen.

Davida, who until that moment had been thinking of Sherban
Vogoride, suddenly realized that her carriage had stopped, that
it was surrounded by a multitude of men, that the nearest were
staring at her with hostility, and that all about her were thousands
of pairs of dark eyes in thousands of rough, bony, clay-colored
faces. On the avenue behind her there was not another carriage
to be seen; only a few pedestrians and, in the distance, a dark, moving block—a group of horsemen approaching at the gallop and
raising a cloud of dust. Above their heads floated the brightly
colored pennons of a small forest of lances.

Mlle Marchand had not moved; her anxious eyes were fixed on
the sea of sheepskin capes that surrounded them. Davida was
about to order Nicolai to turn around and drive home when she
realized that nobody was now paying any attention to her. A

carriage was slowly forcing its way through the crowd, its frightened horses neighing. In it were two gentlemen in frock coats and
top hats, and a policeman carrying a drawn saber stood on each of
its steps. One of the gentlemen stood up and, raising his hat,
shouted, "Good people! Stop!"

In the distance, and apparently coming from the villages about
the lake of Baneasa, appeared a line of covered farm wagons. The
crowd was beginning to mutter. A young man with a big bony
frame tore off his fur cap and shouted, "We've been waiting long
enough for our answer! Go to the Prince, sir, and tell him that
we're here!"

"What's happening? Is it a riot?" Mlle Marchand asked in French.
In the same language Davida said, "It's nothing—just some peasants."

"Good people, return to your homes! His Highness the Prince
knows the cause of your misfortunes!"—This from the man in the
carriage, shouting himself hoarse. Before he could go on, a man
with a heavy mustache and a hard, lined face interrupted him:
"Well he may. But before we can get to him, we'll be gobbled
up by your lot!"

The peasants laughed. A young man in white trousers and a
black jacket, perched on one of the lowest branches of a linden
tree, shouted, "Don't argue with that fellow! He's Vogoride's
agent! To the palace, men! To the Prince! The Prince must be
spoken to. He's on your side. It's Vogoride who stops him from
helping you!"

He seemed gay enough—with the madcap high spirits of a
firebrand. The young peasant who had snatched off his fur cap
took him up: "Let him show himself here, then! We'll give him
some coffee, lads! And tobacco! He asked for it; he shall have it!"

These words evidently had a double meaning, for a cruel light
flashed in his eyes as he spoke. There was a burst of grim laughter
from the men nearest to him. Davida started and seized Mlle
Marchand by the arm. "What insolence!"

Davida was choking and pale with rage; she had just realized
that Nicolai and Vasili were laughing—the same mirthless and

hostile laugh as the mob. Her fierce glare quickly put an end to their hilarity.

In the other carriage the two men in frock coats gave an order to one of the policemen, who, saber under his arm, shoved his way through the crowd to the linden tree where the young man in white trousers was sitting. Above the rising murmur from the crowd he was still shouting, "To the Prince, good people! And then to the Chamber! We'll collar these boyars! Let's get our hands on Vogoride!"

Meanwhile the peasants had closed up to make a solid front against the policeman, who was pressing forward with his *képi* pulled down to cover his forehead.

"You can't get through! Sorry, no room! Where do you think you're going?" There was malevolence in their derision. Some of their number were helping the young man down from his perch; a few seconds later the agitator had disappeared. Davida was listening to an exchange of opinions among the peasants nearest to her carriage.

"Hey, you there—what are we going to do? Hi, Costica! What do you think?"

A man, invisible in the crowd, shouted, "These people are only small fry. To the devil with them! Let's make for the town, lads! To the Prince!"

"No, really, good people . . ." It was one of the men in the carriage again. He held out his arms to them, but his voice broke and his eyes were dull with terror. A low, dull growl came from the crowd.

Near the offside rear wheel of the carriage, almost in Davida's ear, a peasant bawled, "Let me just get my hands on that Vogoride one of these fine days! I'll show him."

Another yelled, "Get your hands on him? Not likely! He needs a pickax in his skull. What about it, lads?" he went on violently. "What are we going to do? Stay here all day?" And turning to those in his immediate vicinity, he explained in a fury, "I've nobody to do my work, what with the wife being ill—all I came for was to take a slash at the boyars and then be off back home. It ain't likely any boyar can know what I feel inside—but I'd show him. Oh, I'd show him all right!"

The young man who had flung his fur cap away clambered up onto the steps of Davida's carriage. He had a good look at the green silk upholstery, then at Davida's dress and at Mlle Marchand's. Then he stared in their faces, laughed, quite at his ease, and gave them a wink. Both started away from him and clung to each other. Vasili, still clinging to his place behind the victoria, said gently, "Now come on, get down, there's a good fellow."

The shrill voice of the man in the other carriage was raised again. "Listen, good people!" The police had their sabers out. One of them brandished his weapon threateningly. "Whoa, whoa! Ho! Ho! Ho!" the peasants shouted, as if calming a restive horse, and pitchforks were thrust toward the policeman. Then the clatter of hoofs was all around them. Davida saw the gleaming coats of horses on either side of her, and had the smell of leather and stables in her nostrils. Lancers in blue uniforms with red facings were advancing in two closed ranks against the crowd, pushing it back. Angrily they pointed their lances skyward, the red, yellow, and blue pennons no longer floating. As in a dream, Davida saw the young man who had climbed on the step of the carriage and winked at her jump down and slip away between the horses with astonishing agility. The carriage carrying the two gentlemen was no longer visible; it was hidden by the cavalrymen and a threatening forest of lances. Behind the second rank of soldiers, the space, briefly empty, began to fill with tradesmen gesticulating wildly, and young men with long hair and side whiskers, wearing round hats, shouting and throwing stones at the lancers. Horses began rearing; the soldiers turned in their saddles and one of them pulled his horse around and lowered his lance. The crowd gave way in front of him, but kept up the shouting. The soldier seemed at once angry and unhappy, and sweat was pouring down his face. An officer bawled at him, "Rosca! Back into line, you damned idiot!"

But just as the soldier was wheeling his horse and rejoining the ranks—still with the same unhappy expression—the front line of the troop broke and the horses scattered, driven back by a fearful yell. The peasants in their long black coats were in a state of unusual excitement, shouting hoarsely and brandishing pitchforks or axes, which they had kept hidden until that moment.

"Turn the carriage, Nicolai!" Davida cried. But the coachman had already taken advantage of the moment when there was room to maneuver. The carriage was turned, and by the time Davida spoke he was whipping up the horses, which set off at a gallop straight for the group of townsmen who were obstructing the road. They were forced to scatter for their lives; there were angry shouts and a stone whistled past, striking Davida's little sunshade. The horses suddenly went wild, and started galloping so madly that Nicolai was unable to master them until they were back on the Mogosoaïa Bridge and passing a second troop of cavalry making for the Chaussée at the trot.

A few moments later Mlle Marchand turned around and said in a frightened voice, "Why—where is Vasili?" The man was no longer in his place behind the carriage.

"Perhaps he fell off—or he may have run away," Davida said in a tone of indifference. And without more ado she returned to the matter that was exercising her mind, saying, "So he is universally hated." Her smile, compounded of satisfaction, surprise, and loathing, made her look like a grinning old woman. Mlle Marchand realized at once that the girl was not talking about Vasili, but she left the remark unanswered. Nor did Davida say anything more; she appeared to be lost in thought.

When the servant who was sent to look for Vasili reported that he had been found dead, having been struck by a stone, thrown under the horses' hoofs, and then trampled by the mob, Davida showed not the slightest interest. Indeed, she was hardly listening. Seated in her corner, she seemed to be waiting for something. Numerous callers, avid for news, were eager to still the anxiety which this latest assault by the rebellious populace had aroused in them.

The first visitor was the wife of the *vornic* Sturza. She sat down in her usual armchair, in the place of honor in the middle of a circle of younger women, like an insect in the heart of a flower.

There, bent double, wearing a highly romantic hood in the fashion of 1830 and with her ample black skirts covering the gilt chair, she sat leaning on the ivory knob of her cane, waiting while the other ladies, entering at the far end of the drawing room, walked some thirty paces to reach her. Each visitor paused for a moment on the threshold of the huge drawing room lit by the three enormous chandeliers; then, toying with a fan in one hand and lifting a fold of her skirt in the other, she advanced majestically across the room, smiling to right and left. Having reached the *vornic's* wife, each lady curtsied and kissed the old woman's hand. The latter, as soon as she saw a newcomer enter, and throughout the entire progression across the room, maintained a gay patter which was the joy of the ladies already seated around her: "Ah, here's that idiotic Greceano. I've been told that she likes playing leap-frog in monasteries with the old rams who call themselves monks. I can't think why Radu Greceano hasn't yet put a padlock on her. . . ." And then, changing her tune as the victim swept into her curtsy: "I am so happy to see you, child. And looking so pretty tonight! That blue dress suits you to perfection. Like a little madonna, is she not? Come closer, my dear, I must give you a kiss. There! Now sit here, beside me. . . ."

Mme Greceano took her place, with all the grace and gravity proper to a young matron known for her piety. Meanwhile, another lady had appeared at the far end of the room, and the old Princess merrily began her acid commentary: "Look at the silly goose! She's borne seven children, and if you ask her how she got them she titters like a cretin—Tee-hee! Tee-hee! At her country place they say she entertains gypsies in her bedroom. Don't ask me what she wants of them! All anyone ever overhears is Tee-hee! Tee-hee! and then, 'Well, you ruffian, what are you waiting for?' . . . Good evening, my dear Matilda, I'm delighted to see you. You will be able to enliven our circle a little. All these dear girls are a trifle stupid, you know; they seem to have no conversation. Sit down here and give me a kiss. Now tell me, what books have you been reading lately?"

The question was designed to produce an embarrassed silence

on the part of the lady, who hardly opened a book and spent her time at the card table.

Sophia Coziano busied herself among her guests. Davida remained silently in her corner. When Vogoride arrived she raised her eyes to look at him. The Minister's entrance was noisy: he was accompanied by Prince Ioan Grigori Ghica, the Minister for War, who had laid a friendly hand on his arm, and behind them came several deputies and Prince Ghica's aides-de-camp. Vogoride was laughing, and his face bore an expression of ruthless cruelty.

"What happened? Why nothing, nothing at all!" he exclaimed in answer to the ladies and gentlemen who swarmed around him the moment he appeared in the room. "An attempt at armed rebellion, like that of last winter—the day I was booed when I entered the Chamber, and Apostol Arsaki was stoned. As it happened, His Highness and I were in conference at the time—" Vogoride turned to Ghica, who stroked his pointed beard and bowed gravely—"so that I was able to beg him to send two squadrons of lancers straight away. They arrested about two hundred of the rebels. The scoundrels are being questioned at this very moment—and I'll answer for it they'll tell all they know! Even what they think of the milk they were suckled on!" And, turning to the old Princess Sturza, he asked her without preamble, "Well, Princess, what do you say to a rubber of whist?"

"Sherban, my dear boy, what happened this morning? The whole town's in an uproar! Mark my words, my dear, one of these days we shall wake up with a revolution on our hands, just like we had fourteen years ago."

"Fear nothing, Princess," Vogoride said, separating the skirts of his tail coat to sit down, while a footman set up a card table between them. "Fear nothing. If they dare to raise a hand I'll call in the Austrians, appeal to the Turks, and telegraph Prince Gortchakov. If I can't master them with our native bayonets, I'll swamp them in foreign troops." And, turning to Ghica, "By the way, my dear fellow, how did your troops behave?" Ghica too had taken his place at the card table, Sophia making the fourth. When they were among friends, Vogoride, an old friend of the Minister for War, did not call him "Highness."

Ioan Grigori Ghica shrugged his shoulders. "How would you expect them to behave? A soldier is bound to obey his officers' orders like an automaton. The slightest protest means solitary confinement in irons. I issued an order of the day to that effect and clapped a few rascals in irons by way of example. They've all sworn in the presence of a pope to carry out orders received and to obey their superiors. Let them abide by their oaths! If not, they can take the consequences."

"So you're not in the least uneasy?" Sophia Coziano asked, shuffling the cards.

Vogoride and Ghica exchanged a look; then Vogoride, putting in his monocle, said, "Why, the fact is, there would be nothing to worry about if we hadn't elected a republican as our reigning prince. When we crowned him three years ago, we crowned a revolutionary. With Couza over us and the peasants and their ringleaders under us, we're bound to have trouble. Of course we've got bayonets—and one can rule very well with bayonets." Vogoride laughed and went on: "Louis-Philippe did not dare to use them; nor did Charles X. Which is why both of them were overthrown. But General Cavaignac didn't hesitate to make use of them in July 1848, nor did Napoleon III in December 1852, nor Czar Nicholas in December 1825. And they never had cause to regret it. That is the lesson of history. Your play, Princess: I warn you that I have good cards and that I propose to win."

The rubber was played quietly, while gypsy serving-maids and footmen carried around trays of sweetmeats and French wines. Spurred and braided aides-de-camp with gilded aiguillettes and trailing swords mingled with the gentlemen who, chests thrust out and hands posed in waistcoat fronts, clustered about the ladies, while the ladies themselves played with their fans, and smiling graciously, determined to forget the steel-and-whalebone corsets beneath their silk dresses, constricting their ribs and cutting short their breath.

Davida, still thoughtful in her corner, stole stealthy glances at the tall and imposing Prime Minister, repeating to herself mechanically and for the thousandth time, "Everyone hates him—he is universally hated."

Only one person in the room kept an eye on Davida at that moment: Mlle Marchand. To all those present Herminie Marchand remained as she had always been: stiff, forbidding, and colorless in her simple black dress. None of the guests had yet spoken to her. Suddenly she noticed that M. Lascari was coming toward her. M. Lascari had always been polite to her, and even amiable. He sometimes addressed her as "Mademoiselle Herminie," and at times even went so far as to pay her a compliment. When he had reached her side he drew her into a quiet corner and said in a low voice, "Mademoiselle, there is something I should like to talk to you about as a friend, something I have on my mind——"

Mlle Marchand mastered her confusion. Her face revealed not the least emotion as, barely moving her thin lips, she said, "What is it about?"

"A business matter," Lascar replied with an enigmatic smile. "Shall I come and see you, or would you rather come to my house? There are always so many people here."

"Tomorrow afternoon the ladies are going to the theater. As for me, I am not feeling very well, which means that I expect to remain at home." With which murmured reply, and a very slight bow, Mlle Marchand moved away.

On the following day Lascar's coupé drove up to the Cozianos' residence half an hour after Sophia's carriage had driven away from it. Davida had not been able to avoid going with her mother, but she sat huddled into her own corner, as far as possible from Sophia and avoiding all physical contact.

Lascari went in, asked if Madame was at home, was sorry to hear that she was not, and wanted to know if there was really nobody in. Only the French mademoiselle, he was told.

"Excellent. I shall at least have company until the ladies return."

A few minutes later Mlle Marchand entered the drawing room.

Her hair was drawn back with marked severity, and she was wearing a starched collar and a dark dress buttoned up to the chin.

Lascar Lascari, his face twitching, sat fidgeting in a large armchair, stroking his greasy whiskers with a hand whose fingernails were dirty and bitten. He talked of the weather, of the unrest in the city, where both partisans and opponents of agrarian reform were holding meetings, and he observed that the peasant movement seemed on the point of breaking out into violence. The flame was being fanned by the "red" Liberals, and even by unknown revolutionaries, come, it was thought, from abroad and affiliated to the general European revolutionary movement. At last he came around to the subject of Mlle Marchand herself, of her family and her want of fortune.

"It is obvious that you are perfectly well-bred and of excellent family, though your circumstances are a trifle straitened at the moment—a situation which you carry off with remarkable dignity," Lascari said. Then, without looking at Mlle Marchand, he went on as if casually: "I might be in a position to insure you a modest—er —competence—a little capital, shall we say?—with a small income."

"I hope that you will ask me to do nothing but what is honorable in exchange," said the governess, after a short silence.

"Oh, nothing could be more honorable! I am happy to see that you are as intelligent as your behavior led me to expect. . . . Perfectly honorable, you have my word for that. Here it is in a nutshell. I am very fond of Davida, and I am still too young for this feeling to be of a paternal nature. Consequently I am ready to make the utmost sacrifices in order to marry her. I am well aware that my friend Alexander is an ambitious man, and that indeed he even entertains certain dreams of greatness which might appear ridiculous to anyone less fond of him than I am. His ambitions may perhaps be justified by his fortune, which is substantial, but hardly by the name he bears. His is a very good name, of course, but it places him only in the second rank, a long way behind those families whose ancestors reigned over our principalities, as for in-

stance the Cantacuzenes, who gave Byzantium some of her emperors. And the Cantacuzenes are by no means the only ones. . . .
There are other families whose past has been a glorious one,
though it may not have included a throne: the Ducas, for example;
and also, I do not hesitate to say, the Lascaris. Alexander dreams
of a splendid alliance for his daughter, either with one of our
princely families or with a family of the European nobility—so
long as it is among the most illustrious. You have, I think, been
long enough in this house to realize that he could not, without
distress, bring himself to give his daughter in marriage to a person
—let us say, to anyone else," Lascari concluded rather vaguely.
"As for the young lady's own inclinations," he hurried on, "I do
not know them, but you might be able to tell me if I should be well
advised to hope, if there is any chance, even a slight one, or if on
the other hand I should do better to give up all idea . . ."

He fell silent at that, looking at Mlle Marchand with a grimace
of anxiety and clinking the gold in his pocket. Mlle Marchand
thought for a moment, still keeping her eyes attentively fixed on
him. "At the moment," she murmured, "Davida is very far from
any such ideas."

"Good, good," he said forcefully, as if delighted with what he
had just heard, yet still pulling the same face. "That is excellent.
Perfect."

"At the same time, one might perhaps bring about a situation. . . . A mistake made by Davida, for example, could make
her marriage unavoidable. . . ."

"Of course, to be sure . . . a mistake," Lascari cried, in a pleasant, joyful, but polite tone. "That is very good—admirable."

"However, I do not believe, monsieur, that Davida is likely to
be sufficiently attracted by your person—I speak in all frankness."

"Ah," Lascari said, and fell into a deep silence. Then he began
to fidget in his chair again. "But . . . it would be disagreeable
for me to know that . . ."

"The mistake in question would be apparent rather than real,
monsieur," Mlle Marchand said. "It would be sufficient to give her
father cause for suspicion. As her governess, I could by no means

allow my pupil to commit a real error. In this my conscience is at stake. But as to what Monsieur Coziano might imagine, that is quite a different story."

Lascari took a deep breath, seized the governess's hand, and pressed it. Mlle Marchand said, "However, since Monsieur Coziano would never know that my error was trifling and had not impugned his honor, despite all appearances, I should be risking my position."

"You need have no worry on that score," Lascari said. "I will take care of everything." He was secretly determined that this governess should never see a penny of his money. But Herminie Marchand, knowing that she must escape from Nogent-sur-Seine at all costs, was equally determined not to let go the hold she had secured.

"I think it is now your turn to propound a little. I do not know if I make myself clear. . . ."

"Perfectly. A quarter of the sum at once, deposited in Hillel's Bank."

"Half, if you please."

"Very well: one half," Lascari said in a tone of grievous suffering. He consoled himself with the thought that Mlle Marchand would wait until the Greek Calends for the other half.

That evening, when Sophia Coziano returned from the theater accompanied by Davida and several friends, she learned that M. Lascari had called to see her, had spent a quarter of an hour chatting to Mlle Marchand, and had then decided to wait no longer. She paid little attention to this item of news. On the other hand, she was much disturbed when told that a messenger on horseback had arrived from the Cozia estates, bearing a letter from the boyar. She sent for the letter, which was sealed and addressed to her. She opened it: inside she found another envelope, also sealed, bearing the inscription "For Davida." For a moment Sophia Coziano was perplexed. True, Alexander was bent on observing all the forms of courtesy, and no one was to know that he had not written to her personally; but the affront was still calculated: her husband had nothing to say to her, no longer had anything in common with her. And what if Davida's letter contained something about her? She broke the seal and read it. Then she sent for Davida and furiously held the letter out to her at arm's length. "Here. Your father has written to you."

They were in the anteroom. Sophia had deserted her guests. Davida looked at the open envelope, then at the letter, and asked, "Did he send the letter like this?"

Her mother started angrily. "How dare you be so impertinent? Do you want your face slapped? For some time now you have been very insolent. Try to remember your place, unless you wish to be reminded of it."

"For some time now I have actually been keeping out of the way," Davida replied firmly.

Her mother found nothing to reply; she turned on her heel and, with her crinoline rustling, went back to her guests. Davida, with a pallid smile, began to read the letter.

"I miss you very much, my dear child," Alexander Coziano had written. "I am very unhappy, and feel more than ever the injustice of men, the hypocrisy of friends, and the faithlessness of those who ought to be most faithful." And he went on in the same style, trying to ease his bitterness by allusions, without ever suspecting that his daughter would understand them. Davida's eyes filled with tears, and she kissed her father's letter, whispering, "I will prove that I am worthy of you!"

After which she hid the letter in her dress and went into the drawing room. The ladies and gentlemen were animatedly discussing the forthcoming major debate on agrarian reform, which the Prince and his minister, Kogalniceano, were bent on carrying through at all costs. Sherban Vogoride was holding forth, his back to the stove as usual. Withdrawn in her corner, Davida watched him with extraordinary attention, as if he had been a foreigner or some alien creature. At the climax of his speech she sat down at the piano and began to play Chopin's Prelude in C Minor with rather more force than the score demanded. Everyone fell silent and turned toward her. Davida, her back to the room, went on playing.

"Davida! We are talking," her mother protested, very much annoyed. Davida pretended not to hear. Sherban Vogoride said amiably, "Never mind. It's a very fine piece," and appeared to follow Davida's playing with delight, although his taste ran rather to café-concert melodies and the music of the hunting horn. Davida, with a contemptuous smile which no one could see, played the piece through to the end. When she had finished, she rose and bowed sulkily to the guests' applause.

4

Shortly after her interview with Lascar Lascari, Mlle Marchand found the necessary instrument for her project. The following day she went to the Hillel Bank, and on an order from Lascari, had a substantial sum in napoleons, louis d'or, and Austrian thalers transferred to her account. Thereafter the governess relaxed her watch over Davida, particularly when the girl was taking her mathematics lesson, during which Mlle Marchand sat reading or embroidering in a far corner of the room. The spring air, warm and caressing, drifted in through the open window. The only sounds were the voices of the stableboys, the twittering and chirping of birds in the trees, and in the room itself, the low voice of the young man who was instructing Davida in the elements of algebra.

The mathematics teacher was not yet twenty-five years old. He was thin, tightly buttoned into a threadbare frock coat, very shiny at the elbows, hips, and shoulders. He was very pale, and wore his hair long in the romantic style then fashionable among young men. His name was Anghel Popesco, and he was the son of the pope of St. Nicholas-of-the-Clothiers. Some years previously, M. Coziano had sent the two most promising of his sons' schoolfellows at St. Sava's College to complete their education in Paris. Anghel Popesco was one of them. But his lungs were affected and he had been obliged to leave Paris before completing his courses; and while the young Cozianos prolonged their stay in Paris to the last possible moment, he had returned to live at home, where he gave lessons in mathematics while awaiting an appointment—thanks to M. Coziano's influence—as an assistant master at Sava's.

One morning, long before the time when he was due in Culmea Veche Street, Anghel was still in his little room, sparsely furnished with chests covered with Rumanian tapestries. The walls were also covered with tapestries and, on the east wall, with smoke-darkened icons, above which were stuck a few sprigs of basil. The small brick stove, on which a coffeepot stood warming, gave out too much heat for such a glorious spring day. Anghel Popesco was sitting, elbows on knees, eyes fixed on his broken shoes, absorbed in thought. His sisters, Aglaia and Aristitza, were sitting close together on the divan which occupied a corner of the room, laying out cards to tell their fortunes. Their father, the pope Agapit, in his indoor clothes—a waistcoat which buttoned up to the chin, baggy black satin trousers, and slippers—was seated opposite his son and looking at him with an expression of pity and sadness.

"You're a leech, that's what you are, if you want to know," Aristitza informed her brother. Anghel bowed his head a little lower, but said nothing.

Aglaia turned to her sister and said with a look of deep contempt, "He's an idiot, my dear! Any other brother would do everything possible to find husbands for his sisters—introduce them to young men of the aristocracy. He moves in high society all the time, and never even mentions his sisters. That lady didn't even know he had a sister. When I called on her, first she was all wide-eyed amazement and then she laughed. After that she received me properly, you know, asked me to come in by the little back door reserved for her most intimate friends, gave me coffee . . ."

"But next time you called," her sister interrupted with a sneer, "the lackey told you she was not at home, and the third and fourth time as well."

Aglaia shrugged her shoulders. "All right, my girl, but you'll never be anything but Pope Agapit's daughter. You simply don't understand what is customary in high society. If she had guests, she couldn't just leave them to come and drink coffee with me."

Anghel shook his head and said bitterly, "What people! And what a world!"

Aristitza lashed out at him once more. "A bloodsucker, that's what you are! You spend a lot more than you bring in. You weren't even capable of going and asking the boyar for a job! It's always Father who has to go bowing and scraping to get work for you."

Anghel started up and looked at his father. "You're not proposing to go to Monsieur Coziano's? You mustn't!"

"I have already been, my boy. It was necessary," the priest muttered. "Since you would not go, it was up to me to do it."

"I have no need of his charity. I'd rather be eaten by dogs. Have I not had to live in the same house as his sons? For them a furnished apartment, for me an attic under the tiles, with a rickety table and a bed full of lice. That was quite enough for me! I want no more of it. Why do you torture me? Was it for this that you brought me into the world?"

Anghel covered his face with his hands, the better to restrain his tears.

"Why would you not listen to me?" Pope Agapit muttered. "You would be a deacon or a priest by now, with a wife, a house, and an income. Whose idea was it to go away to foreign parts? Who was forever talking of Paris, only to come back from it sick, and without even the faith he took with him? I let you talk me into it, and this is what it has brought you to!"

At that Anghel jumped to his feet. "Well, what has it brought me to?" He was red in the face. "You talk as if I had fallen very low. That's what you think, is it? But I would rather die of starvation and be as I am than become one of their wage slaves! I . . . I . . . One day you shall see who and what I am! We have always lived under the same roof, but you have never known me!"

Aristitza burst into shrill laughter which sounded like neighing. "And whom ought we to have seen in you? Who are you? A simpleton with his head in the clouds. Oh, you're a clever one! What can you do? Nothing at all!"

Anghel looked at her and became suddenly quite calm. "I can do things that your small mind could never conceive." He resumed his seat. "I know how to live, yes, and die, for the good of humanity, and I seek those whom I can serve wholeheartedly, body and soul."

"And you believe you will be able to find them?" the priest asked gently, as if he were speaking to a child. "Had you become a pope, you would already have found what you are seeking."

Anghel shrugged his shoulders. The old priest sighed: "You have even lost your faith. Nothing whatever is left to you."

"Science is left me."

"What can your science accomplish?"

"It can overwhelm the world," Anghel replied with quiet firmness. "Thanks to science, men will live free and happy, like brothers. They will be masters of the earth, all rich, all powerful, and all equal! You wanted to know. Now you do."

"Lord!" Pope Agapit moaned, his eyes full of tears. "Lord God, forgive him, for he knows not what he says."

"I have no need of pity," Anghel said.

"But you've need of money, eh?" Aristitza retorted. "The food we cook and your father's money, you need those, don't you?"

"He gives me no money," Anghel shouted. "Is not what I bring in enough? But don't worry; I shan't be a burden to you much longer. You'll soon be rid of me."

He finished dressing, put on his hat, and went out, slamming the door behind him. No, he could bear it no longer! His patience was exhausted. He would simply have to find some quiet corner, an attic, anything so long as he could be alone to think, to dream of those things he knew, of certain men he had met. . . .

But first, if his troubles were not to choke him, he must open his heart to somebody. Through the teeming streets that led down toward the river, he made for the Dîmbovitza embankment. There, behind Manouc's Inn, was a narrow-fronted house squeezed in between the Zarifu Bank and Gherson's shop. Anghel went in and climbed a dark and narrow staircase to a landing overlooking the inner courtyard. He found a door to which had been pinned a visiting card: "Thomas Alimanesco, *Docteur ès sciences.*" Anghel knocked. The door opened and a bearded face appeared. "Alimanesco—it's me," Anghel whispered.

Inside the room it was quite dark: only a very little light filtered between the drawn curtains. The men Anghel had met sat on chairs around the table, smoking their long-stemmed pipes. Prodan was there, still a student at St. Sava's College, where Alimanesco taught mathematics. Prodan had a small, sparse mustache; he was squat and powerful, and was wearing a very short black jacket, a black waistcoat, and white trousers. His shirt was open at the throat, and his big cravat gave him, in his own estimation, the look of an artist; to further the impression he would have liked to wear a velvet beret as well, had he not been afraid that in certain circumstances it would make it too easy for the police to recognize him. Also there was Lieutenant Maldaresco, an elegant and dignified young man who said little and that little in a cold, decided tone, whereas Prodan, sitting astride his chair, talked loudly and with much gesticulation. By contrast, Maldaresco sat listening with legs crossed and hands clasped on the brass guard of his cavalry saber, perfectly motionless, his narrow face and regular features set in a mask of severity. The third man present was Iovanake, a young man who seemed, like the Lieutenant, to be between twenty and twenty-five years of age. He was smoking a long *chibouc* with a china bowl, and wore a frock coat with three of its buttons missing, so that only the fourth was buttoned and that into the wrong buttonhole. His high collar was secured by a threadbare black tie, and he still wore his top hat, shoved to the back of his head. His rather near-set eyes were bright with intelligence. His ink-stained fingers, and the copy of *The Rumanian,* wet from the press, sticking out of his pocket, betrayed his profession. All present greeted Anghel, and then Alimanesco went and lay down on his bed; he was in shirtsleeves and slippers, and wore no tie.

Prodan resumed an interrupted harangue: "If at that moment the soldiers had made common cause with them, nothing could have stopped them. I was there, mixing with the peasants, and I realized exactly how things stood. One of them said to me, 'What's the likes of you doing here, sir? You don't want them to give *you* land, do you?' I told him man does not live by land alone: he needs freedom, too. . . . Just as we were about to disperse the troops, a second squadron arrived on the scene, and then another, which meant that nothing more could be done. But everything hung by a thread. A thread, I tell you!"

Alimanesco, his head resting on one white hand, spoke up as the other fell silent, watching the rest out of blue, thoughtful eyes.

"*They* are weak. . . . That's why they did not dare send their police infantry: they knew they'd have had to run for it. . . ."

"Yes, but the Army won't serve their purpose either," Lieutenant Maldaresco said curtly. "The soldiers are discontented; they've no wish to charge a crowd of miserable people. As for the officers, they consider such police work unworthy of them. That sort of thing is all right for the Aga's Mamelukes. At the next attempt they'll keep their lances at rest and their swords in their scabbards, as they did today. Consequently . . ." A slight smile briefly lit his cold, severe features, and he concluded, "Consequently, it can be done," without going into details as to what exactly could be done.

"Yes, yes, Maldaresco, it will be done," Alimanesco said thoughtfully.

The Lieutenant turned and looked at him attentively. "How?"

"It will be done," the sick man answered him, smiling.

Maldaresco flushed, seized his saber in both hands, and struck the floor violently. "That's good!" he shouted, then fell silent.

Iovanake pulled the newspaper out of his pocket and threw it down on the bed. "The leader is a protest against the censorship," he said. "Vogoride is snapping his fingers at all democratic liberties. Here, read this." With his ink-stained finger he pointed out to the mathematician the passage on the front page of *The Rumanian.*

"He's not denying himself much, our Vogoride," Prodan said, laughing. "Legal and final union of the principalities—refused; proclamation of the official name of Rumania—refused; agrarian reform—refused. He refuses everything and confines himself to repeating, 'Order, calm, peace!' "

"An 'order' which benefits nobody but the Tombateras and those who wear the *ishlic*," Iovanake cried violently.*

"What we need is the pistol of an Orsini, but a pistol whose bullets reach their target."

Everyone looked at Anghel Popesco.

"Revolutions are never made with a pistol shot, but with barricades in the streets," Alimanesco put in dryly, as if he were enunciating a theorem. Ignoring this interruption, Iovanake continued: "Rosetti has come to an agreement with Arion and Orasano to form a committee of initiative. We shall assemble some tens of thousands of men in the Filaret Plain on the eleventh of June, and nobody can stop us, for it isn't a crime to celebrate the anniversary of the 1848 Revolution. And they can't stop these people taking their midday meal about noon—and in the afternoon and evening—well, anything can happen: fall of government, summoning of a constituent assembly, proclamation of a republic, land reform—everything!"

With a growl of satisfaction, Prodan spat on his hands and rubbed them together, like a peasant. Alimanesco, his head leaning on his hand, smiled. "But what will the Prince do?" the Lieutenant asked. "And Kogalniceano?"

"Why should the Prince mind? He's one of the revolutionaries of '48!" Iovanake said. "Kogalniceano knows it well. Rosetti—but I need say no more about him. And there are plenty of others!"

"Vogoride is very powerful," Anghel Popesco said. "You're not taking account of what may occur to him—he's ingenious and perverse. . . ."

There was a silence. Then, half joking and half serious, Alimanesco said, "If you intend to play Orsini, it's your duty to tell us so, you know. You might do our cause more harm than good."

"Oh no! No, I never thought of doing that," Anghel replied, embarrassed and much disturbed. The idea had not, in fact, occurred

* *Tombateras* means reactionary boyars and *ishlic* the fur cap worn by the boyars.

to him. The gulf was too wide that separated the half-fledged, half-starved teacher, son of the pope Agapit, and the great millionaire statesman, covered with honors, the heir of rich and mighty men, mighty and rich himself. Anghel was suddenly afraid, not of Vogoride, but of the new dimensions that things were taking in his mind; as he considered them, Vogoride's stature began to shrink with dizzying speed, while he, the insignificant Anghel Popesco, suddenly assumed gigantic and terrifying proportions. Then everything returned to normal and he repeated: "No, I had not thought of that," while the others went on talking and did not hear him. And again he was tempted toward that zone of his spirit in which things changed their proportions.

"Why are you protecting him?" he asked defiantly, pitching his voice high. And since the others had all stopped talking, he went on: "Don't you hate him too?"

Stiffly, his movement impeded by his high collar, Lieutenant Maldaresco turned to him and said, "Hate whom? Vogoride?"

Iovanake had his mouth half open, and a thin wisp of tobacco smoke drifted up toward his eyes. Prodan was laughing. Alimanesco answered Anghel, looking him straight in the eye: "Love for the revolution is greater than hatred for an individual. We are not murderers. Vogoride will be cut down only when it becomes necessary to the cause."

Anghel coughed and looked at the worn toes of his shoes. He kept quiet, but he stopped listening to what the others were saying. When the visitors rose—it was time for their meal and they ate at a restaurant opposite Prince Soutzo's palace—Anghel also stood up, but said that he wanted to stay for a moment.

The others separated with mutual embraces, and Maldaresco, more moved than his severe and distant expression indicated, spoke quietly to Alimanesco: "This is not at all the way in which I expected to hear the great news. I expected more solemnity, something more romantic—but all the same, it is well, very well!"

"There is nothing more romantic than a revolution," Alimanesco said in a low voice; and he took the Lieutenant in his arms, pressing his thin chest against the steel plate engraved with twin blazons that embellished the scarlet plastron of Maldaresco's uniform. Then he offered his hand to Iovanake, who, though less demonstrative than the others, to his great surprise embraced him warmly, and, while kissing him on the right cheek, muttered, "Keep an eye on Anghel." He then kissed him on the other cheek, in order to whisper into his left ear, "Stop him from doing anything rash." Then, in a normal voice: "Good-by, my dear friend." And he left the room, taking Prodan with him.

After they had gone Alimanesco was seized by a paroxysm of coughing. He left the room to expectorate, and came back pressing a handkerchief to his lips. He glanced at it before stuffing it into the pocket of his waistcoat. Then, having drawn back the curtains and thrown open the window, he put his hands on Anghel's shoulders and said gently, "I have not long to live . . . perhaps a year, two at the most. But I should not want to die before seeing the revolution triumphant."

Taking him in his arms in a sudden burst of affection, Anghel said, in his dull, broken voice, "I admire you, Alimanesco. If there were no men like you in the world, humanity would be less noble and would not deserve the sacrifice of one's life. You are a man without spot, a crystal-clear spirit."

Alimanesco began to laugh. "My life is too short for me to degrade it by compromises. So you see, the virtue is rather in my phthisis than in me. But what is the matter with you? You seem upset; has something happened to you?"

"Yes. I have been sorely tried by certain people who are sly, backward, and debased. I am ashamed, for my own sake and for theirs. And I yearn for liberty," Anghel cried, "for liberty and acts of heroism."

"Tell me all about it."

Anghel described the scene that had taken place in his father's house.

"You should have expected it," Alimanesco said. "If you like, you can stay here until we find some other solution. But I have nothing to offer except what you see."

He pointed to the couch with its broken springs, the washstand with its china basin, the table, the single candlestick, the cupboard full of books and clothes, the engraving hanging on one wall— General Field Marshal Miloradovitch crossing the Danube at the head of the Czar's army—the icons before which the atheist Alimanesco never prayed, and finally, the narrow brass bed.

For Alimanesco, son of a petty boyar in the Buzau province, this setting was wretched indeed. For Anghel, who had known dire poverty in Paris, it was more than adequate; nevertheless he refused.

"I shall easily find a room in the city, and I will let you know my address. I am impatient to resume our talks, to discuss ideals, to——"

"Tell me, Popesco, why does your mind run so much on Orsini?" Alimanesco demanded, keeping hold of his hand to prevent him from making for the door.

Anghel flushed. "I give you my word, I never thought of him until just now, when there was question of——"

"Orsini accomplished nothing," Alimanesco said.

Anghel replied at once: "His pistol shot forced Napoleon to undertake the unification of Italy, which today is an accomplished fact."

"A revolution is never made by a pistol shot, but by the whole people in arms," Alimanesco replied with tranquil obstinacy, forcing the other to sit down on a chair. "So long as society is not ripe for revolution, tyrants are killed in vain. And when it is ripe, it is no longer necessary to kill them, for the institutions that support them collapse. Ravaillac killed Henri IV and Damiens stabbed Louis XV, but both did their work in vain; whereas, when the Revolution broke out, the trial and execution of Louis XVI was by way of being a mere formality."

"All that belongs to the past," Anghel said. "Orsini was only yesterday."

"What of Fieschi? Isn't that just as recent an example?" Alimanesco demanded, his cheeks aflame. "Who overthrew Louis-Philippe? Was it Fieschi's infernal machine, or the February Revolution? Who put the Bourbons to flight? Louvel's knife, or the July Revolution of 1830?"

He began to cough and went hastily out of the room. When he returned his face was ashen and he had his handkerchief pressed to his mouth. Anghel rose at once and muttered, "Forgive me———"

"Have you understood?" the sick man asked in a weak voice.

"Yes, you are right," Anghel said hastily.

"We are among those who want the real revolution," Alimanesco resumed. "We cannot be satisfied with a few reforms. We want to see the republic installed, universal suffrage, the people . . ." He lay down on his bed and closed his eyes, then went on in the same weak voice: "The people, free and . . . armed . . ."

"Do not exhaust yourself," Anghel said. "Would you like me to stay with you?"

"No. You can go. Go and look for a room. I shall be better in a moment. Just a little weakness . . ."

5

Anghel had suddenly remembered that he had a lesson to give. He walked with long strides, lost in thought. As he was crossing the Mogosoaïa Bridge, a carriage, driven fast, came tearing up. He was so preoccupied that the horses almost ran him down. The coachman shouted, and Anghel jumped backward, his hat rolling in the dust behind him. He stooped to pick it up, wiping it on his sleeve to the accompaniment of laughter from the passers-by. He walked on, his forehead damp and his eyes wild.

He entered the great gateway of the house in Culmea Veche Street and walked up the steps, tugging and smoothing his threadbare frock coat. The French governess opened the door, looking unusually cheerful. Davida, however, barely nodded; she seemed low-spirited and sullen.

"Really, Davida!" Mlle Marchand said, pretending to be annoyed, "your hair is all untidy again." As she spoke she glanced at Anghel Popesco who, still pulling at his frock coat, was gazing at the girl.

"Well, to work! How are you, Monsieur Popesco? What is the latest news? It seems that the Government has again succeeded in postponing the debate on land reform. . . ."

Anghel Popesco's anger was still boiling inside him. For a few moments his timidity was overcome and, his voice hoarse but firm, he said, "Vogoride is fighting with great energy in defense of injustice."

"What? Oh, how admirably put! 'With great energy in defense of injustice.'" Mlle Marchand was delighted, and repeated the phrase once again.

"Almost an epigram," she said. "You are quite a wit, monsieur!"

Davida had raised her eyes. She looked at Anghel Popesco and seemed to be seeing him for the first time. She took her exercise books out of a rosewood secretary and asked him, "What injustice do you mean?"

"I can tell you what Monsieur Vogoride means by justice and injustice. For him justice means privilege and abuse of power; injustice, the struggle for liberty."

Somewhat alarmed at what he was saying, Anghel thought, *Now I shall not even be able to remain one of their servants. Vogoride is a friend of theirs; they will certainly be angry and dispense with my services. I shall never see her again. And then? Well, at least I shall be out of my pain. . . .* His heart ached; he was sorry that he had spoken, but powerless to stop himself. Which is why, when Mlle Marchand said, "And what, in your view, is justice?" he replied, "Justice, mademoiselle, is the happiness of humanity."

"Bravo, monsieur! One can see that you have lived in France. What do you think, Davida?" The girl had not taken her eyes off

Anghel Popesco. "I think," she whispered, "that it is a very elevated sentiment. Yes, it is nobly thought."

Anghel Popesco had been expecting an icy coldness; instead, his words had been received with admiration. It was the first time such a thing had happened to him, and he felt a surge of gratitude toward Mlle Marchand and Davida. But for that very reason he became incapable of saying anything more profound. After a few attempts to revive the conversation, to all of which the young man answered with a "yes" or a "no," Mlle Marchand rose.

"Davida, I have a little shopping to do. If you want tea, just ring for it. I will tell Anastasia." Very dignified, she withdrew.

Anghel Popesco gave Davida her algebra lesson, but his thoughts were in a whirl. He was possessed by a vibrant happiness. Could it be, perhaps . . . ? Was it possible that . . . ? But Davida did not ring for tea and they soon parted, both silent and morose. On his way home Anghel became aware of the spring for the first time. In the gardens surrounding the stucco-porticoed houses the birds were singing in the linden and chestnut trees. Children were playing in the dust of unpaved streets. Long files of ox-drawn wagons were on the move, frequently overtaken by smart carriages carrying ladies in silk dresses and big hats trimmed with ostrich feathers. Gentlemen on the pavements swept off their top hats as the ladies drove by, then made their way among the shopboys in dirty aprons who were laying the dust by drawing figure 8's with water poured through a funnel, before vanishing into their shops redolent of coffee, dried fish, and spices. The bells clamored from every church belfry; hawkers, bending beneath the weight of carrying yokes, cried their wares. Young men from the suburbs stood talking and laughing at every street corner. Anghel Popesco stopped outside a window which displayed a "To Let" sign.

He looked about him, then entered a courtyard as damp and dark as a well. There must be a series of small rooms with flaking plaster, inhabited by students, office workers, clerks retired on pension. Anghel found the door and knocked. A fat woman in a red flannel dressing gown, her hair wrapped in a mauve rag, opened it. He asked if there was a room to let.

There was. He was taken up to the top of the house, under the shingled roof, to a sort of landing with an iron railing off which opened a room loftier than it was wide, a sort of cell with a bed, a table, a chair, and a worm-eaten chest of drawers.

"Be careful when you open the drawers. They're not very strong and it won't be me as pays the carpenter. Any repairs come out of your pocket." The rent was ten lei a month. Anghel paid in advance and went to fetch his things from the house. The pope was at his church. Anghel's sisters greeted him with gibes. But when they saw him putting his things into a bag and realized that he was really going, they were astounded. They were so taken aback that they had not even the curiosity to follow him and discover where he was going.

Anghel Popesco settled into his lodgings. *I am free!* he told himself, trying the drawers of the chest and finding them ready to fall to pieces in his hands. *The poverty is even worse than in Paris, but here, at least, I am not living on any man's charity. Here I have no master.* He sat down on the rickety bed, which smelled of damp and poverty, lay back with his hands clasped behind the nape of his neck, and dreamed. Courage! It was courage that he had lacked until now. Here, as in Paris, he had sometimes had the conviction that certain events would open the doors of life and destiny to him. But his own awkward timidity had restrained him from entering those doors. *My sisters are right,* he told himself with an ironical smile. *I am in the moon. Or rather, I was. But now that's all over.* He had just made a great discovery, he had found a solution. Henceforth nothing could prevent him from living as he considered himself endowed to live, that is to say with nobility, purity, passion, and heroism. (At this very moment Davida Coziano was thinking of him. But Anghel Popesco was never to know that.)

That night Anghel went to Alimanesco's to give him his new address. They talked for a long time. "You seem very pleased with yourself," Alimanesco said. "You look like a man in love."

Anghel did not bat an eyelid and changed the subject. But he could not hide his excitement. He paced the mathematician's room, holding forth, maintaining the need for violent action, and uttering fine phrases in extravagant terms, while Alimanesco confined his rare interruptions to propounding from time to time one of his mathematician's axioms for revolution.

Anghel went often during the next few days to Culmea Veche Street. Mlle Marchand seemed always to have something to do about the house, work which could in no circumstances be postponed, and she disappeared, leaving him alone with Davida. One day, when Sophia Coziano was also out of the house—she was visiting Princess Sturza who was ill—and Anghel was trying to explain the mysteries of descriptive geometry, Davida put down her pencil and, with a thoughtful expression, said, "I'm tired today. Wouldn't you rather talk to me—about Paris?" And she rang for tea. Cup in hand, Anghel Popesco made an effort to overcome an excitement which was making his hands shake.

"The Paris I know is not the Paris that rich people know," he said, with a sad smile. "I am thinking of the vile dens in the neighborhood of the great theaters, cellars rotten with damp and reeking of spirits. Men with ravaged faces and glassy eyes come there to drink absinthe and forget their wretchedness. I didn't go there to drink, but to meet certain friends. . . ."

He fell silent. Ought he to go on? Only boldness could save him. In all things it was best to press on to the end.

"You cannot even imagine it, Mademoiselle Davida. But I must talk to you about it, because it seems to me that you are the one person who might understand me. I hope—no, I firmly believe, I am certain—that you will understand all the nobility of the revolution. And it is there, in the cellars of Paris and in wretched little rooms in her suburbs, that the explosion will occur. Bonaparte is sitting on a powder barrel and one of these days he will be blown to pieces. And he knows it. He knows it perfectly well. Only two or three years ago Orsini gave him a sharp reminder."

"Orsini was the man who fired a pistol at him?"

"Yes, that's the man. I was in Paris and I went to see him guillotined. I never saw a man who seemed to me as proud, as fine, as Orsini when he mounted the scaffold." Anghel was paler than usual and Davida gazed at him.

"Tell me about Orsini," she said, with a ghost of a smile.

For a long time she listened to him without interrupting. She played with a lace handkerchief as he talked, but at last put it into her sleeve, saying, "There are no men like him in our country."

"Oh, yes, there are. They exist here too," Anghel replied. There was a long silence. Suddenly, Davida hid her face in her hands, trembling. Anghel Popesco jumped to his feet, appalled. "Mademoiselle Davida—what is it? What has happened? What have I done?" He took a step toward her and held out his arms. Davida uncovered her eyes and looked at him. She was very pale. "Do I have to tell you . . . ?" she asked. It was not really a question and Anghel Popesco did not answer it.

"I hear somebody coming," Davida said. "Sit down and pick up a book."

They pretended to be working. Anghel Popesco was trembling. Davida watched him out of the corner of her eye. Nobody was moving in the house. Davida rose and went to the bell. When the servant appeared, she asked where Mlle Marchand was. The governess had gone out. Anghel Popesco waited until the maid had left; he felt deeply disturbed and his heart was beating wildly. He was preparing himself to face one of the supreme moments of his existence, without having the faintest idea of what was going to happen.

"Now," Davida said, "I want you to go. I have to think."

"But—but—why?"

"No, don't ask me anything, leave me, go away. We'll talk about this again. Come . . . come tomorrow."

When he was at the door she said, "Until then I shall be thinking of you."

She did, in fact, think of him, but only to decide the extent to which she could take him into her confidence.

As for Anghel, he shut himself into his little room and did not leave it all day long. Sometimes he got off the bed and paced around like a caged beast until he was giddy. From time to time he drank a glass of water and then resumed his pacing around and around the table. The floorboards creaked hideously. Several times the people in the room below knocked on their ceiling. Finally, somebody banged on the door. Anghel opened it, and found himself face to face with an old man in a satin skullcap, wearing a dressing gown reminiscent of an American shopkeeper's caped greatcoat. The old man complained that he could get no rest.

"I am ill and the doctor has ordered me to walk ten hours a day," Anghel said, and pushed his neighbor out onto the landing. He wanted to laugh. It seemed to him that his life was only just beginning, that it was marvelous, incredible, that reality was now giving him things he had hitherto known only by hearsay and from his reading. He could not sleep all night. The vision of Davida's delicate brown hands covering her sweet face haunted him. *She needs me. I will save her. I will help her, and ask nothing in return except the right to see her and talk with her as I have done up till now. What happiness! Ah, what happiness!* He wanted to express his gratitude, to offer thanks. But to whom? To life, to chance—or to himself?

The next day Anghel arrived a quarter of an hour too early and spent the time walking up and down the street before the house. Three carriages drew up at the house, and a number of elegant gentlemen went up the steps and indoors, while the carriages drove out of the other gate and stationed themselves at the curb. Anghel Popesco watched these arrivals without envy. If these people could have known what was passing in his mind, could have guessed who he was, all would have envied him. He was almost sorry for them.

Now it was his turn to enter the house, and he followed a footman through rooms full of people who chatted together without even noticing him. He knocked at Davida's door, and she herself came to open it. She was alone. The governess had gone out, doubtless to make some purchases, as she seemed to do so often lately.

"I have been thinking about you a great deal," Davida said in a low voice. Anghel Popesco had made up his mind to cast himself at her feet, to kiss her hands, but he was incapable of doing so; he was as if paralyzed.

"I have thought about you . . . and I still don't know . . ."

"Don't know what?" Anghel said, his voice almost failing him.

"I still don't know . . . if I dare trust . . ."

"Davida——" Anghel whispered. He slipped from his chair to kneel at her feet. Imperceptibly Davida stiffened, as if she wanted to draw back but had no room to do so. "I do not know whether you are the man that I dream of finding," she said.

The tone of her voice was carefully calculated: in point of fact, she had not been "dreaming of finding" a man of any kind. She leaned toward him and said, "Did you see who is here, in this house, at this very moment?"

"N-no—I did not . . ."

"The most odious, the most infamous, the vilest of men!" Davida hissed, leaning still nearer. Anghel caught the sweetness of her breath and the scent of her hair, which her gypsy maids had washed in an infusion of linden flowers and camomile. "The man who dishonors our country," she continued, "defiles the name of our greatest families, a tyrant, a debauchee, and a hypocrite, a man who shames the very earth he spurns beneath his feet!"

"Who?"

"Can you still ask me that? You do not know? I expected better of you," Davida said, turning away.

Anghel remained silent for a few moments and then, in a hesitant voice, said, "Vogoride?"

Davida looked into his eyes. So transformed was she by passionate feeling that Anghel Popesco completely lost his head. "Has he offended you personally?"

"Me? How dare you think such a thing! Do you think I can be touched by the insults of a dirty little Greek like him? Leave me at once! You are good for nothing but fine phrases! You call yourself a republican; must I teach you that personal insults and petty self-interest do not count, that all that matters is a higher and a nobler cause? I find I was mistaken in you."

Both were silent for a few moments.

"Sit down. Here, take this chair. Perhaps you would like me to ring for tea?" Davida said with a coldness that went to his heart.

Anastasia brought the tea and went out without a word. Nothing was to be heard but the purring of the silver urn. Davida poured the tea into cups and added sugar. In the silence a teaspoon tinkled against a saucer.

"Everyone hates him," Davida said. "Who does not hate him? Do you know anyone who does not hate him?"

"Yes," said Anghel curtly. "The great boyars whose interests he defends certainly do not hate him." And he suddenly began to examine the girl with a new curiosity. Appalled by an idea which he did not dare to formulate even in his own mind, he asked, "Mademoiselle Davida, what have you against him?"

Davida began to cry with exasperation, fury, and impatience; things were not going to be as simple as she had fancied.

"Have I not also the right to love liberty?" she said, her voice broken by sobs. "Must I be like all those people whom you saw as you came in? Am I condemned to live without an ideal?"

These last words were uttered with passionate anger. Davida was furious. Not, of course, that her "ideal" was Anghel Popesco's. But since, for the time being, she deemed it necessary to say that she had an ideal, everyone had to take her at her word. This wild girl with her long hair in disorder and her eyes flaming in a thin, pale face overwhelmed Anghel Popesco. He again threw himself on his knees at her feet, kissing the small brown hands which Davida snatched away, shuddering. Anghel did not even notice this movement of repugnance. He was laughing, happy, almost beside himself. Davida sat down and allowed him to hold her hand. Then she said with a frown, "I should not have told you. . . ."

"Why?" Anghel demanded, suddenly uneasy.

"You are not the man to risk your life for an ideal."

"On the contrary, I am perfectly capable of it," Anghel replied, curt and firm.

She stared at him and murmured, "You're lying."

Anghel went white. "Do not humiliate me. I am a poor man. I have nothing in the world but my honor."

Davida's face expressed contempt and Anghel went on, emphasizing every word: "Mademoiselle Davida . . . be very careful what you say."

Despite her youth, Davida concentrated in a single look more poisonous irony than a whole battalion of elderly ladies could have achieved and, distinctly articulating every syllable, said, "Orsini."

Anghel flushed; then his face became livid, and in despair he cried out, "The time is not yet—I have thought about it very carefully. No, no, it is not yet time . . ."

Davida burst into mirthless laughter.

". . . but if our cause requires it, it is *I* who will do it!"

"Our cause!" Davida cried, rounding on him. "And when will *our* cause require it? After *he* has done as he likes and done evil for years to come? Obviously it is easier to hide behind the interests of *our* cause than to risk one's life!"

Anghel caught hold of her wrists. "Tomorrow," he cried. "Do you hear me? Tomorrow I will show you what I am capable of. But why am I saying tomorrow? Today—now! But I have no right to do so."

"Orsini," Davida replied with a challenging laugh. "Orsini!"

"You must understand me, I have promised my friends to do nothing without their knowledge."

"Then tell them! Why not——"

Davida stopped in mid-sentence. No; nobody must know anything about it.

"They would not agree. They see things differently."

"You're lying! You're afraid!" Davida cried, forcing the sobs into her throat and hiding her face in her hands. "I am sorry I ever spoke to you about it," she wailed through her tears. "I should have kept silent and tried the thing myself, with my own hand!"

Anghel Popesco put his lips to the small clenched fist and, with a shade of hesitation, said, "Very well, I will do it."

Davida looked at him squarely, and smiled. Deeply moved, almost terrified, he fixed his eyes on her, tried to say something, but succeeded only in moving his lips. His eyes filled with tears. Davida took his face between her hands. He trembled at their touch and closed his eyes, while the tears ran down his cheeks. When he opened his eyes Davida was no longer facing him. Slender and supple, she was standing at the old rosewood secretary, looking for something. She took a pistol from a drawer and handed it to him.

"It's Father's and it is loaded."

It was a dueling pistol with a long, hexagonal barrel, and the stock was inlaid with mother-of-pearl.

"You must aim it like this."

She showed Anghel Popesco how to hold the weapon. Anghel let her guide him, saying nothing, as if in a dream, listening passively while she told him where Vogoride was to be found and which was the best place to lie in wait for him.

"During the next few days I will let you know the time at which you are sure to find him."

Anghel Popesco stood motionless. Davida pressed herself against him, resting her head on the young man's chest, and he stooped to kiss her, dazed with happiness. She offered him her cool, velvety cheek. After Anghel had gone she wiped her face. It was not enough, and she poured water into the basin and washed. She even changed her dress.

Anghel Popesco returned to his lodgings without knowing what he was doing. He let himself fall upon his bed, and all that evening, all that night, all the morning of the next day, he remained there, motionless, pale, covered in sweat and with his head on fire. Then he returned to Davida's and found Mlle Marchand with her. The governess, after a long look at the young man's haggard face and at Davida, secret and silent as ever, left the room to make the tea herself, remarking in French that the servants had no idea how to make a good pot of tea.

"Are you afraid?" Davida asked Anghel.

Her words were accompanied by a mocking and arrogant smile. Anghel drew himself up. "Not at all," he said, adding unhappily, "I wanted to see you once again."

"Listen," whispered Davida, talking fast, "I will see that nothing bad happens to you. Manage it so that nobody sees you. And afterward—we should be able to see each other again."

Anghel Popesco placed his hand on his heart. The pain he felt there came from a strange happiness which he had never before experienced and had not even heard of.

During the following days Anghel came again. They exchanged a few words, hastily and in secret. At last a decision was taken: Anghel Popesco was to lie in wait for Vogoride on the following day at a certain place.

But nothing happened on that day, and late in the afternoon Anghel Popesco again called at Culmea Veche Street. The footmen informed him that Davida had gone out. Anghel waited outside the house, watching for her carriage to return. He waited until past midnight, but still no carriage appeared. He called again the following day: "Mademoiselle Davida is out." And in the afternoon it was "Mademoiselle Davida is engaged." On the third day he tried once again to see her, and at last realized that Davida was refusing to receive him. He left the house and walked slowly down the street toward the center of the city.

He had not been back to Alimanesco's. But now, despite the fear with which the idea of seeing his friend inspired him, he found himself following the streets that took him ever nearer to Alimanesco's lodgings. And in due course—it was nightfall and the lamplighters were at their evening rounds—he knocked at his friend's door.

"Come in quickly," Alimanesco murmured, drawing him into the room. The atmosphere was dense with tobacco smoke. The blinds were drawn. There were many more visitors than on the last occasion: the student Prodan had brought a number of fellow students. Iovanake had brought a member of the Chamber of Deputies, a man with gray whiskers and bushy eyebrows, who had voted for Balcesco and Ion Ionesco, leaders of the revolutionary movement in Wallachia, in the provisional government commissions of 1848. Lieutenant Maldaresco had come with three or four other officers, one wearing the white facings and scarlet epaulets of the Second Lancers and another the navy blue of an infantry line regiment. Maldaresco was talking, his back against the four-columned, white-tiled stove. As usual he was calm and precise.

"We cannot be certain that the whole Army will go over to the revolutionaries, but we can be quite certain that it will not open fire on them. We have more or less won over the Lancers regiment and the infantry regiment of the line. That is all I can say positively." Maldaresco finished speaking and looked coolly around.

The deputy growled, "We need no more than that——"

"We must count only on those elements we know and are sure of. We have, at this moment, enough of that kind to be able to fight. Thereafter, the will of the people will bring in the rest. And whoever dares to oppose it will be crushed." Maldaresco looked around again and said, "My dear friends, the matter seems to me to be settled."

One of the officers shouted "Hurrah!"—and everyone turned on him, laughing, to silence him. They might get themselves arrested at any moment, although for the time being the police were busy with the peasants demonstrating at the city gates. "Monsieur Alimanesco, I guarantee that on Monday we shall be able to assemble at least fifty thousand peasants on the Filaret Plain," said Prodan.

"You yourself will go from village to village?" Alimanesco inquired.

"Yes, I shall go. And these young men will go too."

Leaning against the wall, a prey to indescribable excitement, Anghel listened silently. Suddenly he cried, "Suppose the police forbid the meeting?"

Everybody looked at him. Alimanesco smiled and said, "Don't be afraid! Some tens of thousands of men are not going to be stopped by a police cordon. They'd need the Army for that. If the Army breaks in the Government's hands, there will be no other obstacle to oppose the people's will."

There was an approving murmur. Anghel lowered his eyes before Alimanesco's clear blue gaze. His heart was beating as if it might burst. So he was to be given no great part to play in all this? He would remain an obscure supernumerary. It was a heavy blow to his vanity. And Davida would despise him. Things were turning out in such a way that instead of becoming a giant crushing tyranny he would remain what he had always been—the son of old Pope Agapit: a revolutionary, no doubt, but a revolutionary lost in the multitude of others and much less important than, for example, Lieutenant Maldaresco, or Prodan, who was a clever agitator. He suddenly felt that he hated the lot of them, that he was jealous of their resolute cheerfulness, their firm, active attitude. He slipped away among the first to leave.

Meanwhile Iovanake, taking Alimanesco on one side, was saying quietly, "Do you know that Kogalniceano and Rosetti are a good deal worried by the proportions this business is likely to assume? To say nothing of Bratiano and Carada. Kogalniceano is all for reform, but not revolution. Rosetti took fright in Paris in '48 when he saw that the workers had got out of hand. As for Bratiano, Carada, and company, all *they* want is land for themselves. You realize we'll have to force their hand?"

"I have always known it. And even afterward, we shall have to watch them. . . ." Alimanesco sighed. He was pale, but there was a flush over his cheekbones. "Only three more days," he said.

6

Summer was come and a dry wind blew from the Baragan Steppe. Lascar Lascari was in a state of rising excitement. In dressing gown and slippers, hands in pockets, playing as always with a few golden coins among shreds of tobacco, he drank innumerable cups of coffee and paced nervously among the dusty furniture of his bachelor house, whose curtains were impregnated with cigar smoke and the smell of coffee. He wiped his forehead with a crumpled handkerchief and then mopped between his neck and his shirt collar. His hands were damp and clammy. Finally his patience gave out; he threw open a door and clapped his hands to summon a servant. "Tell Nicolai I want the carriage."

Lascari put on a tie, took off his dressing gown, slipped on a gray jacket, and picked up a bowler hat, cursing and swearing at every object he handled. He got into his carriage and the horses trotted off through the quiet, dusty streets, between rows of houses with closed shutters. From time to time Lascari fancied he felt cold; next moment he would be sweating again. Why had he heard nothing from her? What had happened? Outside the Cozianos' three carriages were parked along the pavement in the shade of the mulberry trees.

Lascari gave his hat to a footman. "Your master and mistress are at home?"

"Madame is at home, and Mademoiselle Davida, monsieur."

"They have visitors?"

"Monsieur Vogoride is here, and His Highness Prince Ghica, and Madame's sister."

Lascari waited for no more; he went in, dabbing at his fat white neck. The house was cool. In one corner of the big drawing room Sophia Coziano, in white, and her sister, Mme Otetelesano, in pale green, sat fanning themselves. The men were standing by one of the windows, talking in low voices.

"Oh, is that you, Lascari? What a good thing you've come!" exclaimed the ladies. "You can talk to us about something other than what we've been hearing for the past hour. These gentlemen have gone quite mad with their eternal politics!"

"Why, you know . . . You will have to excuse me, but I shall be no better. Madame Coziano, I kiss your hands; and yours, my dear Hortense. The whole town is in a ferment. Beneath the ashes the fire is smoldering. Something is in the wind, with our Prince sending for politicians every hour of the day. The leading opposition men are meeting at Rosetti's every evening, and they plot and conspire till the small hours. Kogalniceano no longer conceals the fact that he believes a *coup de force* is necessary. In short, everything hangs by a thread. Prince, my respects. Good day to you, Sherban. Well, what is to become of us? Will the volcano erupt?

Are you going to let them hold their meeting on the eleventh of June?"

Sherban Vogoride drew himself up to his full height and thrust out his chest. "I cannot, in any circumstances, tolerate such an assembly. They are trying to unite the masses and work them up with the kind of revolutionary ideas that did us so much harm twenty years ago. I won't have it. I'm too old a fox to swallow their nonsense about everything going off in good order and nothing serious happening. In a matter of hours we could very well have a real revolution on our hands, here in Bucharest. And the Prince would not be displeased. I know him. He's in the mood to put himself at their head. No—never!"

His Excellency Prince Ghica shook his head and stroked his whiskers; the oracle had spoken and there was no more to be said. Lascar Lascari looked around the room. Where was the governess? He stopped listening to what was being said and sat down, wiping his face with a crumpled handkerchief. He fidgeted in his chair, and answered at random such questions as were put to him.

"What is happening to our dear Lascar? What's the matter with you?" Sophia Coziano asked him in surprise, accompanying the question with her deep, voluptuous laugh.

"It's the heat, madame, the heat—and my worries," Lascari answered, truthfully.

"Surely you are not afraid? You must take Sherban as an example. He's like a rock."

"He has not so many worries as I have," Lascari said. And seeing the ladies raise their eyebrows with an expression of astonishment, he corrected himself: "I mean, he has more courage! As for me, I feel the earth quaking under my feet. What's happening is serious, very serious."

He was not referring to the political situation but the two ladies thought that he was, and his uneasiness spread to them. There was a sound of wheels outside and a few moments later other guests appeared—friends of the Cozianos'; among them, two members of the Moldavian Assembly, anxious to see Vogoride before the afternoon session, and the Mlles Gradisteano who, with their governess,

Mme d'Aubigny, had come to see Davida. There was a slight bustle, and then the men grouped themselves around Vogoride in a corner of the room. Davida appeared in a short-sleeved yellow dress, and took the two girls into another corner. Sophia Coziano remained the center of a group of ladies and older men. Lascari, with his hands in his pockets, strolled about the room looking at the pictures without interest, and glancing sideways at Mlle Marchand, who, dressed in black as usual, was talking to Mme d'Aubigny.

What is she up to? Is she losing her head, making a fool of me? Everyone stayed for lunch, and still he had no opportunity of talking to the governess. Lascari ate a great deal, gobbling the food and shooting occasional furtive glances at Mlle Marchand. When they rose from table to take coffee in the drawing room, Lascari stayed behind. Mlle Marchand, passing close behind him, murmured, "Good day to you, Monsieur Lascari. How are you? I should like a word with you."

She walked away without waiting for an answer. A few moments later, when the gentlemen were lighting their cigars and Davida and the other girls were looking for some piece of music among the scores scattered on top of the piano, Mlle Marchand came up to Lascari as if by accident. He promptly accused her: "What are you doing? I have heard nothing from you. You undertook certain obligations. Why have you not been in touch with me?"

He very nearly reminded her of the sum he had paid into the bank, but controlled the impulse for fear of offending her and thus seeing all his good money thrown away and the deal come to nothing. He was trembling with avarice, desire, fear, and rage.

"Perhaps you will explain . . ."

"Certainly, if you will give me time instead of making me waste it with a lot of pointless questions. I believe that Davida is losing her head over that insignificant little fellow, that nonentity, her mathematics teacher. You must have seen him about, a young man dressed in black, a pauper and a protégé of the family. Have you never noticed him?"

"Mathematics? A teacher? Ah, yes, the young man Coziano sent to Paris. I know whom you mean. But what can she see in him? I should have thought he could inspire nothing but pity; it's quite painful to see him, he is so ridiculous! I know him very well. . . . Besides, he has a sickly look. Of course I know him! But have things gone very far? You've kept a close eye on them? I do not wish to come too late! I do not trust——"

He very nearly said "you," but once again stopped himself just in time.

"I have no confidence—and besides, I am very dissatisfied with you. Why have you not kept me informed? Had you told me, I should never have agreed to such a course. It's a serious mistake!"

"It is exactly what you asked me to do," Mlle Marchand replied coldly.

"No, I asked you to do nothing whatever," Lascari whispered. "And what are we to do now? What will you do? What remains to be done?"

"She is becoming more and more nervy; she has fits of crying and she will say nothing. Today she asked my permission to have the carriage to drive into town. I refused. She then agreed to come with me, but begged me to let her get out and pay a visit alone—to call on him, I'm sure. I was to wait for her in the carriage."

"Unheard of! And dangerous! You realize what could happen?" Lascari said breathlessly.

"Nothing whatever will happen. I shall follow her one minute after she enters the house, bring her back, and write to her father the moment we return. Monsieur Coziano will arrive tomorrow. And the day after, you have only to call on him and make your offer. . . . Yes, madame, it is a very pretty piece and your daughter plays it angelically," she said, smiling, to Mme Gradisteano, who was approaching them.

"This weather is very trying, isn't it, Monsieur Lascari?" Mme Gradisteano said.

"Intolerable. I feel it is driving me mad," Lascari replied, with unexpected conviction. Mme Gradisteano looked at him in astonishment but said nothing. The men began to take leave, it being time for the afternoon session of the Assembly. Sophia Coziano kept Vogoride back for a moment and they exchanged a few words in low voices.

"I shall expect you tonight. I have missed you very much these last few days."

"As you know, I am not to blame—I shall be here tonight without fail."

"And I want your advice, too. I am very worried about Davida. I don't know what's the matter with her, but she has become impertinent, very odd, quite intolerable."

"Very well, we will also discuss Davida. But suppose we wait," he added, smiling, "until a decision has been made about the big demonstration on the eleventh of June."

"You're making fun of my little worries."

"I am not making fun of them," Sherban Vogoride said, "but everything in its place—and time, in its order of importance. We will talk of it again tonight, my darling."

He bowed, kissed Sophia's hand, and left. Lascar Lascari again contrived to pass close by Mlle Marchand, and paused to whisper, "Be careful. Your future depends on what happens. Above all, nothing irreparable." And he went quickly out of the room, much disturbed, taking Vogoride's arm and clinging close to him.

"Now for the great moment, Sherban!"

The other deputies were joking nervously. The general opinion was that today's debate, and tomorrow's, would be decisive, and that the agrarian reform project could be postponed or modified to suit the Conservatives, provided their party got a majority in the matter of the demonstration planned for June 11.

Lascari, in Vogoride's carriage—his own following at walking pace—was looking at the crowds which had gathered on both sides of the street. Suddenly he had an impression that a man whom he knew was staring at him with extraordinary intensity. Who was he? He had no time to search his memory, for at the same moment he felt something strike his hat, which fell to the floor of the carriage. He promptly crouched down in a huddle of fear.

"They're stoning us," he stammered. Vogoride did not hear him, however, for the crowd began booing and jeering. The horses took fright and broke into a fast trot up the hill. At the summit of the rise the coachman stopped them. "I'll give them a taste of bayonets—to teach them a lesson," Vogoride grumbled, white of face.

He walked into the Assembly, looking to neither right nor left.

Lascari, gazing fearfully at the crowd, followed him, still wondering about the man who had stared at him. Surely he knew that face . . . ?

The city reeled under the heat. A trickle of oily, dirty water coming from the tanneries quarter carried a stench of decay. The air was dry. Dust hung above the roofs of the houses, and the towers of a hundred churches were half obscured by its yellowish mist. Groups of men formed and massed in the neighboring streets. There were sudden outbursts of shouting. In the direction of the Manouc Inn and the Lipscani quarter the crowd was very thick, and from time to time people broke away from it, running; it was impossible to tell why, or where they were going, yet they seemed to have a definite goal, a secret and imperative purpose in fighting against the torpor of this overpowering summer day.

A line of carriages came up the hill at walking pace and drove under the archway beneath the tower of the Metropolitan Church. Numerous deputies were arriving on foot. Crowds had gathered along both sides of the street, cheering politicians of the popular party and breaking out into furious imprecations and insults whenever a Conservative minister appeared. The tall trees and bushes that grew all the way up the hill right to the foot of the monastery's ancient walls were covered with dust, and the hot breezes coming up off the plain did not even stir their petrified immobility. Right at the top, between the Metropolitan Church and the Assembly building, there was a confused mass of men and vehicles. The deputies going in greeted one another, exchanging looks and gestures of understanding with political friends, of ironical politeness with political enemies.

In the great hall, with its large portrait of the Sultan and its smaller one of the reigning Prince, the air was stifling. At first the

windows had been opened, but as soon as the speeches began faces
from the mob had appeared in the openings, and the President
of the Chamber had given orders to close them again. Thereafter
the debate was carried on in an unbearable atmosphere, which
greatly aggravated the nervous tension. Speeches were interrupted
by shouts from both sides of the Chamber. The President kept
ringing his bell. Even the prelates, with *potcaps* or monastic veils
on their heads and crosses set with amethysts hanging on their
chests below full beards, showed uneasiness and some agitation,
though they never normally departed from their ecclesiastical
calm. Kogalniceano, plump and bald, stepped up to the tribune
with a number of books under his arm. He polished his glasses
and began to speak. In the midst of his highest flights of oratorical
enthusiasm and generosity, while his warm voice rolled out grandi-
ose figures of speech, he cast an occasional quick glance at the
ministerial benches, where Sherban Vogoride sat with his chin sunk
on his chest. Lascar Lascari, raising his head with an awkward
movement, dabbed at his sweating neck. His neighbor leaned toward him and said, "The lion of eloquence is afraid of only one
person here——" A member of the Opposition, who overheard
him, retorted more loudly, "The lion is Vogoride, and it's he who's
afraid of Kogalniceano. Your lion is face to face with a man!"

There were cries of "Hush!" from the neighboring benches.
Lascari fidgeted constantly. A torrid sun glared through the windows, cutting the Chamber into slices of light and dense shadow.
The President, the secretaries' and stenographers' desks, and the
tribune itself were in the shade; Kogalniceano's glasses flashed.
The Government front bench was in full sunlight, and two of the
ministers kept wiping the sweat from their faces. Vogoride sat motionless, head bowed.

Lascari had lost the thread of the speech and was no longer listening. Then suddenly, he saw Vogoride stand up and realized that
a great silence had fallen. Kogalniceano had left the tribune to the
applause of half the Assembly. The Government was to reply, and
their best speaker was to do so on their behalf. As was his habit,
Vogoride did not go up to the tribune but spoke from his seat. He

straightened his massive body and turned toward the deputies on his left, bestowing upon them a look of withering scorn through his monocle.

"Monsieur Kogalniceano has spoken with the skill we expect from him. But, let us be quite frank—even were I twice as great an orator as you, monsieur—oh, yes, I admire your talent—though I had the voice of a siren and a golden tongue, I should never, monsieur, persuade your partisans. They have adopted the words of Mr. Disraeli: 'A good speech has sometimes changed my convictions, but never my vote.' "

There was some ill-natured laughter from the right; the great prelates smiled, their long beards turning toward one another. There was angry muttering from members on the left, and one of them cried out, "You're describing yourselves, not us!"

"Gentlemen, why hide the facts behind generous principles? Your object is to bribe the peasants into silence with a gift of land, so that you can put up to auction the vast estates of the monasteries and the even vaster lands of the State—to be bought by you and yours!"

The muttering grew louder. "Of all the cynical twists!" Kogalniceano said angrily. Several members protested, two of them rising to their feet and shouting. Their voices were drowned by the President's bell.

"Do you want to climb still higher? Who is stopping you?" Vogoride asked, laughing. He had removed his monocle and was talking easily, as if he were in a drawing room. "All the public offices are at your disposal. But you want to have them all at one go. And you do not want to start at the bottom; you want to climb on our shoulders, and from there reach the eaves, and so finally the roof. You will fall, gentlemen, and break your necks!"

There were two or three indignant exclamations, but on the whole the silence was broken only by mutterings. Vogoride had struck hard at most of the Liberals present. It was by striking openly at his opponents' weakest points, uncovering their venality and hypocrisy, that he succeeded in keeping the Conservative Government in office.

Sensing that the moment was propitious, Constantine Filipesco, a right-wing deputy, rose in his place and, with his hand thrust in the open front of his white waistcoat, began to ask a question: "It is rumored that, on the eleventh of June, there will be an attempt to organize a celebration in the Filaret Plain, the so-called Field of Liberty, which will bear the name of National Festival——"

He uttered the words "bear the name" with icy disdain. He went on to ask if "such a festival" would be tolerated by the present Minister; the year before, the previous Minister, Golesco, had done nothing to prevent the holding of a banquet in the same place, a banquet which had taken a political turn. Filipesco looked toward the left-wing members, one of whom shouted, "What of it?" Turning to Vogoride, Filipesco went on: "For my part, monsieur, I should like to see an end to such meetings, which can lead to nothing but disorder."

He sat down without another glance at Vogoride, although the latter had, in fact, written the question. Lascari, who was in the secret, cast curious looks to right and left. The Opposition benches were silent. Vogoride rose to answer. He had at first resolved to allow the meeting, but owing to the tone adopted by the organizing committee in announcing it, he had decided to forbid it.

On the extreme left, Anton Arion rose, his long black hair in a tangle, his gestures lively. "I have conformed to the terms of a circular issued by Monsieur Dimitri Ghica's department," he said with heavy irony.

Prince Ghica, seated beside Vogoride, jumped to his feet. "Let the order issued by me be read!"

"Send for the *Official Gazette,* and you will see!" Arion replied with a mocking laugh. Prince Ghica's graying eyebrows came down in a scowl as he tried to parry the thrust; at last he said, "The order was not for the eleventh of June."

"I did not say it was for the eleventh of June," Arion cried, delighted to have caught the Prince out.

Vogoride realized that he would have to intervene. He rose, and said sadly and gravely, "No private person has authority to assemble a crowd, on any pretext whatsoever."

"Five or six men," Prince Ghica growled, "and they call themselves the representatives of the Nation."

A "red" deputy rose and shouted, "The people have the right of assembly! There is no law against meetings."

Vogoride turned toward General Floresco. For sessions of the Assembly the General wore a black frock coat. Nervously stroking his pointed beard, Floresco rose and read the following motion:

> In every civilized country there is a law against the assembling of a mob. We are in urgent need of such a law in our country also, and the Government will be submitting a suitable bill to the Assembly as soon as possible. Signed: I. Floresco, Prince Mavrocordato, G. Valeano, Corlatesco, Castroian, Sherban Vogoride.

"One liberty less!" Kogalniceano shouted. A number of members stood up. Arion shouted, "And you call this a civilized country! In your language, civilization means the Inquisition!" He was quivering with indignation. Vogoride rose again, and a silence descended.

"Gentlemen, the people who intend to demonstrate on the eleventh will not be carrying bunches of roses, but axes, swords, picks, pitchforks, and even firearms. We must not allow roses of that kind to grow in our country's soil, for their scent is mortal poison to our society. The salvation of this country, gentlemen, is social pacification, and I would rather die than infringe or see violated a single one of our laws."

The reigning Prince's son, much moved, turned to his neighbors and said, "Poor Sherban—he has tears in his eyes."

"I ask the Assembly to close this discussion," Vogoride concluded, "or to adjourn it until tomorrow, the ninth of June." He sat down.

"Adjourn it until the ninth, the tenth, or the Greek Calends!" Kogalniceano said. "What a tactician! What acting!"

"Continue the debate! Debate! Debate!" shouted the members

surrounding him, while the Conservatives were vociferating, "Vote! Vote!"

The Assembly voted in a tense atmosphere which at any moment might erupt into violence, and the Conservatives, who had a majority, carried the motion to adjourn. The deputies rose and the Chamber became noisy with footsteps and general conversation. Kogalniceano and his friends remained in the confined space between the ministerial benches and the tribune. Vogoride polished his monocle. Prince Dimitri Ghica came up, shook his hand, and said, "You were tremendous, Sherban."

Vogoride shrugged. "I am defending a fallen bastion, step by step." He forced his way through to the exit, followed by a swarm of his political friends. There was a dense crush at the door. With some difficulty, Vogoride and his friends made their way through the crowd that had gathered on the steps, from which a handful of policemen were trying to dislodge it. Hostile stares and a heavy silence greeted Vogoride's appearance. He put in his monocle and called for his carriage. There was no reply. Lascar Lascari asked one of the policemen what had happened to His Excellency's carriage.

"It has gone, sir."

"Who told the coachman to leave?" Vogoride asked. He was standing a couple of paces behind Lascari, arm-in-arm with Prince Ghica.

"A very pale young man, dressed in black. He said they were Your Excellency's orders, so I passed them on and your man drove away."

"Come in my carriage," said the Prince, "or better still, go in Lascari's; he can drop you on his way."

The three men made their way to Lascari's carriage.

"Until tomorrow, then. Or perhaps at Sophia's this evening, eh, Sherban?"

"Very well, Highness, this evening." Vogoride got into the carriage. The people pushed and swayed around them, and coachmen were shouting at the crowd to make way. The horses snorted, and seemed ready to trample the people pushing in between the vehicles.

As the carriage, moving behind two or three others, made slow progress toward the arch under the Metropolitan Church tower, Vogoride turned to Lascari. "I wonder who's responsible for the joke—this business of my carriage, I mean?"

Lascari was about to answer, but instead remained silent. Just at that moment the carriage passed under the arch and emerged. Below lay the city, a vast spread of roofs, the dark verdure of parks and gardens, church towers gleaming in the setting sunlight. And there, at one pace from the carriage, with his back pressed to the wall of the archway, stood a young man dressed in black, whose wax-white face and dark eyes Lascari instantly recognized as those of the man who had stared at him when they were driving to the Assembly. The young man raised a pistol and took aim. Lascari shut his eyes. The shot rang loud in his right ear. He caught a whiff of burnt gunpowder.

For a moment he lost all idea of what was happening. Then he thought, *He's missed me! He's missed me! He's missed me!* And an overwhelming happiness mingled with terror possessed him, for there might be a second shot. But no! Nothing. Lascari opened his eyes. The white smoke of the gunpowder was drifting away. He looked to the left; the bushes shook for a moment, and then became still again. *He's made off.*

"What has happened, Sherban?" Lascari stammered. Sherban Vogoride was sitting on his right, with his chin sunk on his chest, just as he had sat on the Government front bench. But his hat was gone. It had fallen into the hood of the carriage. Sherban's face looked strange: his eyes were half closed and he seemed to be deep in thought. "Whatever is the matter, Sherban?" Lascari stammered. At the same moment he heard quite clearly, but as if from a great distance, a voice shouting, "It's Vogoride they were shooting at!"

Lascari realized that the voice was Dimitri Ghica's. But for a moment he no longer knew what was happening: men were running toward the carriage, there were confused questions and cross-questions, the shouting increased, policemen bustled about as the prefect of police, Nicolai Bibesco, issued his orders: "Close all the gates! Nobody is to leave the precincts of the Assembly!"

But none of this succeeded in rousing Lascari from a state of bewilderment in which he could do nothing but mutter incoherent words. For the space of fifteen minutes all was excitement, amazement, and confused activity. It was not until much later that a squadron of lancers arrived to restore order and clear away the crowd. Even so, groups of idlers kept forming in the neighborhood until far into the night.

In the courtyard of the Metropolitan Church at the top of the hill, Lieutenant Maldaresco dismounted and gave his bridle to a trooper. He went up the steps, his saber rattling against the stone. As he came on the scene he had spotted Iovanake in one of the groups; he appeared disturbed and had given the Lieutenant a questioning look, to which Maldaresco, still in the saddle, had replied by an almost imperceptible shrug to convey his ignorance. He went into the Chamber, threading his way between overturned chairs. Papers lay scattered on the desks and on the red carpet that covered the floor. There was nobody about. Maldaresco looked around, his expression harsh and ill-tempered. Was this the people's revolution, the barricades in the streets of Bucharest? He went out again, his saber trailing on the red carpet. Outside, in the twilight, a trooper of his squadron came smartly to attention, his spurs clinking.

"Good evening, Rosca," Maldaresco greeted him.

"Lieutenant, sir—if you'll excuse me—is it true they'll be giving land to the people now?"

Maldaresco made out a group of people standing in the shadow behind the soldier and listening. They were waiting for his answer.

"I think they will," Maldaresco said. He turned away, feeling as if his high red collar were choking him.

7

Lascar Lascari went home and drank several cups of coffee, pacing the length and breadth of the room as he did so. Did Mlle Marchand know what had happened? What part had she played? And Davida, did she know? What had Davida to do with all this? Lascari feared for his plan, for his passion; he was afraid of all the unknown things that might happen. Late in the evening, his patience exhausted, he called for his second carriage—the one in use that afternoon had its upholstery stained with blood, and he had decided to have it reupholstered and then sold at the best possible price. At the Cozianos' only two windows showed light. As a friend of the family he was admitted without difficulty. But "Madame was indisposed." He asked to speak to the governess. Mlle Marchand, very pale, and with her hair screwed into a tight little bun, came to him in the deserted drawing room.

"It is terrible," she said in French, "poor Madame Coziano is suffering terribly." She had no word of sympathy for Vogoride. Lascari, his face pallid, watched her with troubled eyes.

"Yes. Vogoride was one of their best friends."

Tight-lipped, the governess said nothing. Lascari made one or two more attempts to bring their conversation around to Vogoride, but Mlle Marchand remained obstinately silent. At last she said, "He was a wicked man."

She knows nothing, thought Lascari, and began talking of other things. "Did you go *there,* this afternoon?"

"Yes. Admittedly the young man was not at home, but the visit in itself was compromising enough. I wrote to Monsieur Coziano, sending him both items of news."

"Splendid! Splendid!"

"Monsieur Lascari—you have not forgotten me?"

"Never fear, mademoiselle. As soon as the thing is done you will be an independent woman. You will not be rich, but your material well-being will be assured," Lascari said emphatically.

Mlle Marchand bowed her head slightly in acknowledgment. "Thank you. You are very generous."

"That is our nature, you know—we Easterners. What is Davida doing?"

"She is in a state of nerves. Like her mother, but for a different reason, I fancy. She is crying and will see nobody—she is almost out of her mind."

"Ah, indeed," Lascari said thoughtfully. "Good. Good night, mademoiselle. I will call again tomorrow."

On the morrow and the day after, Lascari, who had spent the night in thought, pacing his rooms and clinking the coins in his pockets, drove hither and thither all over the city. He learned that Prince Couza had been furious on hearing of the murder, and had demanded that the culprit be discovered at once: as a result a number of people had been arrested and imprisoned at Plumbuita. Everyone was sure that the assassination had been planned in Kogalniceano's and Rosetti's entourage, although both men had emphatically denied the accusation. Lascari, to their great surprise, called on them as well. He asked for a private interview and showed himself favorable to their ideas, declaring that he had long intended to go over to them and to abandon the Conservative side in the political arena. Moreover, he gave them to understand that he knew perfectly well who had planned and who had carried out the assassination. Fidgeting ceaselessly in his chair, exposing his greenish teeth in a smile, and contorting his face into amiable grimaces, he persuaded Rosetti to believe that the step had been decided upon by Kogalniceano and that the Prince himself was no stranger to the project. At Kogalniceano's, on the other hand, he insinuated that he, Lascari, had unquestionable proof of Rosetti's responsibility, "and perhaps even of Couza's." Thus it was that suspicions and vague rumors, born of a couple of conversations between the two men and consisting of hints and shrugs, had the effect of creating an atmosphere of uncertainty which put an end to all investigation and drew a veil over the immediate causes of Vogoride's assassination.

Thanks to these circumstances, Lascari won the esteem, mixed with fear and repugnance, of the Opposition leaders. After Couza's *coup d'état* simple-minded persons were astonished to find Lascari sitting with Kogalniceano and C. A. Rosetti's party in the Chamber. His rise to power among his new political friends was as surprising as it was unostentatious, especially after Bratiano had begun to acquire his absolute dominion over the Liberal Party.

On the day after the crime, Lascari did not go to Culmea Veche Street; but he saw Coziano, who had returned from the country, among the crowd of black frock coats, ladies in mourning, and officers in full-dress uniform with black crape on the handles of their swords, which had assembled opposite the Sarindar Church. There Vogoride's body lay in state, clad in formal dress and with a candle burning in its hand. While Prince Couza, followed by the officers of his court and by his ministers, was doing honor to the dead, Lascari went over to Coziano, who was shaking hands with various friends and kinsmen.

Coziano was a prey to a kind of strange excitement. He realized, like everyone else for that matter, that the land reform plan would not be long delayed now that its principal opponent was no more; on the other hand, he rejoiced to see Vogoride stretched on a bier. His expression of tragedy was constantly giving way to a sort of sneering smile which appeared altogether out of place. To some, he responded with lugubrious solemnity: "A great misfortune, my dear fellow. A disaster for the country. And a shocking loss to all of us." But to others, with the cheerfulness of a man who can hardly prevent himself from laughing, he said: "He'd nobody to blame but himself, my dear fellow. I warned him time and again but he wouldn't listen. . . ." Then would come the question that plunged him into gloom again, and his answer: "Sophia? Making herself quite ill. Overdoing it, you know . . ."

And, with a frank laugh, quickly suppressed, "She ought to realize that we're all mortal, ha! ha! ha!"

Lascari, speaking discreetly, said, "Alexander, I want to see you on a matter of some importance. . . ."

"Very well. Come this afternoon."

During the afternoon Lascari went to Culmea Veche Street, and before having himself announced to the master of the house, asked to speak to Davida. He was in morning dress and carried a bunch of white roses. Davida sent word that she was not feeling well and could not receive him.

"Never mind. I will just go and knock at her door," Lascari replied. And thrusting aside the startled footman, he walked straight into Davida's room. The girl rose from her chair in one swift movement. She was carelessly dressed in a light olive-green dress, the neck and sleeves unbuttoned. Her face seemed paler than usual, her large eyes glittered feverishly, and her silky hair lay in confusion about her shoulders. Mlle Marchand also rose, protesting.

"As an old friend of the family, I think I can permit myself a word in private with your pupil," Lascari said pleasantly. "I have something of the utmost importance to say to her. Please leave us alone for a moment."

"Don't go," the girl said sharply. "I have nothing to say to anybody."

"I will inform your father," Mlle Marchand murmured. She slipped out and sat down in one of the drawing-room armchairs, leaving Davida alone with Lascari, who put his bouquet down on the table and said, "You know that I was in the same carriage with him. Nobody—*nobody*—has any idea of his assassin's identity. But I know it. I was in the same carriage."

Davida stiffened. Standing very erect, she stared at Lascari fixedly.

"Are you very fond of your friend?"

"What friend?" Davida said in a whisper. Her voice came with difficulty through dry, colorless lips.

"The one who killed him. You know perfectly well whom I

mean," Lascari said in an easy, almost paternal tone. He sat down in the armchair which Mlle Marchand had just vacated. "I know everything," he added.

"How do you know? Who told you?"

"That is none of your business. But there is one thing I can tell you. The Prince is beside himself. He wants to have the assassin and his accomplices hanged."

There was no death penalty in the penal code of the United Principalities. But Lascari was counting on the probability that Davida would not know that and that it would not occur to her at the moment to check it. She was nothing but a child. To his great surprise she blenched, and stuttering with fury, burst out, "Let him hang! Let them hang him! I'd like to see him cut to pieces. Hacked to pieces. Like that! And that! And that!" Her hands slashed at the empty air like a madwoman's. Her eyes, inflamed and reddened with tears, seemed sunk in their sockets.

"He dared to—the infamous vermin—the vile lackey! He must hang! The cur! Worm! Let them kill him!"

"What?" Lascari cried, astonished and skeptical. "You didn't know?"

"I went to his lodgings that afternoon to tell him he must not harm Sherban, to tell him I did not want him hurt, that I loved Sherban, that I loved him, loved him . . ." Davida buried her face in her hands and burst into tears.

"So that was why you went there with the Frenchwoman," Lascari muttered.

"Yes . . . Yes . . ." Davida sobbed. "Let them kill him! He must be killed!"

"Things will not be quite so simple as you would like, little girl," Lascari said coldly. "You'll be caught in the net too. If he is arrested he'll confess everything. The Aga's* people will know how to make him talk. He'll tell them everything he did, and even things he did not do. Your name will come out. It will be a shock-

* Chief of Police. As Turkish dependencies, the United Principalities had Turkish names for some officials.

ing scandal. Your father will blow his brains out and your mother will go mad."

Davida sat down, her hands on her knees. She looked at Lascari, bewildered, her mouth half open. Lascari took her hand between his own, but that small, cold, fragile hand disturbed him; he dropped it and moved away. At all costs he must keep his head.

"As a politician and a citizen, it is my duty to say that I saw him aim his pistol." Davida was trembling. So, for that matter, was Lascari, though he showed his dirty teeth in a smile. "However, I am fond of you and your family, and I shall not do my duty. I am going now to your father to ask him for your hand."

Davida rose and said weakly, "No . . ."

"What did you say?" Lascari asked pleasantly. Davida fell upon her bed and began crying again. Lascari stroked her hair, her shoulders, her back, her waist. "Now, now, stop that, it doesn't matter, it will all be forgotten soon. You will be saved. I will save you. And him too. I'll even save him. . . ."

Davida's weeping grew louder, desperate, broken by deep, shuddering sobs like a child's. Lascar Lascari opened the door and shouted for Mlle Marchand. She appeared immediately.

"Stay with her. Don't leave her for a moment in case she does something foolish."

He sought out Coziano and they shut themselves into the latter's office. Coziano was at once glad to be rid of Vogoride, filled with hatred for his wife, and appalled by what Mlle Marchand had told him about Davida's passion for a nobody. He almost fell on Lascari's neck when his friend asked him for Davida's hand in marriage.

"You're a true friend, Lascar," he said, embracing him. "But have you spoken to Davida?"

"Yes, and she accepts me—that is, if you consent."

"I am glad that *she*, at least, really loves me," Coziano said, frowning.

"We must also speak to your wife."

"At the moment she is far too desperately stricken to think of her children," Coziano said with a hard and bitter laugh. "Her opinion is not necessary."

Anghel Popesco came several times to Culmea Veche Street to see Davida. But the servants, to whom Mlle Marchand had given orders, would not let him in. He asked to speak to the governess, who received him coldly and with the utmost disdain. "I am surprised that you should have the audacity, after your shameful conduct, to show your face in your benefactor's house."

Anghel tried to see Coziano, but the footmen told him, "Monsieur Anghel, don't come back any more! The boyar is furious with you."

He went home and to bed without eating. When he pulled himself together sufficiently to go out again, he returned to Culmea Veche Street once more; to be told that the Cozianos had gone to the country, where Mlle Davida was to be married to M. Lascari. He went back to his lodgings, hardly aware of what he was doing, went to bed, and stayed there. A few hours later he was tossing in bed, raving, in a high fever and with agonizing pains in the head. Soon he lost all idea of time; he thought he was surrounded by human figures who spoke to him and accused him. To one of these threatening faces he cried, "Go away! You're a phantom."

It was Alimanesco. With troubled eyes and chattering teeth, his whole body shaking, the sick man made signs to him to go. But the phantom would not go; on the contrary it leaned over him and said, "Why didn't you listen to me?"

Anghel raised his head a little; his eyes were glassy.

"Why did you not listen to me?" Alimanesco repeated mournfully. Anghel let his head fall back on the pillow and closed his eyes.

"You have played into the hands of the moderates, those who wanted nothing beyond land reform. They were afraid of the rest —the republic, universal suffrage, the people in arms. The demonstration has been put off, everything has been stopped. I begged and pleaded, but they replied that it was no longer necessary. They have put it about in the villages that land reform is now certain, and that the peasants must keep calm. Ah, if only we had tried! If we had only tried!" And Alimanesco grumbled to himself in despair: "They are snatching the revolution out of our hands. The demon of cowardice, selfishness, and compromise possesses them. I shall never see liberty, Anghel!"

But Anghel, with his eyes turned toward the ceiling, did not hear him.

Alimanesco went hurrying off to look for a physician. When he returned with one, the doctor diagnosed brain fever and held out no hope. Anghel Popesco died two days later. As for Alimanesco, Doctor of Science and artisan of the revolution, he was carried off by tuberculosis in the following spring.

Alexander Coziano dismissed Mlle Marchand, although the governess proudly declared that she had nothing with which to reproach herself. She had watched over Davida's conduct and reputation; over the girl's feelings she had no control. However, the governess put up no serious resistance: she was hoping to be able to go home to Nogent and live on the small capital, the second half of which was now due to her. Needless to say, Lascari refused to consider paying her a penny, and even contrived to get a deportation order issued against her. Mlle Marchand found herself with twenty-four hours in which to cross the frontier of the United Principalities. Nothing is known of her after her departure.

M. and Mme Coziano lived for several years in the country, Coziano never speaking to his wife unless it was absolutely necessary. In 1870 he died after eating a dish of mushrooms. Very little credence was given to the rumor which went the rounds at the time to the effect that Florica, the gypsy with the ruined teeth, had poisoned him. Sophia Coziano remarried in Vienna, her husband being the Baron von Bodman. She is believed to have been happy with him.

In the early years of their marriage Lascar Lascari and Davida had five children, whose descendants are still living. Lascar became Governor of the National Bank. Much has been said and written about that enigmatic and sinister figure, Eugene Carada, who, ever in the shadows, controlled the "Occulta," the secret directory of the

Liberal Party. Yet Carada was but a pale shadow of the gross and pallid Lascar Lascari, the real originator of most of the political maneuvers carried out by the Liberals during that period. Today, he is completely forgotten; even in his own time he was virtually unknown, but he was nevertheless all-powerful. He died of cancer in Switzerland, and Davida survived him by only a few years. There exists a portrait of her, a daguerreotype taken in 1860. There is also another picture, taken in 1899, a year before her death. The daguerreotype shows a girl of about eighteen dressed in a crinoline, with narrow bands of lace at neck and wrists. The face is delicate and rather childish, the head held high with fierce pride; the dark eyes seem to look out at some heroic future, a world in which everything will be hers by right. The photograph shows a woman in her forties, lean, angular, and thin-lipped, with dark circles about her eyes. She looks obstinate, hard, and sharp; and her gaze is full of the desperate weariness of a woman who has understood nothing, who understands nothing, and who is never going to understand.

PART TWO

Childish Things

I

One spring morning, about the year 1875, Lascar Lascari was just
thinking of leaving the Liberal Party Club and going home to
lunch. Lascari had changed a great deal during the past ten
years. He had a paunch, and the hips and buttocks of a sultan. His
complexion was suety, his hair sparse and of a dirty white. No one
would have been particularly surprised to learn that he was suffering from a serious illness, that his white waistcoat concealed the
scabs of leprosy or something similar. He ate and drank enor-
mously, smoked too many cigars, and drank too much coffee. At
home he dragged himself from one easy chair to the next, and, if
he went out anywhere—in his carriage—it was only to collapse
into yet another armchair.

Those members of the Club who were not gathered around the
gaming tables or reading the papers in the next room were sitting
in groups, talking. A number of them had gathered around Lascari,
who was sitting well back in his chair, his paunch resting on his
thighs, his eyelids drooping, and a cigar in his mouth. His right
hand hung limply, trailing on the carpet a newspaper: *The Eastern
Echo*, with the French subtitle "L'Echo d'Orient." The gentlemen
surrounding Lascari's chair were silent, waiting for the oracle to
pronounce. Lascari often remained silent, not, as some claimed, to
give more weight to what he said, but because he had become extremely lazy.

When he did bring himself to speak, it was with so many
reservations and half-hints that his political friends had formed the
habit of meeting immediately afterward to discuss and interpret

what he had said, so that Lascari, no longer needing to explain what was in his mind, spoke less and less. A number of deputies and senators were standing about his chair on this occasion, affecting a familiarity which he received with a kind of regal indifference. His white waistcoat emphasized his great bloated paunch. He looked like some fat insect lying on its back.

"Tell us, my dear Lascari," asked Dumitru Vasesco, thrusting his enormous thumbs into the armholes of his waistcoat, "tell us the position regarding the railroad which is to connect N—— with the Danube? Is the Government going to acquire it?"

Lascari seemed to be deep in thought, as if he had forgotten the answer he wanted to give. After a while another member of the Assembly, a man with a mustache of the kind made fashionable by the President of the Third French Republic, Marshal MacMahon, concluded that Lascari wanted to avoid answering and would be grateful to anyone who changed the conversation. He therefore remarked, "I suppose you know the Opposition are preparing to ask a question? They are going to ask why the railroad should not run directly to the loading port on the Danube, instead of wandering all over the plain. They are protesting against the plan of the track, which they claim has been adopted solely to please the big landowners, since it runs through the estates of Coziano, Lascari, Mavromihali, and others—all of them on the board of the Agricultural Bank of N——."

Lascari leaned forward and, levering with his hands on the arms of the chair, got to his feet. He dropped *The Eastern Echo* beside the copy of *The Rumanian* which already lay on the floor, seized his eyeglasses, which hung from a black silk ribbon fastened to the lapel of his frock coat, and holding them between thumb and forefinger, looked smilingly around.

"Will you kindly tell me, gentlemen, what harm you see in that? The railroad has to satisfy our citizens, surely, and not the rules of geometry or geography. Moreover, in this case it is not only the interests of our citizens which are at stake, but the interests of the country. The idea is to export grain by using the Danube. What grain, may I ask? That which is grown and harvested in the plains. As you can see, gentlemen, there is nothing shameful in all that. The gentlemen of the Opposition can formulate their question in any way they like: we shall simply tell them the truth—which is what we usually do in everything pertaining to public affairs."

Turning his back on them, Lascari made for the door; his frock coat was as badly creased as if he had slept in it all night. The deputies followed him. Vasesco pulled at his sleeve. "Tell us once and for all the real facts about this railroad. You're keeping us on the rack."

Lascari, having made a sign to the footman on duty in the hall, turned on the threshold and smiled at Vasesco in a manner at once innocent and crafty. "Now, what is all this? You seem to expect me to know absolutely everything. My dear fellow, I'm not a politician, I'm a banker—a financier. I shall die a simple deputy, which will certainly not be the case with you gentlemen. What can I tell you? Do you think that the Cabinet is in the habit of divulging its secrets? And especially to me?"

He laughed as he struggled into the ulster which the footman was holding out for him. He put on his worn and dirty gloves. (Lascari washed his hands only rarely, his face still more rarely, and his body not at all.) He took his top hat and walking stick from the servant's hands and concluded with a short laugh: "For my part, I know nothing and the matter does not interest me in the slightest. All I can tell you is that my brothers-in-law, the two Cozianos, have bought shares in this railroad. Don't ask me why, nor at what price; I know nothing whatever about it. Au revoir, gentlemen; your servant."

He walked out. After his departure the others exchanged a long look. As they heard the wheels of Lascari's carriage driving out of the Club courtyard Vasesco said, "If I understand it correctly, the company's shares will be acquired by the State—or else the State will be a shareholder in the business. So the dividends are assured! Are you coming into town, gentlemen?"

They hurried out. That day every share on the market was bought up. Shortly afterward the Government passed an act by which the State became owner of fifty-one per cent of the shares in the company building the railroad between N—— and the Danube. This act was the origin of many a great fortune.

After leaving the Club, Lascari sprawled on the padded seat of his coupé, which rolled silently through the streets on its rubber-tired wheels. The windows tinkled. Lascari half dozed, the cigar in his mouth filling the dark-blue velvet interior with pale-blue smoke. He was sweating gently; the dullness of mind which had overcome him was a symptom of intoxication, and he enjoyed it. He felt himself strong, heavy, full of the brute contentment of an animal that has eaten too much and can hardly breathe and lies stretched on its side, grunting with well-being. With half-closed eyes he watched a parade of mental images depicting other fleshly pleas-ures. He thought of his sister-in-law, Cleopatra, and his desire for her made him catch his breath. *I'll soon have her in my bed,* Lascari assured himself with satisfaction.

The carriage turned into the courtyard of the Coziano house, which Davida's father, Alexander, had given to his daughter when he distributed his fortune among his heirs. Nothing had changed. At most, the spearpoints of the iron railings had lost a few flakes of their gilding. The same footman who had formerly opened the carriage door for Alexander Coziano hurried down the front steps, lowered the carriage step, and watched his master climb out. Lascari always went up the front steps slowly, yet he was out of breath when he reached the top. For the umpteenth time he de-cided that they really must make up their minds to move. He was a little less decisive than he had been in the past. All the fuss and bother there would be, what with builders, mortar all over the place, decorators, painters, furniture damaged, china broken, cold, the smell of paint and whitewash, and a dozen other things . . . No, no, it was better to stay where they were. Later, perhaps, they would see. . . . At the same time, he knew perfectly well that this procrastination was nothing but pretense, to cover the failure of his will. *Formerly, when I got an idea into my head,* he thought, *it was as good as done. Now I say "We'll see." I'm getting old. Yes, I'm getting old. Or am I old already?* No. But having looked at himself in the big double looking-glass which covered a whole wall of the hall, he saw his double chin, and his fat, hairy jowls, his forehead made unnaturally high by incipient baldness, and was forced to recognize with bitterness and anger that he was not yet old but was beginning to be; there was no escaping the fact that he was on the verge of old age.

He went into the anteroom and through to the drawing room, rubbing his hands. *Shall I still be able to please Cleopatra?* he wondered. Then: *Whether she likes me or not, she's going to give me what I want.* Showing all his greenish teeth in a smile, he went forward to kiss Cleopatra Coziano's hands. She was the wife of Davida's eldest brother.

Cleopatra, who was alone in the drawing room, was a very young woman: eighteen or twenty, plump, dimpled, with large black eyes, arched brows, a willful chin, and a full lower lip. There was something secret and restless in her, as if she were forever trying to recall some important matter which she had forgotten. But this expression of absorption gave a very exaggerated idea of Cleopatra's mental activity.

She rose from her chair and hurried to meet Lascari and kiss his whiskers. The rustle of silk, the play of light on the taffeta gown, and the scent of youth went to Lascari's head. He pressed her to him and gave her a long kiss. The girl did not draw back with that expression of disgust which Lascari's demonstrations of affection usually provoked; she merely shifted a little to one side, so that she could see over her brother-in-law's shoulder.

"What are you thinking of, my dear?" she stammered. "Suppose Davida were to see us?"

"What do you expect, when you are so provocative?" Lascari muttered, letting himself sink into an armchair.

"I wanted to thank you," she said, with a naïve expression. "To thank you for what you have done for us in this railroad business. . . . Titi has gone to the bank to make the final payments . . . he was delighted. And I am very grateful to you too!" She had sat down close to him and was making an effort to appear childlike and spontaneous.

Lascari pinched her cheek. "If you are really grateful to me you can prove it, dear little Cleopatra."

"How?" she asked, still naïve and innocent, wide-eyed, brows raised and mouth half open.

"Oh, she's such a sugar-stick!" Lascari exclaimed, excited. "Just a simple little maiden! You know very well what I mean. . . . You may be young, but old people indulge in certain childish things that you understand perfectly. . . ."

"I don't know what you're talking about," Cleopatra cooed.

"Oh, yes, you do!"

Lascari, comfortably settled in his armchair, his paunch thrust well forward, laughed, sure of himself. Cleopatra owned herself beaten and changed her manner: the ignorant child suddenly became a woman, who by her laugh and by her bold and provocative glance seemed to be saying, *Oh yes, I know that I must pay, and pay I will: it is, after all, a bargain.* Gaily she said, "You can hardly want me to demonstrate my understanding here in the drawing room."

"Very well, then, we'll certainly find a place where we can come to terms," Lascari answered her, laughing. "I shall visit you in the country this summer. Keep your gratitude for me until then."

He turned his head to see who had come into the room: it was Eustace Coziano, Davida's eldest brother, a man in his early forties, tall, well built, inclined to fat, with a round, clean-shaven face, large plump hands, protruding eyes, full lips, and a high color— a cheerful, good-natured fellow, wearing a close-fitting gray frock coat and a green silk waistcoat embroidered with flowers.

"My dear Lascar," Eustace said, "we shall have to erect a statue to you! Do you know that the shares have already started to rise? My brother sends his apologies—he has an unavoidable engagement; he sends his respects to Davida and best regards to yourself. Know what he said to me about you 'Even hand-in-glove with the Liberals, a boyar is always a boyar!' What do you think of that?"

"Why, he must allow me to answer—that I'm fond of him in spite of it," Lascari said, laughing.

"What do you think they'll go to?" Coziano asked.

"Think what will go to?"

"The shares, man, the shares!"

"Now don't keep thinking of them all the time. Give them time to ripen," Lascari said sardonically. *I'm talking safely,* he thought, *like a wise ancient; I'm expressing myself in maxims, like an elder.* He glanced suspiciously and anxiously at Cleopatra, with a trace of humility none the less. But Cleopatra gave him a charming smile in which he could discern a hint of perversity. *You're a pretty little whore, my girl,* he thought with contempt, affection, and contentment.

"Where's Davida? Isn't it time for dinner?" Eustace asked cheerfully. Then, turning to Lascari: "Besides, the position of the stars is favorable to business, too. Mercury is in the ascendant, in trine with the Sun and Jupiter, so I can hardly help but be making large profits. Though that doesn't mean that I'm any the less grateful, my dear Lascar."

He was in high spirits and full of plans and projects. "You realize that the railroad will send up land values in the Danube plain? As soon as I get back to the country I shall start buying up some of that completely uncultivated land—used to be the property of the Porte, you know. That will make my place at Dobrunu worth ten times as much."

"What have you done about the peasant Community there?" Lascari inquired.

Eustace laughed. "The case is still going on in the courts. . . . Meanwhile, I'm still buying land . . ."

"And the peasants are letting you?" Lascari asked.

"Not the peasants as a whole," Eustace said, with a roar of laughter, "but individual peasants—yes. Let's not talk about it. The land is virtually mine. In a year, two at most, you'll see dozens of grain cars rolling toward the Danube."

"Aren't we ever going to eat today?" Lascari demanded. "Where are the children?"

"Davida sent them for their morning walk," Cleopatra said. "They should be back by now."

Discontentedly Lascari looked about him. He was hungry and

thirsty, and he was impatient to be back in that state which followed every meal, when, his stomach laden with highly spiced food and his wits a little dulled by wine, he began to sip his brandy and to feel a comfortable fullness pervading him. Waiting for it made him peevish.

"What are they doing? Can't we begin without them?"

Just at that moment a footman announced that luncheon was served. They went into the dining room, Lascari gallantly offering Cleopatra his arm and squeezing her hand against his fat-lined ribs. Cleopatra took her husband's arm with the other hand. She moved forward simpering, swinging her hips with a movement that set her whole body swaying.

Davida was at table, waiting for them. She was now a woman of thirty—looking forty or more—pale, thin, her once blazing eyes now empty and dulled, with dark circles under them. She was unbecomingly attired in a plaid dress with a narrow band of lace at the throat; her cheeks were hollow, her cheekbones prominent. She still held herself well, from habit. She asked the others to be seated, and without further word began to eat. There were only the four of them.

"The children are having dinner in their own room," Davida said, not looking at anybody to avoid speaking directly to Lascari. She seemed weary, bored, and abstracted. Eustace, who never paid attention to anything that did not concern him personally, talked to her animatedly about the railroad business.

Lascari had tied a table napkin around his neck and was eating with an expression of disgust. Nevertheless, he asked for second helpings of every dish, and drank glass after glass of wine. Throughout the whole meal he never once glanced at Davida. They seemed to be infinitely remote from each other, while at the same time treating each other with perfect politeness.

"As I was telling our dear Lascar just now," Eustace continued, "my calculations cannot go wrong."

"What is all this stuff about calculations?" Lascar cried, after emptying a glass of wine. He replaced the glass on the table, pulled the napkin from his neck with a grunt, and turned to Eustace again. "Really, I don't understand you. A man in his right mind and the prime of life giving himself over to this astrological childishness!"

"That can happen to quite elderly people; they sometimes indulge in childish things. Didn't you know that?" Cleopatra cooed, her double meaning aimed at Lascari alone.

Lascari felt a pleasant warmth take possession of him and replied indulgently, "Yes, that's true. We all come to it."

"There, you see!" Cleopatra said, smiling.

Lascari felt himself cheered and rejuvenated by her smile. *So that's that,* he told himself, suddenly filled with happiness. *The thing is settled!* Benevolently he turned to Eustace, saying, "You see, my friend, your wife has convinced me. Calculate as much as you like according to the stars, if that's what amuses you." And in a sudden burst of high spirits, he asked, his eyes shining, "Can you cast my horoscope?"

"Why of course, my dear fellow! This very moment, if you like."

"And predict everything I am going to do?" Lascari persisted.

"Absolutely everything! Broadly speaking, of course. But if necessary, I could even go into details."

"Oh, that's a good one, that's really a good one!" Lascari burst out.

Surprised and somewhat vexed, Eustace looked at him. "I can't see what you find so funny in that."

"Now don't be angry, my dear fellow; I just felt like a laugh. No, no, I shan't trouble you to draw my horoscope. I don't want you to know all I've done and all I shall be doing from now on. And I'd far rather you didn't know too much about my character, nor—ha! ha! ha! ho! ho! ho!"

And wiping the tears from his eyes with his table napkin, he went on, shaking his head: "No, no, I really can't have you casting my horoscope. Oh, no, you shan't do that. . . ."

He began laughing again at the thought. *The stars might tell him that I'm going to fit him with a pair of horns! Better not run any risks!*

With lowered eyes, Cleopatra went on eating. Davida seemed to be in another world.

"I can't see what you find so funny," Eustace persisted. "You'll see for yourself that there's more in it than you think."

Suddenly serious again, Lascari nodded his head, ready, like the good politician he was, to accept a compromise. "No doubt it is all quite possible," he said, "and since you assure me of it, I'm ready to believe it."

"Then why not let me cast your horoscope?"

"You shall—but some other time. You shall do it, and tell me my character and all that the future has in store for me. As I understand it, the past doesn't interest you, eh? Right, then you can cast my horoscope—say, next autumn."

"I don't understand a word of what you're talking about," Cleopatra said.

"We're just talking," Lascari replied. "The childish prattle of the aged."

2

The children (Eleonora, thirteen, rather backward both physically and mentally; Alexander, eleven, silent and cowed; Helen, eight, pretty, fair, and quarrelsome; Sherban and Sophia, seven and six respectively, cheerful, turbulent, and happy) piled into the big landau, whose two half-hoods were lowered. They were accompanied by Miss Rose and Mlle Kessel, who held the two youngest on their knees. The carriage passed the Scaune Church and drove down the Boulevard Coltea toward the Chaussée, between two rows of boyars' houses, most of them dilapidated, low built, and very ugly, surrounded by large gardens full of trees. Helen was standing, looking out at the people and the carriages and carts, which were coming from the market or making for the station in long files. Then she turned her attention to Eleonora, who was immediately opposite her. Eleonora was the eldest, but she was a torpid creature, flabby and soft.

"Silly!" Helen muttered.

"I'll slap you," Eleonora retorted, speaking through her nose.

They got no further because each governess pulled the ear of the nearest little girl, and said, in French and English respectively, that they were not to speak Rumanian.

Later, after Miss Rose had signed to Constantine, the coachman, to stop the carriage and they had all got out, Sherban began demanding a hat like Constantine's, a tall black hat with a wide yellow ribbon.

"You certainly cannot wear a hat like that. You are a gentleman. Constantine is a servant. His hat is a servant's hat and no gentleman would dream of wearing one like it."

"But I like it! I want one too!" wailed Sherban. Then he began to cry in good earnest. Miss Rose gave him a couple of taps on his behind and told him that a gentleman never cried, whereupon Sherban's sobs changed to howls. Ladies, passing at a gallop in their open carriages, en route for the Mogosoaïa Bridge, turned to stare at the children through their lorgnettes. Helen whispered to Eleonora, "You're a big silly!"

"I'll slap you!"

"Are you going to give me Zoë?"

Zoë was a very large and beautiful doll which Eleonora had received for Christmas.

"No, I'm not going to give her to you," Eleonora replied.

"You're a silly fool, you're a silly fool," Helen said spitefully, staring at her sister, her pretty little mouth distorted by a sneer. Eleonora hesitated a moment before throwing herself upon her. But Helen was already out of reach and, hopping on one foot, had regained her place with her brothers. Ranged according to their age, hands behind their backs, and followed by the two governesses, they began their walk. The governesses talked together in English. The children loitered, staring at the people, the carriages,

the dogs, and the nursemaids. Helen was the third from the left.
First came Eleonora, then Alexander, then Helen. She was taller
than the little ones and shorter than the big ones. But the two
eldest were stupid, only half awake. *I'm not afraid of silly old
Eleonora,* she thought. *I'm going to trip her up. Then I'll punch
her in the belly. She won't forget it! Why won't she give me
Zoë? At her age she doesn't need a doll any more. I'm the one
who needs dolls.*

She was seized with overwhelming pity for herself and indignation at Eleonora's selfishness. Slipping between Alexander and her
elder sister, she kicked Eleonora's legs and in a flash was back in
her place, hands still clasped behind her back. In tears, Eleonora
turned to the governesses. They all came to a halt. Helen looked
at her sister and thought, *How ugly she looks when she cries.*

Helen was a fair little girl, with long curls falling down her
back. She wore a blue ribbon bow on top of her head, and a satin
dress of the same blue, with a Van Dyck lace collar, and high
buttoned boots. She loathed Eleonora—this wretched, stupid,
frightful creature who yet had the effrontery to refuse to give her
Zoë. So intent was she on vowing eternal hatred against her sister
that she did not even notice Miss Rose's approach, and the slap she
received came like a bolt from the blue.

The children set off again, Eleonora still sniffing and crying.
Helen's eyes were full of tears but she had been told a hundred
times that a young lady does not cry. However, that was not the
reason she restrained her tears: she did so because she was angry
and because her head was full of plans. *I won't cry,* she was saying
to herself. *You can all croak, but I won't cry. I'll show you!*

Eleonora went on sniveling and sniffing. Her shin was hurting.
Suddenly she was overcome by a wave of anger. She rushed at
Helen and slapped her sister's fresh pink cheeks. Helen, without
a moment's hesitation, gripped her hand and bit it as hard as she
could. The governesses hastened to part them and punish them;
the other children began to cry too. Finally, Miss Rose took Eleonora and Alexander, Mlle Kessel Helen and the little ones, and
the whole walk was ruined. Getting back into the carriage, the

Englishwoman contented herself with a sigh, her eyes raised heavenward, but Mlle Kessel, shrugging her shoulders, exclaimed, *"Que voulez-vous? Chassez le naturel, il revient au galop!* We'll talk about it this evening."

They made no further allusion to it before the children. They were obliged to be discreet in order to keep their places with these half-civilized aristocrats; after all, they were paid in gold—napoleons and sovereigns—which made it worth while to hide their contempt. Helen, her face flushed and her eyes reddened, was telling herself, *I am not crying. I'm never going to cry. You're going to learn to respect me. I shall be an empress and have your head cut off. And as for silly old Eleonora, I shall* . . .

She was not quite sure what she would do to her sister. Helen was only a child, and moreover, a child of good family, who knew nothing of life's brutality. But something she had seen in the kitchens one day gave her an idea. *I shall disembowel her,* she concluded.

3

Contrary to all expectations, Eustace Coziano and Lascari had no more to discuss that afternoon. The business had been efficiently put in hand and promptly executed. Everything was clear. Lascari —sprawling in his easy chair—was sipping brandy, smoking a cigar, and casting occasional sly glances at Cleopatra. Cleopatra was chattering idly and nobody was listening to her; but there were two little dimples in her cheeks, her rather thick black eyebrows were in constant movement, her brilliant eyes darted restlessly about, and her rosy mouth was opened constantly to reveal small white teeth. All this irritated Lascari, who began to feel that the summer was still very far away. Consequently he merely grunted at Eustace, whose astrological theories had the knack of exasperating him. Davida, seated in an armchair, erect, hands crossed on her chest, stared unseeingly out of the window.

Eustace realized that the time had come to take leave. He turned to Cleopatra. "My dear, Davida is expecting guests this evening."

Lascari, who was pretending to be half asleep, muttered, "Don't forget that we are counting on you. Don't go accepting some other invitation."

"Oh, no, we shall be coming," Eustace said. "But we must leave Davida some time to rest."

They rose, took leave of Davida and Lascari, and withdrew to their room. Lascari concentrated his thoughts on something which was not very clear to him but which he felt intensely. After some time he rose; the ash of his cigar, scattered on the lapel of his frock coat, fell to the carpet. Crossing to Davida, he put his hand on her shoulder and said, "I should like to take a siesta. . . ."

Davida followed him through the anteroom and the study, into their bedroom. She drew the curtains, then began to unhook her dress. She went behind the tapestry screen which hid the door into her boudoir, and twitched the silk bell-rope. A gypsy girl, her head covered by a kerchief, came to unfasten her corsets. Davida put on a dressing gown and reappeared from behind the screen. Lascari was in bed, lying on his back, his shoulders propped up by two pillows, and warmly covered with rugs and eiderdowns. He was waiting. Davida lay down beside him. But when Lascari reached out to take hold of her, in a gesture so old, so much a matter of course that she had learned to bear it as if some alien and inanimate object were in question and not her own body, Davida began to tremble.

All day long she had been expectant, on the alert for something without knowing what it was. And now all this pointless tension was discharged in a moment, transformed into despair and revolt, into an agony that shook the unresponsive body that Lascari held in his arms. Davida began to cry. Thrusting Lascari away, she jumped out of bed and sank to her knees beside the night table. Clutching at it blindly for support, she let her head fall forward, striking her forehead a violent blow on the edge of the table, but feeling no pain. She stayed there, crouched in her long white night-dress richly incrusted with lace. She wept bitter, convulsive sobs. She felt in every fiber of her being the long years of disgust and shame, beginning with the first days and nights of her married life, with their blend of the hateful and the ridiculous, of weariness and revulsion.

Lascari climbed out of bed with difficulty, seized Davida by the shoulder, and shook her. "What is the meaning of this childish-ness?" he demanded.

"Leave me alone! Don't touch me!" Davida moaned. Lascari felt suddenly ignoble, lecherous, and disgusting. "You shall pay for this," he said, putting on his clothes.

Davida began to be afraid. She knew Lascari: she knew the kind of sly tortures he could devise to punish anyone who dis-pleased him. "It would be better if you killed me," she sobbed.

Lascari was tying his black cravat. His braces hung down over his fat buttocks.

"I'm a decent, law-abiding man," he said. "I don't kill people. In your family there may be murderers. There are none in mine."

Alexander Coziano, Davida's father, had died after eating a dish of mushrooms. Both of them knew the rumors which had gone the rounds in consequence.

"A decent man! *Decent?* Filth, muck with a human face, that's what you are. Filth! You're nothing but filth!"

4

Helen had been deprived of the sweet course. She felt this punish-ment to be atrociously unjust. After the meal she went and played by herself. The two governesses had retired to a corner and were talking in low voices. Helen was able, unseen, to slip into the dressing room. A number of cupboards stood against the wall; some of them were always kept locked and none of the children knew what was in them. Wide-eyed, Helen walked slowly forward. The light was wan and diffuse, and there was a strange scent in the air. What was it? Patchouli? Naphthaline? Tea? Tobacco? At one moment one scent seemed to predominate, at the next another; then all mingled again into one, mysterious and unfamiliar, which seemed to be that of the reddish, gleaming old wood of the cupboards themselves, stuffed with all sorts of inconceivable things.

One of the cupboards creaked. Helen stopped short and caught her breath. She waited to see if anything would happen, if the cupboard would open and start talking, or if someone would step out of the dark old mirror which looked yellow in the half-light. Outside it was raining, and the drumming of the raindrops on the metal gutters sounded clearly. No, nothing had moved. Helen went up to a massive cupboard. She stood on tiptoe to open it. The door made no noise. Inside were hanging dresses belonging to her mother, packed tightly together, and other dresses that Helen had never seen before. Some of them were of velvet, much worn. On the shelves there were hats, a great many hats. There was a smell of mustiness, of lavender, orange-flowers, and age. Helen pulled out the bottom drawers; they were crammed with cotton and leather gloves, with veils and shawls. She started rummaging among them. She put on a large white hat lined with green silk, and draped a heavy, brightly colored Venetian shawl over her shoulders. To these she added a pair of long white gloves that reached to her armpits. Thus arrayed, she began parading up and down, backward and forward, before the tall mirror. She was no longer unhappy. It seemed to her that she looked grown up, in fact very old, twenty or even more, and that she was very beautiful. *This is what I shall be like when I am an empress,* she told herself, *like the Empress Eugénie that Mademoiselle Kessel keeps talking about. I am an empress. And now that I'm empress, I'm going to punish all those vipers. They'll soon find out who they're dealing with!*

She decided to ask her mother if she would give her all these things. *You have quite enough already, more than you need; and they suit me perfectly,* she pointed out to her mother in imagination as she tapped on the door of the boudoir, not carelessly and noisily with her knuckles, but discreetly, with the tips of her fingernails, as she had been taught to do. Receiving no answer, she walked in. She was sure of a welcome; so much beauty could not fail to charm her mother.

But her mother was not there. She was next door, in the bedroom. She was talking, talking very strangely and in a hoarse voice. "Filth!" she was saying. "You're nothing but filth!"

Draped in the shawl—the shawl which, fifty years later, Maria-Theresa Dumitriu, who was to inherit it from Sophia, Helen's sister, was to lose in the streets of a small provincial town—Helen crept to the door left ajar by the maid a few minutes before, which was shielded from the bedroom by a screen. The door swung open, impelled by a draft. Helen paused and listened. In a curt voice her father was saying, "It's you who are filth, since you accepted our life together and have lived with me for the past thirteen years, eating at my table and sleeping in my bed."

"You forced me to it by your threats," her mother moaned.

"Because, my dear, you had got yourself involved in a very dirty business."

Her mother seemed to be crying; or perhaps she was laughing, but whichever it was, she was doing it so strangely that Helen was seized by a kind of terror.

"Oh, what have I done to suffer like this? What have I done?" Helen could barely recognize her mother's choking voice. And then, with a sob: "What harm have I ever done? What wrong?"

She cries just like Eleonora, Helen thought.

"You can always hang yourself," came her father's calm, cold voice. "Why don't you?"

Her mother's voice came again, but now harsh with fury: "I'd do better to kill you! Ah, what a pleasure that would be!"

"You're not made of the same stuff as your mother," her father's voice replied, still cool and contemptuous. "Oblige me by restraining yourself and behaving as if you were not out of your mind. You are no longer a child, but a mature woman with a house, a husband, and a family. Have the sense to behave accordingly. I want no more of this childishness! Remember that you have people coming to dinner tonight. Control yourself, you mad fool!" he concluded in a sudden burst of brutality.

A silence. Then Helen heard clearly: "Is that understood?" Another silence. Then abruptly, the sound of two ringing slaps, and again the question: "Is that understood?"

There was another moment of silence; then her father's voice, pitched low, almost as if he were laughing as he spoke: "Don't pretend you've fainted; it doesn't fool me. I'm going out and I shall leave you here. I shall be back in the bosom of my family at half past seven."

"I should like to kill you! Ah! How I should love to kill you!" moaned Helen's mother.

Her father seemed highly delighted, to judge from his voice. "I know you would, but you're not capable of it. The only satisfaction I could give you would be to die before you; no doubt I shall, in view of the difference in our ages."

"How I shall laugh when that day comes! How I shall laugh!" she replied, pronouncing each word separately and clearly.

Her husband's tone was unchanged as he replied: "Not at all! It's I who will do the laughing, even on my deathbed, because, my dear, I have possessed you, and all has come to pass as I desired. As *I* desired, let me remind you. Your servant, ma'am, your servant!"

The far door of the room opened and closed. In the bedroom someone sighed.

Helen withdrew silently and returned to the room with the cupboards. Thence she proceeded to the nursery, where she made her appearance hatless, gloveless, and without the shawl. She was particularly good all that afternoon. It was only toward nightfall that this strange and unusual tranquility forsook her. Children are creatures of quickly changing moods. Moreover, Helen had seen Eleonora playing with Zoë, the big crinolined doll. Eleonora was playing with an air of sulky and apparently casual defiance as Helen came up. Five minutes later the governesses were startled by heartrending shrieks. They rushed to part the two little girls. Zoë lay on the floor, minus an arm. Helen had knocked her sister down, and holding her by the throat, was banging her head against the floor and shouting furiously, "I'd like to kill you! Ah, how I'd like to kill you! How I should enjoy killing you!"

Alarmed, the governesses went to tell Mme Lascari that, as the children's mother, she ought perhaps to have a talk with Helen. But Mme Lascari, very pale, with lackluster eyes, and dressed in gown of pearl-gray crêpe and Brussels lace, was giving the final orders for her dinner party. She hardly listened to them and merely said, "Don't bother me with these childish things."

Then she turned her back on them and went to make sure that the roses had been put on the table and that the place cards were correctly arranged. M. Kogalniceano was to sit at her right and Menelas Gherman at her left, while Bratiano was to sit on Lascari's right and Vasesco on his left. She liked to place the cards herself: it was safer. The smallest mistake might have very tiresome consequences, and Lascari would not forgive her for weeks.

PART THREE

The Position of the Stars
on July Nineteenth

I

The small town of N—— was, in 1885, the capital of a province bounded by the mountains, the Danube, and the plain. In the center of the public gardens was a statue of Constantine Mavromihali, who, as reigning prince, had rebuilt part of the town after it had been burned by the Turks in 1794. Several of the streets were avenues of chestnut trees, and the old single-storied houses, each enclosed by a fence or a wall, were overgrown with creeper and wistaria.

The air was limpid that day, and the slowly moving clouds were few and high. Peasants, their trousers decorated with braid like those of the *pandours,* the Hungarian mercenaries, were making their way toward the law courts. Their wives followed them, wearing long veils of a delicate material woven of raw silk and called *borangic;* their feet were bare and on their heads they balanced a bundle containing provisions for the journey. Shopkeepers stood on the thresholds of their shops, under signs bearing such legends as "The Gentle Lamb," "The Rainbow," or "Café Moca (Proprietor: Aznavor Aznavorian)." At the Orient Hotel bedding was being shaken out of the windows regardless of a group of gentlemen in top hats who were standing on the curb and talking politics, each leaning on a walking stick. In the courtyard of the Hotel Europa, whose name had recently been changed to Grand Union Hotel, the stagecoach which went from N—— to Bucharest three times a week was just setting off with a clatter. Eustace Coziano, his hands clasped behind his back, was strolling down Pejba Avenue, keeping to the pavement, which was sometimes bare earth, sometimes paved with brick. His somewhat protuberant eyes looked out upon the world with an expression of benevolence. From time to time he put up his monocle to stare at people, or gaily twirled his silver-knobbed ebony stick.

In the course of his walk Eustace passed beside a number of shrunken, wizened old women, seemingly made of some other clay than his own, whose faces were yellow and covered with wrinkles. These old witches were crouched along the edge of the pavement. Cloths embroidered with large black flowers were spread out before them. The cloths were as dazzlingly white as their blouses and head veils, and on each cherries were spread out—two handfuls per cloth. The old women were quite silent.

"How much for your cherries?" Eustace Coziano inquired.

"Two a penny, sir."

"Two cherries, or two heaps?"

"Two heaps, sir."

Eustace Coziano went on his way. He was neither hungry nor thirsty. The old women did not even watch him go.

Eustace passed the house which was now the Conservative Club; it had formerly belonged to Take Buzesco. He saw two carriages in the courtyard and tried to recognize their horses: were they Manolica Horoveano's and Nicolitza Jiano's? Or did the second team belong to the Bishop? Eustace did not go in. Politics no longer interested him. *My hair is turning gray. I am getting old,* he thought. *What do I want with this fleeting fame bought at the expense of such endless worry and trouble? Land—that is the only thing that matters. To be sure, banking and industry have their own kind of prestige. But land is still the soundest investment. In my case, Jupiter is in conjunction with Saturn and Mercury in the eighth house, and the Sun is in the ascendant in the Sign of Aquarius. I know exactly what I still have to do, what I must avoid, and what I should look for.*

Four barefoot peasant women, wearing skirts drawn in at the waist and reaching to their ankles, were walking in Indian file, carrying enormous bundles on their heads; another, behind them, had placed a hatchet on her head. She followed her companions at a steady, stately pace.

Eustace laughed aloud. *Ah, the minx! What a way to carry an ax! What a thing is habit, to be sure!*

Then he resumed thinking about his affairs. He could guess what Plavanesco's answer would be. But he wanted the satisfaction of hearing it with his own ears. He felt the need of assurance that his striving had not been in vain. He was already savoring the pleasure that springs from the certainty of having an absolute fortune (to add to the one he already possessed). And that thanks to his own shrewdness and perseverance. Anyone else would have long since lost heart, would have given way to entreaties, threats, or sheer fatigue. But not he! He had persevered, and now Sava Plavanesco would be bringing him the reward of his tenacity. Not that he had anything to boast about: he had merely followed the guidance of the stars.

Eustace Coziano halted. Three bullock carts were coming toward him from the direction of Winkler's pharmacy. Winkler was a German, one of the three foreigners in the province, the others being Aznavorian the café proprietor and Mercado the money-changer. In each of the carts a young man was sitting, his *caciula* as tall as a *pandour's* cap. Each had a white, black-braided cloak thrown over his shoulders. One of the youths had a panpipe stuck into his wide leather belt which was adorned with a pattern of large copper studs.

The three young men suddenly rose to their feet, crossed themselves composedly, and then carried on at the lumbering pace of their oxen. Stretched out across the pavement lay a little old woman, her face the color of earth: she was dead. Another, younger woman knelt beside her; at the dead woman's head she had set a lighted candle stuck to a flat stone.

Eustace Coziano also crossed himself and raised his silk hat. "Who is the deceased?" he inquired.

"My mother," the woman said, without raising her eyes.

"What did she die of?"

The woman shook her head and made no answer.

"And what are you going to do now?"

"I'm waiting for my husband to come back with a cart; he's gone to borrow one from some people at our place."

Coziano took a piece of gold from his waistcoat pocket and placed it on a stone beside the body. "For the repose of the souls of my dead," he said.

"May God reward you," the woman muttered. Coziano replaced his hat and went on his way.

He had not gone twenty paces when he remembered the old woman with the cherries. *Fancy trading in nothing but two hand-fuls of wretched cherries,* he thought. He retraced his steps to look for the old woman and give her a few coins. He found her, gave her the money, and refused the cherries. She too said in a toneless voice: "May God reward you." It was as if someone else spoke for her, someone strange and utterly indifferent. M. Coziano went on his way, walking more quickly, his mind at ease. *One should try to merit one's luck by doing good deeds,* he thought as he strode along with his head high and his hat a little tilted toward the back.

Sava Plavanesco had a new house freshly painted yellow and roofed with corrugated iron. On a panel between two brick pilasters above the front door the letters *S.P.* and the date *1882* were carved between stucco garlands. When he had built the house, on the site of a garden bought from Manolica Smadoviceano, Plavanesco had left the lilacs and pine trees untouched. Coziano pushed open the wrought-iron gate, climbed the steps to the front door, and rang the bell. A servant opened the door and showed him in; everything was very clean and perfectly hideous. The red-brown floorboards looked as if they had been painted with dried blood; the carpets, woven at Braila, were attempts to imitate the masterpieces of Khorassan and Bokhara; the furniture was massive and somber, the pictures atrocious—representations of farmhouses, churches, or gentlemen clamped into high starched collars. There were also two enormous engravings, one depicting the crossing of the Danube by Prince Carol I, the other a troop of Cossacks at the gallop. The tables were covered with yellowing lace, and a samovar stood on the aggressively new-looking piano. Everything reeked of dankness, and slightly, almost imperceptibly, of mold.

Sava Plavanesco came out of his office with his hand extended, but he did not smile. He was squat, pot-bellied, with the face of a bulldog. A massive watch chain spanned his black waistcoat. As a lawyer Plavanesco was second only to M. Mihuletz, who was the best in the town. Deputies and senators for local constituencies were obliged to reckon with him. The interminable lawsuits between the peasants and the landowners of the province had enriched him, and he was growing daily richer.

"Good day to you, Monsieur Eustace. Come into my office, if you please. Have the goodness to take a seat."

Coziano put his gray top hat and stick on Sava Plavanesco's desk, then threw his gloves after them. Crossing his legs and clasping his hands around one knee, he asked cheerfully, "Well, how is business with you? You're busy, are you not? Very busy?"

"Why, as to that—I find time for things as best I can. Will you take a cup of coffee, Monsieur Eustace, and a little to eat?"

Plavanesco's bearing, however, was disquieting. With his low forehead, he had the air of a bull about to gore someone. An ugly smile revealed uneven teeth as he watched his boyar visitor, graying maybe, but young-looking in spite of it, sipping his coffee and eating Turkish sweetmeats.

When Eustace Coziano had put down his glass of ice water, Sava Plavanesco picked up his own cup of coffee and, still gazing at his visitor, emptied it at a gulp, smacked his lips repulsively, and put the cup down again, still with the same apparently stupid smile on his face. He said nothing.

"Do you know why I have come?" Eustace Coziano began.

"No."

"Really? What possible business—apart, of course, from the pleasure of meeting you—could bring me to your office?" Coziano asked with a touch of insolence. "Come now, have I any lawsuits pending?"

"You certainly have."

"One lawsuit, one only."

"One only, but that one serious. On what date is judgment to be given? Isn't it today?"

"Today it is," Coziano agreed lightly.

Sava Plavanesco fell silent once more. He did not stir, but his head was still down as if he would certainly gore his visitor at any moment.

"You know I am certain to win."

"As to that . . ."

"Why 'as to that'? Do you think I shan't win?"

"Oh, you'll win all right. That's quite certain," Plavanesco said with an expression of envy.

"Right. That is what I have come to see you about. I wanted to ask you if you are still in the market."

Plavanesco remained silent for a few seconds, then said, "I do not understand why you are in such a hurry to sell. The case is not even over."

"It is virtually over."

"If you say so. Let us grant that that is so. But I still do not understand your haste, my dear sir. I do not understand it in the least."

"Perhaps it suits me to be in a hurry. Perhaps I have another deal in mind. Perhaps real estate no longer interests me," Coziano said. And in a tone once more tinged with insolence he went on: "Are you suggesting that I should place the administration of my property in your hands? Thank you, but for the time being I prefer to manage it myself. I am not one of those who waste their time in politics or spend it abroad. Consequently . . . Well, are you, or are you not?"

"You mean, am I in the market?"

"Exactly, in the market," Eustace said, putting on his left-hand glove.

"Indeed I am, Monsieur Eustace. If they had not built the railroad to the Danube, nothing would have induced me to meddle in that region of mud and dust. As it is—yes, I am in the market."

"Very well, but you see——" Coziano carefully buttoned his gloves, and then looked Plavanesco frankly and squarely in the face. "You see, I have thought over the question of the price I propose to ask, my dear fellow. According to my calculations, it ought to be higher than the figure we mentioned the other day."

Plavanesco's smile disappeared. "What do you mean?"

"Simply that I am now asking sixteen thousand louis," Coziano said, picking up his hat. Plavanesco fixed his small, red-veined eyes on that elegant object. Still without rising, Coziano picked up his stick and sat waiting, motionless, his gloved left hand holding the other glove and the hat, his right hand clasped over his left, and both hands resting on the stick. Plavanesco stared at the silk-edged lapels of Coziano's frock coat. He was still silent, but at last he said: "I did not expect this. I shall have to think it over. . . ."

"Think it over, my dear fellow, think it over," Coziano said benevolently. "I'll tell you what: you shall give me your decision after the judgment is pronounced. If we get it today, give me your answer this afternoon or tomorrow. If the judges give us their verdict tomorrow, let me hear from you in the afternoon, or the following day. Will that suit you?"

"Perfectly, very well indeed," Plavanesco stammered. He rose to escort his visitor, who, upright and slender, thanks to a tight-laced corset, had risen and was moving toward the door. "Till to-morrow, or the day after."

"My respects, Monsieur Eustace, my respects. Be so good as to convey my kindest regards to Madame Cleopatra," Plavanesco growled, waddling along beside him. He shut the door behind his visitor and returned to his chair, muttering oaths. *That's your boyar all over! Because he realizes that I'm dying to own Dobrunu, he raises the price. But it is still a bargain. The place is worth even more.* Plavanesco smiled. *A few years' development and Papa Sava will be the winner as usual! He'll bring in steam plows and seed-ing machines and threshing machines—and he won't have to do a thing except sit back and watch the gold flow into the till. Let's hope Coziano doesn't lose his case!*

Eustace Coziano strode home, his spirits raised by what he had just learned. It was obvious that Plavanesco would accept. And who knew whether the new price was not still far below the real

value of the property? That was worth considering. Coziano almost wanted to laugh at the thought of the trick he would play on
Plavanesco at their next meeting. Yes, the idea was amusing. . . .
Three hundred and twenty thousand francs—quite a sum! Especially when one considered that he had bought the land piecemeal,
almost without noticing it. A few acres one day, a few more the
next, and so on over the years. The whole lot had cost him about a
hundred thousand francs. Yes, it had been a bargain all right, and
he had every reason to be satisfied.

The Bishop's carriage, with two episcopal croziers painted on
the door, drove past him; the prelate was on his way home from
the Conservative Club. *What can he have been after there?* Coziano wondered, bowing to the old man in the *potcap.* Further on,
outside the Michael-the-Brave High School, Coziano met his lawyer, Mihuletz, a man whose hair was turning gray, whose mustache
was already white, and whose back was unbelievably round. His
top hat, worn perpendicular, made him look like a figure 5 without its horizontal stroke.

M. Mihuletz was the scion of an impoverished boyar family.
Distinguished and serene, he greeted his client composedly.

"Good morning," Eustace greeted him in return.

"Your servant."

"How's it going?"

"It will go all right, don't worry. We're going to win this case,
not they."

"What time does it come on?"

"The court is in session from eleven o'clock, but the proceedings
will go on until late in the afternoon."

"Good. I shall go and have a quick meal and then rejoin you."

"As you prefer. It would look better, though, if you were not
there at all. After all, what difference can it make to you? The
case is as good as won."

Almost doubled up by his stoop, the lawyer looked his client
up and down from under his vertical top hat. He appeared so
calm that Eustace felt completely reassured. "It does me good to

talk to you, my dear friend. Well, *à bientôt!* You'll come and see me, I hope, immediately it's all over?"

"Of course. Your servant, my dear sir, your servant," Mihuletz murmured, sweeping the pavement with his hat, after which he turned on his heel and made for the law courts at a steady pace.

Coziano could not contain his joy. *At last! After twelve years.* He took out his watch. *In five hours, perhaps four, it will all be over. Twelve years it's lasted, and in four hours there'll be nothing left of it.*

He walked on a little and then halted. *It's no good, I'll never be able to stay in the house. I simply must go to the law courts.* He set off again hastily; he would have an early luncheon and then return to the law courts.

The house which the Cozianos had built in N—— fifty years before had been designed to serve simply as a *pied-à-terre* when they went into town. The family seat was the ancestral manor house on the Cozia estate which had been built beside the ancient *coula*—the fortified house of the old Rumanian boyars—a tower-like construction of dressed stone with loopholes just wide enough to take the barrels of those long Albanian muskets called *shu-shanea.* The Cozianos also owned country houses on their other estates and, in Bucharest, the mansion in Culmea Veche Street. Alexander Coziano, Davida's father, had left the ancestral house and the house in N—— to his son Eustace, as well as the best of the landed property. Other estates had been left to the younger son, Boniface—so called according to the romantic fashion of the 1840's, his mother having read the Baroness d'Arnoult's *Boniface, Marquis de Monferrat* shortly before he was born. The house in Bucharest was left to Davida on condition that she provided a home for her mother, who, however, had left the country and married again in Vienna. Sophia Coziano never made the slightest attempt to keep in touch with her children, who saw her only *en passant,* when they went abroad and happened to run into her on the Promenade des Anglais at Nice, or in the casino at Biarritz.

The house in N—— was a one-storied building. French win-

dows opened onto a garden behind the house. By way of entrance
porch there was a sort of cage made of wood and glass, very ugly,
but most useful in winter, since the cold could not accompany
visitors into the house. In one corner of every room towered a
solemn-looking stove of whitewashed brick. The green-and-white
striped silk which covered the upholstered furniture had been
imported from Vienna by Alexander Coziano in 1830. The furniture itself, of which the rounded lines were not without a certain
massive grace, was in a rather German style. Into an interior by
no means spacious had been crammed commodes, wardrobes, occasional tables, card tables, clover- or lyre-backed chairs, a big
clock which played several bars of Schubert's "Serenade" every
quarter of an hour, portraits of ancestors, some with daggers thrust
into their wide cashmere sashes, wearing the fur cap (*ishlic*) and
the long olive-green frock coat (*anteriu*) peculiar to the boyar
class; others wearing conventional evening dress and sprouting
Turkish, Russian, and Austrian decorations. There were also pictures of ladies in low-cut dresses with leg-of-mutton sleeves, their
faces surrounded by those sausage curls which, at that time, were
known as *anglaises*. Such was the house in which shade and cool-
ness reigned that day, despite the heat of summer. Through the
French windows of the drawing room the roses could be seen coming into flower, and at the far end of the garden were the servants'
quarters, beside the stables and coach house.

Eustace entered the house and was greeted by a number of
hunting dogs, who began dancing around and jumping up at him
as soon as he appeared. "Good dog, good dog! That's enough,
now!" Eustace cried good-naturedly as he removed his hat and
gloves. He went into the drawing room; his wife rose and came to
meet him. Cleopatra was now a young woman of thirty, with
round pink cheeks and, beneath thick eyebrows, bright eyes which
Eustace gallantly called "Andalusian."

"Well? All settled?"

From another easy chair their friend Walter Apostolesco rose
to greet his host. The handsomest man in town, he was also its
arbiter elegantiarum. He was tall and slim, with long curly hair. A

low, very wide shirt collar *à l'artiste* revealed a blue silk cravat. His chestnut side whiskers, short blue velvet jacket, white waistcoat, and wide-brimmed gray felt hat, everything about him, in short, was designed to give him a "Bohemian" appearance—or what would pass for one in society. A former cavalry officer, he had resigned his commission because he preferred peace and quiet and was satisfied with his rank of major. Too lazy to go into politics and possessed of an adequate fortune, Walter Apostolesco spent his time very pleasantly: when he was not at home reading novels and smoking, he was calling on friends, enjoying a day's shooting, or playing cards at the Conservative Club, where he was held to be one of the town's most influential electors; after which he would repeat his customary round of visits. He said little, but he said that little pleasantly, without ever raising his voice, asking questions, making personal remarks, or speaking ill of anyone.

"I should like to lunch early so as to go to the law courts," Coziano said. "Where is Davida?"

"In the garden," Cleopatra replied, drawing back the curtain at one of the windows. Outside, beyond the iris beds, under one of the old walnut trees, Davida, in a black silk mourning dress, was sitting in a wicker armchair.

"Poor Davida," Eustace said.

Cleopatra shrugged her shoulders. "I don't understand her. Oh, granted Lascar was a delightful man, but to be so utterly inconsolable . . ."

"She loved him passionately," Apostolesco said in a tone of deep feeling.

Davida sat warming herself in the sunshine. She was not thinking of anything. She was bored. She saw her brother, her sister-in-law, and their friend coming toward her, and returned their greeting with indifference. Ten paces away the servants were setting up a table in the shade of the walnut trees. Eustace turned toward them to count the number of places being laid.

"Whom are we expecting today?"

"Smaranda and Aristitza promised me to come. They are alone. Their husbands have some political luncheon or other, so they

thought they'd come and see me," Cleopatra replied. Eustace Coziano made a face but said nothing. The footman came up and
said, "Some peasants are asking to speak to the master."

"What sort of peasants?" Eustace demanded.

"They say you know them, sir, that they come from Dobrunu."

"Peasants from Dobrunu?" Cleopatra said, surprised. "What do
they want with you?"

"They are probably hoping to arrange a compromise," Apostolesco suggested, laughing comfortably.

"Now? Just as I'm about to sit down to lunch?" Eustace complained, frowning. "Oh, well, since the ladies haven't arrived
yet . . . Excuse me a minute."

The peasants were waiting on the pavement outside the house.
There were twelve or fifteen of them, their clothes ragged. Some
had no shoes and their feet were covered with mud and dust. As
soon as Eustace appeared, they all removed their hats or *caciula*.
Their faces were bony and lined, their hair and mustaches black,
their eyes dark and melancholy. They looked at Coziano as if he
was a being from some alien planet, unfamiliar and remarkable.
For his part he looked at them with good-natured condescension.

"Good morning, my good men."

"We greet you, master."

"What do you want with me?"

The peasants looked at one another in silence. One of them, a
sickly, swarthy man with a small triangular face, started to laugh.
The laugh was completely unexpected. His companions appeared
uneasy, even frightened. "What do we want?" he said, still laughing. "Your lordship knows very well what we want."

"No, I don't know," Coziano said with a touch of irritation. "I
can guess; and I can be mistaken. Tell me what brings you here;
then I shall know."

This conversation took place in the courtyard, behind the
wrought-iron fence enclosing the house and garden. Outside in the
street hawkers came and went, carts clattered past, and a yellow
cabriolet drawn by a black, high-stepping horse.

"Don't keep me too long, my men. They are waiting for me to begin luncheon."

One of the peasants nudged the man who had already spoken, and said in a mournful voice, "You tell him." The swarthy man looked all around him and then turned to Coziano. "It's like this. We've come . . . well, to talk about our land."

Coziano's manner became icy. "There is nothing for either of us to say about that. Go to the law courts, they'll be giving their verdict now. The land is no longer yours, except for the holdings I have not bought." And looking the swarthy man in the eyes, he added, "As for you, I know you. You're Nitza Negrea. You sold me nothing. What are you interfering for?"

The man smiled politely with his head on one side, and explained, as one explains to a foreigner or a child: "We're a Community."

"A Community, are you? That's all very well for you in your village," Eustace shouted. Then abruptly, resuming his former benevolent attitude, and adopting in his turn the air of an adult talking to a child, he explained: "Your Community exists only for you. In law it has no existence. The law recognizes only persons, individuals, landowners."

"We've been a Community since the time of Michael the Brave, master," said the oldest and most melancholy of the peasants. "We're descended from a certain Nitza the Captain. We've never been subject to any boyar. . . ."

"I've known all that ever since our lawsuit began," Coziano said, laughing. "I know it all by heart. Tell me quickly what you want. I'm in a hurry."

"Master, don't stifle us," Nitza Negrea returned gravely. "What is to become of us?"

"That's a good one!" Coziano said. The manner in which these peasants spoke to him, the way they eyed him even while standing bareheaded in front of him, was beginning to vex him. *They exaggerate their despair,* he thought. *They can hardly have supposed they were going to be able to keep the land! If I hadn't bought*

*it from them someone else would have done so, sooner or later.
Once capital is brought into it, they can't possibly hold out. Heaven
knows that's easy enough to understand!*

"Yes, that's a good one, all right! So I'm stifling you, am I,
Nitza? Didn't all your people come to me, one after the other, to
sell me their plots of land?"

"That is true, master, they did come to you, but there was the
drought, and some of them had lost their livestock, and others had
borrowed money from you and then they weren't able to pay it
back," the old peasant murmured.

Coziano looked at him severely. "Will you kindly tell me what
business that is of mine? I still have not grasped what you want
with me, and my meal is getting cold."

Nitza Negrea gave him a crooked smile. "No danger of *our*
meal getting cold, master. We shall all end up begging our bread,
like the blind at the city gates."

"Nonsense! Don't worry: there'll always be work for you with
me," Coziano replied genially. Would he really have need of so
many hands? His idea was to use steam-driven machinery, harvest-
ers, in a word to make Dobrunu an up-to-date farm like the kind
he had seen in England, Brandenburg, and Pomerania. He could
not, therefore, employ all these peasants. But after all, there were
other estates in the neighborhood. Coziano accordingly brushed
this consideration aside.

Nitza Negrea knew nothing of these thoughts of Coziano's. He
had simply heard him say "Don't worry: there will always be
work for you with me." And he smiled, still with his head tilted
to one side, as if to say "Ah, you sly one!" This was by no means
to Coziano's taste. "Well? Anything else?" he demanded.

The men still looked at him with the same expression of resigned despair. Then suddenly something utterly unexpected happened, making Coziano shudder: the oldest peasant fell on his
knees before him and, raising clasped hands, said, "Lord, let us
keep our land!"

Coziano's monocle fell from his eye. But he was not given time
to pull himself together, for, one after the other, all the peasants

fell on their knees. Last of all, Nitza Negrea went down on bended knees to him also, and said, "We will give you back all the money you gave the men who sold their land."

Coziano, at first disturbed, was seized with terror at the sight of all these men on their knees to him, especially the old one who was so emaciated and had such sunken eyes. Then he took himself in hand; he was even tempted to laugh at the way in which Nitza Negrea, from his knees, had made him a practical proposition, offering to buy back the land like a real businessman.

"A fine joke! Where would you find the money? Come, on your feet! It doesn't suit men of your years to be kneeling. Up with you!"

"No, no! Let us kneel, lord, and implore you! We are lost without our land. We shall die." The old peasant's voice was tearful, yet utterly toneless and dull. The others remained on their knees, their faces grave, looking at Coziano, and waiting, as if they were taking part in a ceremony that would have to end in a prescribed fashion, with a ritual gesture.

"Have I not told you once and for all that I will give you work?" Coziano repeated. "Our interests, yours and mine, are identical: we want a fine harvest. Why do you think they have built the railroad right down to the granaries on the Danube? So that our wheat can be loaded onto barges which will carry it to Galatz, and from there into vessels which will take it to England and Holland, where they do not grow wheat of their own."

The peasants looked at him and listened, but Coziano could feel that his words were making no impression.

A carriage drove up at a trot, making for the gate into the drive which a footman was hastening to open. There were three ladies in the carriage, each holding a light-colored parasol. Coziano hurried forward to help them alight. The peasants remained kneeling outside that sumptuous, alien house which, with its drawn blinds, looked somehow deserted. The ladies alighted, holding wide skirts clear of the ground with one hand. Talking and laughing, they walked around the outside of the house, toward the garden. The coachman, turning the horses in the space before the caged entrance, shouted to the peasants to get out of the way. They stood up, but they were still forming a compact group near the veranda when Coziano returned to them, smiling at a remark made by one of the guests.

"So we're agreed, are we?" he said. "Go in peace, and in the autumn we'll talk about it again. I'm certainly not going to take away the wheat you've grown this summer! In the autumn we'll come to an agreement."

The peasants remained motionless. They were capable of standing there for a hundred years in the hope of making Coziano give way by their mere silent presence. He therefore bade them good day, and went through the house to the garden, where the others were already at table.

The peasants remained for a few minutes longer in the courtyard. Then Negrea said, "Come on, lads, our coffee will be getting cold."

2

Even as they were alighting from their carriage, the three ladies were congratulating M. Coziano. Mme Smaranda Buzesco, married to a descendant of Preda Buzesco, one of Michael the Brave's captains, was short and dumpy. She looked as if she had been kept in a press: her face was pushed down into her double chin, the back of her neck disappeared into her round shoulders, and her whole body slumped downward to her hips. Constance, her daughter, was still unmarried, although she was twenty-two years old—something as unusual as it was considered reprehensible in the N—— of that era. Constance was a lanky girl with a big, clownish nose, inherited from her mother, and a sad little mouth in the shadow of this nose which her mother described as "Bour-

bon," but which prevented her from finding a husband. Mme
Horoveano was a woman of about thirty, placid and shy, and
married to one of the biggest landowners in the province. She too
murmured her congratulations.

"And how do you feel about it, my dear man?" Mme Buzesco
said. "After twelve years you must be sick and tired of this lawsuit. Well, it's an open secret that it's all settled. So all that's left
is to wish you good luck and prosperity at Dobrunu. Good morning, Davida. Good morning, child"—this to Cleopatra Coziano.
"Good morning, my black-haired beau. Do you know how we
found Eustace when we arrived? He was outside the front door,
delivering a sermon to the kneeling peasantry! My dear man, I
knew you were an astrologer, but you seem to have gone up in
rank; you've been promoted saint! When do the miraculous cures
begin?"

They had Chablis with the trout, wine from Balotesti with the
lamb, then Burgundy, and finally armagnac with their coffee. Coziano, red in the face, glass in hand and napkin tied around his
neck, declared that the outcome of his lawsuit could not have been
otherwise. "The stars predetermine everything."

"Look, my dear," Smaranda said, "couldn't you cast this child's
horoscope and tell her when Prince Charming is going to appear?"

"Of course I could."

"Good, then that's settled. But frankly now, isn't all this business of the planets a pack of lies?"

"No," Walter Apostolesco replied with an air of conviction.
"It's not lies: Eustace has given me evidence which frightened me,
but which won me over to his side."

The children appeared. They had had their meal and the governess brought them in, leading them by the hand. The little boy,
Manolica, was thin and gawky. He kissed the ladies' hands and
then, mechanically, kissed Walter Apostolesco's. Everyone laughed.
This put Manolica out of countenance and he ran into the house.
The girls—Olga was ten and Zoë eight—started chatting to Constance. Those who were sitting around the luncheon table pushed
back their chairs and moved to the wicker chairs set out on a big

Oriental rug in the shade of the walnut trees. The gentlemen smoked cigars. The ladies read their fortunes in the coffee grounds at the bottom of their cups. Walter Apostolesco hummed a song which he had heard in Paris a year earlier.

Smaranda tapped his face with her fan. "Quiet, you wicked man! Look, Eustace, I simply can't believe in all this astrological nonsense. . . . In fact, I refuse to believe in it until you give me some kind of proof."

Coziano glanced at Apostolesco: it was the look which one sage exchanges with another in the presence of some ignorant unbeliever.

"How shall we convince her?"

"The only way is to cast Mademoiselle Constance's horoscope," Walter replied. "We must touch the maternal chord in Madame Smaranda's heart. It's her only weak point! For the rest, Madame Smaranda is a strong-minded woman."

Adroitly he evaded the closed fan, which brushed his nose.

"Make fun of me, if you like, and think me an idiot. . . . The fact is, I have difficulty enough in believing in the next world. Do *you* believe in it—a life after death where we'll all meet again?"

Up till then Davida Lascari had not said a word. Now, breaking the thoughtful silence which followed, she said, "After we have all got rid of one another at last, are we really going to be obliged to meet again?"

The ladies exchanged looks. Nobody said anything, and Davida stared at nothing. Then Smaranda Buzesco proposed a game of cards. Cleopatra clapped her hands and the servants brought out a card table.

"Will you be good enough to excuse me?" Coziano said, rising. "I must go to the law courts to see how things are going."

Apostolesco also stood up. "I'll come with you. I am curious to see what happens."

"No, no, stay here and keep the ladies company. Please!"

At this moment a footman appeared to announce that M. Mihuletz was asking for him. Eustace's face lit up.

"That means it's all over. You can congratulate me."

Agile as a boy, he ran into the house, while the ladies all rose, disturbed and curious also. Only Davida did not move from her chair. The others had not reached the door of the house when Coziano reappeared, his face livid. He spoke in a hoarse voice to Apostolesco: "Walter, come here a moment, please. I need you."

Calmly but quickly nevertheless, Walter threw his cigar into the long grass, rose from his chair, shaking off the ash that had fallen onto his velvet jacket, and went into the house. Cleopatra was much agitated, and Smaranda Buzesco was trying to soothe her.

"It's probably some trifling technicality. Nothing serious, I'm sure."

"I'm not afraid of that, and besides, it would not be so terrible. In the past twelve years we've foreseen every possible outcome." Cleopatra's cheerfulness was obviously forced. Her guests suggested taking their leave so that she might join in the discussion with Mihuletz. Cleopatra politely urged them to stay, but they would not hear of it and left at once, walking around the outside of the house. Mme Smaranda kissed Cleopatra.

"Tell Eustace not to worry. I'll have a word with Take and tell him to give the presiding judge a hint—the old man's gone quite gaga lately, can hardly hear a word and his brain's not much better than his hearing. . . . Thank you for the lunch, child; it was perfect. I'm sorry Eustace frets so much. Tell him not to take things so seriously. It's bad for his health."

They exchanged kisses under their little silk sunshades, then the guests got into their carriage. Mme Smaranda surveyed the other carriage which was waiting for Mihuletz, with its matched pair of English dapple-grays, and said philosophically, "That's the way of things nowadays. Mihuletz is ugly and misshapen, and yet his horses are nothing short of miraculous. Console yourself, Constance: the kingdom of this world belongs to the hideous!"

Constance's eyes filled with tears. Her mother did not even notice, and prodded the coachman in the back with the point of her parasol. As they drove out between the gateposts, she waved to Cleopatra and said, "Talking of hideousness, what do you think of Cleopatra's children, Aristitza?"

"Monsieur Coziano is such a handsome man. . . ." Mme Horoveano said timidly. "And yet the little girls are not like their mother, either. . . ."

"Oh, come now! Allow me to point out that each of the children is exactly like its father," Smaranda insisted, much amused.

"Really, Mama!" Constance protested, embarrassed.

"I can see no resemblance, none whatever."

"You're mistaken, my dear," Mme Smaranda replied, delighted. "The resemblance is striking. Each of them is like the father!"

"I don't understand," Mme Horoveano said.

"Now don't be silly! The boy—well, you saw who he was like: Eustace. But Zoë is the spit of Eustace's brother, Boniface. As for Olga, the eldest, she is the daughter of her old hog of a brother-in-law—Cleopatra's, I mean—Lascar Lascari. He spent the summer at their house at Cozia, just about the time . . ."

"Oh!" Mme Horoveano was appalled.

The signs of her distress appeared to alarm Smaranda. "Heavens! What have I done?" she exclaimed. "You mean you didn't know, and I am the first to tell you? I would never have said a word, never, had I thought you didn't know—but you're the only person in the whole town who doesn't, my dear! You ought to be canonized! Is it really true that you didn't know? My dear, you must have been living on the moon! Well, there it is, poor Cleopatra is like that: it's her one weakness. Nothing vicious about it, you know. It's no more than a weakness. Fortunately, she controls herself—never gives way to the desire to give herself to her stable-boys and coachmen. That's something. At least she can be said to keep it in the family."

Mme Horoveano was literally overwhelmed. "You mean . . . with her brothers-in-law?"

"One after the other!" Mme Smaranda proclaimed in a martial voice. "Not all at the same time! In order of age."

Mme Horoveano had still not recovered when her friends

dropped her at the house where she was living, her father-in-law's. She was from Bucharest, and was simply visiting her husband's constituency. Mme Smaranda gazed after her, and said to Constance, "Nice girl. More or less half-witted, of course. . . ." Whereupon she again prodded her coachman in the back with the point of her parasol, and bawled "Home!"

Meanwhile, Mihuletz was trying to soothe Coziano, who, in a state of great agitation, was pacing the room, gesticulating and repeating as if he were out of his mind, "Impossible! Absolutely impossible! I spent whole nights over my calculations. Jupiter and Mercury are in conjunction in the fourth house. Twelve years at law, and now another adjournment? How many more times will they adjourn the case? When shall I be able to call what I've bought and paid for my own? It's immoral! It's unjust!"

Suddenly he halted, and stared at Walter Apostolesco. "I suppose I misinterpreted the aspect of Saturn in square to Mars. That's probably where the trouble lies."

"The hitch is of no importance," Mihuletz said soothingly. "It's a mere formality."

"Saturn in square to Mars! So that was it!" Coziano exclaimed, mopping his face with a large wine-colored silk handkerchief.

"Please listen to me," Mihuletz insisted quietly. "It is a matter of proving that at the time of your first purchase of land at Dobrunu, the Community's right of pre-emption was respected. Evidence of witnesses to the first purchase will be accepted as proof. And you have the very man you need for that in the person of Turcou Sake: the first contract was signed in his presence. All you have to do is to send for him."

"Is that all?" Walter Apostolesco asked, putting a hand on Coziano's shoulder. "Then don't get in such a state. You hear what Mihuletz is saying: it's nothing, less than nothing!"

Cleopatra did not take her eyes off them. Seeing that Walter was restored to his usual smiling serenity, she felt calmer and came toward them the better to hear the lawyer's explanation. She stood by the window overlooking the garden, and could see Davida as a little dark patch against the green foliage of lilacs and walnuts.

Coziano was still boiling with exasperation. "It's yet another postponement, don't you see, another adjournment! How much longer must I be patient? What date was fixed?"

"July nineteenth," Mihuletz said placidly. "I was unable to obtain an earlier date."

"July nineteenth! But that's an eternity!" Coziano shouted. "However—you guarantee that this case will definitely be over by July nineteenth?"

Grave and dignified, the lawyer bowed his head in affirmation. "Rest assured that the verdict will be ours," he said, getting to his feet. "Madame Cleopatra, my respects. Monsieur, your servant."

Bowing to Cleopatra and Walter, hat in hand, bent almost double in the black satin courtroom gown which he had not had time to remove, Mihuletz left the room. Coziano followed and saw him into his carriage, glanced at his horses, and then, leaning toward him, said, "Listen, Mihuletz; you have some fine thoroughbreds there, but if everything is settled by July nineteenth, I will make you a present of four horses beside which this pair of yours will look like a couple of broken-winded hacks!"

Mihuletz gave one of his rare smiles. "Excellent. I accept with thanks. But order the horses at once. Let them be there without fail on the nineteenth. Your servant, monsieur."

The carriage moved off toward the gates.

Walter Apostolesco, meanwhile, was whispering in Cleopatra's ear. "I turned astrologer for love of you. Now behold me turning jurist in the same cause!"

She laughed, throwing back her head.

Coziano returned. "Walter, let us take another look at that horoscope. I'm sure we can't have made any mistakes in our calculations. It must be an error of interpretation. . . ."

3

Tanasake, who was also called Turcou Sake, meaning Sake the Turk, shaved only once a week and wore a sheepskin hat even in summer. He had a bony head and a prominent chin. His small mustache was squeezed between his nose, which looked as if it were collapsing into his mouth, and his thrusting lower jaw. His body always seemed to be leaning slightly backward, and he kept his backside well tucked in as if he went in constant fear of having it kicked; none the less, he carried his head high. Sake had had his house built at the far end of the village, apart from the rest. His example had been followed, and soon there was a huddle of daub-and-wattle cottages. Sake talked a lot and was listened to. He talked about city life, and what was to be seen in foreign parts, in the boyars' houses or those of the merchants, and a great many other things of which his own knowledge was by no means exact.

One evening in June some peasants were seated on a bench in front of Sake's house, their bare feet covered with dried mud. Others stood around, leaning on their cudgels, and still others sat at the roadside with their feet in the ditch. They were all Tanasake's neighbors and friends. Nitza Negrea passed that way and stopped to hear what was being said. Tanasake did not seem to notice his presence. He was talking in an easy, carefree manner.

"What's wrong with having a boyar? It's he who'll pay the tax. We'll have his land for a share of the crop and he'll have to find us in seed and stock. If anyone needs anything he'll just go and ask him for it: 'Master, be generous, give us some maize,' or 'Master, I've come to ask you to lend me some money.' And then he'll say, 'Very well, my good man, call in at the bailiff's office and ask the bailiff to put you down in his ledger. We'll settle up next harvest.' Of course he'll skin us a bit. Wouldn't be a boyar if he didn't. But at least we'll know there's someone there we can turn to. Is it any use asking our own people for anything when we're in need? No. It's not possible because they've got nothing either. The Community never lends anything, not even a handful of flour. Nowadays, come to think of it, we're not really a Community at all. Besides, we've had his money, haven't we? What's the use of regretting it? Some of us have still got a bit of it in hand. And now those who didn't sell are angry with those who did because the boyar has no use for their plots of land now. That's clear enough, isn't it?"

In the fading light the others muttered uncertainly, dully, like ignorant and defeated men. Nevertheless, they felt more enlightened now, more intelligent. They were moving with the times; they belonged to a boyar. Henceforth, in their Community things were going to be different.

Night fell; the air was hot and dry.

"It's clear enough," Tanasake resumed. "It's no good counting on one another. The boyar is too powerful. We're certainly not going to try to fight him, are we?"

There was a silence. Then some of them murmured that it was true: they could not fight the boyar. They could hardly see one another in the darkness. Above their heads glittered innumerable swarms of bright stars which seemed very close to the village.

Tanasake laughed. The peasants could not see him, but they knew that spiteful laugh of his which was accompanied by a contortion of his jutting, pointed chin.

"Besides, you can always rob a boyar! You can't help yourselves to the neighbors' goods; they'd spot it at once. But it's different with a boyar. He's fat enough to nourish a lot of fleas, the rascal!"

The others laughed too, softly. "We're as lean as grasshoppers. No good the fleas trying to live on us!" someone said.

For a little while all the peasants talked at once; then the hubbub died down. Much later they set out for their own cottages in groups of two or three, separating at the little bridges which crossed the ditch, one in front of each house. One man remained at the roadside, arms crossed and pipe in mouth. From time to time a red glow as big as a hazelnut shone out as he drew on his pipe. Until then Tanasake had pretended not to see this man and had talked as if he were not there. But when he rose to enter his own yard, the peasant called him:

"Sake!"

Tanasake halted and turned around. "What do you want of me?" he asked coldly.

"Hey, Sake, I wonder if you know what you're doing?"

"What do you mean, what I'm doing? I'm not doing anything," Sake answered.

"Take care, friend. You're falling foul of our Community."

"Let me alone, Nitza Negrea! There's no Community worth the name. Have I quarreled with Radu, or with Prosteala, or with Cogar? What do you mean—falling foul?"

"That lot don't count. You're falling foul of the others—the most of us—right enough, my little Sake," Nitza Negrea said in a good-natured voice.

"It's always the same when a man doesn't go with the herd. Those who do get angry with him. But I've got my own ideas about it, I've no need of anyone else's. . . ."

"It seems *they're* going to call you into court as a witness," Nitza Negrea murmured.

"That's their business," Tanasake said proudly, like a man who, after all, did not trouble himself about the case, the boyar, or the village; a man completely independent and sure of himself.

"If you are called, what are you going to say?" Nitza Negrea demanded, as if he thought the question unimportant and the answer even more so. He drew on his pipe and expelled the smoke in a number of small, quick puffs. The glow of the burning tobacco lit his face for a moment: it was angular, and divided by a thick mustache.

"What am I going to say? Sly, aren't you? I shall say what happened. The truth, that's what: I'm no liar. Never told a lie in my life and not going to start now. People can say what they like—they can go and croak, even—but I'm telling no lies."

"Good." Nitza Negrea coughed and knocked out his pipe against the palm of his hand. A few sparks glowed on the ground. Nitza Negrea stamped them out with the callused sole of his bare foot and said, "In your place, I'd lie."

"Why should I lie? I don't want to dirty myself with lies, d'you hear? Not for anything in the world!"

"I'd lie, you know. I shouldn't want to harm the others, so I'd say I hadn't taken into account the right of pre-emption—see? That means you haven't begun by asking people if they themselves wanted to buy—you get me? The boyar would lose his case, and we'd keep our land. How about it, Sake?"

"I want nothing to do with you. I sold my plot and I've had my money. I'm no perjurer and they'll make me take an oath. . . ."

"So you *are* going to give evidence?" said Nitza Negrea, suddenly pleased.

Sake shrugged. "Did I say so? I'll go if I'm called. If I'm not called, I shan't go."

Nitza Negrea was silent for a moment; then he shook his head. "You're a sharp one, Sake."

"Perhaps I am and perhaps I'm not," Sake said sneeringly. "I wouldn't know. I am what I am, and I'm not going with the herd."

"Good," Nitza Negrea said. "God be with you."

"God be with you," Tanasake replied cheerfully.

"God be with you," Nitza Negrea repeated mechanically. He moved away from the little bridge and went down the village street.

Tanasake ate his meal and went to bed with his wife and children. Nitza Negrea went home, had supper, and went out again to call on some neighbors. He called them by name from the street, and they came out and spoke to him over the fence. Then he went on his way. Two or three men went with him. They stopped to talk for a while and then moved off again toward the far end of the village. They stopped when they were fifty paces from Tanasake's house.

"You two will stay here," Nitza Negrea said calmly. "You don't know how to stop the dogs from barking." He went on alone, drawing on his pipe. When he came near to the fence, a dog rushed out at him, snarling and showing its teeth. Nitza Negrea murmured a few words in a voice so soft and even that the dog quieted down. The other dogs also behaved in an unusual way: they wagged their tails and watched in silence as Nitza opened the gate and went into the yard. He threw them some bones. In the darkness it was impossible to see anything, but the dogs went sniffing after the bones. Nitza Negrea walked around the thatched cottage. He walked slowly, almost too slowly. He was incredibly peaceful. Above his head in the serene June sky great stars gleamed greenishly. Nitza Negrea drew on his pipe, then took it in his hand and turned the bowl upside down so that the burning tobacco fell out upon the thatch. He retraced his steps, crossed the yard as slowly as he had come, closed the gate behind him, and made off down the street. When he had rejoined the two men who were waiting for him, he turned around. When they saw flames licking the thatch Nitza Negrea said, "Let's go."

4

The Buzesco Theater at N—— was named after the great *Logothete* Buzesco who had built it at his own expense in 1842 out of philanthropy and public spirit—or, according to evil tongues, to avoid leaving anything to his children because he had quarreled with them and wanted them to feel as chagrined as possible. The theater was a long, single-storied building separated from the Buzescos' house by the arch of a wide porte-cochère. The façades of the house and the theater were identical. Beyond the big gates was a passage lit by an ancient wrought-iron lantern. On the right a few steps led into the house; on the left, into the foyer of the theater. Straight ahead was a vast courtyard planted with horse-chestnut trees, and on the far side of its central lawn, the Buzesco stables and coach houses. At the time—1885—the courtyard was ill-kept: stable doors were off their rusty hinges, the grass was withered and trampled, and servants in ragged clothes lounged about on the lawns. The house, however, was always full of guests, who came there to play cards, from early afternoon until dawn. The theater was let to Iani Iorgo, proprietor of the Orient Hotel; and he sublet it for municipal balls, or dances given by the Hussar regiment quartered in the town, or by the Rumanian Ladies' Charitable Association. From time to time he also sublet it to theatrical companies, musicians, conjurers, or other performers on tour.

The auditorium of the theater had only two hundred seats, and one tier of boxes with slender Corinthian columns. Pastoral scenes were painted on the ceiling. Above the boxes hung portraits of ancient and modern dramatic poets up to and including Schiller. On either side of the proscenium arch was a grinning mask, which persons of education knew to be that of a satyr, but which ladies and the rest of the audience took to be that of a devil. The boxes were furnished with Louis Seize chairs upholstered in red velvet, the rest of the house with hard seats.

Only the stage was lit, but that in a manner quite fairylike, by about thirty oil lamps installed on each side of the prompter's box. The society ladies sitting in their boxes held supple ostrich-feather fans in one hand and mother-of-pearl opera glasses in the other, which enabled them better to inspect the jewelry of their friends and relations, to assure themselves that the ladies of the merchant and professional classes in the stalls looked ridiculous, and to admire the slender elegance of Captain Lampenmacher, Master of Music to the Hussars, as he conducted the overture to *Robert le Diable*, an act of which was about to be given by amateurs of good family, under the aegis of the Rumanian Ladies' Charitable Association.

Walter Apostolesco should have been on the stage, in a medieval costume which would have suited his romantic face to perfection. But he had refused a part with gentle obstinacy.

"It is Cleopatra who forbade it," Mme Smaranda Buzesco

whispered behind her fan to her neighbor. "The trollop's jealous!" As she spoke, she nodded amiably to the Cozianos, who occupied a box where Cleopatra was enthroned in white satin and lace, the color contrasting happily with her black fan and the rubies at her throat and ears and on her fingers. Coziano raised his eyes to the ceiling, then gazed fixedly at his knees. Apostolesco, seated beside them, pale, making play with his long eyelashes, his side whiskers carefully groomed, was listening to the music.

Coziano was trying to reconstruct in his mind a map showing the positions of the stars on July 19. He had drawn it a hundred times and knew it by heart. *Yes, but I may still be mistaken,* he argued. *I've been wrong once. It's all a question of interpretation.* Anxiety brought him out in a cold sweat. What could be the meaning of the journey? Mercury in the ascendant meant financial gain, and, associated with Uranus and Saturn, a journey. Did that mean the case would be adjourned again? More interminable delays? Or even that the case might be lost? But no: his calculations showed that this was out of the question.

Coziano felt that he had not patience enough to wait. He whispered to Cleopatra, "Will you excuse me? I'm too hot. I'm going out for a breath of air. I shall walk back to the house. Walter will bring you home in the carriage."

Cleopatra nodded; Eustace tiptoed out, made his way along a corridor to the foyer, walked out under the arch of the passage, and drew a deep breath. When he reached home the footman was dozing in a chair on the veranda.

"Bring me a glass of cold water," Coziano ordered. He crossed the drawing room bathed in moonlight, and went into his study, whose walls were lined with books. There were innumerable treatises on astrology and cheiromancy, the complete works of Saint-Martin, Swedenborg, Franz von Baader, and Theophrastus Paracelsus, and a copy of the extremely rare *De Occulta Philosophia* of Cornelius Agrippa. Eustace lit his oil lamp and sat down at his worktable, which was littered with open books, charts of the heavens, and pieces of paper covered with figures. The footman brought him a glass of water on a tray and spoke to him.

Eustace Coziano swallowed the water at a gulp and put the glass back on the tray.

"What do you wish me to tell him, sir?"

"What? Tell whom? What are you talking about?"

"The peasant, sir. What is he to do?"

"What peasant?"

"A peasant from Dobrunu has arrived with his wife and children in a cart, with their cow tied behind it. He claims he has something to tell you."

"What? Where is he? What does he want of me? I must look into this," Coziano said, rising.

"I told him to leave the cart in the street. Did you not see it as you came in? He is with us, in the pantry. Waiting."

"Go and fetch him."

Eustace went into the garden and sank into a wicker chair. Two forms approached from the servants' quarters: the footman, and a peasant wearing a sheepskin *caciula* which he removed, saying, "Greetings to our master."

Eustace Coziano looked at him, trying to recognize him.

"Good evening. But who are you, my good man?" Coziano turned to the footman and added, "Bring a lantern and put it on the table."

The footman vanished. Cap in hand, the peasant bowed low. "I am Tanasake, at your service. Tanasake of Dobrunu, from whom you bought a plot of land."

"Ah, yes, I remember you. Well, what do you want?"

"Ah, master, what a disaster has come upon me! You don't know what those scoundrels in the village have done to me," the man whined in answer. "They set fire to my house, and I was nearly burned alive and my wife and children with me."

"When did this happen?"

"Yesterday, your honor, yesterday, about this very time as you might say. Fast asleep I was, and then all of a sudden, in my sleep, I smell smoke . . ."

In great detail Sake told how he had tried to extinguish the fire, how it had spread to the cowshed, then to the barn beside the cowshed, and how the flames had then shot up from all sides before he had been able to rouse the neighbors, so that everything had been destroyed.

"And it was that blackguard Nitza Negrea who did it!"

"How do you know?" Coziano asked.

"Why, master . . . he was at my house the evening before."

Sake gave an account of his conversation with Nitza Negrea. ". . . And he said, 'God be with you,' twice. And then he goes and sets my place on fire. Ah, I know him, the blackguard."

"Why do you call him that?" Coziano said, not understanding why the incendiary should be Nitza Negrea rather than anyone else. True, this Nitza Negrea had seemed an insolent fellow, but all the same . . .

"Why, they're a family of bandits. His father was a forest *haidouk*—died in prison, come to that. His grandfather was a *pandour* at the time of the Greek Revolution. It's just the same nowadays: they're all rebels in that family, him and his brothers. They tried to force me to tell lies in court."

Coziano skillfully questioned the peasant until he was sure that there was no more to be got out of him. "Now take your cart and go and install yourself on my estate at Cozia. I will give you a letter to my bailiff. He will find work for you. You'll be housed and fed, but only until the end of the lawsuit. Because after that, you'll be Mayor of Dobrunu. Is that clear?"

"I thank you, master," Tanasake said, standing to attention. Then he added meekly: "It wasn't for that I came to you. I came to tell you the sort of people they are at Dobrunu. I'm an honest man. I am, I tell the truth . . ."

"Yes, yes, I understand. That is just why I have need of you as Mayor of Dobrunu. You at least will not tell me lies to shield those rascals. I need an honest man who doesn't lie. You can go now. Take the lantern."

Coziano rose from his chair and strolled around the garden. *I shall have to put the screws on them. Extraordinary! This poor devil is innocent and honest and won't agree to bear false witness just to please them, so they set his house on fire. A fine thing to have happen! But I'll show them what I'm made of. In the first place, I'll make him mayor of the village: that'll let them see at once what they're up against. And to think these are the people who were on their knees to me, the scum! Could anyone imagine the hypocrisy these simple peasants are capable of?*

He was still walking up and down the garden when he heard the carriage drive up to the house, then Cleopatra's voice saying, "Where is your master? In his study?"

"No, madam, in the garden," the footman's voice replied.

Cleopatra and Walter found Eustace in the darkness, guided by the gleam of his shirt front and white tie.

"What are you doing out here in the dark?" Cleopatra asked, drawing off her gloves. Eustace did not answer. "So you are back?" he said indifferently. "Tell me, Walter, how do you explain the fact that the stars say nothing about the lawsuit, but on the other hand foretell money and a journey?"

"I can't say. But if you like, we will recast the horoscope," Walter offered, patient and courteous.

"Here we go again!" Cleopatra muttered, turning her back in exasperation. Walter squeezed her hand and whispered, "Patience . . ."

While Cleopatra was hurrying into the house, lifting her skirts in her fingertips as her short train swept the gravel path, Walter waited for Coziano to emerge from the shade of the walnut trees.

"Come into my study. And ask Cleopatra to have some coffee sent up. There must be an explanation. I haven't found it, but it must be there. Otherwise the thing simply isn't possible! Not possible!"

5

As the slow and torrid days of June passed, Eustace Coziano became increasingly nervous. By the time there were only a few days to go before the court passed judgment, he could not even sleep at night. He had still not discovered a satisfactory interpretation of the position of those stars which in his view must determine his fate on July 19. At night he paced the garden in dressing gown and slippers. Belated citizens even saw him out in the street in the same attire, talking aloud to himself and gesticulating. At meals he ate and drank a great deal, without noticing what was set before him. It was necessary to speak to him two or three times before he heard. On the evening of July 18 he dressed and went into town after dinner.

"Are you going out?" Cleopatra asked him, surprised. The children were in bed, Davida had gone to her room, and Walter Apostolesco had already left. His wife's very natural question seemed to irritate Eustace, who mumbled something unintelligible in reply. Cleopatra was sleepy, and in any case at heart she did not care what her husband was up to. She did not repeat her question, and went to bed. The following morning she found Eustace in his study; the lamp was burning, although the sun was shining brightly outside. Coziano was livid, his eyes were bloodshot, and he had obviously not had his clothes off. He rose from his worktable.

"I have not found the answer," he said gloomily and, head down, hands clasped behind his back, resumed his interminable pacing.

"Never mind, you will," Cleopatra said, yawning.

"I don't know. I know nothing, nothing, nothing!" Coziano repeated.

"What don't you know?"

"I don't know whether I shall not end by losing my case after all. Do you realize what that will mean? All that money, all that energy, all that hope expended—and for what?" He came to a halt in the middle of the room and added, "We own four times as much land as we have at Dobrunu, yet if I do not get Dobrunu, it will be as if I had nothing at all."

"You will get it all right. There's no need to get into such a state!"

"I'll get it, I'll get it! You're saying that for the sake of something to say. How do you know I'll get it?"

"Were you born yesterday?" Cleopatra retorted, bored and irritated. "Have you ever heard of peasants winning this sort of case? Where should we be if they did? You know all this as well as I do, but your stupid calculations have made you lose your head. Astrologer, indeed! You've got your head in the clouds, all right!"

The last words were almost shouted, with hands on hips and in a voice harsh with anger. Cleopatra turned on her heel and walked out of the room to dress. A quarter of an hour later, looking out of the window, she saw Eustace emerge into the street, still wearing the black alpaca jacket and white trousers he had kept on all night.

"Where are you going?" she called.

"To the law courts," he replied absently.

"It's too early."

He stopped, looked at her for a moment, and said, "I shall call for Mihuletz."

Two hours later Walter Apostolesco arrived. Cleopatra was in the drawing room, wearing a low-cut, sleeveless dress, and fanning herself.

"Where are your master and mistress?" Walter asked the footman.

"Only the mistress is in."

Walter appeared in the drawing room. "All on your own?"

He went to her, holding out his arms. She motioned him aside with her fan.

"No. Let me alone. It's too hot. Have you seen the madman?"

"No. Where is he?"

"With Mihuletz, or at the law courts. . . . Can you ever tell with him? Darling, do go and look for him. See that he doesn't do anything stupid and make us look fools. He's been virtually out of his mind for some time. I give you my word, he frightens me."

"Very well, I'll go, like a docile *cavaliere servente*. But will not my lady deign to reward my obedience?" Walter asked, giving her a languishing glance from beneath his long eyelashes.

Disturbed, Cleopatra was on the point of rising from her chair; then she changed her mind and again parried his advance with her fan. "Let me alone for the moment. Off with you!"

"One kiss!" Walter said.

"And more; but first go and do what I ask."

"Little flirt! You'll be the death of me," Walter said, bowing gallantly. He was wearing a sky-blue jacket and lavender-colored trousers, a lemon-yellow cravat, and a wide-brimmed straw hat. In the same hand as his hat he carried a thin bamboo cane with a gold knob.

"Off with you!" Cleopatra ordered, with a complacent and proprietary look.

When he reached the door she called him back. "Come here."

She put her arms around his neck, hugged him, kissed him passionately, then once more thrust him toward the door. When she was alone again the voluptuous smile faded from her lips. *Surely we are not going to lose Dobrunu?* And for the first time she felt a touch of anxiety. *No, no, it isn't possible,* she assured herself, looking out of the tall window that opened onto the garden where she could see the children, dressed in white, at play among the foliage flecked with the brilliant July sunlight. Davida, waxen-faced and still in deep mourning, was also in the garden.

What can she be thinking of all the time? Cleopatra wondered. *What are her plans? What does she mean to do now that she's rid*

*of him? He was certainly disgusting, but thanks to him we're twice
as rich as we were. And now Dobrunu—how can we possibly lose
it? I've spoken to everyone, they've all promised their help. . . .
No, we're not going to lose it.*

But so long as the game was not definitely won nothing was
certain. The presiding judge might go mad; a witness might change
his mind. The slightest incident might suffice to change the whole
situation. For a moment Cleopatra was tempted to call for her
carriage and drive to the law courts. But that would hardly be the
thing. Her business was to control herself, and wait.

She had been waiting three or four hours, tormented, powerless,
when she heard the carriage. She rushed to the door. At the same
moment the gentlemen came in, talking noisily, with loud bursts
of laughter. Coziano, purple in the face, was sweating freely. He
lifted Cleopatra clear off the ground, kissed her, set her down
again, pointed to Mihuletz. "And now give him a kiss," he commanded.

Gallantly, Mihuletz offered his white-mustached countenance. He
was gayer than usual.

"He was stupendous! A second Demosthenes!" Coziano cried,
clapping the lawyer on his hunched back, still covered with the
black courtroom gown. Walter too was laughing.

"The whole thing went on oiled wheels! The witnesses—especially that ugly devil who kept on saying he was a truthful man,
he was, the presiding judge, everybody—not to mention our Demosthenes here! Our opponents looked pretty sick, I can tell you!"

"And now, monsieur," Coziano said, "I am going to prove that
my word is my bond; come with me." He spoke with the feverish
excitement which had of late characterized everything he did. He
seized Mihuletz by the hand and led him away toward the stables
in such a hurry that he nearly tumbled the lawyer down the steps.
The stableboys sniggered at the sight of the boyar dragging along
this funny old man with a black nightshirt over his clothes.

"Open this door, you! There, monsieur—they're yours."

Four dappled horses with slender hocks, long necks, and delicate
heads turned their moist eyes on the newcomers.

"Oh, but—they—they——" Mihuletz stammered, unable to take his eyes off the gleaming animals. He turned to Coziano and took his hand. "I shall never forget this," he said simply and sincerely. Coziano kissed him and set out for the house again, still dragging the lawyer behind him.

"And now let's eat," he cried, with exaggerated gaiety. And to Walter Apostolesco, who was talking to Cleopatra, he said, pointing to Mihuletz: "Tomorrow we drive down there with this gentleman so that I can take formal possession of my new property!"

Walter looked at Mihuletz, then at Coziano, and started to laugh. "The journey foretold by the stars wouldn't be your drive to Dobrunu, by any chance?"

Eustace was speechless. He turned first pale and then red until at last he burst out, "But of course! That's it! The very thing. Come here and let me kiss you! Cleopatra, Davida, listen! Here, quickly."

He dragged them into his study, to explain the horoscope. "Here, you see—Mercury! And Jupiter in opposition. Hence—no judgment."

"Because the case was already judged," Mihuletz said.

"Exactly! Of course!"

"Don't get so excited," Cleopatra said anxiously. "It can't be good for you."

"How can it be bad for me? I'm in excellent health. Nothing can happen to me. Look here at Mercury in the eighth house and in square to Uranus."

Cleopatra asked Walter under her breath, "Is there any sense in all this?"

Walter shrugged his shoulders, made a barely perceptible grimace of contempt, and whispered, "Sheer nonsense!"

At table, Eustace, with a napkin around his neck, held forth, explaining for the twentieth time this horoscope which indicated that he could not fail to win his case; in talking, he managed to forget that the interpretation had not been discovered by himself and unblushingly took all the credit for it.

"When I decided to go to Dobrunu tomorrow, it was like a sudden revelation. That was it! The solution I had been seeking lay there! And there was I, not knowing that I was going to decide on something already preordained by . . ."

"Monsieur Plavanesco is asking for you, sir," the footman said.

"What? Who? Ah, good! I'll come at once. Ask him to step into my study. Kindly excuse me." He rose, knocked over two glasses and a chair, made for the house, reeling slightly, and bumped into the doorpost as he went in.

"I've had a glass too much. . . . No harm in that, on a day like this. How are you, my dear Sava? Good day to you. Take a seat. Well, what good wind brings you here?"

Plavanesco, all in black as usual, was sweating copiously and wiping his face on a checked handkerchief. Coziano clapped his hands; a servant came running and was ordered to bring cold water and sweetmeats. Coziano sat down beside his visitor and looked at him with every appearance of solicitude.

"Now tell me, what can I do for you?"

"Why . . . I think you know. I am sure you know very well what you can do for me."

"Upon my word, I've no idea. . . . Ah! Perhaps you're referring to Dobrunu? Would that be it? I dare say you want to buy it, eh?"

Coziano laughed until the tears came. It was some time before he could control himself. Head lowered, Plavanesco gave him a furious glance and said, "Happy to find you so merry, my dear Monsieur Eustace. What is funny about our business? I promised to call as soon as you had got your judgment, to let you know if I would agree to your new price. Well, here I am! And I am ready to pay what you ask."

"How much will you pay?" Coziano asked him, still laughing.

"The price you asked: sixteen thousand louis. But, my dear sir, what is the joke?"

"Merely this. I have reconsidered the matter in the meantime, talked it over with this one and that, and decided that Dobrunu is worth much more. Think about it yourself. That estate is worth twenty-five thousand louis at the very least."

There was a long silence. Coziano studied Plavanesco with a smile of gentle benevolence. Plavanesco looked the other man slowly up and down, and at last, in his deep, coarse voice, demanded, "How much did you say?"

"Twenty-five thousand louis."

"Very well," Plavanesco bellowed. "I agree to twenty-five thousand."

Coziano became more serious. "Now look, brother Sava, we'll discuss it some other time. Why be in such a hurry? I dare say you're not in that much of a hurry to buy, nor I to sell. . . ."

Plavanesco settled himself more firmly in his chair and his face darkened. "So that's it." And after a short silence: "Is that your last word?"

"It is," Coziano said calmly.

"Good. Very well, I'll be going. My respects."

Plavanesco took his hat and made for the door. Coziano accompanied him as far as the veranda and took leave of him rather casually, then went back to the garden. On his way through the house he started laughing again.

Meanwhile Plavanesco was hammering the pavement with the ferrule of his stick and growling: "Devil take you! So you're making a fool of me, are you? Put me to the expense of valuing the place, and then bring me out in this heat for nothing! Hi, cabby!"

A passing cab drew up and Plavanesco climbed in, the vehicle sagging under his weight.

"Put up the hood! This heat's enough to drive a man out of his mind."

"Lord, sir, it's Saint Elias's day," said the driver, a fat, gray-haired gypsy. "Saint Elias's, you know—the dog days."

6

The lawyer Mihuletz lived in a house as old as the Cozianos', but rather smaller. It stood in a garden of trees, with lawns and clumps of irises, beyond which were the servants' quarters, coach house, and stables. It was in the stables that the lawyer spent his afternoon, talking to the new horses, and patting their long, graceful necks. Mme Mihuletz, a white-haired lady with a round, good-humored face, asked him if he would not like the team harnessed for a trial drive. "We could go as far as Preajba," she suggested.

Mihuletz looked at her thoughtfully, then shook his head. "No, no. Not yet."

That night at bedtime he said to his wife, "Tomorrow when Eustace Coziano comes to call for me, he is to be told that I am ill, that I have eaten something that has disagreed with me, that I've been sick all night and have a temperature—in short, that I am very ill."

She lowered her eyes and said quietly, "Very well."

It was by no means the first time she had helped her husband out of a difficulty. She never asked him for explanations: as a rule she understood, in due course, without them.

Which was why, when Coziano's carriage stopped before the house at seven o'clock on the following morning, July 20, Mme Mihuletz, wearing a dressing gown and a muslin kerchief around her head, met Eustace at the door with a very long face. "I am so terribly sorry. And so is he—most upset! But if you only knew the state he's in. . . ."

And she embarked on a laborious account of her husband's indisposition. For a moment Coziano's face was clouded: then he became his normal cheerful and benevolent self. "I will call and see him on my way back tonight. Tell him I wish him a speedy recovery. I kiss your hands, madame. Whip up, coachman!"

The horses set off at a brisk trot, causing the carriage to sway on its springs. Eustace, lolling back on the cushions, called to his coachman, "Stop at Monsieur Walter's, Nicolai." He had a headache and there was a constant ringing in his ears, but he was happy. The weather was fine; before leaving, Eustace had put on a clean, starched linen shirt, and had drunk several glasses of light and refreshing Chablis.

Walter Apostolesco's house was sheltered by some fine old horse-chestnut trees. When the carriage stopped, Coziano jumped out to go in and get his friend out of bed. But Walter, wearing a red dressing gown, a fez embellished with a long gold tassel, and morocco leather slippers, was relaxing on his divan, smoking a Turkish pipe, and reading the latest number of the *Revue des Deux Mondes.*

"What nonsense, smoking that contraption!" Coziano said jovially. "My dear fellow, why do you put on this act? Have a cigar, man, and get rid of all that apparatus!"

"Are we going?" Walter asked, rising and starting to untie the cord of his merino dressing gown.

"No, that's what I've called to tell you. Stay and keep Cleopatra and my sister company. If they're left alone together, Davida is apt to say the most unpleasant things to Cleopatra. I shall come home to find Cleopatra in tears, and there'll be a scene. I'll go to Dobrunu alone, make all the necessary arrangements, and return as fast as I can. Au revoir, and do give up this posing, there's a good fellow; smoke what any sensible man smokes, and not that childish affair!"

Smiling, he ran down the stairs, got back into his carriage, and gave Nicolai the address of the bailiff into whose hand he had slipped twenty pieces of gold the day before in the law courts. The fellow would have kissed his hand then and there, if he had not been afraid of being seen.

The carriage drew up outside a small whitewashed house in a

narrow street planted with acacias. The bailiff was waiting for him, a short, stout man dressed in black, with a watch chain draped across his waistcoat. At the sight of the man's drooping mustache, round eyes, plump cheeks, and dull, sickly complexion, Eustace thought: *The Moon and Saturn in the ascendant.*

"Get in, Monsieur Ionitza, come along!"

The man came out of his little garden. "I have the honor to wish you a good morning. Hasn't Monsieur Mihuletz come?" As he was about to climb up next to the coachman, Coziano said, "No, not up there. Sit here beside me."

"No, really, monsieur, I shall do very well . . ."

"Not at all, I am asking you to come and sit with me. Where have you put your files? Ah, good. Off we go, Nicolai! To Dobrunu! Monsieur Mihuletz is unwell, Monsieur Ionitza!"

The little man looked at him, suddenly attentive, his cheerfulness fading; but he said nothing.

"I fed him too well," Coziano explained, laughing. "As you can imagine, we had a little celebration."

"Very naturally," the bailiff said, smiling again and reassured. He leaned timidly back against the cushions as the carriage, swaying gently, took the road toward the Danube.

A little later Coziano asked Nicolai to stop and raise the hood. By leaning forward a little he could still see fields in bright sunshine, golden-brown ears of wheat, a vast acreage of maize, fields of sunflowers, each flower a dark disc surrounded by a wreath of flamelike petals. He saw pastures too, and irrigation wells, the long lean arms of their lifting gear pointing heavenward; and, in the open grassland, great herds of sheep and cattle drowsing in the heat.

"What abundance, eh, Monsieur Ionitza? But just wait and see! All this land only needs a bit of capital invested in it to give a really worthwhile income. Yes, my dear sir, a very comfortable income!"

They talked of this and that: Ionitza's family troubles, and various lawsuits between peasants. "They're capable of cutting each other's throats for half an acre of land. They'll take to pickaxes over some worthless corner. Savages, Monsieur Eustace, real savages!"

"Poor devils!" Coziano said with a good-natured laugh. "But how could it be otherwise? The land is their living. Look at the quality of the maize here—just look at it! It's unbelievable!"

"You've certainly done a good stroke of business, monsieur," Ionitza said with an ingratiating smile. "May God give you good health to enjoy its fruits for many years."

"It was worth keeping a lawsuit going for twelve years, wasn't it?"

"Indeed it was. How the Dobrunu villagers must have groaned when they heard the verdict! They knew what they were losing."

"They'll get over it. I saw something of what they felt. But I told them there would always be work for them with me. I shall not let them starve," Coziano said ponderously. And once again he looked out at the rich black earth, where wheat and maize, grass and bush, grew thick and strong and vigorous. *What I shall be able to make out of it!* he thought, and began to calculate the income he might expect from it. Reckon the estate at what Plavanesco had valued it—half a million francs (the recollection made him burst out laughing again): his net income per annum would certainly not be less than twenty-five thousand lei. *Not bad, not bad at all,* Coziano thought, drawing on his cigar, his eyes still fixed on the wheatfields, above which the air shimmered in the merciless July sun. Whirlwinds of dust rose from time to time in the middle of the road, frightening the horses. Toward the Danube, heavy, motionless clouds obscured the sky, casting vast, dark-blue shadows. A blinding flash of reddish-violet light ripped through the air.

"It looks as if we may have a storm," Ionitza said. "That's always the way on Saint Elias's Day! However, we run no risk, for here we are at Dobrunu."

Cottages of daub or mud, roofed with thatch, crouched in the thin shade of willows and acacias, or in the dense and fragrant shade of linden trees, on each side of the road. In fields dotted with dried cow-pats cattle dozed and chewed in the sun, watched over by several children. Not far away, thin and white as an old bone, rose the lifting gear of a well. Brown dogs, made snappish by the heat, gathered in the road to bark at the horses. As the carriage drove on toward the center of the village between rows of low fences, scattering whole flocks of wandering geese, Eustace Coziano, his mind dulled by the journey and by the nights of insomnia which had preceded the final hearing, became slowly aware that something was happening. When the carriage arrived in the neighborhood of the Town Hall he understood what it was: groups of peasants were gathering by the railings. They were talking together, and all turned around to watch his carriage pass. What Coziano did not realize was that, as he passed, these peasants fell in behind the carriage and began to follow him to the Town Hall.

When the carriage stopped, Coziano got out and looked about him. He recognized more forcibly the strangeness of this gathering of peasants. They were very numerous. Coziano recognized one of them whom he had seen before somewhere. What was his name? A thin-faced, hollow-cheeked man, with a heavy mustache and lively eyes. An insolent fellow. What the devil was his name? The peasants were innumerable. Dressed in coarse brown home-spun cloth, barefoot, sweating in their rough shirts, they waited in silence. Everywhere there were eyes—black, hostile eyes. Where was that worthy man who had been such a good witness at the trial? Ah, yes, of course; he had gone to Cozia to fetch his wife and children. After that he was to return and take up his office in the Town Hall as Mayor of Dobrunu. For the time being the acting mayor would have to do.

"Good day to you, my good men."

Two voices muttered some formula of greeting: only two. Three at most. Coziano started and looked about him. What eyes these people had! Brigands' eyes. Well, he would show them what he was made of.

"Where is the Mayor?" he asked.

Nobody answered. The bailiff leaned close to him and said, "Listen, Monsieur Eustace, we had better send for the policeman.

These people are up to something. It would be better to leave. . . ."

Coziano looked at him in surprise. The little man was trembling. What was the matter with him? Policeman? What did they want with a policeman?

"What do you want a policeman for? Your job is to make known the court's verdict and——" Coziano went on talking, meanwhile thinking, *What a lot of them there are. Ragged, ill-fed, penniless. They can't work the land as it should be worked. There's one who looks as if he had pellagra. Hideous sight, poor devil. Nothing I can do for them, except give them work, and even that . . .*

Bang! A short, sharp sound, dull, like someone striking a piece of wood. Coziano turned his head to see what was happening. But he could see nothing; he hardly had time to, for immediately there was another dull bang, similar to the first. He turned sharply to see the bailiff with his hands raised to the level of his watch chain and poised there in mid-air. He was staring at Coziano with his round eyes starting from his head. His face had gone ghastly white. A piece of skin the size of a leaf was missing from his brow, near the left temple. Beneath was a pinky-white surface being swiftly dyed by trickles of blood. At the same moment Coziano heard something whistle past his ear. A big stone had barely missed him and struck the wall of the Town Hall, knocking off a strip of plaster and a little clot of dried whitewash before falling to the ground. It was one of those large stones from the bed of a stream, rounded and polished by the water, grayish-white in color and about the size of a fist.

7

M. Mihuletz spent the whole of July 20—St. Elias's Day—at home, and the whole of July 21 likewise: he even stayed in bed. On the morning of the twenty-second, when, like everyone else in the city, he heard the news, he rose, dressed in black, and, with his back bowed as usual and his top hat set upright on his head, went to the Cozianos'. The great porte-cochère and the front door of the house were draped in black; the footman who opened to him wore mourning.

Cleopatra was alone in the house with Walter Apostolesco; they were in the drawing room, where the furniture had been shrouded and the looking glasses covered with black crape. All around were vases filled with fresh flowers. Walter was pale, his face was haggard, and there were dark circles around his eyes. He was sorry for Eustace's death, and when he saw the body he had been deeply moved. Now he was murmuring absently, "If only he had cast his horoscope for July twentieth as well . . . would he perhaps have taken some precautions?"

Cleopatra raised her eyes—she had been staring dully at the floor—and said sourly, "Are you starting that nonsense too? Didn't I have enough with one madman?"

Walter smiled awkwardly and muttered, "I was only joking. Can't you see a joke any more?"

At that moment Mihuletz came into the room and made his bow to the widow, who immediately burst into tears.

"I am sorry I did not accompany him," Mihuletz said with great simplicity.

Davida, wearing the mourning she had worn for Lascari, entered the room, returned the lawyer's bow, and sat down beside Cleopatra. Cleopatra gave her a quick glance through her black veils, and promptly wept with greater moderation. Mihuletz, accompanied by Apostolesco, withdrew discreetly. As he was passing through the small drawing room where Coziano's body lay, he heard a group of ladies being shown from the hall into the drawing room, then a fresh outburst of sobs and cries of grief in several voices.

Eustace Coziano's body, laid out in a massive, bronze-handled coffin and wearing a black suit covered with decorations, was almost smothered in flowers. One bruised and purplish hand was visible; the face was covered with a handkerchief.

"You can't imagine the state he was in when we found him," Apostolesco said. "He was lying on a table in the Town Hall, covered with earth and mud and blood. He was pounded to pieces. The odd thing was that they had put a lighted candle in his hands, and there was another one burning by his head. Do you know what they were saying? 'We had nothing against the boyar. But since he wouldn't leave us in peace, there was nothing else we could do.' They're absolutely incomprehensible."

"Savages," Mihuletz observed. "You did well to have all these flowers. With this heat, one begins to . . . What has been done at Dobrunu?"

"The procurator has gone there with a platoon of armed police. He has arrested eighty people and started his investigation. I've sent a message to Bucharest, so that Boniface should be here for the funeral. I think he will stir the authorities to action."

"If there's anything I can do," Mihuletz said, "you have only to let me know."

"Thank you. You are always the same—so devoted," Apostolesco said, pressing the lawyer's hands in both his own. He escorted the visitor as far as the courtyard, where once again he pressed his hands.

At luncheon, Mihuletz told his wife what he had seen. "It is probable that Apostolesco will marry Madame Coziano, so that he will be the master of Dobrunu. He will have a large fortune in his hands. Why do you look at me like that?"

Mme Mihuletz, kindly, aging, and gray, studied her husband with admiration. "I was just thinking," she said, "that you are a very clever man."

"Enough of your nonsense! It would be better if you gave orders for the carriage to be washed down. We'll go for a little drive this afternoon, to try out the new horses."

PART FOUR

The Life of Boniface Coziano

I

In 1876 Boniface Coziano, Davida's younger brother, was thirty-four. After taking his degree in law at the Sorbonne he had returned to his own country, done his military service, and risen to the rank of lieutenant in the Reserve. Since then his life had consisted of paying calls, hunting, shooting and fishing, going to balls, traveling, and spending the summers in the country houses of his friends. He was usually to be found sprawled in an easy chair, looking bored; or sitting at a card table, holding his cards and looking bored; or dancing with a lady, smiling with good-natured indifference and looking hardly less bored. He was also to be met with in the hunting field, equally placid and bored; and at fashionable watering-places abroad—in France, Austria, or Italy—very correct, and still unutterably bored. He was of use to nobody, neither to others nor to himself. His existence, while not displeasing or noxious to anyone, gave no one any particular pleasure. Had he died at this time, no one would have taken much notice of the disappearance of this particular soul from among the four million three hundred thousand inhabitants of the United Principalities.

Short, slight, with cold eyes of a very light gray, and chestnut hair waved and pomaded: such was Boniface Coziano, Bachelor of Law, landowner with a good rent-roll, and lieutenant in the Reserve, and such he appears in the family album, in a sepia photograph whose darker areas have acquired a curious rusty tinge. He is young, stiff, frowning, and mustached; he wears the uniform of a lieutenant in the Hussars, and holds himself as stiff as a ramrod, his whole body tense, his head held high and turned slightly toward the camera with an air of defiance. This is the earliest photograph of Boniface. Others were taken later, and make it possible to follow the changes wrought by time; but, better than all the rest, this first photograph reveals how he started out in life: with an energy, a vanity, and an aggressiveness which had no manifest goal or object, but were attributes of his very nature and bound to shape his destiny. In due course his temperament ceased to appear in his attitudes and declared itself in his acts, which caused him to be hated by many and feared by all.

Not even his sister-in-law Cleopatra loved him, although she experienced a strange, persistent impulse—which she herself never managed to understand—to fight him, scratch him, and strike him. One morning during the summer of 1876 she was at Cozia, and Boniface was sitting beside her. He was leaning back in his chair, his long fingers thrust into the armholes of his white linen waistcoat, one leg crossed over the other, one foot swinging idly in its patent-leather spurred boot, and his eyes fixed on the house. Swallows were twittering under the eaves and on the first-floor balcony pigeons, discernible through the balustrade, were strutting and cooing. Above the heads of Cleopatra and Boniface the hanging foliage of the weeping willows stirred in the wind, casting shadows back and forth across their faces with the regularity of a pendulum. Beyond the weeping willows stretched a small wood, where the shade was dense and green; it was cool in there and full of the pleasant scents of earth. A woodpecker was hammering at the trunk of a willow, and here and there starlings squawked.

Cleopatra studied the straight nose, thick eyebrows, and full lips of her brother-in-law's profile. How fresh and immaculate his clothes looked! Boniface was still swinging his foot. Cleopatra too turned her eyes on the house: windows closed, curtains drawn, and the first-floor French windows open onto the balcony. The doves persisted in their stupid cooing, the swallows kept up their twittering. The sky was empty. Not far from the house rose the square *coula*, its windows high and narrow as loopholes and the door so small that one could hardly get through it. At the top of the *coula*, beneath the pointed roof, there was a *pridvor*, or open

terrace, whose rounded arches rested on short stone pillars. It
was there that Eustace had installed his astronomical telescope and
his library, and spent his time studying the map of the heavens.

Boniface said nothing. Without knowing why, Cleopatra kicked
his swinging foot as hard as she could with her small pointed shoe.
Boniface turned his head with a sharpness that startled her. He
began to laugh impertinently. Cleopatra's answering laugh was
nervous.

"What's the matter with you, swinging your leg like that?"

"Why shouldn't I? However, I can stop if you like."

"And are you going to go on sitting there and saying nothing?
You're hardly entertaining, and you're being a bore. You're even
boring yourself. You ought to find something to do."

"What? I have nothing to do. Wherever I see something to
be done, there's already somebody else doing it, and nothing for
me to do but withdraw. . . ."

Boniface looked at Cleopatra less absently than usual: something in his look seemed to give a new meaning to the words he
had uttered. Cleopatra seemed ready to accept anything. Her eyes
held a question. Then both looked away from each other. After a
long silence Cleopatra said, "Still tongue-tied?"

Boniface responded promptly, with exaggerated politeness, making as if to get up from his chair and render whatever service
she might ask of him.

"Forgive me. What must I do? I am yours to command."

"Let's go for a walk," Cleopatra said, with lowered eyes. She
stood up.

"Would you like to go fishing? I'll go and fetch the rods."

"Yes, bring them." *First he hasn't a word to say for himself,* she
was thinking, *then he's all polite and obliging and invites me to go
fishing. Fishing! The simpleton. But he is no simpleton—far from
it. Devil take him!*

Boniface was coming back to her, his step brisk and elastic, as
if he were mounted on springs. In one hand he carried a wide-
brimmed hat, in the other two fishing rods. Cleopatra stared at
him fixedly, then turned unhurriedly and walked toward the little

wood, keeping in front of him so that he could see the black chignon of her hair, the matte white skin of her neck and shoulders bared by the low-cut dress, the mole on her back, and the pretty movement of the light summer dress itself. Boniface caught up with her, but said nothing. Side by side they made their way through the long grass and the undergrowth. A smell of rotting wood came from the worm-eaten willow trunks, mingling with the penetrating scent of the cow-parsley and plantain leaves which grew in the green shadows. The woodpecker rattled on the tree-trunks, and the starlings chattered high in the poplars, whose silvery foliage quivered and glittered in the blue air.

"Why do you never so much as glance at the things around you?" Cleopatra asked. They were walking beside a bed of reeds, slender and tufted, straight as swords.

"I never so much as glance at the things around me?" Boniface repeated, making a sweeping gesture with his hand as if to draw the whole countryside within his range of vision. Then he put on his hat, leaving only his straight nose and mouth showing, the too-fleshy lips thrusting out like a muzzle and covered by a drooping mustache.

"Of course you never look at anything," Cleopatra said. "You haven't looked at me once today."

"Forgive me. You know what it says in the Bible: 'Whoever looketh upon his brother's wife, it is as if he had committed adultery in his heart.'"

"But I wasn't inviting you to commit adultery! I was simply requesting you to make yourself agreeable in the company of a lady." Cleopatra spoke like a woman snubbing a man who has been insolent. Boniface looked at her and laughed. She halted and suddenly changed countenance. She was not much shorter than he, and they were face to face.

"You are an impertinent fellow," she said, boiling with rage.

Boniface went on laughing, a light, casual laugh which put folds into the skin at the outer corners of the eyes. "I am indeed."

"I'll slap your face," Cleopatra shouted. She had lost control of herself.

"For the moment you have no reason to do so," he said, perfectly serious. They walked on in silence. Dry twigs cracked under their feet, and the undergrowth rustled at the passage of Cleopatra's skirt.

"Do you mean that I am going to have reason to slap your face some other time?" Cleopatra demanded.

"No, I hope not. . . . What makes you think that one day you may have cause to slap my face?"

"Because you said 'for the moment.'"

"So I did. By mistake. Simply by mistake," Boniface said, serious and preoccupied. They had reached the edge of the lake, which was almost dry and full of large stones. There was a bench beneath a willow tree. A little farther along, the banks became marshy and covered in wild plants with enormous fleshy leaves. Frogs were croaking, crouched on the round leaves of the water lilies whose open flowers looked like white cups floating on the stagnant waters. Sedge grew dense on the opposite bank, and beyond were fields, a fence, and the winding road upon which four hay wagons were moving, one behind another.

A boat, just big enough for two people, was moored to one of the willows. Boniface untied the painter and hauled the boat in to the bank. He held it steady with one hand and offered Cleopatra the other to help her in. Lifting her skirts to show a black-stockinged leg, Cleopatra stepped aboard. Boniface put the fishing rods into the boat and unshipped the oars. He set to work, rowing easily and looking at Cleopatra with a remote and severe expression.

"Why are you looking at me like that?"

Boniface smiled and said: "Just now you were rebuking me because I never looked at you."

"Look at me as much as you please, but not that way!"

"What's so unusual about this way?"

"I can't explain exactly—something I don't like. What were you thinking of just now, when you were looking at me?"

"I'll tell you some other time."

"That's just a pretext for never telling me. I know you."

"I promise I'll tell you," Boniface said gravely.

Nevertheless, Cleopatra was dissatisfied and uneasy. *No matter what he says or does, he simply exasperates me. Not a word to throw to a dog all morning, and now he stares at me as if he had God knows what ideas at the back of his mind. . . . But just you wait, my friend! I'll get the better of you!* Although she was only twenty-one, she knew perfectly well how to twist a man round her little finger. But where Boniface was concerned, she did not feel at ease. His reactions were so disconcerting! Cleopatra could never be sure what was in his mind. She understood nothing of his character. Perhaps she had not, hitherto, paid enough attention to him? But although she explained it thus, she knew perfectly well that this was not the reason for her uneasiness.

"You have a ridiculous name," she said abruptly.

Boniface raised his eyes and said coolly: "So have you, my dear."

"My name's historical," she retorted.

"So is mine," Boniface said, smiling.

"Yes, but Cleopatra is a beautiful name, whereas Boniface is ridiculous." She was trying to provoke him, but he said: "That is so," adding with an air of indifference: "What of it?"

"Nothing."

"No, I thought not," Boniface said, with an impertinent smile.

Cleopatra looked at the water lilies. She let her fingertips trail in the water; one of her rings was set with an emerald. The emerald was a luminous mineral green, while the green of the water was dirty and clouded. The reflection of the jewel glided over the surface of the water, a moving point of brilliance.

"Do you want to fish?" Boniface asked.

"No. I'm going back."

"Why do you say 'I'm going back' and not 'We're going back'?" Boniface asked.

"Because, you see, I don't in the least care about what you do," Cleopatra answered, in a tone intended to hurt him. Boniface laughed.

"Why do you laugh? You have a very silly laugh."

"No. Not silly at all. You'll realize that later."

" 'Later! Later!' You're always saying that. Such nonsense!"

"It's not nonsense," Boniface said, his levity tinged with seriousness.

"Yes, it is nonsense!"

"As you wish——" Boniface reached out to catch hold of a willow root and stop the boat. He jumped ashore and held out his hand to Cleopatra, but she pretended not to see it, followed suit and jumped to the bank unaided, and walked on ahead. Her white dress moved rapidly through the alternating light and shade of the undergrowth. Boniface moored the boat, picked up the fishing rods, and moved toward the house. Cleopatra had disappeared. Boniface passed close to the two wicker chairs standing on the lawn, but she was not there. No doubt she had gone into the house. He went to put the fishing rods away.

Cleopatra was in the drawing room on the first floor; concealed by a curtain, she was looking out at him. She had the impression, just as she had had in the garden, of looking at him for the first time.

What an extraordinary way of walking the wretch has, she thought as he reappeared with his easy, arrogant gait. Boniface gave the impression, when on the move, of being ready to leap aside at any moment, although he held his body erect and tense, and his head high. *He isn't handsome, but there's something attractive about him, a je-ne-sais-quoi,* she concluded. But the impertinence of him! No other man had had the same capacity to infuriate Cleopatra. *I'll pay you out,* she promised. She already knew exactly what she proposed to do. For the time being she was waiting for him to start looking for her.

She waited for perhaps a quarter of an hour and then prepared to go in search of him, wondering what in the world he could be doing. *If he's gone to his room, I'll go and rout him out,* she thought. Then suddenly she heard a clatter of hoofs, turned quickly back to the window, and stood there flabbergasted: Boniface was just disappearing around the corner of the house, on horseback. He was riding Samson, an Arab horse but larger than horses of that strain usually are—and coal-black, literally so, with the same blue highlights as coal. The horseman, dressed in white, looked small and fragile. He leaned slightly to one side, and had an easy, casual seat, but his long, tight-fitting trousers revealed the tensed muscles of the thighs. The spurred boots made a slight movement, and Samson broke into a trot, entered the little wood, and disappeared from Cleopatra's sight. She swore between her teeth. *God! the vermin! Wait till I get my claws into you!* She spoke half aloud, for she was alone in the great drawing room, all in shadow behind its drawn curtains.

But Boniface avoided her claws. He did not return until lunch-time. He had taken a cold shower and had changed his clothes (he was now wearing a shantung jacket, black trousers and waist-coat, and a high silk cravat). He was as placid and bored as ever. Eustace, running with sweat, his eyes tired by too much reading, was silent and preoccupied. Cleopatra tried to master herself and to avoid looking at Boniface too often or too insistently; she kept her eyes on her plate. She noticed, however, that Boniface, con-trary to his usual practice, was watching his brother very closely and with unaccustomed seriousness.

"Who is coming to dinner?" Eustace inquired. He had noticed nothing. Cleopatra named their guests and he made a face of mild disgust. "Just when the skies are so clear at night . . . However, I hope that tomorrow night, at least, we shall dine alone."

"Quite alone," Cleopatra said, laughing. "Your brother is going to be very bored with only me to talk to."

"I am never bored," Boniface said crisply.

"He's right, my dear Cleopatra. I know him better than you do," Eustace said jovially. "I've been personally acquainted with him for thirty-four years."

He chuckled to himself and went on: "He is a man who has never been bored in his life. I have often been astonished to realize that he is capable of remaining idle for hours on end."

"On the contrary," Boniface retorted, "my time is fully occupied. I dress, I ride, I pay calls, I shoot, I keep the ladies company, I am my sister-in-law's *cavaliere servente,* and so on and so forth."

"All foolishness!" Eustace replied. "Do you call those serious occupations? You're nothing but an idler."

"Do you call astrology a serious occupation?"

"Of course. It's very much more serious than you can possibly imagine."

"Well, I don't want to argue the point with you. Come to that, I don't want to argue with anybody," said Boniface placidly. Cleopatra looked furtively at her brother-in-law as he turned his head to drink a glass of wine.

Later in the afternoon Boniface was playing patience in the drawing room when he saw Cleopatra pass close beside him and stop at the French window which opened onto the balcony. A warm, reddish-yellow glow came through the open window, giving new life to the reds of an Ispahan carpet and shining warmly on the smooth surface of an old bow-fronted cabinet standing against the wall. Above the cabinet the portrait of a *ban** of Craïova who had married a Coziano was nothing but a dark patch.

Cleopatra stared out at the garden. Boniface turned his head toward her. "It's getting cooler," he said.

"Yes," Cleopatra replied cuttingly.

"Would you like to go for a drive?"

There was a moment of silence before her answer came, and when it did the tone was no longer cutting but carefully indifferent.

"Why not?"

"I'll go and have them harness the trap," Boniface said, rising.

Ten minutes later he came back for Cleopatra and offered her his arm down the stairs. A groom was holding the horse. Boniface handed Cleopatra into the trap, squeezing her fingers quite deliberately. Cleopatra was gathering up the wide folds of her skirt as he did so, and wondered how to interpret the gesture. Before she could decide, Boniface had let go her hand, climbed into the trap, put on his gloves, seized the reins, taken the whip from its socket and cracked it. The horse set off at a brisk trot down the

* Title of the reigning prince of Little Wallachia or Oltenia until 1700, and thereafter of the governor of that province.

avenue of lindens which connected the manor with the main road.

They bowled along a little-used beaten-earth road. Dust rose in small brown clouds under the horse's hoofs. The rubber-tired wheels made no sound: the silence was broken only by the muffled dup-dup-dup of hoofbeats.

"What are you thinking about?" Cleopatra asked. Boniface smiled.

"At the moment, nothing."

"But out in the boat, what were you thinking of?"

"I'll tell you one of these days."

"You're lying! You won't tell me! You've already forgotten."

"No. I know perfectly well what I was thinking about and I give you my word I'll tell you."

They fell silent. On their left was a small wood; beyond it they could see the white gravel of the Zlatistea, which meandered between hillsides covered with vineyards. Still farther away was another wood, and thereafter the gorge which the Zlatistea had carved through a limestone hill.

"Would you like to get out and take a walk?" Boniface asked, his voice serious.

"We can do," Cleopatra said, without enthusiasm.

Boniface drove on until they reached the little wood overhung by the gorge, and drew up; he put on the brake, jumped down, and held out his hand to Cleopatra; but when she leaned forward to get out, he seized her below the armpits with a swift, adroit movement, swung her clear of the trap, and set her down on the ground. "What are you doing?" Cleopatra cried, before her feet touched the grass.

"Nothing. It's done," he said, as if nothing had happened, and offered her his arm. They walked toward the outskirts of the little oak wood; the grass was sparse. They scuffed through last autumn's dead leaves, and the ground was soft underfoot. Both were silent. Through the trees came the distant sound of running water—the Zlatistea flowed over a bed of pebbles, and babbled and whispered and gurgled incessantly.

Boniface halted, seized Cleopatra by the shoulders, turned her toward him, and with eyes closed, made as if to kiss her. But his nose came suddenly in contact with the palm of Cleopatra's hand, while with the other hand, she pushed him firmly away. "What are you doing, sir? Are you mad?" she demanded, in a tone cold enough to cool the most passionate impulse. And she went on: "Do you realize what you are doing? With your brother's wife? Do you want me to complain to Eustace? I thought you a man of honor, and you're behaving like a fool!"

Boniface fell back a pace; he had turned pale. With a short, embarrassed laugh he said, "Please forgive me. Tell Eustace everything if you wish. I give you my word never to be wanting in respect toward you again."

Cleopatra lowered her eyes. She felt her whole body invaded by a keen and delicious sensation. *I'll teach you to behave, my lad,* she promised herself. *I'll show you what it is to be eaten up with thwarted desire and driven half mad! It's time you realized what sort of woman I am!* She was delighted.

"Tomorrow," Boniface said, his manner grave and measured, "I'll invent an excuse to leave Cozia without arousing Eustace's suspicions, and I'll return to Bucharest."

Cleopatra did not answer at once. All her pleasure evaporated. This man had the gift . . . No, it wouldn't do! Was she to be left alone with Eustace? Anything but that! Boniface was not going to escape just as she was beginning to tame him.

"Why leave?" she said. "If you behave yourself honorably, you can stay."

"I'll do whatever you like. For instance, if you like, we'll continue our walk. If not, why we'll go home at once. I'm afraid that my company must be disagreeable to you, after what has just happened."

His voice is quite altered and he's talking nonsense. What's happening to him? Cleopatra thought. She replied harshly, "On the contrary, I wish to go on walking. You have only to behave yourself properly." And she went on, walking at his side beneath the motionless oaks under the violet sky of evening. Boniface walked half a pace behind her.

"Give me your arm," Cleopatra commanded curtly. But to her great surprise she found herself seized by the shoulders, spun around, and thrown to the ground. Struck dumb by this sudden attack, she felt obliged to defend herself with all her strength. Their struggle set up a rustling in the withered oak leaves. "I'll shout for help!" Cleopatra moaned.

"Shout away," he said, panting.

"I shall bite you and scratch you!" He made no answer, but gave her a couple of well-placed slaps which made her relax suddenly, defeated and happy.

On their way out of the wood they were better friends than they had been on their way into it. From time to time Cleopatra put her arms around Boniface's neck, stopping him so that he could kiss her. He was cool. "Oh, I can't bear you! I loathe you! I hate you!" Cleopatra said suddenly.

He laughed softly. "Excellent. What of it?"

She hesitated, half minded to scratch his face, but smiled instead and once more put her arms around his neck for a kiss.

"You can be too revolting!" she said, pulling his ears. "You horror!"

"Let me light the lamps. It's beginning to get dark."

The evening star had appeared in the sky. The Zlatistea rippled over its bed of pebbles and gravel. Boniface lit the carriage lamps, untied the horse, and taking Cleopatra by the waist, lifted her into the trap. She asked for a kiss as he did so; then, when Boniface sat down beside her, she snuggled up to him and they set out for home. The darkness was deepening.

Cleopatra began to laugh. "Revolting creature! What were you thinking about this morning?"

He laughed in his turn. "It's no business of yours, you know."

"You promised to tell me."

"What if I did?"

"Please, please tell me," she begged in a childish voice. "What were you thinking of when you were looking at me in the boat?"

"I was thinking that you must be a pleasant armful and asking myself 'Shall I? Shan't I?' I was also thinking that you are my brother's wife and wondering if I could make you my mistress. I was just deciding that I could," he added, phlegmatically. Cleopatra said nothing. Her brother-in-law took a cigar from the leather case which he carried in the breast pocket of his jacket, lit it, and started to smoke.

"What were you thinking of when you were looking at him, at luncheon?" Cleopatra asked again.

Boniface turned and looked at her. "I did not promise to tell you that."

"Come on: tell me."

He drew on his cigar and the end glowed red. "I was thinking that Eustace is not at all to my taste. He's mad, and he's an ass. Why should I take any account of him? If husbands don't know how to look after their wives . . . Why should I deprive myself of a pleasure for Eustace's sake? He means nothing to me. To hell with him!"

Cleopatra drew away from him and leaned against the back of the seat. In a tone that was much less wheedling (he was beginning to exasperate her again, and she detested him so much that she would have liked to hurt him), she said, "So when your own selfish pleasures are in question, you take no account of anything?"

"What is there to take into account? My business is to avoid doing myself any harm, and that's all there is to it."

"So, apart from yourself, you don't care a rap for anyone in the world?" Cleopatra was now openly hostile.

"No, of course I don't," he said succinctly. And he added quite cheerfully, "You can all go to the devil!"

Thereafter Cleopatra held her tongue. The night was mild, the darkness like velvet. A warm breeze blew softly. The lights of the manor house came in sight and the dark bulk of the ancient *coula*.

"You really are a cad!" Cleopatra said.

With his cigar between his teeth, the reins and whip in his gloved hands, Boniface retorted promptly, "And what does that make you? What did you do with Lascar? Do you imagine I don't know?"

On that topic Cleopatra kept silence. The trap entered the avenue of linden trees leading to the house.

2

Cleopatra tried to resist the pervasive and urgent desire which had brought her, after weeks of hesitation and evasion, to agree to that drive in the trap with Boniface. But she was bored in the country and her husband bored her even more than rustic loneliness. Although she felt a kind of resentment against Boniface and detested him with all the strength of her nature, she was his mistress all that summer. Their affair dragged on intermittently throughout the autumn and winter, and into the spring of 1877, when the Russo-Turkish War broke out. Cozia happened to be on the line of march of one of the Russian armies. The manor became the scene of innumerable parties, in the course of which Mme Coziano rejoiced the heart of many an Imperial Russian officer, and so forgot Boniface.

As for Boniface himself, having taken part in all the balls and receptions given in Bucharest that winter, and shown himself as courteous, as bored, and as insignificant as ever, he was called to the colors as a reserve officer in the army of the United Principalities. Shortly afterward the regiment of hussars to which he belonged crossed the Danube. The period which followed had a decisive effect on Boniface. The change did not take place at one stroke—nothing happened to bring about a sudden and violent alteration in his character and opinions. The change came about gradually, in the course of long, exhausting days, sleepless nights, and advance-guard skirmishes, at the time when the Russian and Rumanian armies were investing the Turkish fort at Plevna. Nevertheless, it is possible to date very precisely the moment when

Boniface was first able to formulate the idea which for some time had been taking shape in his mind. He himself, when—much later —he looked back over his political career, attributed its origin quite definitely to a particular incident.

The weather that day was wet and cold. The abandoned fields and hills of heavy clay were transformed into a gigantic sewer of mud. There was a rumble of gunfire in the distance. The Russian batteries were bombarding the forward earthworks of the fortress, to open a way for the pioneers who were prolonging the trenches leading to the bastions. Boniface knew this: he also knew that he, Lieutenant Coziano of the Second Regiment of Hussars, was in charge of one of the reconnaissance parties sent out by the hundred in advance of the Rumanian Army, which was taking up its position in the ring of besiegers, while repeatedly engaging the Turkish forces facing it and driving them back toward the line of redoubts defending Plevna. All this Boniface knew, but he remained profoundly indifferent. He felt himself overwhelmed by an immense boredom and weariness. He was dissatisfied and angry, but could not explain why, nor sort out what it was that disgusted and even revolted him. He sat on his horse, as usual, a little to one side, gripping firmly with his knees, and with his heels turned slightly outward. He was making his way along a road, among innumerable puddles. Drops of water were dripping from the peak of his *képi*. A gust of icy wind flung a squall of rain in his face, and the water gathering on the edge of the peak was dashed into his eyes. Boniface blinked. He was sleepy, for he had spent the night, half paralyzed with cold, playing cards with several other officers in a Bulgarian peasant's cottage with a floor of beaten earth.

The regiment was advancing slowly, far to the rear, between hillsides channeled by heavy rain. Beyond the hills the air was quivering with the thunder of the cannonade. But here everything was still and lifeless, except for the crows picking at brownish heaps—the carcasses of dead horses—in the fields beside the road. The cold damp wind carried the stench of rotting bodies. Boniface felt his horse's spine quiver under him. The animal's hoofs, striking the muddy road, splashed water out of every puddle. On the left, a broken ammunition-box had been thrown into the ditch, and beyond it, sprawled on the sodden earth, lay the body of a Turkish soldier in a blue uniform soiled with mud; it lay face downward, the cheek pressed against the earth, as if the man had set his ear to the clay to listen; the feet were bare, the head clean-shaven and the color of ashes. The hands were half clenched, the nails seeming to claw at the ground. The soldier's fez had fallen into the grass; whoever had taken his boots had had no use for a fez. Boniface averted his eyes from the dead man with the same disdainful indifference that he had shown when passing the dead horses which the crows were eating. Clenching his teeth, he put his horse into a trot. *How beastly,* he thought; *I could have done without that.* And he cursed certain persons silently for a gang of filthy brigands.

Farther down the road three scouts were approaching a miserable wood of stunted trees and sparse foliage which extended for several hundred yards on both sides of the road. Boniface was staring into vacancy over the tense, arched neck and drenched mane of his horse. *Swine, all of them! But they're clever,* he thought. *They're quite right. Anyone who doesn't follow their example is a fool!* Furious, he gave an involuntary tug on the bridle; his horse jibbed, then broke into a light, dancing trot, and suddenly shied violently to the right, jumping with all four feet off the ground. Any other rider would have been thrown; but Boniface, his knees gripping his mount firmly, merely leaned a shade to the left and a moment later was squarely back in the saddle. At the same time he gripped the riding crop which hung from his wrist by a plaited leather thong and slashed his horse on the crupper.

"What startled you?" he asked. Almost at once he saw for himself—three bodies lying across the road, deep in the mud, stretched out full length and practically stuck together. One of them had a hand completely submerged in the mud, crushed in, no doubt, by the wheels of carts and gun-carriages or by horses' hoofs. The second had his face cleft obliquely in two by a gaping wound which had turned blackish brown. The third had his feet in the ditch and one arm raised stiffly; the hand had been cut off at the wrist, leaving only a purplish stump with something white poking through it.

How easily their fezes come off when they fall, Boniface thought, securing the chin strap of his *képi.* Then he began to doze. Behind him he could hear the clatter of horses' hoofs and the rattle of sabers. A cutting wind blew icily down his neck; drops of rain dripped down inside his collar. He had forgotten to pull the hood of his cloak over his head, but the hood was by now wet through and there was no point in trying to use it. Boniface felt dirty: he had slept in his clothes, not even removing his boots. His hands were damp inside his gloves. His eyes were itching and burning with fatigue. *I smoked too much last night,* he thought, moving his tongue in his furred mouth. Should he light a cigar now? There were two in the leather case which he carried in the inside pocket of his tunic. He passed the reins into his left hand and thrust the right inside his cloak to unbutton his tunic.

Suddenly he stopped, withdrew his hand, and reined up sharply. "Halt!" he commanded softly. The horse stopped at once; it was nervous and kept pawing the ground. Boniface raised his right arm, and behind him the sound of hoofs and the jingle of harness stopped at once. One horse only continued to advance at a fast trot and drew up beside the Lieutenant. Its rider, a young second lieutenant with blue eyes, a pale face, and thick side whiskers like those of the Prince, looked at Coziano. He was the son of a land-owner from the same district as the Cozianos, and the estates of the two families adjoined. The young man's grandfather had farmed land as a tenant; his father had bought the land; and the youth himself, Walter Apostolesco, had been reared like a boyar of ancient lineage. Boniface and his brother had known him since they were boys. Nevertheless, in the army there could be no question of making exceptions for an old neighbor, or even a friend, and one day when Walter had called him by his name, Boniface had put him in his place.

"They've spotted the Turks," Walter Apostolesco announced. And in fact the scouts had halted and regrouped: one of them was coming back at the gallop; the other two went one to each end of the little wood, whose trees were so stunted that they barely screened the riders. The two officers waited in the middle of the road. Boniface did not even look at Walter Apostolesco. He noticed, however, that the other was keeping his horse on the move, turning him first one way, then the other. *He's nervous,* thought Boniface. Walter Apostolesco was by nature pale, but today he was positively livid and his eyes, ringed with dark shadows, glittered unnaturally.

The scout reined in his foam-flecked horse when he reached them. He replaced his carbine in the saddle holster and saluted. "I've seen them, sir."

The trooper, a sergeant, was a lean, swarthy fellow with a small mustache twirled upward at the corners. His hands were large, thick, callused, the hands of a laborer. He had raised his voice to report and spoken with a kind of mechanical liveliness, as if they were on the barracks square.

"How many of them? Infantry?" Boniface asked.

"Cavalry, sir. Ten to fifteen, coming up from the valley, in line."

"Anything else?"

"Nothing, sir. A few carts moving along the road, down there." The man pointed to a range of long, low hills.

"How many carts?"

"A lot, sir. Like back home when they're bringing the wheat to the mill," he added, laughing shyly. Boniface looked at him. Embarrassed, the sergeant blinked. Why didn't the Lieutenant say something? He saw Lieutenant Coziano pass gloved fingers over his heavy, drooping mustache and turn to Second Lieutenant Apostolesco, who kept backing and turning his horse. *Why the devil does he keep his horse on the dance like that,* the sergeant thought, *instead of letting the beast rest? He'll need him soon enough.*

"Monsieur Apostolesco, this will be a patrol covering a convoy of munitions or provisions making for Plevna. The patrol will certainly not be alone. There'll be another force of cavalry to protect the convoy."

Boniface said no more. He had pulled himself together, but he was cold and from time to time his body shivered inside his clothes. His temples were burning. He looked at the sergeant, who was waiting, hands on knees, for orders.

"Nothing else to be seen in the neighborhood?"

"There may be, sir, but farther on, in the village. There's a village on the main road. I've seen nothing up to that."

"Let's attack them, sir!" Walter Apostolesco said, his eyes shining. Boniface looked at the sergeant, raising questioning eyebrows, as if inviting his opinion. The man laughed, with his head on one side. "It could be done, sir. All we need do is form into two parties, one going to the left of the trees and the other going to the right, and we've got 'em—like that!"

Boniface studied the little wood and the deserted fields. It was still raining. *The horses will slip. Had I better go and see for myself? But if I do, we lose time and they may get away.*

The trooper was still waiting, wiping his wet face on his coat sleeve. He seemed quite calm. *A good soldier, brave, intelligent,* Boniface thought. *A decent fellow—one can trust him. Ah well, having come this far, I might as well do the thing properly . . . for those gentry in Bucharest, fool that I am! What the devil can I have been thinking about all my life? How did I land myself in this mess?*

He emerged from his thoughts to say, "Apostolesco, take half the platoon and move off in that direction. You'll attack at once and drive them back toward the right. I shall be over there, and I'll show myself two minutes after hearing the first shot. Forward!"

Walter Apostolesco saluted. "At your orders!"

He had turned paler than ever and his fine blue eyes had darkened. He murmured "Adieu, monsieur!" in French.

Boniface looked at him, smiled, and said, "Come, embrace me."

The young man held him so tightly that both of them nearly fell off their horses. The sergeant seemed to pay no attention.

"There! Now away with you. Forward, march!" He backed his horse and said to the sergeant, "Take the other half of the platoon and follow me."

Without more ado, he spurred his mount forward. The horse started off briskly, but was slowed up by the heavy, sodden ground. Boniface stared straight ahead. He saw a scrubby wood, a trooper, an empty field, the horizon. Below, clay soil and patches of puddled, marshy land; above, a livid sky and lowering black clouds. From behind came muffled hoofbeats. Then he saw the other trooper who had been sent out as a scout, near a small clump of dwarf oaks, with his carbine across his knees. Boniface had time to recognize the foliage of the trees: they were oaks all right. He had reached the prearranged point. To his left, a group of mounted men wearing gray cloaks made their way with difficulty across heavy plowed land and came to a halt at the far extremity of the wood. Behind him the half-platoon was forming up in line. The sergeant, at the far end of the line of troopers, put his thumb against one nostril and blew his nose. Boniface moved on. When he came up with the scout on the edge of the wood, the trooper stiffened in the saddle and saluted, carbine on hip. Boniface took out his watch. He did not want to leave the cover of the trees for fear of scaring off the enemy. Drops of rain slid over the face of his watch, and he wiped it with the tail of his cloak. At that moment the first shots were heard. Boniface saw the trooper beside him start. He looked at the man. He was tall, and his round cheeks were flushed on the cheekbones. Boniface laughed. "Feeling a bit cold, eh?"

"A bit cold, that's it, sir," the trooper replied, smiling.

"Don't worry, it will warm up presently," Boniface said, putting his watch back into his pocket. He turned to his half-platoon and gave the order. "Sabers at the ready, lads!"

One or two laughed. All leaned forward to draw their sabers. Boniface drew his own from its scabbard, slipped the sword knot over his wrist, drew the pistol that he wore on his hip, and touched his horse with the spurs. He started to ride for the barren land which lay beyond the far extremity of the wood. When he got there he turned to take another look at the men who were following him, and caught a glimpse of the lad he had spoken to. This soldier, who was immediately behind him, was very pale, and the saber which he carried resting on his right shoulder had a dull, grayish gleam, like the rain-charged sky. Boniface cleared his throat, rose in the stirrups, and, pointing with his pistol toward the deserted plain to their right, shouted, "Forward, at the trot!"

Some seconds later he passed the last tree of the wood. In front of him, beyond the wood, were fields and, in the distance, the road with its endless line of carts. In the uproar of carbine fire and shouting a few cavalrymen in blue cloaks were riding toward him, crouching close to the necks of their horses. Boniface could see one of them furiously flogging his horse with the flat of his saber. Once again Boniface rose in his stirrups and cried, "Charge! Hurrah!"

Scattered cheers answered him from the ranks. Boniface rode at a gallop toward the horsemen who were coming toward him. He heard the earth groan beneath the hammering of many hoofs. *Lucky that the water has run off,* he thought; *the ground's on the slope.* He checked his horse a little, and a whirlwind of hussars rode past him. He followed at a slower pace, watching the sabers rise and fall. Then Apostolesco's men were in front of him. The skirmish was over. He reined in his horse. At the same moment he saw a horseman riding toward him at a gallop. A moment later he realized that the man was a Turk: he recognized the blue uniform, the fez; he could see the face. The Turkish soldier saw him and swerved his horse aside just in time to avoid a collision. Boniface could have let him pass. For a split second he hesitated. The fight was over; a man riding that way, or any other way, was of no importance whatsoever. Why shoot the fellow? To hell with him! Let him get clear if he could.

Boniface could not have said why, but at the exact moment when the galloping Turk passed closest to him, he raised his pistol, aimed, and fired. He saw the man sway forward and caught a glimpse of his long, sallow face. A moment later the Turk had turned his horse and, swinging up his saber, charged straight at Boniface. Through the smoke which was beginning to drift away, Boniface aimed in the general direction of the stomach and fired a second time, followed immediately by a third. The horse swept past him, shying, and at the same moment its rider keeled over and

Boniface saw the man's boot dragging across the saddle. He heard
the dull thump of the body striking the earth, but a second horseman was riding at him, saber raised. Again Boniface aimed and
fired. Not a sound; he pressed the trigger again. Still nothing. The
second Turk was within ten yards, brandishing his saber. Boniface
hurled his pistol into the man's face, dug his spurs into his horse,
turned the beast violently to the left, and seized his saber. He felt
the hot sting of a steel point graze the scalp above his right ear. He
swung his horse about and raised his saber. The Turk had drawn
rein to face him and was returning to the charge. Boniface Coziano
could see the nervous snarl which had bared his teeth. Abruptly
the Turk drew a rein, forcing his horse to rear, threw down his
saber, and raised a hand, shouting something that sounded like
Aa! Aa!

That was all he heard, and in any case he could not have stopped
himself. He swept past the Turk and aimed a blow with all his
strength at the man's head. The Turk ducked and put up his arm.
And it was only as he galloped past that Boniface realized that
the man was shouting *"Aman! Aman!"*—the Turkish for "Mercy!"
Boniface checked his horse, turned it about, and saw the Turk
sprawling on the ground, his arm lacerated and his head bowed
into the mud. Boniface charged, leaned down, and dealt him another blow with his saber, this time on the nape of the neck. The
man collapsed completely, flat on his stomach, and after a convulsive movement of the legs as if he were trying to thrust himself forward, lay still. His horse trotted off toward the little wood and
stopped by the first trees. Boniface returned to the field where his
hussars were regrouping. Walter Apostolesco galloped up to him;
his eyes were haggard and he was laughing like a man in delirium.
Boniface felt warm sweat running down his face, and wiped face
and neck with his gloved hand. When he looked at his hand he
saw that the glove was sticky with blood. He took it off and threw
it away, took out his handkerchief, and pressed it to his face. The
soldiers crowded around him. One of them took out a large handkerchief and bound up the Lieutenant's head, but the blood continued to trickle around his ear and down his neck.

"Have we lost any men?" Boniface asked. Apostolesco looked at him bewildered, as if he did not understand. Boniface glanced around. One or two hussars were coming up, leading riderless horses. Here and there Turks lay sprawled on the ground. A number of troopers had dismounted and were stooping over the dead. It was not possible to see clearly what they were doing: searching them for money, no doubt.

"Sergeant!" Boniface shouted. "Where's the sergeant?"

He had forgotten his sergeant's name. Five minutes ago he had known it. Now he had forgotten it.

"There's the sergeant, sir, look!"

Boniface looked at the man who had spoken: it was one of the scouts—the one he had asked before the skirmish began if he felt cold. His face was scarlet now, and he was wiping his saber on the sleeve of his tunic.

Boniface made for the group of men, some on horseback, others dismounted. Seeing him come, they made way for him. The sergeant lay in the midst of them, on his back in the mud, with eyes wide open and glassy. His face was ghastly white, the head leaning toward one shoulder. His cloak was bunched up under his hips. He did not seem to have a scratch on him. "He fell off his horse and broke his neck," one of the troopers volunteered.

"To horse, men!" Boniface ordered, his voice hoarse.

As the men were mounting, he heard a confused groaning and looked about for its source. The man he had shot was dragging himself, moaning, by the hands toward the wood. When Boniface, Walter Apostolesco, and several troopers came up with him, the Turk rolled over on his back, hands above his head, his face disfigured by terror. Plaintively he said, *"Aman! Ama—a——"*

"Shot through the spine, I fancy," said Apostolesco: he was beginning to recover his spirits. "We can't take him with us."

"You've taken none of them alive?" Boniface asked. He could feel the blood running onto his shoulder now, and down his side.

"No. They were bolting and we were cutting them down too fast," one of the troopers said.

The Turk looked at them. His eyes were already two large black holes, as if he had been dead a long time. His mouth, with a trickle of saliva drooling from the corner, moaned *"A—a—a—"*

"We can't take him," Boniface said. "—— him! Follow me! Platoon, forward!"

He led the way back, skirting the end of the wood. He was over-heated, sweat was running down his back, but he was shaking. *What idiocy!* he was thinking. *What idiocy! This sort of thing is all very well for those poor devils of peasants, and that half-witted sergeant whose trade it was, after all. But for me? No, no, gentlemen, try elsewhere if you want someone for this job, it isn't my line. You see, I claim, like you, to be a privileged person. That's it, gentlemen—and to hell with the lot of you!* Such were the ideas passing through the mind of this taciturn cavalry lieutenant as, minus his *képi,* with his bare head wrapped in bloody rags, he jogged along in the pouring rain at the head of a troop of hussars, reeling from the weariness and revulsion which always follow the joyous fervor of battle.

Coming toward them along the road was a patrol of bearded Cossacks wearing tall, shaggy fur caps and voluminous black cloaks, their long lances swaying. The officer commanding them was a fair young man, with a silky mustache and whiskers, rosy cheeks, and blue eyes. His cloak and boots were immaculate. The patrol halted, and the bearded horsemen asked a question in Russian; their voices were deep and powerful and they smiled cheerfully at the hussars. The elegant officer rode forward to salute Boniface smartly.

"Bonjour, mon lieutenant," he said, and continued in French, "Allow me to introduce myself: Lieutenant Count Wenden. You have had a saber fight? I envy you!"

Boniface replied politely, but with a gloomy countenance. The Cossacks were talking and shouting happily. Boniface asked their officer what they wanted.

"They are asking if you have a headache. Cossack humor, you know!" Count Wenden's cheeks became pinker than ever as he gave this explanation, and his smile was embarrassed.

"Indeed?" Boniface said sourly. *Gang of savages,* he thought;

let's hope someone makes a hole in your skins. Aloud, he said, "Monsieur, I saw convoys of carts moving along the main road. They may perhaps interest you."

The Russian thanked him, saluted with a bow, and turning, shouted something to his Cossacks, who immediately gave a yell of joy. The whole patrol broke into a fast trot, riding off in the direction from which Boniface had come. Boniface Coziano's expression was hostile as he watched these bearded giants ride past him. *If that's what you want, you're welcome,* he was thinking; *but they won't catch me having another saber fight with half the riffraff of Anatolia. This is no place for me. Why on earth didn't I realize it before?* He was cold; from time to time he shivered. Apostolesco, riding beside him, said, "Do you think we shall attack that column of carts?"

"We'll see what the colonel has to say about it," Boniface replied. Then, suddenly striking himself on the brow with his fist, he shouted, "Good God! What an imbecile I am! What a fool! Me! Me! to be engaged in . . . What madness! Well, they won't catch me again! Never!"

He repeatedly struck his forehead with a clenched fist. Walter Apostolesco stared at him, surprised and distressed, particularly when he saw that the clot of dried blood which had closed the Lieutenant's wound had been dislodged and that a fresh flow of bleeding had begun. But Boniface Coziano's face was so pale, his jaw so set, his expression so ferociously ill-humored that Apostolesco, who had long admired him as a great boyar, a man of distinction, and a hero, held his tongue. Besides, he soon forgot what he had heard, for that same morning the regiment took part in an attack and thereafter was withdrawn from the front line when the infantry had occupied the newly won positions.

Until the end of the campaign the hussars occupied the local villages, but took part in no important action. Meanwhile, Boniface Coziano was awarded the highest Rumanian and Russian military distinctions. Then he was recalled to Bucharest. In the evening of the day of his very first engagement with the enemy, he had written to his brother-in-law, Lascar Lascari:

My dear Lascar,

A fortunate opportunity having been offered to me and the Turks for cutting each other's throats, I took profitable advantage of it, whereas they merely scratched my scalp, although a very little more would have laid open my head. But after these feats of arms I realized that I was wasting my time here. You see, there are two kinds of men: those who issue orders to the rest to kill each other, and those who receive and execute those orders. It is my wish to pass from the latter into the former category, to be hammer rather than anvil, rider rather than horse. Will you help me? My eternal gratitude can be expressed only by remaining your faithful brother-in-law and your devoted and humble servant,

Boniface Coziano

3

Back in Bucharest, Boniface did not see Lascari until a month had passed. They met one evening at a political dinner in Lascari's house. It was late; the guests were rising from table and adjourning to the drawing room. Outside, rain was beating against the windows; but inside, tall, pot-bellied stoves gave a pleasant warmth. Conversations pursued their course, someone was playing the piano, grave and reverend elders were making up fours for cards, and the ladies plied their fans. Lascar Lascari and Boniface Coziano, paying little attention to the guests, had withdrawn into a deep window embrasure, half hidden by the yellow silk curtains, where they stood smoking and talking. Boniface had begun by saying, "Thank you for inviting me to this political gathering, even though I am not myself a politician. . . ." He smiled; he had said it as an opening gambit. Lascari, meanwhile, was mechanically chewing his cigar. Only his eyes showed any liveliness when he said in French, "That, of course depends entirely on yourself. Have you really no wish to become a politician?"

Boniface assumed that Lascari was being tactful in making no allusion to his letter, and was pleased.

"Why, yes. I should like to immensely. I said as much in a line or two I wrote to you. And, in passing, I'd like you to know that I'm very grateful to you—eternally grateful to you—for having got me out of that filthy war business. Only, I wrote the substance of this in a rather—immoral note which . . ." He looked at Lascari, waiting for a response.

"Yes, you certainly called a spade a spade. A politician should not write such letters," Lascari said with the utmost seriousness. Boniface smiled engagingly, then looked his brother-in-law squarely in the eyes.

"That will be my last letter as a private citizen. It will also be the last occasion on which I put myself unreservedly in another man's hands. Besides, you realize, I am sure, that you can count on me for the rest of your life. You hold, as it were, very good security. . . ."

Lascari looked out through the streaming windowpane at the row of black carriages drawn up before the house in the rain. He seemed not to have heard what the other was saying. Nevertheless, with an air of affability, he asked, "What would you like to do?"

The pact was made. Henceforth, for as long as Lascari lived, they were to be allies. Boniface coughed to clear his throat. "What I have to say may surprise you. I want to enter politics, but with the Conservatives. Not with you and your friends. The other would suit me better. You see, my own interests—contrary to yours—are in land rather than in banking. Would it not suit you to have an ally among the Conservatives? And one, moreover, who would be your brother-in-law? The higher he was placed, the more useful he could be to you. Thanks to him, a door could always be open to you, whatever happened. One never knows . . ."

Lascari was still looking out of the window. At last he turned to face Boniface, glancing at the room and the guests assembled there. Boniface said nothing. "And in what way can I help?" Lascari asked him.

"Financially," Boniface said simply. "I need money to get into the Chamber and I am going to raise a loan on my estates, but I want to deal with a bank where I have friends. Not only do I want to avoid being fleeced, but I want to be sure of extensions whenever I need them."

At the following general election Boniface was returned as a deputy on the Conservative side. Thereafter, he was to be returned at every succeeding election and to remain a member of the Conservative Party for a very long time. In the course of his first electoral campaign he experienced one of those profound moral disturbances which are major milestones in a man's life, and whose cause must, as a rule, be sought in some external influence.

At the time there was no railroad between N—— and Bucharest. Boniface therefore traveled by stagecoach. Sleet was falling from an ashen sky. The dark and naked trees, stark and sparse in the muddy landscape, the peasants bundled up in their sheepskin coats with their fur caps pulled down over their mistrustful eyes— everything, in short, combined to be depressing. The town itself looked like a village half sunk in mud. The main street was paved with large round stones taken from the river bed.

Boniface got out of the coach at his brother Eustace's house, and there found the former lieutenant Walter Apostolesco, who had resigned his commission when the war ended and now seemed very much at home. On his first evening, tired and cold, the newcomer ate his meal in silence, while Eustace chattered about a celebrated clairvoyante, Mlle Lenormand. Cleopatra and Walter Apostolesco were listening with the keenest interest. Boniface studied all three of them by the light of the oil lamp set on the table. He understood why Cleopatra had received him as she had done, pleasantly, but without a shade of intimacy, as if he had never been and never could be anything more than her brother-in-law. Well, that was her business; he had not come to resume their idyll, but to get himself elected to Parliament.

On the following day Boniface met the local Conservative Party leaders, Take Buzesco, a man with a grizzled, square-cut beard and a gleam of madness in his eyes, and Manolica Horoveano, who was stout and strongly built, had a deep voice, and always wore hunting costume. The two men, ensconced in armchairs in one of the Club's smaller sitting rooms, were smoking cigarettes and watching the blue, wavering smoke. Fires roared in the stoves. Outside, the weather was vile. A Club servant had just fetched them cups of Turkish coffee from the Café Panaït around the corner. Boniface, with his hands in his pockets and the skirts of his frock coat swept back—he had decided, upon entering politics, to dress badly and without taste, except for great social occasions—was standing with legs firmly astride, looking down on the other two with an air of contemptuous amusement.

"Really, gentlemen, what sort of an organization do you call this? In Bucharest I was told that we could be sure of the election result, that everything in this constituency ran on oiled wheels, and that you had never come a cropper. I am bound to tell you that I find the reality very different. I find you helpless and in despair. And why? Because Monsieur Ienake has been taken ill. A fine state of affairs, don't you think? To be candid, this is not what I had been led to expect. A pretty kettle of fish when we're dependent on Monsieur Ienake! Congratulations, gentlemen!"

The two men fidgeted uneasily. Horoveano muttered that there was no occasion to take that tone, and Boniface rounded on him sharply: "The election is three days off and we're certain to lose. It's time you heard a few home truths. Handle the election properly, and you'll find me reasonable enough. You'll have me eating out of your hand."

"We can't canvass the electors without Ienake," Manolica Horoveano sighed with an air of dejection, stroking his graying whiskers.

"But who is this fellow Ienake, for heaven's sake?"

Eustace came in, burly and elegant; he was an elector in the first electoral college and ready, at a pinch, to be active in the Party cause. A number of other well-fed, well-dressed, red-faced gentlemen arrived and exchanged greetings with those already present. All seemed equally uneasy.

"What is he up to? Is he still unwell?" Eustace inquired, as if at that particular moment there could be only one sick man on the face of the earth.

They talk of this Ienake as if he were God Almighty, Boniface thought, and promptly proceeded to fall into the same error.

"Who is this man? And why can't we manage the election without him?"

Eustace shrugged. "He's the best election agent in the whole province. It rains or shines as he wishes. The only reason you don't know him is that you haven't been home since we were boys. Ienake is the son of Balaban, who was our Great-uncle Take's farmer at Buzesti-de-Zlatiste. He made his pile . . ." Eustace was thoughtfully silent for a moment, as if admiring the beauty of M. Balaban's self-made fortune, and then resumed: "Yes, a very nice little pile. And his son, this Ienake, grew up without even going to primary school. The fellow knows nothing, has read nothing, but he knows what's behind every move and how to pull every string in the constituency. I thought this business of being ill was all a blind. But I see I was wrong. And I don't like it. It's not good. And yet the horoscope . . ."

"Spare me that nonsense," Boniface said. He looked at the others with an absent-minded stare, and then said curtly, "Gentlemen, I bid you good evening. I will see you here tomorrow." With that he went out.

"He's going to get Ienake out of bed," Horoveano said. "He's sheer quicksilver, that young man."

"I hardly recognize him myself," Eustace admitted. "He's quite changed—active, busy, talks well—he's been like this ever since he went in for politics. Before, he was as lazy as they come."

"Lazy? Him? He's the Devil incarnate," said Manolica Horoveano.

Old Buzesco laughed and merely said: "Nonsense!"

"What's the matter with you? Why do you say 'Nonsense'?"

"Even if he were God Almighty," Buzesco replied, "instead of being the Devil incarnate, he wouldn't be able to get Ienake back on his feet." After a moment's thought, he added naïvely, "Unless he's a doctor. . . ."

Meanwhile Boniface's carriage, lurching over the bad road, was driving through the rain, while inside it Boniface was reflecting that he had wanted to be independent, his own master, and now he was dependent on one Ienake. Worse still, on M. Ienake's cold in the head or dyspepsia!

He alighted before a large, ill-designed house with a porch over the door and a dog kennel beside it, out of which the dog hurled itself, barking ferociously. From the threshold a woman called across the yard, "Who's there?"

"I'm looking for Monsieur Ienake," Boniface shouted, shaking himself; his clothes were already drenched with the rain that was drumming noisily on the crown of his top hat.

"Who are you?" the woman asked.

"Monsieur Coziano, from Bucharest."

The woman shut the door and left him standing in the rain and face to face with the dog, which was strangling itself on the end of its chain in a frantic effort to get at the intruder and tear him to pieces. Boniface set his teeth and waited. At length the woman came out again, her head covered with a shawl, and crossed the yard to open the gate, meanwhile endeavoring to quiet the dog. She showed Boniface into the house where, with sympathetic familiarity, she clapped her hands together and exclaimed, "Heavens, how wet you are!"

Boniface could have struck her. He growled, "Never mind that. Where's your master?"

"Be so good as to step this way," the woman said, going first. Candle in hand, she led him past ranks of tall dark cupboards. In the shadows Boniface saw close beside him the immense head of a wild boar, stuffed and fixed to the wall. They climbed a creaking wooden staircase and went along a dark corridor, the servant still preceding him. *The fool must come from the mountains,* Boniface reflected, *probably from somewhere near Panaghia.*

The woman opened a door. "Come in, sir."

Boniface found himself in a lofty room which smelled of stale air, tobacco smoke, charcoal, and cooking. An oil lamp, its blue china stand embellished with bronze ornaments, gave a feeble yellow light. There was a bed with the bedclothes in disorder, bedside tables covered with beakers and glasses and medicine bottles (which included a bottle of brandy and a soda-water siphon), a number of pedestal tables laden with dirty plates, trays, bottles of wine, and used glasses. A dog, curled up in an armchair, growled at Boniface. Clothes were hanging at the window, and there were piles of law books ranged on top of the cupboards. Sitting up in bed, looking very dignified with his hands clasped over his stomach, was a stout man with gray whiskers and a double chin. His embroidered nightshirt was unbuttoned to expose a hairy chest.

With deliberate casualness Boniface said, "Good afternoon, Monsieur Ienake."

"My respects, Monsieur Coziano. Forgive me for not rising to receive you. But, as you see . . ."

"It doesn't matter at all," Boniface said easily, tipping the dog out of the armchair and sitting down in its place. "And how are you feeling?"

"Poorly, very poorly," Ienake said, glancing slyly at the young boyar who had arrived in the provincial capital as candidate in the election. Boniface took out his case and offered Ienake a cigar. The old man looked at him and groaned that really in his condition . . .

"That doesn't matter. One of these will do you no harm. Do take one—you won't often find a cigar as good as this in these parts."

Ienake took a cigar, sniffed it, nodded in sign of approbation, and put it down on his bedside table.

"Your health may be bad, but our election chances are looking even worse," Boniface said good-humoredly.

Ienake sighed.

"So you're letting us down? I can hardly believe it."

The old man gave Boniface a mournful look and shrugged his shoulders. "You must blame this illness. Can a man know when God is going to afflict him with disease?"

With an air of straightforwardness, Boniface said, "How unfortunate that I'm not a doctor! There is nothing I would not do to cure you. I'd cover you with gold if I knew it would do you any good!"

Ienake sighed again. His enormous belly wobbled under the blankets. "You say that because you're young. . . . The other boyars of our party . . . they don't even trouble to ask after me."

"Is it possible?" Boniface said benevolently. "I find it hard to believe."

"And yet it's true. Do you suppose they have ever granted me what I asked of them? Never, Monsieur Coziano, never!"

"Well, *I* will. I'll do whatever you ask," Boniface said crisply.

Ienake studied the young boyar, weighing him up. "Bah! They all say that. And then they let you down, drop you . . . Ah, things were very different in poor Monsieur Sherban Vogoride's time! I'd say to him: 'Look, Monsieur Sherban,' I'd say, 'we mustn't forget the folks here, there's so-and-so wants a place, and old what's-his-name would like a pension, and someone else has got a lawsuit. . . .' Well, he'd never even answer me, just hold out his hand to me for the petitions, sign them, and that was that. What a man! That's all I can say, what a man! They don't make them like that nowadays."

"Well," Boniface said, "where are these petitions of yours? Let me have them. One month after the Government's formed you shall have them back, duly signed and sealed."

Attentive, mournful, Ienake gazed at him like a great frog. "Then there are my nephews wanting places in the schools . . ."

"Write it all down for me."

"Yes. But there are also my cousins who have a lawsuit against the town council . . ."

"Let's get this straight," Boniface said. "You make out a list of everything you want."

M. Ienake raised himself heavily in bed, felt about under the pillows with his fat, hairy hand, and brought out a sheet of paper folded in four.

"Here is the list, Monsieur Coziano," he said simply.

Boniface nearly burst out laughing, but controlled himself, took the paper with a look of severity, almost of rebuke, and rose. "Try and get better quickly!"

"Call here tomorrow morning, Monsieur Coziano. If I am well enough, we'll make a round of visits, pay a few calls. . . . You see, I am prepared to do anything for you because you're young, and because I used to know poor Monsieur Alexander and Madame Sophia, and because Monsieur Eustace is very fond of me, too. I'll manage the election for you, never fear. Good. So until tomorrow morning."

Boniface went home and to bed without bothering to stop at the Club and put the boyars' minds at rest. The following morning he and Ienake set out in the carriage, driving through rain and snow and broken, muddy streets. Ienake was freshly shaved and decently dressed; he wore massive rings on his fingers and a gold chain across his waistcoat. He was very talkative and his breath reeked of good brandy.

"This is what it's like here, as you see—mud, bullock carts in the streets, and peasants. Fridays, when they come to market, it's up to your knees in cow-dung. And in wet weather it's a dog's life. Still, there's money to be made in these parts. And afterward you can go to Carlisbad [sic] and strut about with an emery walking stick ogling the girls! High life, eh? Only you've got to live this sort of life, up to the ankles in mud, to get the wherewithal to live the other sort."

Boniface, trying to avoid the old man's breath, was wondering what kind of walking stick Ienake meant. Ebony, perhaps? He stopped listening to Ienake, who was still comparing the ugliness and poverty of this little provincial town with the splendors of Carlsbad and Vienna.

". . . and then there was one, a blonde, fresh as a rose, swaying as she walked, like this, see——" Ienake mimicked the Viennese beauty's gait. "Well, when I came up to her, I said . . . Stop!" The last startlingly unexpected word was addressed to the coachman. Then, turning to Boniface, the old man said, "Here we are. We shall have to talk a bit longer to this one. These electors in the third electoral college aren't like the boyars in the first electoral college, who know what they want and vote the right way. They're peddlers and such, and you have to *explain* to them where their interests lie."

They stepped from the carriage onto a pavement of beaten earth and went through the garden gate onto a brick path. A curtain was thrust aside and a woman appeared at the window; then the door of the house was opened to reveal a man in slippers and shirtsleeves.

"Why, it's Monsieur Nicolai," Ienake cried heartily, sweeping off his hat. Boniface followed suit, more restrainedly. He went into the house, talked with the trader, and made a fuss over his children, who stared at him as if he had been a calf with two heads. Of this interview Boniface retained nothing but a memory of low ceilings, a smell of stew, and a great many people all gaping at him wide-eyed.

When they returned to the carriage, M. Ienake spread himself over the seat, nudging Boniface with his elbow. Boniface drew away into his corner.

"It didn't go badly," Ienake said. "You made an impression. A pity you weren't wearing your medals. Have you any?"

"I have," Boniface said tranquilly. "I'll wear them the next time."

"Fine, fine . . . Now what was I telling you, my dear fellow? Ah, yes, it was about . . ."

This torture lasted two days. At last the adoption meeting took place on a wet evening in the auditorium of the Buzesco Theater, where, amid icy drafts, a crowd of men forgathered, keeping their hats on. The place was lit only by half a dozen oil lamps. At the central table in that dim and ruddy light, and likewise with their hats on, sat M. Ienake with Boniface Coziano on his right, and on his left, the burly form of Manolica Horoveano in corduroy jacket, high-laced boots, and a soft hat.

"Gentlemen—my dear fellow citizens! We are going to discuss and vote upon the amendments which have been rejected," Ienake began, rising and speaking suavely. A wind from behind the scenes whistled freezingly from the stage. Horoveano leaned toward Boniface and in his husky, asthmatic voice whispered, "You're a miracle-worker, young man! How did you manage to get him out of bed?"

"I have become my servant's servant," Boniface whispered in reply. The words were not uttered in bitterness or disgust, but with his usual expression of dignified reserve. His neighbor did not understand and said, "What was that?"

Boniface, who was preparing to deliver his electoral speech, did not answer. He had in any case made up his mind not to.

"Dear fellow citizens . . ." M. Ienake was saying unctuously; he stopped suddenly, appeared uneasy, and looked behind him into the wings. He then cast a glance over the auditorium, looked at the pipes of the central heating which was the envy of neighboring townships but was at the moment stone cold, picked out one of the servants, and attracting his attention by raising one fat, hairy hand, said in the same soft, oily voice, "If you please, citizen, be so kind as to ask someone to light the sentry heating." Not a soul smiled.

One morning when the electoral bustle was at its height, the Prefect of the constituency summoned the principal officials of the prefecture to his office on the first floor of the Town Hall. The Prefect received them standing, with his back to the windows. His officials listened to him respectfully. Suddenly they all turned as one man: the door had opened behind them.

"What? What's he doing? I know perfectly well what he's up to. Out of my way!" cried a cold, hard, angry voice. And there appeared on the threshold, followed by an astonished policeman, an usher, and a woman with a broom, a gentleman who still looked young despite the gray at his temples, short, slight, clad in a black frock coat and carrying his top hat in one hand. His pale-gray eyes flashed lightning at the Prefect, who, clearly upset and recognizing the intruder, began to protest. "Monsieur, what is the meaning——?"

"Monsieur," the other interrupted, "what is the meaning of the unwarranted behavior of your police officers in the Buzesti-de-Zlatiste district? Speak up. What does it mean?"

"What behavior? I have no idea what you're talking about," the Prefect stammered.

"So you know nothing about it? What sort of Prefect are you? It's time you resigned."

"Monsieur Coziano, I cannot allow you——"

"But you can allow illegal pressure to be put on the electors," Boniface said ironically, still standing in the doorway.

"There is no illegal pressure in my prefecture!" the Prefect shouted.

"Yes, there is."

"No!"

"Are you calling me a liar? A scoundrel of your kind can doubtless hear himself given the lie without batting an eyelid. But I am a boyar and I will not stand for it. Go —— yourself! Do you hear? Go —— yourself!" Boniface was crimson and choking with rage.

"Monsieur Coziano, you shall answer for this!"

"Had you been a boyar, I should be at your disposal with either swords or pistols. If you dare—it is up to you. But you will not dare!"

Boniface laughed derisively and walked out, slamming the door behind him; small pieces of plaster fell from the wall.

"Constable!" the Prefect shouted.

A policeman entered and, wide-eyed, stood at attention. The Prefect looked at his petrified officials, and in a voice hoarse with rage screamed at them, "Out! Get out! The lot of you!"

The officials made a disorderly rush for the door. Only the policeman, appalled at the scene, stood fast. The Prefect turned on him, yelling, "You, too! Outside!" and striking him violently in the face. The policeman made for the door.

The incident had no consequences. The Prefect did not dare fight a duel with Boniface, nor bring a legal action against him. Boniface Coziano was elected, took his seat in Parliament, and kept it for many years. But in the coach on his way back to Bucharest, he thought of Ienake with revulsion. *In future I'll give him money to take care of everything,* he thought. *I want nothing more to do with that pack of petty tradesmen.* . . .

But to lead the kind of life Boniface dreamed of required a great deal of money. He had already been obliged to borrow a considerable sum from the bank. And the large fortune he needed could not be made in politics. The only rapid and radical solution to his problem was marriage with a rich heiress.

4

Constantina Mavromihali was an insignificant blonde with pretty blue eyes—albeit rather small and shortsighted—in an irregular, triangular little face with ill-defined features. Her hair was piled on top of her head in the fashion of the times—1883 or 1884—and on it she wore a black toque with a little white veil. The very full skirts of her riding habit were spread out over the flanks and crupper of her horse. Holding reins and riding crop in gloved hands, she kept her horse at a walk in the linden-bordered ride running parallel to the Chaussée Kisselev. M. Boniface Coziano, the young Conservative deputy—though he was in fact twice her age—rode at her side. Constantina was rising twenty, but she looked older because of her serious and even melancholy expression.

The foliage of the trees was rust-colored. The thickets and coppices over toward the Herestrau ponds were turning from red to yellow. A few hardly noticeable drops of rain were falling from the cloudy sky. Carriages passed at the trot, escorted by gentlemen on horseback, while a few other horsemen, alone or in pairs, were using the rides and bridle paths. Boniface gave frequent salutes, whereupon Constantina would ask, "Who is that?" and he would answer, "Marghiloman" or "Blarenbergh" or "Madame Soutzo" or "Madame Ipsilanti," or some other name of political or social notability. When they reached the end of the avenue, Boniface inquired, "How about a gallop? Toward Bordei?"

"If you like," Constantina replied. They spurred their horses and set off across the fields, sweeping past lines of willow trees, fields with cows at pasture, and herds of sheep. Then, still following bridle paths among the willows, they made their way back toward the Chaussée.

"That was pleasant!" Constantina said. Boniface was silent. His seat in the saddle was easy and casual. Constantina looked at him furtively. Boniface took her back to the Chaussée and then turned for home, saying little, raising his hat to more acquaintances. Ladies smiled at him pleasantly. But Boniface did not once relax his guard. From time to time Constantina looked at her escort's muscular thighs, revealed by the tight fit of his trousers, as they gripped the gleaming black sides of his horse.

"What a beautiful horse," she remarked, for the sake of saying something. "I had never looked at him properly before."

"From noon today he is yours," Boniface returned.

"Oh, no! The very idea! He is far too lively for me. . . . Thank you very much, but you must not give him to me. I should not know what to do with him."

"Very well, then I won't give him to you," Boniface said calmly. Constantina looked at him, surprised and amused.

"But you have already given him to me—a moment ago."

"True. But you would not know what to do with him. So I shall keep him."

"But suppose I want to have him just the same? You'd be obliged to give him to me now if I asked you."

"You should have accepted straight away."

Constantina admitted this unresentfully, saying, "Very well, just as you like."

Goose, Boniface thought. A horse at the trot came up with them and a voice said, "Good morning, Constantina, I kiss your hands."

The newcomer was a tall, slim young man, with dark hair

and an olive complexion, his deep, velvety eyes surrounded by dark circles. Like Boniface, he wore a drooping mustache. He did not look strong.

"How are you, Ionas?" Constantina said kindly.

"Very well, thank you. Just out for a ride. Good morning, Monsieur Coziano."

"Good morning," Boniface said coldly, offering two fingers. The young man blushed. *Serve you right and do you good,* Boniface thought, and deliberately ceased to pay any attention to their new companion.

"Did you know," Constantina said, "that Ionas is trying to organize a stag hunt, strictly according to Hunt Rules, only instead of a stag we're to hunt a man on horseback?"

"Ridiculous!" Boniface said curtly. "I suppose afterward we're to feast off a haunch of cardboard venison. Personally, I like to kill real game when I hunt." He looked at Ionas, who blinked and looked away.

"Now that you have company," Boniface went on abruptly, "allow me to withdraw." He raised his top hat to Constantina, turned his horse, and left them.

"What's the matter with your friend?" Ionas said, with hostility in his voice. "Is he mad?"

Constantina turned to watch Boniface riding away and then turned on Ionas. "It's all your fault!" she said furiously. She turned her horse and set off at a gallop in pursuit of Boniface. When she caught up with him, both checked their horses to a walk.

"You force me to make myself ridiculous by galloping after you," she said in a low voice. "Why can't you behave like a rational human being? What will Ionas think of your behavior? And what will people say about me? Is it because we're friends that you do this sort of thing, and make me run after you? Next time I shan't! Next time I shall stop seeing you," she said, almost in tears.

Boniface smiled imperturbably. "Why don't you stay with Monsieur Hagiopol? He loves you to distraction, he worships you, and wants to play the stag. He has every virtue, you see."

"He has a noble heart!" she said, blushing and indignant; and, taking her courage in both hands, she added: "I very much fear that he has a better heart than you."

"Then why abandon him and run after me? Your behavior is absurd."

Constantina gasped. Her eyes filled with tears. "Aren't you ashamed? . . . I am not running after you. I'll never speak to you again!"

"Oh, yes, you will!" Boniface said. "Your servant, mademoiselle." He set spurs to his horse and galloped off. Constantina began to cry. She returned the way she had come, at walking pace. Several people saw her, but as she was shortsighted she did not realize it. She rejoined Ionas Hagiopol who, greatly upset, rode by her side in silence. Between sobs she kept repeating, "The wretch! The beast! Of all the unkind . . ."

Between his teeth Ionas Hagiopol said, "I shall challenge him to a duel."

Constantina turned on him. "Are you mad? If you do, I'm finished with you!" After a moment she added, "Do you want to get yourself killed?"

She rode on sulkily, her eyes still clouded with tears. Ionas Hagiopol kept glancing nervously at her profile; with a pleasure verging on pain, he felt his heart melt within him. Suddenly Constantina checked her horse.

"Let's go home. He's ruined everything."

They trotted toward the city. When they drew near to the first houses, with their shingled roofs and high fences, all half hidden by flamboyant autumn foliage, they slowed their horses to a walk. Constantina was silent and gloomy. "Do you realize that—that I love you?" Ionas Hagiopol murmured.

The lump in his throat hardly allowed him to get the words out. Constantina remained silent; after a few paces, she said, "Do leave me alone. I can't think what's come over you. . . ."

Boniface went often to his brother-in-law Lascari's house. They got on well together and talked for hours at a stretch. That day and on the days following he went to Lascari's several times. But he no longer called at the Mavromihalis'. However, Lascari, having encountered Prince Mavromihali in the Parliament building (the Prince was senator for the Arges constituency and was just leaving a session of the Senate), asked him, "Am I to congratulate you? Is there any truth in the report that your daughter and my brother-in-law are to be married?"

Mavromihali's face flushed but all he said was, "Nothing has been decided yet."

Back at home, Mavromihali went to his wife for information; she knew nothing and went to ask her sister, who said that Constantina was constantly in Coziano's company; she seemed to take offense that she, Constantina's own aunt, had been told nothing of what was happening. That evening Mavromihali had an interview with his daughter, who promptly burst into tears.

"He hasn't said anything to me. I know nothing about it . . . I've never thought about it . . . No, I don't love him."

"At least make an effort not to fall in love with that good-for-nothing Hagiopol fellow," Mavromihali growled. He now had rather more to go on. And turning to his wife, he added, "Grandson of one of Vogoride's tenants, if you please! The scum is rising to the surface!"

He turned back to Constantina. "You will kindly see no more of that confounded Hagiopol. Understand?"

"But he's so nice," Constantina sobbed.

"He is not a fit person for us to know!" the old prince thundered.

Two or three days later Boniface sent the Prince a note asking for an appointment. He turned up for it in morning dress and white gloves and formally asked for Constantina's hand in marriage. Mavromihali, who knew that Boniface would be given office in the forthcoming Cabinet reshuffle, nagged his daughter for several days.

"I don't want to marry him! I don't want to!" Constantina wept.

"Do you love him or don't you?" her mother asked her.

"I don't know . . . I tell you I don't know . . ." Constantina replied between sobs.

"After all, why force her to marry him?" the Princess asked her husband.

"Very well, she shall not be forced," Mavromihali replied.

Constantina rose from the chair where she was sitting in floods of tears and said with resignation, "Since you wish it, I will marry him."

Boniface met Ionas at Capsa's, the fashionable café-restaurant of the day, after the engagement had been announced. He went up to him and offered his hand. He was short, stiff, upright, and muscular; the other was tall, thin, and drooping. Hagiopol accepted Boniface's proffered handshake.

"I want to ask you," Boniface said, "because I know you're attached to Constantina and that she has a great affection for you—I want to ask you to remain our friend. I am asking you this for her sake."

He looked Ionas Hagiopol squarely in the eyes and his smile was almost naïve. Hagiopol also tried to smile but could produce nothing better than a sort of painful rictus. He stammered, "Yes, of course . . . that goes without saying."

"Thank you. So we are friends?" Coziano asked, taking the other's hand again and squeezing it vigorously. Ionas Hagiopol could not even answer. But the delighted Boniface had already left him and was making for the cloakroom to reclaim his overcoat. *So much for you, my fine gentleman,* he told himself. *You've got your deserts. That'll teach you to get in my way!* He looked as pleased as Punch while the porter helped him into his coat.

The wedding took place in the Scaune Church, in a quiet and aristocratic quarter of the city. A long file of carriages, most of them bearing a coat of arms discreetly painted on the door, brought ladies in velvet coats edged with sable or mink and gentlemen in silk hats, for the most part notabilities of the Conservative Party: Prince Dimitri Ghica, General Floresco, Alexander Lahovary, Vasili Boeresco, Prince George Cantacuzene. Among the representatives of the other political party were Lascar Lascari and his wife.

The bridegroom's expression was stern. He had little cause to be satisfied: he had just learned that Prince Mavromihali would not give Constantina the Neaga and Bereni estates until after his death; until then she was to enjoy only a part of the income derived from them.

The ladies stared at Davida. "My dear, it's incredible how ugly she's become! You remember her before her marriage? And as for him! Have a look at him. Is he ill?"

"There's nothing the matter with him—he's just poisoned by his own ill-nature."

"No, really. He's a sick man."

"Not him, my dear! Believe me, he's bursting with health!"

Lascari was pallid and too fat; the back of his neck seemed to have become one with his shoulders and he was huddled into himself, defeated at last by some mysterious malady. He had become completely bald and his big dull eyes stared vacantly. He was tortured by the desire to smoke a cigarette: he left the church, and the first puff relieved him. General Vladoiano, the Mayor of Bucharest, was there too, wearing a black overcoat with a velvet collar and a silk hat.

"What's this, monsieur? Not able to go without a smoke even for this long?" he inquired, laughing.

"Life is short," Lascari replied, "and I have no intention of going without my pleasures for anyone's sake. Will you have a cigar?"

"What is it? Corona? Flor Fina? Thank you, my dear fellow. Fine day, isn't it? Almost springlike."

At this moment the guests standing outside the church made way, and the bride and bridegroom appeared, followed by their sponsors,* the bridesmaids, the parents and relatives. Cleopatra Coziano hurried forward to congratulate the bridal pair, but Boniface, cold and distant, turned away. One after the other the carriages moved off, amid the laughter of ladies and the bustle of footmen lowering and raising carriage steps.

* In Rumania weddings are performed according to the Greek Orthodox rite, in the presence of sponsors or godparents, usually a husband and wife.

Reception at the great house on the Mogosoaïa Bridge; then another procession of carriages to the Filaret station; a railway compartment to Giurgiu; the port, and the little ships with their tall funnels; the Bulgarian bank in deep shadow; the Danube at twilight, a coppery mirror; then night, and the stars in an icy sky. Boniface was silent; he was furious. *I've made a bad bargain. She isn't even pretty and at bottom I don't particularly like her. Of all the damn-fool things to do!* They were sitting on a bench overlooking the Danube, which was turning the color of red-hot iron when it begins to cool. Constantina took Boniface's gloved hand, removed the glove, and pressed the hand to her soft, cool cheek. Boniface remained passive, indifferent.

Later, toward eleven o'clock at night, they saw the Danube Steam Navigation Company's ship *Empress Elizabeth* breasting the current. Ringing of bells, bustle of sailors and porters, the captain in a frock coat with gold epaulets and peaked cap—(*"Sehr geehrt, bitt' schön, gnädige Frau; gute Nacht, mein Herr"*)—the staircase down into the bowels of the ship, the white doors of cabins and the smell of fresh paint, warm air, and well-scrubbed decks . . .

At dawn Boniface rose and put on his clothes. Constantina was in her bunk against the bulkhead. She was silent. Boniface put on his waistcoat. Constantina sat up suddenly, and putting her arms round his waist, whispered, "Don't go away. Don't leave me alone. Stay with me. Please!"

"I am going to get a breath of fresh air," Boniface said curtly. "I shall be back directly."

Wrapped in a thick fur coat he went up onto the promenade deck. Ahead the river was violet, shading into the somber gray-blue of the retreating night.

Tomorrow evening we shall be at Basiasch; Thursday afternoon, Budapest; Vienna, Friday evening. Five days. Five hundred thousand days! What a pleasure! Boniface clenched his teeth, facing into the biting wind with hands in pockets, nerves taut, and jaws set. "Doesn't matter," he muttered. "Forward!"

5

In 1885 Boniface was a simple deputy and nothing more, despite being considered in the Chamber as one of the Conservative Party's best speakers. He was living in a big house behind the Pitar-Mos Church. He entertained a great deal, had carriages, riding horses, and numerous servants. One day, while he was drinking coffee with Lascar Lascari, he burst out, "I've been serving these fools of Conservatives for ten years, and I've had nothing in return!"

"You'll have to get used to the ingratitude of the great," Lascari said.

"No doubt—and used, meanwhile, to seeing my estates mortgaged," Boniface growled.

"So long as I live the Bank won't press you," Lascari reassured him. Boniface made an effort to avoid looking at his brother-in-law and thought, *Yes, but how long have you to live?* All he said was, "Thank you, my dear Lascar. A drop of brandy?"

"Thank you, just a drop."

They drank slowly. Lascari's breathing was labored. Boniface, reserved as ever, refrained from asking whether by any chance he was not feeling well.

"Listen, my dear Lascar: what would you say if I were to come over to your party and desert those phanariots?"

Lascari did not seem to have heard; slumped in his chair, his huge belly thrust forward, he seemed to have difficulty in breathing. His chin was sunk on his chest. Prudently, Boniface refrained from repeating his question, and waited.

"Yes," Lascari panted, "yes. We shall see. I'll think it over. We'll talk about it again soon."

Toward the end of the week they discussed the project. Lascari's intention was to raise the matter with Bratiano. A month later Lascari had to take to his bed. Two months more and he was dead of cancer, without having been able to come to terms with Bratiano. The directors of the Rumanian National Bank invited Boniface to call and discuss his financial position. Boniface asked for a short-term renewal of his loan and took the coach to N—— to see his brother Eustace, who had come to Bucharest for Lascari's funeral but returned home immediately afterward. Eustace also asked for a couple of days to think over Boniface's request, and invited him to dinner. On the following day at noon Boniface, who was as usual calm and to all appearances indifferent, sat talking with Eustace and Cleopatra. He realized that Cleopatra was watching him with a strange kind of intensity, and he guessed what must have happened. Eustace took him on one side, and then said to his wife, "Cleopatra, my dear, we have to talk politics."

"All right, I'll leave you," she said, and did so hastily.

Eustace, alone with his brother, broached the business with an air of embarrassment. "My boy . . . I'm sorry . . . I've thought it over . . . looked into my accounts to see whether I have any ready money available. . . . The fact is, I can't manage it."

"Not even in part?"

Eustace turned away his head. "I can do nothing for you. . . . I have had very heavy expenses—buying Dobrunu from the peasants. . . ."

"But, good heavens, you've been doing that for ten years!" Boniface exclaimed.

"Yes, but you see, I've recently had to find the money for the final plots of land. I . . . well, what more can I say? I can't help you. I haven't a penny. Otherwise I'd have lent you the money with all my heart."

"I know, I know, I don't doubt it," Boniface replied. He was visualizing the scene which must have taken place between his brother and sister-in-law: "Don't give him any money, darling. You'll never see it back again. You'll need your money in the spring (or autumn) when you begin to farm Dobrunu. You don't imagine he'll pay it back when you ask him for it?"

Yes, this was Cleopatra's doing, all right. Boniface mastered his bitterness and left hastily, bidding them a chilly good-by.

In the end Boniface was obliged to sell the estates which he had inherited from his father. Old Mavromihali also refused to give his daughter the property which constituted her dowry, saying, "I told him before that he would not get them until my death." The Prince had been treating Boniface with increasing coldness, seeing that his son-in-law had still not received a ministerial appointment. From then on Boniface did not speak to Constantina except in public, in front of the servants, or on the rare occasions when he could not avoid it. He ignored her completely. Since their honeymoon they had occupied separate rooms. Later, Boniface started taking most of his meals at Capsa's or at the Boulevard Restaurant. Whole days passed during which Constantina did not even see him, and sometimes whole weeks during which she hardly heard the sound of his voice. She became increasingly silent and withdrawn.

On July 21 or 22 of this same year, 1885, Boniface received a message from Walter Apostolesco to the effect that Eustace had been murdered by the Dobrunu peasantry. "Much good that will do me," Boniface muttered coolly. Then he thought better of it. *I ought to go; otherwise it will make a bad impression. Besides, what would the electors of the first electoral college say if they saw me shrugging my shoulders over the murder of landowners by their peasants?*

On the way to N——, as his four-horse traveling carriage rumbled along between interminable fields of maize, Boniface Coziano bitterly totted up the balance sheet of his life: *Forty-three years old and nothing accomplished. Nothing.* He was sweating in his mourning suit. His starched collar was limp. He arrived at his destination in a rage. He was polite but curt to Walter Apostolesco. With Cleopatra, who burst into tears at the sight of him, he spent only a few seconds, then left her in disgust. He pretended to be plunged in meditation before his brother's body; a handkerchief covered the swollen face and an unpleasant smell was beginning to be apparent, despite the lilies that were strewn lavishly over the corpse. Stiff and silent, Boniface followed Eustace's body to the grave. On the following day he drove to Dobrunu, accompanied by Walter Apostolesco. They followed the same route that Eustace had taken five days earlier. A few peasants removed their caps. Others did not even raise their eyes, and some looked the other way. Boniface greeted nobody.

"Listen, my dear Walter," he said, "I'm going to ask you to do me a service, the sort of thing one can only ask of a friend. Take care of Cleopatra. Stay with her, don't leave her by herself. See that she isn't fooled or cheated, either over the inheritance or in any other business."

He knew very well that Walter had been Cleopatra's lover for years and that he would be managing her fortune. But things must be done decently, under cover of the noblest sentiments. Walter would have influence with the landowning electorate, and even with the teachers, lawyers, and doctors of the second electoral college; come to that, with the shopkeepers and traders of the third. He could be very useful; he could also be very dangerous.

"In a general way, you and Cleopatra must call on me for anything you may need—anything whatsoever. There is nothing I will not do to be of use to you."

Much moved, Walter took his hand, pressed it, and said, "I thank you with all my heart."

The carriage drew up at the Town Hall. A sentry, carbine on shoulder, was guarding the door. A number of armed policemen were sitting on a bench, and still more were standing about in the shade of the mulberry trees beneath which they had piled their arms. The clatter of hoofs and the sound of voices could be heard from the Town Hall courtyard. But the village itself might not have existed.

It's no use pretending, Boniface was thinking as he got out of the carriage. *That disgusting woman will never forgive me. She hates me! She'll turn this idiot against me and make him into an enemy. And here I am—forty-three, and I'm nothing, a nonentity!*

Inside the Town Hall they heard the sound of voices. The Prefect, the Procurator, a police lieutenant, and a number of his men were grouped around a peasant. The Prefect, recently appointed, greeted the well-known politician cordially. The Procurator was even more fawning, almost servile. The lieutenant clicked his heels, making his spurs jingle.

"Please carry on with your inquiry," Boniface said with statesmanlike dignity. "Do not let my presence embarrass you. I am here merely as a spectator." He sat down on the chair that was offered him—it had been chipped and slashed with penknives, and the paint was flaking off.

The Procurator turned to the peasant and said, "Well, do you confess?"

The peasant avoided looking anyone in the eyes. A rough beard covered his red, sunburnt cheeks. He was a burly man who carried himself well. His big, square hands with their horny finger-nails were posed squarely on his knees.

"I said, will you talk?" the Procurator repeated. The Prefect was smoking a cigarette. The lieutenant stepped closer and struck the man twice in the face. The man's hands did not leave his knees. The police stood at ease, their firearms resting on the ground. The lieutenant had gone red in the face. Everyone was ill at ease. The peasant blinked and sighed. Boniface whispered to the Prefect, "What has he done?" and looked at the peasant, a man in his thirties whose face seemed vaguely familiar. Where had he seen him? He had even spoken to him. But where? When?

The Prefect took a sheet of paper off the ink-stained table and handed it to Boniface: it was a minute of the interrogation.

. . . Petrake Dumitru, Commune of Dobrunu. Nationality Rumanian. Married, three children. Agricultural laborer. Can neither read nor write. "I did nothing. I was at the Town Hall. Everyone hit him. No, I can't identify anybody. I did not hit him. I have done nothing wrong. He is wrong, I was not there, he is not right to accuse me. I was only looking on. I do not know the ones who hit him."

Such were the man's answers. The Prefect then gave Boniface a sheaf of papers which he glanced through. They were minutes of the police interrogations of Culea Pavel, Chireasa Vasili, Arghir

Dumitru, Ion Tirna, Mirea Constantine, Lefter Uzum, Florea Dumitresco-Porcoi, Ene I. Jirlacan, George M. Jirlacan, Vasili Larota, Nitza Geanta, Coman Lixandro, Petrake Todorake—in all some fifty names. "I do not know. Everyone in the village hit him," ran the invariable answer to the question "Why did you strike Monsieur Coziano?"

Vasili Paun, nicknamed the Beanstalk, had replied, "He was harassing us all the time." Only one, Iordake Narfa, had said:

> Since Saturday Nitza Negrea had been telling the people to stone the boyar when he came to take away their land. I have heard it said that he began the attack. And Petrake Nana was with him, the one they called the Fool—not Ionitza Dumitru Nana nor his brother Balabesh.

It was this same Petrake Dumitru Nana whom the police lieutenant had just seized by the hair; he was banging the peasant's head against the wall. The dull thumping was punctuated by the lieutenant's panting breath and the victim's groans. Boniface was wondering where he had seen this man Nana. He turned to the Prefect and asked in a low voice (not that he could have been overheard because the lieutenant shouted "Do you confess?" each time he banged the man's head against the wall): "What about this Nitza Negrea? What have they done with him?"

The Prefect rose and beckoned Coziano to follow him. They went into the next room—a bare cell, its walls covered with scribblings and its floor filthy. A dead peasant lay stiffly on the ground, his nose pinched and his mouth hanging open. Flies swarmed over his face.

"This is him," the Prefect said. "He was the ringleader of the riot, but he would not confess. He was beaten with a sandbag and something must have broken inside him. . . . I don't like this kind of thing, but there was nothing else to be done. They're all a lot of brigands; they cover up for each other. We were lucky enough to find two or three more—er—docile, and they pointed out the guilty men. . . ."

"It is regrettable," Boniface said gravely, looking at the body of Nitza Negrea with the same indifference as he had looked at his own brother's. "It is most regrettable to be forced to use such methods. But we are dealing here with an attack on the very principle of private property, and not only with a murder."

The Prefect acquiesced.

"It is not simply a question of punishing the murder of one man," Boniface went on severely, "but of defending morality, justice, the lives and property of our citizens—in short, of safeguarding the whole social order."

With which he left the Town Hall. As he made his way along the corridor he caught a glimpse of a policeman holding the peasant Petrake Dumitru by the hair, while another threw a pailful of water over him. Blood was flowing from his nose onto his upper lip. He was staring vacantly, with an expression of bewilderment.

Ah, now I remember, Coziano thought. He had seen this man once before, during the war, one morning just before a brush with a Turkish patrol. The man had been sent forward as a scout; Boniface recalled his placid smile—*"Feeling a bit cold, eh?"*— *"A bit cold, that's it, sir." Funny that he pulled through all right in the war, and now they'll have his blood. Ah, well, devil take the fellow!*

Boniface offered his hand to the Prefect. "Congratulations on your zeal. I think it would not be a bad idea to interrogate another score of the ringleaders with the same thoroughness. . . ." He looked the Prefect in the eye to make sure that the man understood him. That the Prefect had understood at once was apparent from his smile.

"Where is Monsieur Apostolesco?" Boniface asked, mopping his face and neck.

"In the courtyard, sir," the coachman said. Boniface went out. The police horses were dozing in the shade of an awning. The steel of the piled gun-barrels was hot from the sun. Policemen with nothing to do were wandering vaguely about. Walter was standing, legs apart and hands in pockets, staring at Eustace's carriage which had been overturned near the fence; the polished wood of the coachwork was smashed and the upholstery ripped to ribbons.

"Here's some of their devil's work," Walter said, pointing to the carriage. "They've been at it with axes. What vandals!'"

"Yes," Boniface said, adding: "We had better be going, my friend, if we are to arrive before nightfall." They got into the carriage and set off.

After some time Boniface said abruptly, "Cleopatra can take possession of Dobrunu without anxiety. Help her to exploit it systematically, using up-to-date methods. It's good land, worth a gold mine." And he added in a tone of melancholy, "It's a great pity I can't take up farming too."

"We might go into farming together?" Walter said. Boniface avoided a direct answer, but gave the other to understand what it was he really wanted: "I shall be very satisfied if we go into politics together," he said.

"That goes without saying. You are our deputy forever," Walter declared jovially.

And yet they did not go into politics together. At the next election Boniface nearly lost his seat. And, tapping him familiarly on the knee, Ienake Balaban told him, "Monsieur Walter has gone out of his mind. You realize that he tried to do us in? Tell me, Monsieur Boniface, why does he bear you a grudge?"

"He has the right to vote as he pleases," Boniface answered dryly.

"Oh, come now, my dear sir! There isn't much anyone can teach me about politics. What have you done to him? Done him some service, I'll be bound, and now he can't forgive you, eh? You know what human nature is. . . ."

Boniface laughed. "Yes, I once did him a service." And he added in another voice, cold and resolute: "And I shall do him another one of these days. Don't worry. The day will come when I'll do him a service he won't forget!"

6

In 1887 Mme Constantina Coziano was a young woman in her early twenties—five-and-twenty at most—but she looked much older. Her melancholy spirit, product of a sluggish body and a slow mind, aged her prematurely. The first lines had appeared at the corners of her eyes and mouth. Her blue eyes were dulled by shortsightedness, and the golden down over her cheeks blurred her face, which had become a little fuller. Her figure too had thickened: the slender horsewoman whom Coziano had escorted along the bridle paths of the Chaussée had become almost stout, and rings which at eighteen she had worn on her middle finger now had to be worn on the ring finger, or even on the little finger.

Always sullen and withdrawn, Mme Coziano dressed in the height of fashion, received and returned calls, rode in the Chaussée, and went to the season's balls with her husband. They would enter a drawing room together, smiling amiably to right and left. But between themselves they exchanged neither a look nor a word; each held the other's arm as if it were a piece of wood. They would separate, dance, play cards, chat with the other guests, he in his corner, she in hers. The party over, they left together, got into their carriage, and from that moment were silent—and remained silent when they were back home. They would part after exchanging two words of cool and indifferent courtesy, he to his room, she to hers. The next day they would meet for meals, say nothing, and part again. M. Coziano went to the Chamber of Deputies, his wife to make her round of calls. She visited her friends, drank tea, listened to conversation, uttered a few words herself, smiled, and departed. She went shopping, bought a statuette, a picture—usually the work of some third-rate French or Austrian painter—material for a dress, silk for an armchair that needed re-covering. She returned to the house to wait for dinnertime, or to dress for the evening and put on her pearl necklace or her *rivière* of diamonds.

Later she became more of a recluse and took to drinking in secret. From Broft the wine merchant she bought sherry which he imported by way of Genoa, a full-bodied wine, fragrant as a whole cartload of muscat grapes. When she had drunk, she sometimes found the energy to read a novel.

Still later Constantina withdrew altogether from the world, became an alcoholic, and died, when she was just over forty, of the consequences of these excesses. But these things all came to pass little by little, and her decline was barely perceptible. It was in 1885 or at the beginning of 1886 that the events occurred which were to lead Constantina, unwittingly, into utter loneliness, alcoholism, and death.

The first of these events happened during an afternoon in November 1885. It was raining and cold. Constantina had not yet summoned a servant to light the lamps. She was sitting near the drawing-room window at a small tea table. Facing her, with his knees together, elbows in to his sides, and a cup of tea in his hands, sat Ionas Hagiopol. He was nearing his thirtieth year and he had let his mustache grow. He was correct in his manner, reserved, and flabby. Two or three times a week he called on Constantina and sat chatting with her for an hour or two. He still loved her, but he never made the slightest allusion to his feelings. Their conversation was devoid of spirit, brilliance, and even vivacity.

"What weather!" Constantina said, watching the rain cascading down the windowpanes.

"Shocking weather, indeed! Are you going to Madame Gradisteano's the day after tomorrow?"

"I think so. . . . Yes, we shall surely be going. Do you know who will be there?"

"Come now, who do you think? The same people as usual. The cream of Bucharest society."

"What a limited society it is!"

"Well, there it is—a small country, a small capital, a small social world. . . ."

"Yes, that's true."

They looked again at the tall window: between the yellow curtains they could see the rain dashing against the glass.

"Anything in the papers?" Constantina asked indifferently.

There was a silence. They were bored, but not excessively so. It was as if they were about to fall asleep, or into an eternal trance of dullness. The door opened and Boniface came in.

"Good evening, Constantina. Are you alone? Ah, you're here too! My dear, why not have the lamps lit?"

Boniface pulled the bell rope which hung beside the door. Somewhere in a remote corridor a bell tinkled faintly. Presently a footman entered.

"Light the lamps," Boniface said, sitting down. "What were you talking about?"

"Society," Constantina said dully.

"What about it?"

"It is very limited. A few hundred families and that's all."

"What about tradesmen, shopkeepers? When they have something to celebrate they invite everyone they know—and the whole party can be held in a small backyard. There are people with no more than a score of friends and acquaintances in all. Why should we complain?"

"All the same," Ionas Hagiopol said, "a few hundred families isn't much."

"Well, there it is—we are not in England," Boniface replied coldly. "Besides, come to think of it, it's the same thing in every country. A few hundred families—a few thousand at most in the bigger countries—and for the rest, the rabble. It is those families which count. Here as elsewhere."

Boniface expressed himself fluently. Constantina and Ionas realized that he thought more quickly than they did, and with more precision and lucidity; that he took a longer, broader, more general view. He had disturbed their silence, the pleasant numbness of twilight. One by one the footman lit the gas lamps. The room became bright. Ionas Hagiopol drew his watch from his waistcoat pocket. "Seven o'clock. I have some friends still to visit."

He rose, bowed to Constantina and, less deeply, to Boniface.

"I did not see your carriage outside. Did you come on foot?"

"Yes. It had not started to rain."

"Take my carriage," Boniface said. "Allow me: I will see you to it." He left the room on their guest's heels, and crossing the anteroom, escorted him into the hall. The footman helped Ionas into his coat.

"Go and tell Ion to bring the carriage around—not the big one, the other—to take the gentleman home," Boniface said. The footman left them, and for a moment they were alone together in the glass-windowed hall. Through the panes the brick-paved courtyard gleamed under the rain, and beyond it the iron railings, the big wrought-iron gates, and the street where a lamplighter, huddled against the cold and with a sack over his head against the rain, was lighting the street lamps.

"My dear fellow," Boniface said, fixing a hard stare on the cameo pin securing Ionas's cravat, "I have a request to make: don't come to this house quite so often. Don't be surprised; I am about to explain. I am very fully occupied by my political work, and am hardly ever at home. Constantina is much younger than I, and so are you. A chivalrous man such as yourself would not, I am sure, want to give the world cause to smile significantly at my expense—even though you have, in fact, nothing to reproach yourself with. You know what people are. . . . Do I make myself clear?"

Ionas Hagiopol changed color. This short, slight man, who was becoming increasingly capable with the years of assuming an expression and bearing not merely aggressive but brutal, inspired Ionas with a feeling which was not exactly fear but something more: a sort of horror, a profound physical revulsion. He stammered, "Yes, of course I understand—of course——"

"Thank you," Boniface said dryly.

The carriage drew up to the steps. Boniface himself opened the front door and stood there until Ionas had gone out. Ionas bowed once again, awkward, disturbed, bewildered, and unhappy. Boniface did not offer him his hand. Hagiopol, not really knowing what he was about, offered his; Boniface touched it with two fingers, assuming a patronizing, slightly contemptuous expression.

"Good-by, my dear fellow. Good-by."

The carriage drove away into the rain. Boniface went back into the house and straight to the library, without going to see Constantina, who bored him.

After that evening Ionas Hagiopol never again set foot in the Cozianos' house. During the first week Constantina hardly noticed his absence. But at the end of the second week, when she and Boniface were eating alone, she said, "What has happened to Ionas? I haven't seen him lately."

Boniface shrugged and made no answer. He had not spoken a word since they sat down; nor did he speak during the rest of the meal.

One evening Constantina, entering Mme Otetelesano's drawing room on her husband's arm, saw Ionas Hagiopol and their eyes met. A moment later Hagiopol had vanished. Constantina looked around for him, and then after M. Catargiu had relieved her of her husband by taking Boniface into a corner to talk politics, she tried, discreetly, to find Ionas in one of the other drawing rooms. She could not see him and did not dare to question anyone about him. Thenceforth she never met him in society again.

One morning during the following spring, Constantina went out to do some shopping and happened to stop next door to Capsa's Restaurant. In front of her, glittering in the sunshine, was a shop window bearing in large gold letters the legend: "Universal Stores. Branch of the Constantinople Bon Marché." The window was full of silk ties, kid gloves, walking sticks of ebony, bamboo, or rose-wood, pyramids of starched collars, panoplies of black, white, aquamarine, and lemon-yellow sunshades, and cashmere shawls. The side windows announced, in smaller gold lettering: "Brushes, Gloves, Perfumery, Paris Novelties, Fancy Goods, Glass, Porcelain, etc."

Mme Coziano stared into the shop window. Passers-by turned for a second to look at this woman whose figure was still good and

whose green-gloved hand rested on the knob of a long gray silk
sunshade. But they saw nothing but a commonplace profile, a
mediocre complexion, a sullen, sleepy expression, and went on their
way. Constantina did not even notice them. She was looking at the
shop window and recalling that she needed a dozen pairs of gloves
to finish the season. She went into the shop and was at once received by the obsequiously bowing shopkeeper.

"Good morning. I want some gloves," Constantina said, looking
at nothing, not at the customers, nor the cut glass, nor the imitation
Dresden figures of amorous shepherds or marquises in hideous
fondant colors; nor at the boxes on the shelves; nor at the iron
stove burning in the corner of the shop. Hearing Mme Coziano's
voice, a gentleman in a black frock coat and top hat had turned to
look at her. The gentleman was Ionas Hagiopol. He stood staring
at her, holding a starched collar in one hand. Constantina, shortsighted though she was, recognized his figure and bearing. She took
three swift steps toward him, exclaiming, "Ionas! You! My dear,
what has become of you these days?"

Hagiopol took off his hat and tried to take her proffered hand
to kiss it; but he was still holding the collar. He lost his head, and
keeping her waiting, turned to replace the collar on the counter.
His olive cheeks had flushed darkly. Constantina, emerging from
her customary apathy, also blushed; she felt suddenly and intensely
happy. She had only just realized how much she had been wanting to see Ionas again.

"What's become of you?" she asked. "Where have you been?
Why don't you come to see us any longer? Why have you given
no sign of life?"

He looked at her, not speaking. The flush had gradually disappeared from his cheeks. He gave a forced smile, but still he
said nothing.

"What have you been doing? Where have you been?"

"In Bucharest—that is to say, I have also been in the country.
Shooting, you know."

She looked at him attentively. "No, I don't know," she murmured. "What's the matter?"

Ionas smiled awkwardly. Constantina said, "Wait while I choose some gloves, then you must come back to the house with me."

He appeared startled at this and stammered, "No . . . that is, you will have to excuse me . . . I am expected . . . I must on no account be late . . ." But he looked at her with a hungry expression, a look of grievous thirst unslaked. "I must leave you . . . I must go at once . . . I am not going . . . not going . . ." And in a half-choked mutter he concluded: "Not going your way."

Yet he did not move. For a moment Constantina was simply surprised, but then her happiness turned abruptly into hurt and bitter anger.

"Very well," she said. "Good day to you, monsieur."

And she walked swiftly to the door. The shop assistant ran after her, saying cajolingly: "Aren't you taking the gloves, madam?" Constantina slammed the door in his face and set off, walking very fast, along the Mogosoaïa Bridge. *Why can't I die on the spot, here and now? Why don't I drop dead?* she thought, choking. An empty cab was passing. Constantina hailed it, got in, gave the cabman her address, and fell back on the seat, exhausted. She was sure she was dying. She felt herself dying. But then came tears, which relieved her.

At luncheon she came to table with red eyes and stricken face. There were no guests. Boniface ate in silence as usual. During the dessert course he studied her face and said, "What's the matter? Have you been crying?"

"I have a headache. I don't feel well," Constantina said, looking down at her plate. Boniface said no more. There was a session of the Chamber that afternoon.

They got up from the table and parted in silence. Constantina went to her boudoir and sat down in an armchair near the window. Outside the sun was shining and the dark branches of the trees were surrounded by a faint cloud of tender green. In the brilliantly clear light of early spring everything looked ugly and poor. Facing the Coziano mansion was a row of little houses, each presenting a blank wall to its neighbor's front, and suggestive of monkeys turning their backs on each other. A ragged glazier was passing along the street, crying "Gla-ass, gla-ass!" in a cracked voice. Everything was boring, stale, sickening. Constantina said aloud, "How lonely I am." Then, in a lower tone, "I am utterly alone."

She began to pace the room, walking on a Shirvan rug rich with golden highlights. She thought of the same things over and over again: her marriage, the life she had led since, the disappearance of Ionas, their encounter. And always her thoughts spiraled back to herself. Sometimes she recalled the faces of her parents and brothers; she could not bear her brothers, had never been on good terms with them. There was nobody to whom she could turn, no refuge. What had happened to Ionas? Why was he behaving like this? Then her mind returned again to the train of her memories, always ending with the same agonizing question: what had caused the change in Ionas's attitude?

Night had begun to fall when she suddenly came to a halt. She must see him, talk to him. He must come to her. If he refused, she would go to his house. She sat down at a small writing desk, elaborately turned and carved like a shell, and began a letter. But before she had finished the footman came in and delivered an envelope on a silver tray: it was a letter from Ionas. Constantina tore it open and crossed to the window to read it; she was afraid of the lamplight.

My Dear Constantina,

I have suffered during the last few hours more than I thought I could suffer in the course of my whole earthly life. My feeling for you is much deeper than I have ever dared to confess. I am yours in the sense that a man belongs to the air and the earth which keep him alive. Why, then, have I voluntarily deprived myself of the air I need to live, of my earthly and heavenly sustenance? For you, my darling, only for you, so that your conjugal happiness might be cloudless. Boniface, with his rather brutal candor, warned me of the danger—I mean the danger of giving rise to malicious and perfidious gossip and by so doing

smirching the honor of someone who, in my eyes, is worth
more than all the world. I can say no more. Words are too
feeble to express what I feel. Only my heart knows all, but it
is silent, and will be so forever. I kiss your feet and the earth
they tread, and remain for all eternity,

Yours,

Ion Hagiopol

P.S.   Please convey my regards to your husband. I am taking the
evening train to Vienna and by the time you receive these
lines I shall be far away. Later, perhaps, we can meet again
without endangering your honor and happiness. In that case
I will return.

At first Constantina stood as if turned to stone. Then she rang
to order the carriage and ask the footman to look up the time of
the next train to Vienna. Departure, seven-ten, with a connection
on the morrow at Roman for Czernowitz, Lemberg, and Vienna,
the whole journey taking three days. The time of arrival was five-
twenty in the morning. The footman stood before her with the
timetable in his hand; he added in a low voice, "Two hundred and
nineteen francs, thirty-two centimes."

"What time is it?"

"It is seven o'clock, madam."

"Very well. You may go."

Constantina remained alone in the dark.

That night Boniface was kept at the Chamber by a late sitting
until far into the night. Constantina had no dinner and locked herself in her bedroom. Nor did Boniface return for luncheon the
next day; he ate at the house of some political friends, and that
evening he again stayed late at the Chamber of Deputies, where the
budget was being debated. He noticed no change in Constantina's
attitude. In any case he paid hardly any attention to her. He considered her simply as a machine for receiving such guests as he
chose to invite. She had been intended primarily, of course, as a
machine for making his fortune, but old Mavromihali had still not
handed over her estates and showed no inclination to die soon. She

should at least have given Boniface children and reared them; but she was barren. No, decidedly, Constantina was not worth his notice. Her duty was to efface herself and not to hinder Boniface in that political business which exhausted him, without (so far, at least) having procured for him the satisfaction he desired. True, politics brought Boniface a certain amount of power; most men would have been well satisfied with that. But Coziano had long been expecting a ministerial appointment. He told his friends that it was due to him as the only capable man in a flock of idle old idiots. And he had not got it; he still had not got it.

That spring Constantina took to drink. Wine opened for her the way into happier lands where everything was beautiful and easy. Sometimes she was driven out of her paradise by nausea; but she soon learned to measure her dose of liquor so as to experience the same euphoria every time, while falling short of complete drunkenness with its unpleasant and all too prompt consequences.

7

The honors of office came too late to Boniface Coziano to give him unalloyed satisfaction. With melancholy vanity he thought, *It was no more than my due; they have realized it at last.* Such was his state of mind as he drove to the palace on a cold, wet day early in the spring of 1888. As he got out of the carriage, walked up the steps to the terrace, made his way under the awning into the guard-room, climbed the stairs leading to the first antechamber, came face to face with his fellow members of the new government to be sworn in, shook hands and exchanged greetings with those who had arrived before him—during all this time he found in his heart only a kind of dismal satisfaction and a pride almost ready to explode in overt discontent—*For, all said and done, am I prime minister? I am not. I am only one man among the many who are or have been cabinet ministers. It isn't much.* And he looked at his colleagues, whom he despised—two or three for their want of character, and the rest—the majority—for their stupidity.

At last the Prime Minister arrived; he was an old man, tall and very dignified. His handsome bearing bore witness to a nobility of lineage which went back to the Byzantine emperors and the princes of Wallachia. In a room which opened off the principal ante-chamber his ministers joined him, standing in a row, facing the paintings which were hung on one wall—El Greco's "Betrothal of the Virgin," the same painter's "A Spanish Grandee" dressed all in black with a white ruff standing out like a plate, and beside it, a Rembrandt, "Esther Receiving the Submission of Haman." Boni-face looked from the paintings to the row of corpulent gentlemen in black tailcoats gaudy with decorations, their waistcoats crossed by the blue, red, or green ribbons of various orders. All had pon-derous jowls and double chins, eyes dulled by age, good living, and nervous exhaustion. Only one or two among them still had a spark of life, because they were not entirely replete, not perfectly com-placent with self-satisfaction. Boniface Coziano, despite the gray in his hair, was the youngest man among them. And meanwhile he was bored and irritated.

The King, in the blue uniform of a divisional general, came into the room. He was short, thin, and wore his hair long and his beard rather full; he had the smooth face of a man without passions and not too much given to thought. He extended his hand to the Prime Minister and that proud old nobleman, descendant of Byzantine emperors and Wallachian *voivodes,* stooped to kiss it.

You have to be a great boyar, Boniface thought contemptuously, *to be quite so servile. Pah! the old bootlicker!* He had heard of this practice of the Prime Minister's, but had never before wit-nessed the scene. He looked at the King with hostile eyes: that petty German princeling, scion of a house that could not compare for antiquity with the Cantacuzenes or the Brancovans, was regard-ing them all with cold haughtiness as the Prime Minister mur-mured a few words of introduction. The King shook hands with each in turn. Ready to follow the Prime Minister's example, each member of the Cabinet bowed deeply. Boniface was the fourth. He bowed less deeply than the others and held out his hand. But he failed to repress a start when he realized that the King was only offering him two fingers. It was too late: under the influence of surprise he pressed the two fingers, and the King passed on to the next man.

The rest of the ceremony held no interest for Coziano. Boiling with rage, he was cursing inwardly. *German swine! Ill-bred lout!* he told the King—in imagination. *You can keep your dirty hand to yourself in future! What do I want with your fingers? Learn manners, or for my part, —— you!* But though Boniface answered only "yes" or "no" to the two or three questions which the King put to him, he did not convey that his personal dignity and the honor of the Cozianos would not allow him to cringe before the royal arrogance. Mute, and with rage in his heart, he left the audience chamber, telling the King—in imagination: *Thus do I treat the bailiffs of my estates—but the relationship between you and me is not the same.*

For several days Boniface was obsessed with the idea that he ought to resign and withdraw from public life. Sitting on the front bench in the Chamber; in his carriage while driving to the Ministry; in his own office at the Ministry—everywhere, he thought with rage, bitterness, and despair of the multiplicity of his masters: Ienake Balaban, the King, the tradesmen and landowners of his constituency, the old boyars of the Conservative Party's central committee, who in turn truckled to the German. Ten, nay, a hundred, a thousand masters whom he despised and loathed, but on whom he was obliged to smile, to whom he must bow and scrape. *Enough,* he thought, grinding his teeth as he sat at his great Boulle desk. *I can stomach no more. It is more than I can bear. Is this what I wanted at any price? What I aspired to? Well, I have it now. Much good may it do me! At the next audience I'll show this German the kind of man I am. I'll offer him two fingers—no more. Only the two of us will ever know, but the German will draw his own conclusions.*

The audience was not granted until much later. During the first week of April peasant risings broke out in the provinces nearest to Bucharest—a situation which gave Boniface some satisfaction—but nothing could appease his colossal and devouring discontent.

One day Boniface arrived at his Ministry and crossed the anteroom quickly. Stout deputies, journalists affecting shirt collars *à l'artiste* and round hats, ladies flaunting the first spring coats and the first flowered and feathered hats of the season, were waiting for the Minister. The ladies and the elderly parliamentarians were seated in maroon leather armchairs. The rest stood in the window embrasures or even behind the curtains, talking quietly and watching the carriages which drove along the street. As he passed among them with his swift, springy stride Boniface nodded curtly to anyone he happened to know. Out of the corner of his eye he caught sight of Walter Apostolesco and turned to greet him with a cordiality which was entirely superficial, pleased to see that the man looked pale, depressed, and anxious. In his own office, Boniface sat down behind his big desk, which was embellished with a figure of Fame brandishing her trumpet. It was raining; the first gas lamps were being lit in the street.

The Minister's *chef de cabinet* was young Alexander Lascari, Davida's eldest son, who, despite his twenty-five years, had a grave and sullen look about him. Boniface had given him the job because Alexander was his nephew. The young man, half smothered in one of the turn-down collars which had just become fashionable, placed a list on his superior's desk.

"Let's see now," Boniface said, and began to read, half aloud, the list of people who had favors to ask. "Madame Ascherliu—the wife of the General, the Crown Prince's A.D.C.?"

"Yes," Lascari replied, "she wants to see you about an estate she has in the Vlashea province."

"I'll see her."

Mme Ascherliu came in, offering Boniface a hand gloved to the elbow. She was a pink-and-white blonde in her early thirties, with brown eyes and a mouth which was beautiful, especially when she smiled. She was wearing a dress of light blue shot with gray, a white hat, and white gloves, and carried a dark-blue muff and a sunshade to match. She cast a laughing glance at the young *chef de cabinet* as he went out and closed the door, then at Boniface, whom she looked straight in the eye in a way which was almost too frank. Boniface realized at once what this meant, and thought that he was hardly likely to refuse.

"I am so worried, Excellency," Mme Ascherliu began, fixing her deep eyes on Boniface. "Our Lespezi and Zilistea estates are threatened by the insurrection. You can imagine the loss it will mean to us if they sack the manor houses!"

"You need fear nothing, madame. I will take all the necessary steps."

"As you would for anyone," she said, smiling. Boniface also smiled and replied, "I will do a great deal more for you than for the others. Madame Ascherliu is not just 'anyone.'"

"You're very kind—but I hardly dare believe you."

"If you cast doubts on my sincerity now, what hope have I that you will believe me later when I talk to you about—much more important things? I am supposing that you may be willing to accept me not only as the defender of public order and of your estates, but also as—an admirer."

Boniface said this very seriously, almost coldly; but there flashed in his eyes that light which in the past used to make his sister-in-law Cleopatra exclaim, "Ah, the wretch!"

"You are being ironical, Monsieur Coziano," Mme Ascherliu replied, laughing. "You are making fun of a poor woman who needs your help."

"No, madame, I am not joking—I am offering a bargain. What would be the use of power if one did not abuse it? You shall have my help and support—at a price."

Boniface's cold smile put a number of ideas into the lady's mind.

"What do you mean? What price can I pay in exchange?" she asked with a nervous laugh, upset by what seemed to her to be coarseness on Coziano's part. She was playing with the small gold watch set with diamonds which she wore hung around her neck on a fine chain, like a medallion. Boniface bowed gallantly without taking his eyes off her and, with an air of submission, gravely replied, "The price I ask is a cup of tea at your house or the first dance at the first ball where we happen to meet. It is for you to choose. If you refuse, I shall send no troops either to Lespezi or to Zilistea."

Mme Ascherliu burst out laughing. "You are a charmer, Monsieur Coziano! You shall have your cup of tea *and* your dance for good measure. Moreover"—this she said in a serious voice and with studied, girlish sweetness—"moreover, you will also have my friendship. Thank you—and I hope to see you at my house soon. I am always at home to my friends on Wednesdays."

"Tomorrow is Wednesday," Boniface said, and bowed again. Mme Ascherliu offered her hand, which he pressed after kissing the glove. She blushed and seemed disturbed, but Boniface at once began talking commonplaces as he escorted her to the door. Returning to his desk, he sat down, thinking, *She isn't bad; it would suit me quite well. How the devil does she contrive her blushing?*

Alexander Lascari returned and Boniface said, "I'll see Monsieur Apostolesco."

Walter came in, visibly anxious. Boniface offered his hand with an air of condescension.

"Well, what's new? Glad to see you. What's happening in your part of the world? You look tired. When did you reach town? Sit down."

"This morning, by the coach. I'm all in and haven't slept a wink. Save us, my dear fellow. Don't abandon us."

"Save you? From what? What's happened?"

"Why—Dobrunu! Anyone would think you'd never heard of the Dobrunu peasants! For three years I've been pouring money into the place, investing in all sorts of equipment, and now there's a risk of the whole thing being destroyed overnight."

"You mustn't take things so tragically," Boniface said, indifferently. Walter Apostolesco looked at him attentively.

"How's Cleopatra?" Boniface asked with cold politeness.

"Desperate. She came with me; she wanted to see you, to tell you how worried she is," Walter explained, with lowered eyes.

Boniface knew perfectly well that Walter had just invented this, and answered with the same coldness, "I shall be very glad to see her, whenever she likes."

"And Dobrunu?" Apostolesco said. Boniface studied a map hanging on the wall, which was picketed with little red, blue, and white flags. "Let's see, it lies towards the Danube," he murmured. "Yes, they're moving that way. . . . Here, you can see for yourself how the risings are spreading."

Walter got up to look and then returned to his chair, appalled. "From all sides! The whole province is up in arms."

"For the time being your Dobrunu is intact," Boniface said placidly, "but it looks very much as if you'll soon be involved."

"But steps are being taken, of course?" Walter asked.

"Naturally."

There followed a silence. Walter Apostolesco watched Boniface light a cigarette. He stammered, "You know that she—that Cleopatra, I mean—is sorry that she couldn't help you that time——"

"When?" Boniface asked promptly, giving Apostolesco a hostile glance.

"You know perfectly well—that time you needed money," Apostolesco mumbled, completely disconcerted by Boniface's strange attitude. Walter was as handsome and elegant as ever, but his confusion made him seem awkward and stupid. The fear of losing the enormous sums that he had invested in machinery, livestock, and farm buildings was driving him out of his senses.

"When was this?" Boniface inquired. "I can't remember. You must have misunderstood what she told you. You're overtired. Go and rest. I'll telegraph to N—— and find out what's happening in your neighborhood, and more particularly at Dobrunu."

With which piece of politeness he rose and escorted Walter to the door. Alone again, he summoned his *chef de cabinet*.

"Alexander, I'll see the journalists. And send a telegram to the colonel in command at N——. Tell him not to concern himself with the defense of Dobrunu—Monsieur Walter Apostolesco's estate—until next week. Word it so that only the colonel will understand, but so that he understands perfectly. I am very anxious that

Dobrunu should come last. Let the colonel do as much restoring of order as he likes, but he is on no account to forestall trouble."

"I understand," Alexander Lascari said. He went out to usher in the newspapermen, but returned immediately.

"Uncle, there's a score or more farmers and country landowners from the Ilfov province asking if you'll see them. They seem badly frightened."

"If you can control your tongue and never call me uncle in the presence of a third party, well and good. If not, you had better get it into your head that I shall dismiss you the first time you 'uncle' me in public. Is that clear?"

"You can rely on me, Uncle," Alexander said calmly, and opened the door.

"Come in, gentlemen. His Excellency would be glad if you landowning gentlemen would come in at the same time."

The room filled with people. Boniface, standing at his desk, nodded to such of the newcomers as were acquaintances—the editor-in-chief of the Government organ, two or three great land-owners. (*Now's the time to collect Constantina's dowry from my father-in-law.*) And while an office boy was lighting the gas mantles of the candelabra under their ground-glass shades, Boniface started to talk. A number of men in the room were newspaper directors and very influential. *I must make them feel that I'm a strong men, which happens to be true anyway,* Boniface thought, and adopted a tone of curt assurance.

"Gentlemen, the Government is in control of the situation. All steps necessary to restore order in the villages have been taken. We shall try persuasion, but if necessary we shall resort to force."

"Persuasion, Excellency?"—this from one of the landowners, a pop-eyed man with a heavy gray mustache. "*They* are burning our sharecropping account books, and assaulting our bailiffs and the village mayors. It won't be long before *they* start sacking our manor houses."

Boniface turned toward the journalists: "Gentlemen of the Press: your newspapers are making a considerable contribution toward preventing me from taking more energetic measures. Some among you, those who confuse democracy with anarchy, are calling us murderers of the peasantry. I give you my word of honor that the director of any newspaper who dares publish such insults again will have to account for them to me personally. I allow no man to call me a murderer."

And, man by man, he looked every one of his visitors squarely in the eye. He read their thoughts and he despised them for not daring to speak out. He went on: "The peasants come to their senses when they see the Army in their villages. But when they are quite certain that the soldiers fire over their heads, and above all when the troops are withdrawn, they revolt again, assuring each other 'Come on, lads! You can see for yourselves they're shooting as if at a fair.' Well, they'll see shooting that's not as if at a fair."

There was complete silence. A farmer with a heavy jaw, a low forehead, and close-cropped hair broke it in a complaining voice, saying, "We must have done with this softness, Excellency, because if you don't put a stop to them in two days at the outside, the insurrection will spread to the whole country!"

"It will not spread," Boniface asserted. "But let the Press stop preventing men of good will from doing their duty and restoring order. And so long as you gentlemen—farmers and landowners— are behind me, believe me, order will be restored!"

"*That's* what I call talking!" one of the farmers shouted from the far end of the room. There was in his *"that's"* such a world of satisfaction and relief that several people laughed.

"If you will be so kind as to come back tomorrow at ten o'clock, gentlemen, I will let you know what we have done in the meantime," Boniface said in a more friendly voice; and he took leave of them with a slight nod. When all the visitors were gone, Lascari came back and said, "They're vastly impressed. You're a fly one, Uncle! You wiped the floor with them!"

Boniface did not even deign to answer, but told Alexander to show another of the persons waiting in the anteroom into his office. And he continued to receive visitors until late in the evening. At last he asked Alexander if there was anyone still waiting.

"Madame Apostolesco," Alexander replied. Boniface looked at

him thoughtfully and said, "Ask her to come in. I'll receive nobody else. Say that I have left the office for tonight."

Cleopatra came in and began to talk very fast. "I'm so glad to see you again. So this is your office? You cabinet ministers do yourselves rather well! I've never seen a minister's office before, you know. Today's the first time. I can't tell you how glad I am that you're a minister—and just at the time when I've so much need of help and we're in terrible danger . . . Walter's quite desperate. . . . Between ourselves, Boniface, why are you still angry with me? Poor Eustace couldn't do a thing for you at the time, I swear he couldn't. I know exactly how things stood at the time, he told me everything. . . ."

"Yes," Boniface said simply. Cleopatra fell silent. Their eyes met, Cleopatra's questioning and anxious, Boniface's expressionless.

"Why do you look at me like that?" Cleopatra asked, with an uncertain little laugh.

"I am looking at you to see if you've changed, and in what way."

"Well, and have I?" Cleopatra said with a sort of uneasy coquettishness.

"You're a little fatter," Boniface said, smiling.

"And you don't like me any more, not as I am now?" Cleopatra was becoming deliberately provocative: she had understood his intention and was prepared to play his game. Boniface rose, walked around his desk, and kissed her hand. Then, without further preamble, he placed his hands under her armpits, picked her up, and carried her gently into a corner of the office where there was a big sofa covered with silk.

Some time later, as Boniface stood with his hands behind his back staring out of the window while Cleopatra pinned up her hair, she said, "Are you very busy? What are you doing tonight?"

"Working," he replied, without turning around. Cleopatra put on her hat, using the glass front of the bookcase as a mirror. "Help me into my coat, will you?"

Boniface went to her, picking up her coat as he passed from the chair where she had tossed it. He helped her into it, and then stood motionless while she smoothed on her gloves. Cleopatra had a feeling that she would do better to linger for a few minutes more. But Boniface, saying not a word, was obviously waiting for her to go.

"Well, I must leave you," Cleopatra said. She was standing in the middle of the room.

"My compliments," Boniface murmured, bowing. She smiled languidly, and said, "Not even a little kiss?"

Coziano stooped over her and, with obvious boredom, kissed her cheek.

"Not very ardent," she said. "Tired? It doesn't take much to exhaust you! Have you aged all that much?"

"No. You're the one who has aged—I find I don't like you as much as I used to," Boniface said, with a cold smile.

Cleopatra turned pale but did not dare hit back: she needed him. A third, perhaps half, of her fortune was at stake.

"Charming as ever!" she said, with a mirthless laugh. "Well, I must be going. I like you as much as before, anyway. . . . Au revoir, my sweet! And don't forget Dobrunu."

"I forget nothing," Boniface said. Cleopatra in the act of opening the door, stopped abruptly. "What do you mean?"

"That I forget nothing," Boniface repeated.

Once again her face lost color. "What? You mean that money business?"

"For one thing."

"And just for that, and after having made love to me, you're going to refuse to defend Dobrunu?"

"Exactly," Boniface replied. He rang the bell. Cleopatra had turned livid. She stared at him out of her great dark eyes.

"You cur!" she said.

"Go and —— yourself," Boniface returned coolly, as Alexander Lascari entered.

"Show this lady out. My respects, madame."

Boniface sat down at his desk and lit a cigarette. When Alexander came back he looked up and said, "The telegrams." Lascari went out again, to return with a stout file of papers. Boniface began flipping over the telegrams, his eyes lingering for a moment on

a phrase here and there: *"At Vidra peasants have risen again . . .
some soldiers wounded . . . At Prundu, Monsieur Bellu's estate
villagers revolted . . . have ordered troops to fire signed Captain
Georgiu . . . Heresti peasants risen claiming bailiff violated several girls . . . Eight agitators arrested one mortally wounded . . .
At Comana rebels demanding farmers distribute maize on grounds
starvation . . . Village near Prundu in revolt. Lieutenant Fulga
seriously mauled . . . Sixth infantry regiment fraternizing peasants . . . Captain Bratu prisoner of rebels at Gradistea . . . One
soldier dead on way brought back in cart another seriously
wounded."*

Boniface returned the file to his nephew. "Alexander, make a
note of this. First a letter to Monsieur Marghiloman, asking that
the reservists who deserted Captain Bratu at Gradistea be court-
martialed; thanks and the usual amiabilities. Telegraph orders to
the officers commanding troops sent into the villages: they're to
call for order three times in quick succession and then shoot—
ruthlessly. A dispatch to Colonel Lahovary, asking him to send a
platoon of cavalry to Leski on Prince Cantacuzene's estates. Find
out who's at Foscani, and see that he takes care of old Marghiloman's property."

He went on talking calmly and clearly, bearing in mind the
interests of every influential member of his party, and those of his
friends and acquaintances, not forgetting the Lascari estates and
those of his father-in-law, Prince Mavromihali. Late at night a
secretary reported with the latest telegrams from prefects in the
disturbed parts of the country. One of the first Boniface looked at
read: *"Dobrunu estate belonging to Monsieur Walter Apostolesco
devastated stop peasants have shared land and started plowing stop
send troops otherwise impossible restore order."* Coziano put this
message on one side. He remembered Dobrunu village—the heat,
the dust, the poplars, a field which gave off a scent of aromatic
herbs, wells dried up by the burning heat of the sun, a dead peasant, and the man who sighed when they struck him, and Eustace's
body under those great bunches of lilies with a handkerchief over

his face. *They'll have to be destroyed,* he thought; *hamstrung and broken so that they dare not move.*

"Telegram to the Prefect at N——: the rising at Dobrunu is to be put down with the utmost rigor. Send a request to the Minister of War for a squadron of cavalry to be sent there at once—but on no account men recruited locally. When you've done that, go and find Monsieur Walter Apostolesco—you'll find him at the Grand Hotel or at Broft's. Show him a copy of this telegram, express my regret, and say that I have given orders to deal with the peasants. He's lost a few thousand louis, but at least in future he'll be able to farm his land in peace." And Boniface thought, *That's one I've mastered—not counting the peasants!* But his own masters were still undislodged.

In due course he had the satisfaction of becoming Mme Ascherliu's lover, as, indeed, he had expected since their first meeting. This pleasure, devoid of surprise, could do nothing, of course, to appease Boniface's devouring pride. At about the same time the King received in audience those ministers who had directed what the *Official Gazette* called "the pacification of villages instigated to revolt by unknown agitators." All night Boniface thought of nothing but the moment when, face to face with the King, he would offer him only two fingers. He was still thinking of it as he climbed the palace steps. *Nobody will know, except himself. There'll be nothing he can do but swallow the insult and hold his tongue. He will not be able to protest, or even mention it to a soul. But it goes without saying that he'll never forget it and never forgive me. When the old man, or some other prime minister, goes to see him with a list of names for a new government, he'll demand that my name be crossed out. Or rather, no: he'll play his hand secretly. Only if I become the Party leader, he'll refuse to deal with me and he'll deliberately call on somebody else to form a government. It will be known that I am not* persona grata *at court. Not having the King's confidence, I shall lose the Party's. . . . And I shall be left isolated, without the slightest hope of ever returning to office. Good God, what ought I to do? Must I, out of prudence, counte-*

nance this German's insolence? Lick his boots like that white-haired old vermin? No. Never! To the devil with the lot of them! I'd rather retire to the country and have nothing to do with this vile political jiggery-pokery. I've had enough of their politics! All I want is to keep my self-respect and my honor!

It was with a feeling of impotent hatred that Boniface watched the German offering the others his hand with an expression of icy haughtiness, not even bowing his head, but looking down on them as they bent double before him. And they called themselves bo-yars!

In his heavy German accent the King said, "Gut tay, Monsieur Coziano." His voice was quite benevolent—he had appreciated the firm and implacable way in which the rising had been suppressed. And he held out two fingers—the middle and index. With a humming in his ears and jaws clenched, Boniface Coziano felt his vocal cords knotting themselves and a cold sweat breaking out all over his body. He wanted to snarl and strike the German in the face, hard enough to break all his teeth. Making a gigantic effort, he started to offer the King two fingers; but as his hand went out the muscles relaxed, as if under the influence of some mysterious power stronger than his own will. And it was with his whole widely open hand that he pressed the King's two fingers, where-upon the King passed on, indifferent, to the next man.

8

The great statesman, eloquent debater, and leader of the Conserva-tive Party was in 1898 a man whose hair was almost white and who stood on the threshold of old age. His body had thickened, the hair on top of his head was sparse, his pale cheeks had become rather jowly, the skin of his hands wrinkled and marked with small brown freckles.

These same hands—the left embellished with a signet ring—were at the moment holding playing cards: Boniface and another elderly gentleman were sitting down to a rubber with two young ladies. The walls of the room they sat in were paneled with fumed oak. Suits of armor in polished gray metal stood in the corners of the room. The walls were decorated with antlers, boars' tusks, and stuffed bears' heads. Dull, predominantly blue English carpets covered the floor, and on them stood Louis Treize and Louis Quatorze chairs, as impressive as they were uncomfortable. A gramophone was playing in the next room, where the aides-de-camp were dancing with the Crown Princess's ladies in waiting. Princess Marie was talking to Mme Theodoru-Kostaki and Mme Ascherliu. The Princess was sitting in an armchair, knitting. Mme Theodoru-Kostaki had an upright chair; there was a book open on her knees, but she was not reading. Mme Ascherliu sat on a silk-covered pouf, her full skirts spread around her; she was well past thirty and had grown rather stout, but her complexion was as clear as ever. At the card table a curt, surly voice said, "You have played the wrong card, madame."

"What a bear the man is!" Princess Marie said in English, referring to Coziano's rebuke of his partner. "He's very nice, but he's a bear all right. That's why I like him."

"Bears *are* very nice—from a distance," Mme Ascherliu said, laughing. "But only from a distance. Or, of course, stuffed."

"They say the Chamber is terrified of him," the Princess remarked. Mme Theodoru-Kostaki said: "Oh, he's not the only one! There are also Messieurs Carp, Maioresco, Filipesco, Alexander Lahovary—all men of parts. There are a great many besides him."

"I said that the others were afraid of him, my dear. I did not say he was the only one," the Princess explained.

"I am sorry, Your Highness. I did not understand. He certainly seems to be feared."

"And he is not much loved either," Mme Ascherliu added.

"What's come over you this evening?" the Princess said, laughing. "You're quite down on poor Monsieur Coziano. What has he done to you?"

Mme Ascherliu flushed and made a trite answer. A few minutes later, when the Princess asked her to go and find out if there was to be any music that evening, Mme Ascherliu rose gracefully and left the drawing room. The Princess watched her until she disappeared.

"What's the matter with her? Don't tell me that a liaison that has lasted ten years is drawing to an end."

Mme Theodoru-Kostaki seemed embarrassed. She said: "Really? I noticed nothing. . . ."

"Noticed nothing, indeed! Did you ever hear her speak of him like that before? Who is the happy successor? Who is *il patito?*"

The Princess laughed. Mme Theodoru-Kostaki said nothing: she stared into space with an embarrassed expression which made the Princess laugh all the more loudly.

"You're so dreadfully conventional. You'll make me die of laughing!"

"It is impossible to play cards in this fashion," Boniface Coziano exclaimed. The four card players rose from their table. Coziano walked away from the others and, alone, hands in pockets and cigarette between his lips, went to watch the young people dance. Seeing him go past, the Princess observed, "If he were younger, he wouldn't be bad."

"But he's always so surly and morose," Mme Theodoru-Kostaki protested. "I can well understand that Madame Ascherliu . . ."

"What do you mean?"

"That she is beginning to find him insufferable," Mme Theodoru-Kostaki murmured. The Princess gave her a look at once questioning and amused, but Mme Theodoru-Kostaki assumed a neutral expression which conveyed quite clearly that she had no intention of pursuing the subject.

"And whom does she find—sufferable—now?" Princess Marie inquired, laughing again.

Boniface Coziano did not even glance their way. The Crown

Prince meant little to him: he was too old to become his prime minister. As for the Princess, she considered him too old to be her lover. Besides, he wouldn't want to sleep with her. He was no gypsy groom to be summoned to her bedroom when the lady felt that way inclined. He cared for nobody. He was bored, discontented, and chronically angry. Without any exact cause, he had been in that state for years. He himself no longer knew how many scores, hundreds, thousands of reasons for discontent and rage had accumulated in his heart, memory, nerves, flesh—in every organ of his body. *I have accomplished nothing. I always have masters to serve. I am forced to do things I don't want to do. I am a servant to Ienake and to the Hohenzollern family. An old servant whom everyone is beginning to be sick of. . . . I'm not liked, I'm hated. They've had enough of me; they'd like to see me dead. But I'm not dead. I'll show you I'm alive for a little while yet. You haven't heard the last of me, not by a long shot!*

A little while later Boniface went to his own room to drink brandy. In this house (the guesthouse of the Crown Prince's Smaia residence) he occupied a room painted in white, very tidy, and full of light, where he was just as bored as he was everywhere else. He drank brandy and smoked. Little by little a pleasant warmth took possession of his cold and weary body. *Poor Constantina, how right she was,* he thought, smiling sadly. (Constantina had died of a liver complaint in 1894.) *It's the only thing to do—make life tolerable even by artificial means. There's drink, and there's women.*

Boniface put on patent-leather slippers and changed his dinner jacket for one of soft chamois leather which he used when he went shooting. He went down the stairs and out onto a gravel path which led to the château of Pelisor. The May night was cool and the dark pine trees on the face of the hill shivered in a light breeze. *Fortunately, I have this woman in my life, at least. What a delicious creature!* And he dwelt with delight on Mme Ascherliu's charms, and on the exquisite skill with which she understood how to yield them, and of their innumerable assignations in the course of the past ten years. *A pity her ass of a husband hasn't the good taste to die, for I'd marry her willingly, and ensure myself a happy*

*old age—at least from that point of view, because as for the
rest . . .*

He entered the château by a side door and went along a dimly
lit corridor, opened the door of Mme Ascherliu's room without
knocking, and shut and locked the door behind him.

Ferdinand von Hohenzollern, the Crown Prince, who was to succeed Carol I on the throne, was at this period a rather shy man
with a small, pointed beard. He had a big nose and the long, ugly
ears of a degenerate. But he was the Crown Prince and future King,
sufficient reason for a number of ladies to consider him handsome.

That same night he put on a dressing gown, slipped furtively
out of his room, walked the length of two corridors, and up some
stairs to knock gently on Mme Ascherliu's door. He had been
courting the lady for several weeks.

There was no answer to his knock, and he repeated it rather
more loudly.

"Who's there?" came the startled voice of Mme Ascherliu from
the other side of the door.

"This is Ferdinand, darling. Open the door!" the Prince murmured, his voice choked by excitement.

"And this is Coziano!" came a man's rough, hard, brutal voice
from inside the room. Whereupon the Prince departed swiftly,
silently, without lingering.

Meanwhile, in Mme Ascherliu's bed, Boniface was muttering
curses in French and Rumanian. His hatred of the Hohenzollerns,
his masters, burst out of him in obscene insults. Mme Ascherliu,
huddled beneath the sheets, lay trembling in terror.

"And what about you? Have you been encouraging that miserable creature? What have you arranged with him? Have you
agreed to meet?" Coziano demanded in such a tone that Mme
Ascherliu began to cry.

"And stop sniveling, or I'll hit you!" Boniface said. The general's lady hastily swallowed her tears and set about proving that
she had not expected the Prince, that he persisted in pressing his
attentions on her, which she as persistently rejected: that it was he,

Boniface, whom she had arranged to receive in her room that night, and that obviously she would not have arranged to receive the Prince as well, since after all she was not completely out of her mind, and so on.

With hair disheveled and a scowl on his face, Boniface sat on the bed, saying nothing, but thinking, *She's lying. It's all over and there's nothing to be done.* Mme Ascherliu had never, it was true, given him anything but the basest kind of pleasure; but Boniface had never known any other. The general's lady was still talking, trying to confound him with excuses, explanations, vows, and lies. Could she not see that it was not necessary? Boniface shut her mouth with a kiss and took her in his arms. Mme Ascherliu abandoned her body to him, passively: Boniface was beginning to disgust her.

Some months later, during an argument which occurred at the Conservative Party Club, Boniface heard his sentence pronounced. It was on a fine afternoon in early autumn: the chestnut trees had turned a dusty yellow and the sky was a delicate pale blue. Well-dressed women and carriages drawn by well-fed, glossy horses passed back and forth along the street below the Club balcony. The day and everything in it seemed calm, warm, and luminous. Only Boniface Coziano was somber. Not one of the Conservative Party leaders seated around the big table was of his opinion. His hands were clasped on the knob of his stick and his chin rested on his hands; he was muttering something under his gray mustache. Suddenly he drew himself up with an energy which petrified the rest.

"Leon Popesco a member of the next Government? What is this wretched country coming to! A Popesco in the Cabinet!"

Two or three gentlemen among the youngest present—they were aged between forty and fifty—laughed. Boniface turned on them with a furious glare.

"If you let Popesco and his kind into the highest places, they will end by overwhelming you. Instead of nipping them in the bud, while it was still possible to do so, we've made terms with them, yielded to them, accepted compromises. One of these days we're going to put a rope around our own necks and hand the end of it to people like Popesco with an invitation to pull."

"But, good heavens," Petre Carp said, "this fellow Popesco is an incomparable orator! He's clever, subtle, widely read—in short, the very man we need. It passes my understanding how you can fail to see it. You're being thoroughly childish."

"My dear fellow, the man is not a boyar. And all this gutter scum will end up on top of you," Coziano retorted. "I say *you* and not *us,* because you're younger than I am. I'm too old to be in that particular danger. It's you they'll wipe the floor with. And so I repeat: no Popesco in the Government."

As he was saying this there was a movement near the door. A note was passed from hand to hand, and Marghiloman delivered it to Coziano, who said, "Excuse me for a moment," and left the room.

A man with a big mustache, a paunch, a pointed nose, a lipless mouth, and small, round, piercing eyes was waiting for him at the foot of the staircase. He was quietly dressed in a lounge suit, with a bowler hat and a cherrywood stick.

"My respects, Excellency," he said discreetly. Boniface inquired, "Well?" They were alone, standing near the staircase. Nevertheless, the man kept his voice low.

"I now know who it is who calls on the lady," he said, and lowering his voice still more, added, "It's the Crown Prince."

"Very well. Thank you. Call at my house tomorrow morning." With that Boniface returned to the conference room, entering as a voice was saying ". . . a case of the old lion trying to stop the young eagle from soaring." *So that's why she can't bear me any more,* he was thinking. *She's had enough. She prefers that wretched minus habens. A poor devil who'd die of starvation as a clerk in some provincial municipal office if he didn't happen to be heir to the throne. She's left me, thrown me out like a bit of rag. Why give herself to a groom when the King's son wants her?*

Aloud he said, "What! Him an eagle? No, gentlemen, he's no

eagle: he's a woodpecker. And a woodpecker doesn't soar: it climbs!"

Alexander Lahovary laughed until the tears came, and the rest did likewise. Only Boniface did not laugh. He was mad with rage. Prince Ghica, laughing like the rest, said, "All right, agreed! We won't have him in the Government."

And that was that. The spectacular rise of the tradesman's son, the great lawyer, the incomparable Parliamentary orator, the Conservative deputy Leon Popesco, had been checked—at least for the time being. But Boniface stared into vacancy, and his face was sad; he was not thinking of Leon Popesco.

Events, however, forced him to think of the man. Leon Popesco's career was not to be broken so easily. His constituents called him "Leon Golden-tongue." Prince Ghica said: "We need fresh blood in our old veins," and Alexander Lahovary: "Their time has come and we can save ourselves only by making use of them." As for Leon Popesco himself, refined, elegant, the affable smile half hidden by a fair and silky mustache, he kept the Party meeting under his spell by the suave gestures of his white hands as he assured them: "We need a new conception of our role, gentlemen, a modern doctrine which will enable the Conservative Party to win all hearts. We should follow England's example, where civilization has progressed so far that servants eat at their master's table!"

Coziano, like an angry bulldog, was on his feet in a moment. "I never saw anything of the kind when I was in England. In all the houses where I was entertained the servants stood behind their masters and poured wine into the glasses. What sort of houses did you stay in?"

In the midst of the storm of laughter which convulsed the meeting, Leon Popesco continued to smile politely, undisturbed, until he was able to continue his speech. Speaking low, Boniface Coziano said to his neighbors, "Real middle-class. Ridicule doesn't even wound him."

It was a fact that Leon Popesco was not touched by ridicule. One day, some time after this incident, when Boniface happened to be a guest in the house of some political friends, he came face to face with Leon Popesco, who bowed deferentially. The chandelier hanging from the ceiling threw a strong light on his fair hair, already thinning on the top.

"Although you don't like me, for my part I am one of your greatest admirers," Popesco said, with a charming smile.

Looking at him, Boniface thought, *I am disarmed. I cannot uproot this weed. I have no means of preventing others from adulating him and pushing him on. They don't listen to me and they don't obey me. But my hand is my own to do with as I please. I am not going to offer it to this manikin who has the impertinence to be stronger than I am. No, I shall not give him my hand!* Meanwhile, Popesco was saying, "Monsieur Coziano, why will you not believe in my sincerity?" His voice was sad and even affectionate. Boniface felt a violent impulse to slap his face.

"Come along, my dear fellow, give him your hand," exclaimed old Marghiloman, propelling Boniface forward by the shoulders. "You must forgive him, for he thinks the world of you and esteems you highly."

"Monsieur Coziano," exclaimed Leon Popesco, holding out both hands with a smile of genuine feeling.

And for the second time in the course of his political career the old leader's hand, governed by some mysterious force, opened and offered itself to the man before him.

What am I doing? What's happening to me? Boniface thought, surprised and weary, mortally weary.

Thenceforth Boniface Coziano gave absolutely free rein to his real nature, for so long held captive deep within himself. He was now an old man with bowed shoulders. Of the man he had been nothing remained but the voice, harsh and abrupt, whose once-famous sallies had now become mere demented outbursts. The crowded, stifling Chamber, thick with cigar smoke, shook to his listeners' laughter when the great Boniface Coziano tore an opponent into shreds and trampled on the remnants. The negotiations which the plenipotentiary Mihail Leordeano was conducting in

Paris seemed to Boniface rather too timid; the old man bawled furiously, "To that pitiful individual in Paris who sits on the edge of his chair instead of banging on the Frenchmen's table I send from this tribune a box on the ears!"

When the Conservative Party committee met to elect a vice-president of the Party and Leon Popesco's name was put forward, the young orator gave thanks in a speech which was sentimental almost to the point of tears. The old man's brutal voice rose in a savage bark: "Crocodile tears!" There was a sputter of laughter. But the speaker went on: "I cannot accept the great honor which you have offered me; there are others, older men, better-known men, more meritorious——" Boniface Coziano's voice was raised again: "There certainly are. But I advise you to accept. Otherwise I'll take you by the seat of your trousers and chuck you out on your ear!"

Shocked but amused, the Party leaders laughed. Leon Popesco smiled gently. But the old man had resumed his seat, rumbling. "Fellow's a huckster!" he growled, heedless of being overheard. "Crafty as a fox."

The spring came round and it was the tenth of May, the national holiday: drums, trumpets, the rhythmic sound of marching troops, the dull rumble of gun-carriage wheels on the cobbles of the Calea Victoriei—the new name for the Mogosoaïa Bridge; ladies in white and pink dresses, boys and girls in sailor suits fussed over by mothers wearing straw boaters and waving white-gloved hands to the marching soldiers.

With the cold dignity which he maintained in all circumstances the King mounted, took the salute. Beside him was the Crown Prince—long nose, pointed beard, looking like a stuffed Don Quixote. A little to the rear, near the General Staff, Mme Ascherliu sat in her carriage, sunshade in hand. She wore a rose-pink veil and a white dress with a taffeta sash. People standing near pointed her out discreetly. "There's Madame Ascherliu. No, no, over there, look! In that carriage. Ferdinand knows she's there, all right—see him turn his head to look at her? She's beautiful, my dear—lovely as the dawn!"

The big drum sounded the opening notes of the Hussars' own march, and to the dancing rhythm of the music the general commanding the garrison of Bucharest trotted up on a black horse, which shied and reared, startled by the noise. The plume in the general's *képi* trembled and his golden epaulets glittered in the May sunshine. A major of the Hussars broke away from the King's entourage. His hair and mustache were white and he sat his horse easily—almost negligently.

"I say, look—it's Coziano who's going to report."

"What's got into him?"

"Well, he's the Minister for War, you know."

"What uniform's he wearing?"

"He's an officer in the Reserve. Look how he sits that horse! He'll be thrown in a moment!"

"Nonsense, that shows how much you know. He's a superb horseman! And look at the horse he's riding!"

A gray mare, a nervous thoroughbred, carried Boniface as if he were a feather. The statesman's aged hands held the reins firmly, and his shrunken old thighs seemed glued to the animal's flanks. The mare was trying to rear, but he mastered her, turned her in her own length, put her into a gallop, then pulled her up short, without fuss, in front of the King and reported the troops present. The King saluted with two fingers raised to his *képi*. Boniface, with knees and a touch of the spur, brought the mare around behind the King and the Crown Prince. Turning his head slightly, he saw Mme Ascherliu not five paces away. His surly grimace became more pronounced; he scowled, and with his head bowed to look down on her, snarled, "Take yourself off, you whore!"

Then he turned his horse and saluted the colors of the Officer Cadet Corps who were opening the march past. The fanfare of the trumpets had not drowned Boniface's voice. On the following day all Bucharest was talking of Boniface Coziano's latest outrage. Prince Ferdinand pretended to know nothing about it. And Boniface himself soon forgot it. He was beginning to forget things very easily now; his mind was no longer as alert as it had once been. He no longer knew how to avoid boredom. He drank alone, in his own room. But it did no good. He hated to be alone; he remembered the woman he still loved, the woman who had consumed the last ardor of his frozen body. To avoid remaining alone in his house he developed a taste for the theater.

9

Lenora Popovici was the best known among the younger actresses, a fame she owed less to her talent than to her majestic beauty. She was seated at her dressing table, removing her make-up. Her corsets had been unlaced and gaped open at the back. The hem of the white velvet gown in which she had been playing the Lady of the Camellias was trailing in the dirt on the floor of the small dressing room, which smelled of face powder, sweat, and stale air. The actress's rounded arms had a slow grace as she tied or untied laces and ribbons. She could hear, outside the door, the voices of actors changing costume, the shouts of scene-shifters at their work, the creak and grind of heavy objects being moved. At her door a number of gentlemen stood chatting. They wore trousers turned up at the bottom, like cuffs, a new fashion started the previous summer at Brighton by the Prince of Wales in an effort to avoid getting the bottoms of his trouser legs wet on the beach; it had been adopted by men of fashion in Bucharest during the following winter.

Lenora did not listen to the conversations; she was tired, hungry, and sleepy. She was a woman of twenty-seven, healthy and strong, and incapable of appreciating even the indifferent wit of the gentlemen who were waiting to take her to Capsa's for supper. She neither knew nor cared whether these admirers were the ones who usually assembled at her door: they were probably Michael Vorvoreano, a retired colonel and the most depraved of them all;

Nico Prodan, a clever and eccentric journalist; two young deputies whose names she had forgotten; the actor Piu Iordakesco; and Bébé Ioanid, the young symbolist poet. Any others besides? One might be absent; or they might have brought a new recruit to be introduced to her. They were talking and laughing together. Suddenly a voice said quickly: "Hush! Look!"

There followed a moment's silence. Lenora was much too busy —she was still removing her make-up and dreaming of an underdone steak and a bottle of champagne—to turn toward her visitors. But the silence was so prolonged that at last she looked over her shoulder to see what was happening. A short, gray-haired, elderly gentleman whose mouth seemed drawn into a grimace of disgust under his heavy mustache was standing in the doorway, his gray eyes fixed on her. In one hand he held a silk hat, kid gloves, and a silver-knobbed ebony stick; with the other he was offering Lenora a bouquet of Crimson Glory roses.

"Good evening, mademoiselle. I should like to thank you for a delightful performance. Will you accept these flowers and allow me to call and pay my respects at your house when you are not so fatigued?"

He handed the flowers to the actress with a very slight smile, malicious, ironical, hardly suited to a man of his age. But the smile vanished almost at once. Mechanically Lenora took the flowers and thanked her visitor with a glance of her green eyes from under the long lashes which fluttered like the wings of a black butterfly. The short gentleman bowed and walked out, putting on his hat as he did so. While Lenora was looking at the flowers, an object fell out of the bouquet onto her lap. It was a little parcel which had been wedged among the roses. She began to undo it, just as the gentlemen who had been waiting for her came into her dressing room.

"Well, are you ready? Come on, my sweet, we're all going to drink your health. You've caught the eye of the great man himself! You've hooked him—the old swine!"

Disturbed and curious, Lenora said, "But who? Who is he?"

"What! You don't know him? It's Boniface Coziano!"

"Him?" she said. She undid the little package and found a jewel box. She opened it to reveal a magnificent solitaire diamond set in a ring. Swiftly she closed her hand on it; then, thinking again, told herself, *To the devil with them! Let them see it! Why not?* She slipped the ring on her finger: it was a little too big for her.

"Oh, look at that! It's all over, friends, Lenora has deserted us! Our congratulations, sweetheart, and good luck. Try not to forget us."

She remained silent, staring at the diamond, then moving her hand a little to set it glowing and flashing. A smile of satisfaction tinged with anxiety touched her lips. She had not liked the old gentleman's strange expression. And yet . . .

"Which of you knows anything about precious stones?" she asked without taking her eyes off the diamond. "Is it six carats?"

Lenora received the old statesman at her house the next day. She was his mistress for three years, with the full knowledge of the whole of Bucharest. In the course of this affair she bought a house, a carriage, horses, valuable furniture; and she was given whatever parts she chose to play.

During this same period of three years Boniface fought his last political battles. He quarreled with most of the Conservative Party leaders, who could no longer put up with his arrogance and eccentricities. He made speeches to his electors which were all but incredible, for he spoke like a democrat and an enemy of the boyars. Buttoned tightly into his frock coat and raising a clenched hand on which gleamed his signet ring, he would shout, "I would a thousand times rather the sheepskin cap of a peasant from the valley of the Zlatistea than the coiffure of a Marghiloman who parts his hair from front to nape and has his shirts laundered in London! Is that what our country needs? No! It needs universal suffrage! It needs the overthrow of the boyars!"

The journalists looked at each other and said in low voices, "He's out of his mind! This is the end of everything!"

But at the Conservative Party Club Leon Popesco was much edified. With his customary benevolent smile, he said, "Gentleman, Boniface Coziano always wanted to pull down the moon.

But the moon remains hanging in the sky. So now he can only bay the moon!"

It was the first time anyone had made fun of Boniface Coziano. When a new government had to be formed, neither Marghiloman nor Filipesco considered giving him office. He had been a minister in every Conservative government for the past twenty years. Henceforth he would be a minister no more. Everyone knew it. He knew it himself. Boniface Coziano was finished.

"What do I care?" he said one day when he was lunching at Lenora Popovici's with a few friends. "Now, at least, I have the right to enjoy life. I am free! The whole world is mine!"

He got drunk, like a young man. And, also like a young man, he was jealous; moreover, he could not be imposed upon. And Lenora Popovici did not much like it.

One morning at about eleven o'clock Boniface, who had passed a sleepless night and was bored with his own company, called for his carriage and drove to Lenora Popovici's house in Strada Polona. It was springtime, it had been raining, and yellowish-gray clouds drifted threateningly across the blue sky. But it was impossible to take them seriously: the sky was too blue, the sun too bright, the green of new foliage too fresh. The rain-washed pavements, the limpid air, the people going about their business, the children noisily at play—all was clean, smiling, full of life. It was a pleasure to be alive. A man felt himself rejuvenated by such a day, and all his hopes seemed justified. Naturally Boniface knew that all this was an illusion, but, lulled by the supple springs of his carriage, he let himself fall into a pleasant daydream.

The horses stopped outside Lenora's house. The footman jumped down from the box and hastened to help Boniface out. Boniface told him rudely to stand aside and got out of the carriage unaided, a thing he had not done for some time. He went up the steps to the door and rang the bell. The housemaid who opened the door remained standing in the doorway, saying, "Madam is not at home, sir."

Boniface looked at her, noticed her frightened eyes and flushed cheeks. He thrust her aside with his stick and went in. There was a *képi* hanging on the hatstand in the hall.

"Tell her to come here!"

Terrified, the housemaid vanished. Lenora appeared five minutes later in a lace negligee—tall, splendid, and furious.

"What's all this? Disturbing people in this fashion! You've become unbearable! You'll oblige me by changing your tune."

She spoke brutally. Nobody had ever dared use such a tone to Boniface Coziano for more than sixty years. But Lenora, sure of herself, massive, her generous bosom outthrust, went on scolding him insolently. The old man blenched. His eyes disappeared into their sockets. With a trembling hand he raised his stick.

"Don't you try that!" Lenora shouted. "If you do, I'll send you sprawling. Come on, now, out of here, you old dodderer! You're in your second childhood. It's not a woman you need, it's a nurse! A wet nurse! And diapers!"

Boniface Coziano covered his eyes with his hand and made his way out of the house as quickly as he could, but Lenora followed him to the door, treating him to other remarks even more unflattering. He climbed painfully into his carriage, groaning, helped by the footman. He was humiliated as he had never been in the whole course of his life. He gnawed his fists and wept softly over his own decline.

10

Some days later Lenora was invited to call on one of the directors of the Agricultural Credit Bank. She dressed for the occasion in a white blouse with a collar, and a navy-blue suit. She wore a sapphire brooch and carried a little sunshade.

The director was one of Boniface Coziano's nephews. His name was Sherban Lascari and he was the younger brother of Alexander Lascari, Coziano's former *chef de cabinet.* Sherban Lascari was squat and had a short brown beard; although he was barely thirty, he had an incipient paunch. He received the actress very coldly, bowing politely but not showing the slightest inclination to take her hand. Without a word, he waved her to a chair.

"Madame," he said, "your account with us is overdrawn to the extent of two hundred and seventy-four thousand, nine hundred and eight francs, and the Bank would like to know when and how you propose to cover this amount."

He regarded her with cold imperturbability. Lenora, gaping, asked him to repeat what he had said so that she could be sure of understanding it, and only when he had done so did she ask him to explain. Her expression changed as she listened to him, and she said, "But I don't understand, monsieur. That money was paid to me by Monsieur Coziano. Why ask me for it? You'll have to argue about it with him!"

Sherban Lascari studied the actress with hostile satisfaction. He wore a suit the color of *café au lait* and an olive-green tie, and kept swinging his monocle around one finger at the end of its silk cord. He had Lascar Lascari's puffy cheeks, prominent eyes, and permanently wet lips. He was neither handsome nor attractive, and Lenora was beginning to look on him with hatred and disgust.

With a cold smile he said, "Monsieur Boniface Coziano is a member of our Board of Directors. He asked us to let you have whatever money you asked for. This request was, of course, made verbally. But he said nothing to us about covering your debt."

That took her breath away. When she recovered it she flung at him, "The dirty old carrion!"

"I must ask you to moderate your language, dear lady," Sherban Lascari said with contemptuous politeness. "I have the honor to be one of Monsieur Coziano's kinsmen, and I cannot allow——"

"That's nothing to boast about!" Lenora Popovici interrupted.

"Considering the nature of your trade," Lascari said pleasantly, "I cannot help wondering whether you are entitled to judge other people."

"I'll scratch your eyes out, you dirty little boyar's brat! You——" She went on for a good two minutes. Lascari rang his bell, and when his clerk arrived, said, "Have this person removed."

"No need. I'm going anyway," Lenora said, taking up the hem of her skirt so that she could walk more quickly. Whereupon she resumed her seat, her expression changing to one of childish consternation, and asked, "What's to become of me?"

"That is not my business. You will be issued with a writ, and your property and income seized until the debt has been paid."

"But what should I do? Put yourself in my place; what ought I to do?"

There was a moment's silence. The clerk was still standing by the door. Sherban Lascari turned to him and said, "You can go, Nicolai. I shan't need you."

Alone with Lenora, he said, "Perhaps if you were to appeal to Monsieur Coziano . . ."

"What!" she said, and looked so genuinely horrified at the mere idea that Lascari laughed.

"It is never wise to burn one's boats. Especially when it means breaking with people of influence."

Lenora looked at him with an expression of complete stupidity. Sherban Lascari could see nothing in the least seductive about her. "Silly and fat" was how he assessed her. Resuming his distant manner, he rose, saying, "Au revoir, madame." And he stood there waiting, ostentatiously, for her to go.

Boniface was at home; he had not left his house since his last call on Lenora Popovici. He was sitting in an armchair, smoking, with a bottle of port in front of him on a small table. His hand was shaky. Sherban Lascari had been to see him and had told him everything. Now Boniface was waiting. He was certain that Lenora would come and ask his pardon. She was not the woman to let her house, carriage, furniture, and horses be taken from her and herself be placed at the mercy of all the jealous gossips of the theatrical world. He began to read, but gave up before the end of the second page. He wandered through empty rooms, going over and over the scene that Lenora had made until he wanted to howl, and

strike, and kill, and die. But all this violent feeling was pent up
inside him; to an outsider he was no more than an old gentleman
walking about his house, knees a little bent, back a little bowed,
groaning and muttering to himself.

At the end of a week of such waiting, his nephew Sherban came
again. They sat facing each other in armchairs, and Sherban said,
"Admirable port, this! Really excellent, Uncle! By the way, we
were finally obliged to bring that woman into court. She'd started
selling her jewels and hiding them. She told Michael, my brother-
in-law, that she'd rather go on the streets than come crawling to
you. Even animals of that species have their pride, it seems. Well,
at least you'll get your money back. Though mind you, *entre nous,*
the proceeding doesn't strike me as being in the best of taste, if
you'll forgive my saying so. . . ."

Boniface Coziano appeared to be turning some private thought
over and over in his mind. Then suddenly, in an unexpectedly
lively tone, he said, "Pour me another glass, please."

I I

Ion the footman stood beside his master.

The old boyar was sitting in an armchair, drinking. For weeks
he had done nothing else. Ion put the old man to bed like a child,
held his head when he was sick, and surrounded him with hot-
water bottles when he lay abed and shivered. Sometimes Ion
would say timidly, "It is not good for the master to drink so
much." And the old man would growl, "Hold your tongue!"

It was a torrid summer day; a burning wind came from outside
whenever a door was opened. Even in the drawing room, with the
curtains drawn, the heat was stifling. Ion could feel the sweat run-

ning down his back and behind his ears. It was weather for sleeping in the shade, wearing nothing but a shirt and drawers, not for
moving about in livery, in shoes and stockings, with a cravat
around your neck. . . . And he had to stand to attention all the
time, just as in the days of his military service when he was on
guard duty. The old man was in a good temper today; that was
something. The heat had put some heart into him.

"I say, Ion, I feel much better now."

What could he say to that? Best keep his mouth shut.

"Go and fetch another glass, Ion. You can drink with me."

"But, sir, it is not . . ."

"Don't argue. Go and fetch a glass!"

Ion went to get a fine crystal glass from a quaint cupboard
whose wood was red and shiny, like copper.

"Come on, I'll pour it myself. Your health, Ion."

"Yours, sir."

"No, no, don't wish me anything, Ion. I have no need of anything."

"Everyone needs health, sir."

"No, nothing. What I need is to be free. To escape from everything. You, you're a brute beast, you think only of your health,
your food, drink, money. Have you drunk that? Swallow it down,
man, and I'll fill your glass. Your health, Ion! Good luck to you!"

"Please God."

"What about you, though? What would you wish for? Supposing you were given a choice, what would you ask for?"

"Well, it would be to get free, sir—no offense intended. That's
what I'd like."

"So would I," the old man said, laughing. The footman gave
the impression of being honest and decent. *Anyone would think
I was seeing him for the first time,* Boniface thought. He felt drawn
toward Ion, almost affectionate. Without losing his poise, the footman persisted: "To get free, sir, to leave your service, that's what
I'd like. And then get a bit of land, perhaps, on the banks of the
Zlatistea, and then . . ."

The old man's voice cut in. "What's all this? Free you? Do you think I'm going to let you go? Don't deceive yourself. Stupid lout!"

Boniface had half risen from his chair. Startled, Ion stepped back a pace. *There, now I've done it,* he thought. *Said too much again! The clout I'd get if he still had the strength!*

But the boyar fell back into his chair, and in a strange, surprised voice, like a man talking to himself in a place where he is all alone, said, "The devil! What's happening?"

He stared into space. Then he muttered a few more words, but Ion could not understand his mumbling. Boniface leaned forward, his chin resting on his chest, his eyes, half closed, staring at the carpet.

"Sir," the footman said, frightened. He pushed Boniface gently with one hand, to set him straight on his chair, but the old man had suddenly become very heavy and fell forward again.

"Sir!"

Only then did Ion perceive that his eyes were absolutely fixed.

"He's dying!" Ion shouted, and rushed out of the room to call the other servants.

12

The Conservative Party newspapers, bordered in black, carried the portrait of the deceased. In the empty house members of the family, the Lascaris and Eustace Coziano's children, received the condolences of every politician of consequence in both political parties. The King's condolences were conveyed by General Warthiadi, officer commanding the Household troops. An enormous hearse with large windows, its black canopy supported at the four corners by silver angels, its horses caparisoned in black trappings

with black ostrich-feather plumes, bore the mortal remains of
Boniface Coziano to his last resting place. Behind the hearse came
the family in deep mourning, then Alexander Marghiloman, Petre
Carp, Leon Popesco, Nico Filipesco, and all the leading politicians
of the Conservative Party. Following them came deputies, senators,
big landowners, businessmen, high-ranking army officers, a long
line of carriages, and finally a platoon of the Hussars, in which
regiment Boniface had served as a major in the Reserve.

It was hot; appallingly hot. The mourners sweated, and inhaled
a torrid, dusty air. One person in the funeral procession fainted and
was taken into a neighboring pharmacy. The pavements were
crowded with people who had assembled to watch the funeral pass
and were pointing out to one another the rich and mighty who
walked behind the hearse.

At the marble tomb in the cemetery the Minister of Justice, Leon
Popesco, looking very pale, climbed onto a big stone and addressed
himself to the shrunken, livid, emaciated man who slept there in
his coffin, face to the heavens, scowling a little as if making an
effort to keep his eyes closed.* The dead man's brow was seen to
be sweating. A fly wandered between the drops, then came to rest
on one of the now purplish eyelids. A second fly flew toward the
first, covered her, and they both took off again. Leon Popesco had
tears in his eyes and his voice shook.

"We can add nothing to your name. For you the words we
speak today no longer count. For us they are of enormous import.
We can indeed say that whereas nothing is wanting to your glory,
you are wanting to ours. You have entered into immortality, having known all the intoxication and all the bitterness of fame. Your
memory will always remain as an example and an instruction
for . . ."

He was forced to pause, his voice broken by sobs. Marghiloman
was dabbing at the corners of his eyes with a white handkerchief.
Nico Filipesco, his eyes drowned in tears, kept swallowing con-

* It is customary in Rumania to take off the lid of a coffin during the
ceremony preceding burial.

vulsively. The ladies of the family, the dead man's nieces, wept and sighed.

The coffin was closed and carried into the tomb, whose iron door was closed and locked. And each mourner turned to go home.

PART FIVE

A Pleasure Trip

I

At about eleven o'clock on a spring morning in the first years of the twentieth century, one of Davida's sons-in-law, Colonel Vorvoreano, was making his way to a brothel. Vorvoreano was a fat, broad-shouldered man, with the bandy legs of a cavalryman. He was in mufti—black jacket, striped trousers, elastic-sided boots, stiff collar. A monocle swung at the end of a moiré ribbon fastened to his lapel. Under the bowler hat centered squarely on his head appeared an insolent and brutal face, with a powerful hooked nose, thin lips, fleshy jowls, and a Kaiser Wilhelm II mustache whose waxed points were turned upward. Vorvoreano strolled idly down the Calea Victoriei with his stick under his arm, raising his hat to the few people of his acquaintance to be met with so early in the morning. He stopped at Capsa's for a glass of rum, and then went on his way with his nose in the air and his bowler tipped forward over his eyes. A slight grimace of disgust curled his upper lip. After more than forty years of existence, to be reduced to waiting on fortune like a schoolboy for his pocket money . . . He sniffed noisily, spat, and kept on walking.

The brothel was in one of the alleys off Lipscani Street; its entry exhaled a damp smell of cellars. A very narrow staircase led to the upper floors. A group of men were loitering on the first-floor landing, leaning against the wall, with their hands in their pockets and cigarettes hanging from the corners of their mouths. Three steps higher stood a plump youth wearing a soft hat shoved back to expose a narrow, sweaty forehead; he was looking at the others with an innocent, smiling expression and saying: "So she says to me, she says, 'What for? One more word and I'll go home to Mother at Ploesti.' 'The sooner the better,' I said, 'and we'll just see how fast you come running back again.' " With that the young man laughed, but no one joined in. Nobody paid any attention to him.

Colonel Vorvoreano walked down the same stairs half an hour later, his head held high and his stick under his arm. He was as sullen as he had been when he arrived, and perhaps even more so. *Filth,* he was thinking, *the whole business is just filth. I no longer enjoy anything. I've lost my zest for life. Ah, she's done for me, the bitch! She's destroyed me. Brought me to this.*

When he reached the landing one of the customers of the house, who was waiting his turn, raised his hat and said, "Good morning, Colonel."

"What? Oh, you, is it? Good day to you."

Vorvoreano went down the last steps into the street and stood there for a while, undecided. Where next? Nothing suggested itself. He had no desire to go anywhere in particular and felt completely at a loss. *She's done for me. Crushed me.* He took a leather case from his pocket, selected a cigar, bit off the end, and lit it. The cigar had a vile taste. He threw it away. *I drink a glass, two at most. And pay occasional visits to third-rate brothels. Apart from that I can afford nothing. Not even the most trifling pleasure! Nothing!* Walking slowly, he set off again, very stiff, his head held high, like a man who is independent and sure of himself.

At about noon or one o'clock Colonel Vorvoreano, having read his newspaper, put it down on his worktable—at which, despite its name, he had never done a stroke of work. It was a massive desk in the Henri II style, the fashion for which had been brought from France by the *nouveaux riches* of Moldavia and Wallachia at the same time as the vogue for Bouguereau's pictures and the novels of Georges Ohnet. The Colonel's surroundings were composed of this desk made of some dark wood carved with lions and satyrs, a couple of leather armchairs, shelves of books protected from both dust and curiosity by glass doors which were kept locked, a panoply of cuirass and helmet, a china tobacco jar, and a large frame enclosing some dozens of small oval photographs. These were portraits of Vorvoreano's contemporaries in the army; some of them were now generals, deputies, or senators; others were still colonels, either embittered or retired; one or two had been cashiered.

The Colonel scowled at his newspaper with a disgust which it did not deserve, then rose and walked out of his study into the next room, which was the drawing room. The street was visible between the heavy fringed curtains; ladies passing outside wore short veils on their hats and carried sunshades in bright, cheerful colors. It was spring; the air that night would be full of the scent of lilac. It would be pleasant to dine in an open-air restaurant, a carafe of chilled wine on the table, a singer on one's right, another on one's left. . . . Or how good it would be if one were starting a journey, catching the night train to Paris. Paris—the cafés with their singers bawling popular songs, the *midinettes,* the ballet girls, the gaming tables—ah!

But none of these delights seemed attainable at the moment. Of course they would be sooner or later; everything would become possible so long as Helen inherited her legacy. Vorvoreano had had a legacy himself once, but he had got through it, just as he had got through the legal minimum that Helen had inherited from her father, Lascar Lascari. (Lascari had refused to leave her any more because he disliked Vorvoreano.) The result was that he and Helen had quarreled with her brothers and sisters, who were furious at seeing a part of the family fortune simply thrown away and foresaw that, sooner or later, Helen and her children would become their responsibility. So there was only one thing left to hope for, and that was long in coming.

Shivering with cold, Vorvoreano pulled his dressing gown more closely around him and glanced about the room. What should he do? Read? There was nothing to read. Smoke? He had smoked so many cigars since the morning. Stay where he was, sitting in an armchair, thinking of nothing? But it was impossible to think of nothing. Even when Vorvoreano was thinking of nothing there was one thing—always the same—that forced its way into his mind. He could not contrive to forget it. Standing on the threshold of the drawing room, he hesitated, a prey to the perpetual disgust that was spoiling his whole life.

Suddenly he heard his wife's grandmother talking in the corridor. He was seized with a desire to flee, to withdraw into his study and pretend to be reading, just as in the past he used to pretend to be asleep to escape from the nagging of his governess bent on hearing him say his prayers at bedtime. He overcame the impulse to retreat and stayed where he was. A forced smile stretched the Colonel's thin-lipped mouth a little. He made for the door and opened it. Helen's grandmother—Sophia von Bodman, the erstwhile Sophia Coziano—came in, leaning on her maid's arm and followed by her granddaughter. At the time of her first marriage, when she had been Sherban Vogoride's mistress, there had been more than one man passionately in love with her; they were all dead now, or in their dotage. She herself, at over eighty, was a plump little old woman with three chins, who moved with difficulty. She wore no corsets under her pearl-gray dress—she had given them up twenty years ago. Her fat, withered, brown-spotted hand rested on the silver knob of an ebony stick; priceless lace embellished her dress at neck and wrists. Her hair, dyed a reddish brown, was thin, and her eyes, half hidden by swollen lids, looked like those of a sleepy old toad, making her an object of fear and repulsion. Those eyes, formerly as deep and limpid as the Bosphorus at night, were dulled now, yet their glance was still keen and inquisitive. When she studied a face that was new to her, Sophia used the ivory-handled lorgnette which hung at her waist; and her look, as she did so, was at once critical, sardonic, and indulgent, as if to say, *Yes, you're an ugly creature, stupid and ridiculous. But it doesn't matter; I'm not holding it against you. After all, you're only a human being and I am not such a fool as to expect anything better from you.*

The Colonel pulled his shoulders back and, albeit unwittingly, came to attention, or almost. A nervous, uncertain smile quivered about his lips. Mme Vorvoreano came into the room behind her grandmother. She was a fair, well-built woman with broad shoulders and white, fleshy arms. Her straight, delicate nose, slightly *retroussé* like that of the Crown Princess, straight back, and splendid, Junoesque body conformed to the ideal of beauty in favor at the time. Few women in Bucharest were more admired; and everyone wondered what on earth she could have seen in the man she had married. The reason was doubtless to be sought in one of those secrets of the nuptial chamber which only the two people concerned can understand. At all events, the reason, whatever it might be, was still valid, although Mme Vorvoreano had realized that the first wrinkles and the first gray hairs were making their appearance, and found a tightly laced corset necessary to keep the Grecian bend which fashion and reputation required of her.

The Colonel clicked his heels, even though wearing slippers, saying solicitously, "I kiss your hands, Grandmama. Did you have a good night?"

The old woman, helped by her maid, sat heavily down on a *bergère* which she had brought back from Vienna, a baroque piece which was sumptuous and heavy compared to the French furniture of the same period. She recovered her breath with some difficulty and then looked about her through her lorgnette. "What is the weather like?"

"Splendid," the Colonel replied, all affability. "The spring has arrived."

Mme Vorvoreano signed to the maid to wheel a small table up to the old lady. A second nod sent the maid out of the room, to return with a tray. The old lady focused her lorgnette and examnined the plate with a critical eye. "What is it?" she asked.

Her granddaughter sat down beside her and replied with a careful smile, "Taste it, Grandmama. You'll be thrilled with it. A salad of mushrooms pickled in vinegar. Help yourself."

The old woman's eyes glistened. She began to eat noisily. The Colonel felt sick and was obliged to look elsewhere. He tried to interest himself in the walls of the room, to think of something else . . . but he could hardly stop up his ears. That was the worst of it: if he could have stopped up his ears, it would not have been so dreadful.

"You're not very chatty today," the old woman said. The Colo-

nel started and cleared his throat. But his wife laughed and remarked quite naturally, "What do you expect us to talk about,
Grandmama? I was just thinking that here I am, feeding you as
if I were after your fortune. But you keep marvelously well. Between ourselves, you're a perfect monster of healthiness! Heaven
grant it may always be so!"

The old woman turned to Helen, smiled, and patted her cheek.
"And you, my dear, you have pluck. You get that from me, of
course. Yes, you have pluck. . . ."

She resumed eating. Mme Vorvoreano blinked; apart from that
she gave no sign of being put out. But then, perhaps there was no
reason to be put out. She said, "I've seen that portrait of Monsieur
Santos-Dumont—you know, the man who's experimenting with a
balloon driven by machine—I mean by motor. Would you like to
see it too, Grandmama? He's terribly chic. He's wearing the costume of an aero—aero——"

"Aerostat," the Colonel said.

"No. Aeronaut. His smartness isn't the elegance of a man of
fashion, you know. Rather, the special chic of the inventor. . . .
You know what I mean: no jacket, a shirt with narrow stripes,
tight-fitting trousers, a very high collar, a big fancy necktie fixed
with a black pearl. He's wearing a straw boater with a black
ribbon. Very smart, but it's a sort of quite personal smartness."

"It all sounds ridiculous to me," the old woman said. "Your
new fashions, with tail-freezer jackets, soft hats, and those collars
which look as if they're made of cardboard, not to mention the
women's fashions, which are neither decent nor dignified. And
what's more, your fashions don't even bring out a man's or woman's natural advantages. What has happened to woman's grace-
fulness? What's become of man's virility? You're all grotesque."

After a moment's thought she added, "All the same, I shouldn't
mind going up in a balloon. Ah, you young people don't know
how well off you are! You can get about in trains, balloons,
motorcars, streetcars. In Vienna they've even got telephones in
private houses, which makes it much easier to exchange insults.

Because all this progress doesn't alter human nature in the slightest. Nice beasts!"

Sophia took a small ball of paper out of her pocket and began kneading it methodically in her plump, wrinkled hand.

"You're so young, Grandmama," Mme Vorvoreano said, smiling. "You even want to go up in a balloon."

"Indeed I'm young," the old woman said. She was manifestly proud of herself. "I was the first lady in Vienna to go in one of Herr Benz's automobile machines. An electric carriage. Not like those which make a lot of smoke and noise like a cannonade at the back. Yes, it was electric—no noise, no nasty smell. A wonderful carriage, there's no denying that. Only, for my part every time I see one, it somehow looks funny to me. When I see the boyars sitting in the tonneau, and the coachman and footman on the box, and not even the shadow of a horse, it always seems to me that there's something missing. A carriage without horses and with smoke coming out of the back is ridiculous. But there's nothing to be done about it, I suppose—it's progress! A sign of the times, that's what it is—machinery, anarchists, socialists. When I was a girl the Liberals were called Reds. They weren't like the Liberals you have now; they were always hatching revolutions, just like your nihilists nowadays. Well, Colonel, why aren't you getting dressed? When are we going to have lunch?"

Mme Vorvoreano rushed to the bell rope; the Colonel hastily left to get dressed; the maid came to help the old lady out of her armchair. Mme Vorvoreano ran to order the carriage, and then hurried up to her room to change her dress. The Colonel was standing in front of the looking glass, knotting his tie.

"Won't the old girl ever make up her mind to kick the bucket?" he muttered.

"How can you say such a thing?" Mme Vorvoreano exclaimed, without the slightest indignation. She powdered her face, bit her lips to redden them, smoothed her eyebrows, passed a brush lightly over her hair which was done in a bun on top of her head, pulled down the cuffs of her silk blouse with its lace jabot, and turned again to her husband: "Well? Ready? Hurry up, Grandmama's waiting for us and you know how she hates to be kept waiting."

"God in heaven, won't she ever croak?" the Colonel groaned. Helen Vorvoreano pretended not to hear, tucked a little green sunshade under her arm, and led the way out of the room.

The old woman was not in the drawing room. Mme Vorvoreano went to her grandmother's room. Surrounded by maids, the old lady was busy adjusting her enormous hat, settling her black velvet bolero, and putting on the white gloves which bore witness to her still active coquetry. One day in Rome, about 1895, Helen Vorvoreano had seen the Empress Eugénie, a little old woman all in black, carrying a sunshade and wearing a violet half-mourning veil. Grandmama reminded her of the former Empress, and she could not help admiring her.

Sophia von Bodman rose, and with a key of carved bronze opened a large secretary decorated with arabesques in marquetry. She took out two gold coins bearing the head of Carol I von Hohenzollern and, without a word, gave them to her granddaughter. Helen, likewise silent, put them into her reticule and took her grandmother's arm, while one of the maids supported the old lady on the other side.

Mme Vorvoreano took her seat beside her grandmother in the carriage, and both of them opened their sunshades. The Colonel sat facing them. The coachman cracked his whip, the carriage passed out through the main gateway and into the streets of Bucharest. Passers-by on foot raised their hats. Mme Vorvoreano bowed graciously; the old woman merely returned a quick, bored nod. The Colonel made his acknowledgments with a bow, which caused his fleshy jowls to overlap his starched collar.

At Capsa's everything was as usual, calm and silent. The light in the restaurant was discreetly filtered. The waiters moved unobtrusively from one table to the next, and the conversations at the tables were carried on in low voices. Even the sounds of cutlery on china and of corks being drawn were muted.

The maître d'hôtel hurried toward the newcomers to conduct Mme von Bodman to her usual table. He murmured into the old lady's ear, "Today, madame, we have *tripes à la mode de Caen* and fresh oysters." A gentle smile lit up his eyes. Sophia von Bodman's gloomy expression became suddenly lively and wide-awake.

"We shall see, we shall see," she said, looking around the room through her lorgnette and acknowledging the bows of several gray-haired gentlemen.

Colonel Vorvoreano was dreaming of a large grilled steak and a pint of *pelin*—a white wine in which leaves of artemisia have been steeped. Instead, he was obliged to eat oysters, *tripes à la mode de Caen,* roast beef, *bombe glacée;* and to drink Moselle, Chablis, and a quarter of a bottle of champagne, while listening to the noise of the old woman masticating. Moreover, he was expected to make conversation to amuse her—it was necessary in his own interests. But if he talked—and talk he did, ceaselessly—it was chiefly not to hear her eating. Furthermore, the old woman herself talked: she was fond of conversation, particularly during meals.

"Tell me all the news," she commanded, forgetting to wipe the gravy from the corners of her mouth. "Doesn't it seem to you that nothing ever happens now? Our society here is so boring that upon my word it's enough to put you to sleep. And this war in China? Didn't you tell me yesterday that it was over?"

"All over, Grandmama," the Colonel said, laughing. "Field Marshal von Waldersee has been congratulated by the Kaiser, by Queen Victoria, by President Loubet—in short, by everyone. He has to pull a little cart behind him to carry all his decorations!"

"I believe I met him at court when I was in Berlin, or rather at Potsdam. A narrow-minded soldier," the old woman said. The Colonel checked the retort which he would have liked to make and went on: "The rebels have already been tried and executed. As it happens, I have the magazine here . . ."

He took a copy of *Le Monde Illustré* out of his pocket and offered it to the old lady. There was a picture across two pages, showing, in the background, a Chinese mandarin and a high-ranking European officer under a kind of awning; on the right, the ranks of Chinese in traditional garb; on the left, European marines standing at ease. In the foreground was a Chinese, on his knees and stripped to the waist, with his hands tied behind his back and a ribbon tied below his chin by means of which another Chinese was pulling his head forward while the executioner flourished a broad, massive cleaver. A headless corpse was sprawled in the grass; the head had rolled to the feet of the European soldier who was standing on the right. Colonel Vorvoreano placed the magazine beside the old woman, who, still eating, stared at the picture for a long time. She swallowed her sweet course absently, and a trickle of *crème au chocolat* ran down her chin.

"What did they want to rebel for, the brigands?" she asked. "Eh, Colonel? What do you think?" The Colonel had not the slightest idea, but he plunged into an involved explanation. Mme Vorvoreano said, "Talking of China, have you heard about the new game, Grandmama, that's all the rage in London? Ionas Ipsilanti had just come back from there, and I met him at Aristitza Romano's. He told me about this game. It's called ping-pong."

"Why 'talking of China'?" the old woman said.

"It sounds like a Chinese word."

"So it does—ping-pong," the old woman agreed. "So that's what they call Ionas now, eh? You mean Nicolake Ipsilanti's son, the one who was agent for the Principalities at Constantinople in Prince Couza's time?"

"No, Grandmama, the grandson, not the son. The son was a general and died twenty years ago, while you were in Vienna. The one I'm talking about is the grandson."

"You breed so fast now I can't keep up with you," Sophia von Bodman said with a touch of peevishness. "And why give him such a ridiculous name? It's a clown's name. Ping-pong, indeed! What does it mean?"

"No, no, Grandmama, it's not Ionas who's called ping-pong. It's a fashionable parlor game that's played after dinner. When the table's been cleared the hostess fixes her veil across it like a net, and the players hit a celluloid ball back and forth across it with little rackets. It seems the game was invented by an engineer, a Mr. Gibbs, at his club. He was playing with friends after dinner, using champagne corks instead of balls and cigar-box lids for rackets. That's why it's always played after dinner, in evening dress."

"The world has become utterly absurd. Colonel, ask them what's happened to my coffee. And you can have a cognac or an armagnac," Sophia von Bodman said. "And take this horror away," she added, pushing the illustrated magazine toward him. Vorvoreano rolled it up and put it into his pocket. They began to talk of something else.

At the end of the meal Mme Vorvoreano discreetly slipped the two gold pieces to her husband to settle the bill. The Colonel paid with an expression of indifference and put the change into his pocket. The old woman did not appear to notice.

Leaving Capsa's, the Colonel and his wife took the old woman home; she dozed in the carriage. After helping Mme von Bodman into bed, Mme Vorvoreano changed into a house dress and joined the Colonel, who was sitting in an armchair smoking a cigar.

"How the devil she manages not to peg out with all the food she eats, is beyond me. It makes me bilious, whereas she seems to thrive on it." This from the Colonel.

Helen frowned. "I've told you a thousand times not to talk like that! I can't bear to hear you speak so cynically. You might show some respect for her age. Why can't you let her live out her life? She may not last more than a few days, especially eating the way she does—and you . . ."

"I hope to God she *has* only a few more days to live," the Colonel said bitterly.

His anxiety was perfectly justified; they went to Capsa's again the next day and the day after, and so on, day after day after day. At the time the Colonel was already having trouble with his liver and his stomach. His chronic rage, the rich food eaten with revulsion and digested during fits of furious temper, were taking their toll. The Vorvoreanos set out for Carlsbad—accompanied by the old woman, of course, for without her they would not have had the money necessary for their journey or any other outlays. As was to be expected, the Colonel's health did not improve in consequence. At night he could not get to sleep and for hours on end repeated his refrain: *She's been the ruin of me. . . . She's been the ruin of me.* And then, changing his tune, *I'll kill her! I'll kill her! I shall have to kill her!*

Needless to say, he did nothing of the kind. He waited; and waiting, aged. The old lady seemed immutable. She still insisted on knowing what was happening in the world, the latest news, the most recent rumor. She read the newspapers, enjoyed conversation, insisted on being taken out and about. Certain old gentlemen called on her, and one or two old ladies who had known Prince Couza well at the time when he was Prefect of Galatzi. Mme Vorvoreano grew paler and paler, her eyes sank deeper and deeper into their sockets, and her features hardened. But nothing whatever happened.

2

It was in 1905 or 1906, during dinner at Capsa's, that Helen Vorvoreano said, "I saw Sophia this morning."

"Sophia who?" the old woman asked.

She was beginning to lose her memory, but otherwise there was no change: she was eating hare *à la crème* and drinking Chambertin.

"Sophia who, indeed! My sister, of course."

"Ah! Davida's daughter . . . And so?"

"So nothing. I saw her drive past our windows in her carriage. She didn't even look up."

"How you two sisters love each other!" the old woman murmured after a short silence.

"Sophia is certainly an odd sort of sister—not to mention her family feeling in general!" Helen exclaimed, taking care not to overdo the expression of indignation she was trying to simulate. "At a pinch I can understand her never coming to see me. She's rich, her rogue of a husband's a millionaire. I'm poor and of no interest. But she might at least show a little respect for you, Grandmama, by calling occasionally. No, really, I don't understand her. . . ."

The old lady cast a quick glance at Helen between her heavy, swollen eyelids. "There's nothing to be done about it," she murmured. "She learned that from her mother. Yes, my dear Helen, your mother behaved to me in exactly the same way. It's from her you've inherited your affectionate heart and filial piety. . . ."

With eyes almost closed, she smiled like a Buddha.

"Oh, but excuse me, Grandmama, that's not quite right. *I'm* not like that. Be fair!" Mme Vorvoreano protested, putting on a show of simple good faith and indignation. Their conversation went on in low voices, surrounded by maîtres d'hôtel and waiters moving silently between well-spaced tables occupied by ladies and gentlemen dressed in dark colors, who spoke softly and hardly moved at all.

"I realize that," the old woman said, smiling. "You are different. But the others?"

"The others . . ." Mme Vorvoreano pretended to reflect, and then with accomplished hypocrisy to admit, as if despite herself: "Yes, you're right. The fact is . . . for two years Alexander has not even been back to Bucharest. He's a strange man. He lives quite alone in the country, wandering through the woods, shooting— nobody sees anything of him for weeks at a time. . . . Yes, you are right, Grandmama. They are all like that. Take Sherban, for instance: he's been back in Paris again for a year, and he has not even deigned to send us a letter. Not a single letter! He might at least have written to you. After all, what other relations has he got in the world?"

Helen fell silent. The old lady, who was eating a *gâteau saint-honoré,* did not answer.

"Really, you know," Helen resumed, "the only one who can be pardoned for forgetting you and us is poor Eleonora. . . ."

"What exactly is the matter with her?" Mme von Bodman inquired. "Is she still dotty?"

"The doctors don't really know what's wrong with her. She's aged terribly and is stupider than ever. You can't conceive how feeble-minded she is, Grandmama. And to think she's so rich! I can't imagine what she can do with her money, in her state of idiocy. . . ."

"She has some kind of rheumatism of the brain," Colonel Vorvoreano declared in an ill-natured voice and without raising his eyes from his plate.

The old lady said nothing. She was smacking her lips over the cream from her cake. Mme Vorvoreano went on talking on the same theme. Once or twice a week for years she had raised this topic in her grandmother's presence. Suddenly, apropos of no matter what, she would manage to start talking about her brothers, sisters, or cousins. All Sophia von Bodman's grandchildren, except herself, were heartless wretches, egotists utterly indifferent to their poor old grandmother's lot.

"What shall we do tonight?" Mme von Bodman asked. "What's the matter with you? You've got nothing to say and you bore me to death. Say something, for goodness' sake. Amuse me! We must decide what we're going to do this evening. I should enjoy a theater but there's nothing to see. Bucharest is such a bore. . . . Get tickets for the circus, Colonel."

3

One evening before dinner the old lady said to her granddaughter, "My dear Helen, I have invited Antofilake to dinner. I have some business to settle with him."

They were in the drawing room, and Mme Vorvoreano was

reading one of Paul de Kock's novels to her grandmother. The Colonel was smoking and, with vacant eyes, trying to keep the ash on his cigar as long as possible. When he heard the name Antofilake he turned his head so sharply that the little cylinder of ash fell onto his jacket. His eyes met the old woman's, veiled and inscrutable, which stared at him fixedly. He turned away his head, pretending to be busy brushing the cigar ash from his lapel and trying to believe that the old woman had noticed nothing.

Helen Vorvoreano had not batted an eyelid; confining herself to saying "Good," she had gone on reading.

Alexander Antofilake was one of the ablest men at the Bucharest bar, although not one of that bright Pleiad of legal stars which included such names as Delavranca, Toma Stelian, and Take Ionesco. He was not a politician nor a man of letters nor a great jurist. But Sophia von Bodman, like many people of fashion, preferred his advice to any other lawyer's. Serious, discreet, and conciliatory, Antofilake inspired confidence. And the Vorvoreanos knew that the old woman could have only one reason for summoning him: she was going to make her will. Scores, maybe hundreds of times, they had discussed the moment when this would happen. They were perfectly familiar with the law of succession, having themselves consulted counsel. They knew what share of the old woman's fortune they could expect to receive; for forty years she had been reinvesting the income from her estates and house property in land, even while she was living abroad, that is to say, between 1867 and 1899. Although she had lived for many years in Vienna and traveled all over Europe, she was not ignorant of the fact that land in the Danube plain was going cheaply and that the law, as well as their own necessity, forced the peasants to grow wheat and transport it to silos on the banks of the Danube, where it was loaded into English ships and paid for as if it were worth its weight in gold. Sophia von Bodman had therefore purchased a vast amount of land and then farmed it out. The management of her fortune had been put into the hands of a man of business recommended by Antofilake. The old woman kept the keys of her desk carefully hidden, but the Vorvoreanos knew that its drawers contained a great many papers and very little cash; all the rest was deposited in the cellars of Hillel's Bank.

Helen Vorvoreano went on reading; and the Colonel went on smoking, his hand trembling. Elvira, Sophia von Bodman's great-granddaughter, came into the room, sat down in an armchair, and kept very still and quiet. She was about fifteen at the time, and her hair was dressed in two plaits which hung down her back. She wore a black dress and a white apron edged with lace, a wide Van Dyck collar, and high buttoned boots. Her breasts, which were just beginning to bud, and her thin legs indicated that she had by no means finished growing. Only her face, very dark, her large green, almond-shaped eyes, the curved nose and well-formed mouth, gave promise of beauty in this girl who would, in due course, endeavor to become the uncrowned queen of Rumania. It had been decided that Elvira, accompanied by a governess, was to be sent to an Austrian convent where the Viennese aristocracy and bankers sent their daughters to be educated. Such was Sophia von Bodman's wish: the Vorvoreanos and their daughter would have preferred Switzerland or Paris.

Mme Vorvoreano was still reading. She had allowed herself one furtive glance at her husband. Each was feeling the need to offer the other advice, and to examine the situation to see if there was anything urgent to be done. They were at once anxious and glad. Not until dinnertime did they get a chance to talk. Antofilake arrived, cordial, with an incipient paunch, his hair white and sparse, his skin yellow and smooth like a eunuch's. When he talked each phrase was emphasized by a gesture. Each of his attitudes could have been cast in bronze and added to the statues of gentlemen in metal frock coats which were beginning to populate the open spaces of Bucharest.

Mme Vorvoreano asked after the lawyer's wife and family, twice over. The Colonel, his mind elsewhere, opened his mouth only to put vast quantities of food into it. Antofilake held forth, questioned, answered.

"And our young lady?" he inquired finally.

Elvira flushed, frowned, but made no answer and did not even raise her eyes.

"She is leaving in a week's time for the convent," her great-grandmother said. "When she comes out she'll be an accomplished young lady. Moreover, she'll learn something about life. She'll meet people of all kinds, different from the people here. I knew such people myself and very useful it has been to me. I have more judgment than I had before. You, too, child, will learn to distinguish, among the people you have to deal with, the gentlemen of the lesser nobility who become officers, are poor, and have no carriage. Their wives do their own cooking, and as to servants, they have at most a maid-of-all-work and an orderly. Some of them actually do their own shopping—with their faces carefully veiled so that nobody shall know that they have no servants. Carriage hired by the month, you know, and the Ladies' Circle and the Gentlemen's Evening—revolting! You'll learn to avoid people of that kind. They're stupid and vulgar, and they always claim to have married beneath them when they take a wife from the prosperous middle class—the daughter of a tradesman or small manufacturer.

"You will be able to know the other kind, the real noblemen, who have a house in town and a manor or castle in the country. And then, of course, there are the people who are received at court, speak French well, are related to the English or Spanish aristocracy—people whose names you'll find in your history books. Their daughters are educated at the place where you are going, thanks to my recommendation, and where you will be on the same footing as no matter who——"

"Elvira," Mme Vorvoreano exclaimed suddenly, "what on earth's come over you, girl?"

Elvira blushed but made no answer, and did not even look at her mother.

"Why have you put my gloves on? Whatever possessed you to do such a thing?" Mme Vorvoreano demanded, taken aback. The lawyer's presence had so disturbed her and the effort to hide the excitement which it engendered was so absorbing that until that moment she had not even noticed what Elvira was wearing. Although she was dressed as a schoolgirl, she had put on a pair of gloves so long that they completely covered her thin arms. The right-hand glove was unbuttoned at the wrist; through this opening Elvira had slipped her hand and in that way was eating.

"It was I who told her to wear them," the old lady said. "She is an obedient child. She must learn to keep her gloves on for dancing, and to eat with one hand gloved and the other not. I am going to write to my friend Adelheid von Taxis who used to take charge of girls who were to be presented at the Hofburg, and ask her to teach Elvira to curtsy correctly—the first curtsy barely indicated, the second very low, the third with one knee on the ground, while holding the dress by the fingertips, or else the hands against the dress, palms outward. . . . It's the most graceful thing in the world, and until I've seen you do a curtsy properly, I shan't be easy in my mind. . . ."

Mme von Bodman fell suddenly silent. Antofilake was thinking, *She's beginning to fail—age will tell.* . . . The Vorvoreanos looked at each other, then at the lawyer. Elvira, her eyes lowered, was imagining herself making a deep curtsy, a smile on her lips, knee bent, back erect, head high, at the Hofburg or at Schoenbrunn. And the old woman was remembering that Adelheid von Taxis had died in 1880. No doubt about it, her memory was beginning to desert her. And she caught herself talking, talking on and on until the moment when she lost her train of thought. Yes, the time had certainly come to get Antofilake to do what was necessary: she might not have much longer.

After the meal Sophia von Bodman drank her coffee, sent Elvira to her room, and asked Helen and the Colonel to excuse her: she had business to transact with her lawyer. She took Antofilake to her own room. The Vorvoreanos were left alone, under the gilded bronze gas bracket hanging from the plaster wreaths and garlands of the ceiling. Somber and massive, the Henri II sideboard winked and gleamed mysteriously with all its tiny lead-framed diamond panes. A bronze cupid on a console table in one corner smiled vacantly. Mme Vorvoreano was drumming her fingers on the table. Suddenly she asked, "Why did she send for him?"

The Colonel shrugged and did not answer. His wife fidgeted nervously with the lace of her collar. She looked at the drawing-room door, then stared at a point in the middle of the table, muttering, "I'd give a lot to know what she's saying to him."

"You've only to ask her."

Helen looked at him in exasperation. "The military brain—a cavalryman's at that! The company of horses sharpens the wits."

The Colonel mumbled an insult into his Kaiser Wilhelm mustache.

"Always the perfect gentleman with the ladies! Ah, my father was only too right to be angry when he saw that I'd lost my head over you!"

"And not only your head," the Colonel said dryly. "The head's no great loss. But a fortune's another matter."

Mme Vorvoreano, having no retort ready, remained open-mouthed, until, with a sigh of discouragement, she rose and began walking around the table, her hands clasped on her breast. Her dress rustled and swept the carpet. The Colonel concentrated on his cigar. Mme Vorvoreano came to a halt and said, "I might go and listen at the door."

"If she catches you at it the efforts of years will be thrown away in a second," the Colonel said. Mme Vorvoreano resumed her perambulations.

Meanwhile Mme von Bodman was settling herself in an armchair in her own room and inviting Antofilake to draw up a chair beside her.

"You've been here before, haven't you? You remember my secretary . . . ?" She pointed to a small rosewood desk. "Sherban Vogoride sent it to me from Paris, full of chocolates. . . . You were still a child at the time. . . . You can open it; I don't keep chocolates in it now. Take out the paper you'll see there. That's right. Have you read it?"

Antofilake, spectacles on nose, had read the document and was looking at his client in some embarrassment.

"Why are you looking at me like that, monsieur?" the old woman demanded angrily. "You are not, I hope, going to ask me for explanations. Such is my will and I shall be glad if you will cast it into legal form so that all my good-for-nothing relatives are unable to get round my wishes after my death. Your business is to obey me and not to ask me why I am doing what I am doing. The fact is, I can't stomach any of them."

"Come now, don't be angry, Madame Sophia," the lawyer said, with a conciliatory smile. "The idea of asking for the motive of your decision never so much as crossed my mind. You are sole mistress of your fortune. Only, you see, the law has requirements too. Thus, in the matter of this will of yours, my advice is to burn it rather than leave it as it stands. Even if you draw up another, you would have to burn this one. Because after your death—from which Heaven preserve us, and really, by the look of you, you'll be with us for twenty years yet . . . but, as you know, one has to think of everything . . . after your death, you see, the courts would refuse to grant probate of a will such as this. They would simply set it aside as being contrary to the law of succession."

"What! You mean I haven't the right to dispose of my own property? I'd rather set fire to everything I possess! I'd rather give all my property to the poor!"

"You are free to bequeath your property to whomsoever you please, but not to the beneficiary named in this will," asserted Antofilake. Then, resuming his conciliatory manner: "Come, come, Madame Sophia, don't be upset. We shall find a way round. . . . I'll explain what the law requires of you. You want to leave your whole fortune to one of your granddaughters, to the exclusion of all the others. The law, however, allows you to dispose of only half your property, the other half being reserved to your natural heirs. The law's object, Madame Sophia, is to safeguard property and family fortunes: it was drafted with that aim in mind. One half, then, is reserved and the legal beneficiaries are your five grand-children, issue of the late Madame Lascari, and those other grand-children, offspring of your sons by the late Monsieur Coziano. So that you are not free to leave the beneficiary of any will you may make—such beneficiary being likewise entitled to her share of the reserved half, more than . . . let's see, exactly how many grandchildren have you?"

"Nine," said the old woman with an expression of disgust.

"Right. Then the party concerned will receive half your fortune plus one-ninth of the other half, that is, approximately fifty-six per cent of the whole. That is all the law allows you to leave her, not a penny more. If you make a gift of all your property to the beneficiary, then, after your—er—after your decease, your other grandchildren will have the right to demand from her their share of the reserved half, and possibly of the other half as well. So you see that it would be to your advantage to draw up a will more in conformity with the spirit of the law."

"I don't like it, Antofilake. I don't like it at all! Don't tell me that a man like you can't find a loophole, a way round, a lawyer's trick. Think it over, my boy, think it over!" said the old lady, extremely vexed. "For example, how would it be if I sold everything I possess to a man I can trust, and he sells it back to my poor—beneficiary, as you call her. Eh?"

She looked at him searchingly, her hands on her knees like a Buddha. Antofilake shook his head with respect and indulgence.

"Very vulnerable to attack. . . . It really wouldn't do, Madame Sophia. The other natural heirs would call upon the beneficiary to prove that she had really bought the property, and even if she managed to do so, it is probable that she would lose her case. The surest way is to make such a will as I have suggested."

Sophia von Bodman became dejected. "But that won't achieve my object, Antofilake," she objected. "It's true that, come to think of it, each of them would get only a ninth part of one-half, but even that is too much." She was thoughtful for a while, and then went on: "They inherited property from Alexander; they inherited more from Lascar Lascari, and then from my daughter. They are all rotten with money, excepting my two poor wretches here because Lascar happened to loathe them and they've lost all they had from my husband and Davida. The others are stuffed with money. For many years they haven't even recognized my existence.

It's true that I've ignored theirs too; but they might have shown a little affection for me, or at least politeness. Ah! I know them! They're all the dead spit of my daughter and that horrible Lascari!"

"You can, if you like, bequeath one-half of your property to charity, Madame Sophia," Antofilake said.

She gave him a hostile look. "Monsieur, I have my reasons for insisting that there be a beneficiary under my will, and that the others regard her with envy. Yes, let them envy her, let them die of disappointment, poisoned by their own bile and spite, and screaming with rage! Do you understand what I want, Antofilake? If you cannot find the answer, my boy, there's nothing for it. I shall have to seek advice elsewhere. But if you can find the solution you can count on my gratitude, as always. . . . I need not go into details, eh? You know that in important matters I don't count the cost. Well?"

Antofilake spread the skirts of his frock coat, and thoughtfully smoothed his mustache.

"Very well, then. The simplest method would be to liquidate all your assets and buy negotiable securities, since negotiable paper can be passed from hand to hand, that is, can be transferred directly by you to the beneficiary."

"You mean I should sell my land, my houses?"

"I can see no other way. Since, at whatever cost, you insist . . ."

Mme von Bodman reflected. Smiling, Antofilake shrugged his shoulders: "Buy gems with part of the money, and shares in the National Bank, the Bank of Austria, any established business of indisputable stability, with the remainder. In that way all your land and house property will go into a single document bag."

"Transform my good land into jewels and printed paper? You're frightening me, my good man."

She was trying to make a joke of it, but her very flesh suffered at the notion of her estates ceasing to belong to her and becoming someone else's property.

"I am trying to help you, Madame Sophia. I have never allowed myself to offer you advice, knowing how you dislike it. Therefore I now have only one thing to say to you: my first solution is good and, moreover, easy to achieve; my second is more complicated, but it goes to the heart of the matter."

The old lady, suddenly more cheerful, smiled at Antofilake. "But if I give her my fortune privately, how will the others know about it?"

Curiosity and excitement had brightened her eyes. Antofilake shuddered at such deep, obstinate, implacable hatred. *What on earth can they have done to her?* he wondered. He felt ill at ease, as if he were being made party to a crime. Hardened by his trade as a lawyer, he would certainly not have felt anything of the kind had he not realized that this time he was being required to serve a passion amounting to ferocity and made use of as an instrument of vengeance. He could easily imagine the torments which the old woman's grandchildren would have to suffer. For a few moments he entertained the notion of betraying her, of getting money from the heirs by drawing up a will which would not be upheld by the courts, and which would consequently result in their receiving that share of her fortune to which they were legally entitled. But the operation would be a tricky one, and if it ever became known, his clients would cease to trust him. It would be hazarding his reputation for a few thousand louis. The game was not worth the candle.

"Madame Sophia, my professional obligation ceases with what I have just told you," he said, ill at ease, "and most lawyers would stop there. But, because I want to help you and am anxious to give you satisfaction in all circumstances, I will undertake to inform the others, since you insist on it, of your decision and the manner in which it will have been carried out."

The old lady took the lawyer's hands in hers. "You will see what my gratitude means, my boy! But listen: I should like to keep one of my estates—Ciobanesti, which is smaller than the others. And for that one I will make a will on the lines you suggested just now."

As she said this, Mme von Bodman was thinking, *If only you were still here among the heirs, my little Davida! You'd have struggled and fought like the rest—a live fish on the grill! You escaped that, though, little viper. . . . But if ever we meet again,*

*I shall have at least one pleasure in the hereafter: it will be my
turn to laugh. . . .*

Hesitating, Antofilake said, "The joke will be a cruel one for
the other heirs, Madame Sophia."

The old lady looked at him from under the heavy eyelids which
half covered her prominent eyes, smiled, and replied, "Now listen
to me, my good man: just now you claimed that you never offered
me advice. . . . I am not asking for your advice, but for your
opinion as a lawyer. Leave it at that. Let us now consider how best
to arrange things."

They began to make plans for the sale of her lands and houses.
M. Hillel would have to be told, so that his bank could set about
buying the shares she wanted. No doubt the banker would also
recommend a jeweler. They could also order jewels in Paris,
whence they could be brought, accompanied by certificates of origin and insurance policies, by a trusted agent of the diamond
merchant—Cartier, or some other firm in the Rue de la Paix. As
for a suitable real-estate agent, Antofilake had someone in mind
already. He himself might also be able to get in touch with
prospective buyers.

"I'll have a word with the Fischer brothers. I know they're
buying up a lot of land at the moment."

"Everything is to be kept in the vaults at the bank. The key
will be in my granddaughter's name and nobody will know what
is in the strongbox except Hillel," Mme von Bodman stipulated.
Antofilake was taking notes in his memorandum book. The deep,
rounded armchairs covered with yellow silk, the portraits of
Sophia's ancestors in their oval frames, the yellow Maréchal Niel
roses in their vases, the silver candlesticks with their candles wilting
in the summer heat, the book lying open on the table (*Les Secrets
du Palais-Royal,* an indecent work by an anonymous author using
as a pen name the nonexistent title "Marquis de Bourbonne")—
everything around him was pleasant, graceful, peaceful, and superficial. And yet Antofilake experienced a feeling of fear. He himself
could not have explained what was happening in his heart: con-

fronting him was a stout old lady still full of life, wearing a
house dress of faded silk; he heard her giving him her instructions
while he took notes in his memorandum book, answered her
questions, and found the swiftest and most convenient means of
executing her wishes. And yet there was an enduring impression
that all this was happening in a dream, one of those dreams in
which you seem to be floating and are surprised because you do
not fall into the frightful pit which you perceive opening beneath
you. Antofilake did not fall, but he was afraid. Late at night he
took his leave, kissed the old woman's hand, and left her, carefully
closing the door behind him.

He knew his way. He crossed the empty corridor, whose floor
was covered with linoleum, and went into the dining room. On
the threshold he stopped, taken aback. The Vorvoreanos were
there and they seemed to be waiting for him. The Colonel gave
him a long, penetrating look through a cloud of cigar smoke, but
said nothing. Mme Vorvoreano, much agitated, was pacing the
room with long strides, her arms crossed on her chest. For an
instant all three remained so, looking at one another. Helen Vorvoreano was the first to recover. She went up to Antofilake and
in a tone of forced liveliness said, "Finished at last? You look
tired. Sit down with us for a while and have a glass of port to
restore you."

"No, really, it's extremely kind of you, Madame Vorvoreano,
but I am tired, and I don't want to be any later."

"Oh, but you must stay a few minutes and have a chat with us."

"You can't go like this, damn it," the Colonel exclaimed, rising
heavily from his chair; he forced a laugh to soften the vehemence
of his injunction.

"No, you really must excuse me. I should enjoy it, but it's
quite impossible for me. My wife is waiting for me and my grandson is ill. I suspect it's measles. Indeed I cannot stay, I assure
you. . . ."

"We've seen so little of you," Mme Vorvoreano said in a tone
of regret. "Grandmama carried you off so soon after dinner. It's

such a long time since we had a little gossip together. . . ."

"I should very much like to, whenever you wish, the sooner the better. . . ."

Mme Vorvoreano gave way with the suppleness of a skilled wrestler. The Colonel, insensitive to such refinements, would have persisted but his wife checked him, and taking the lawyer by the arm, said, "I will show our visitor out. I want a word with him."

In the anteroom, still holding Antofilake's arm which was rigid with uneasiness—he was not sure of being able to keep his client's secret—Helen forced the lawyer to face her, caught hold of the lapels of his frock coat, drew him to her, and, assuming the expression of a naughty little girl, looking straight into his eyes and almost mouth to mouth, pleaded: "Please tell me. Grandmama has been making her will, hasn't she? Don't try to conceal it; I know. She told me. Come now, don't try to evade the question. What's in the will? Tell me what's in it."

Confused and upset, Antofilake thought, *She's lying. The old woman hasn't told her anything.* But there was nothing he could do; Mme Vorvoreano would never have believed him if he tried to lie. He decided to tell her the truth.

"I can only tell you this," he said. "She is arranging matters in such a way as to benefit one of her granddaughters at the expense of all her other descendants. But I must ask you not to breathe a word to a soul. My respects, dear lady, and good night to you."

He left the house quickly, with difficulty restraining himself from running. He slammed the iron gate in the railings behind him and set off quickly, keeping close to the street lamps which glowed in a darkness heavy with the perfume of lilacs and the smell of garlic sausage.

Mme Vorvoreano sighed as she left the anteroom, her eyes wide and her hand to her mouth. At last it was done. She returned to the dining room to fling her arms around the Colonel's neck. "Oh, Michael!" Laughing, she repeated the whole conversation. At once the Colonel shed his starchy manner and joined in her laughter.

"I feel as if I must go and kiss the old carcass!" Helen Vorvoreano said.

"That would be quite out of order. Not a word, not a wink! It's been our discretion above all that she's appreciated. Our disinterestedness. Our attitude must remain quite unchanged. Come, ring to have the lights put out, and join me in our room. We'll talk about it up there."

Some hours later, sitting in their conjugal bed, they were still talking about it. The Colonel was smoking a cigar whose ash was soiling his long starched nightgown, its collar tied with a tape.

He wore a mustache-binder—a band of waterproof canvas tied behind his neck. His wife had her hair in curlpapers and covered by a lace-trimmed nightcap. Propped up against fat pillows, they had discussed every aspect of the question until they were tired out and bored with it.

The Colonel was saying, "What are you talking about? Money, travel, a life worth living—we may still have to wait twenty years for all that. We shan't be able to enjoy them till we're old. . . ."

A moth fluttered around their lamp. On the marble top of the bedside table the stub of the Colonel's cigar sent up a thin streamer of smoke.

"Why do you say that?" Mme Vorvoreano asked. "She's eighty-two or three, remember."

"She's been eighty-odd since God knows when. Don't you see that she may live for years yet?"

"But she's ill—she has heart trouble."

"With that kind of ailment she may live to be a hundred," the Colonel growled.

"Do put out the lamp," Helen murmured. For a little while they sat motionless in the dark, still propped up by their pillows. A little later the Colonel began to talk again, but as if to himself.

"I've had enough. She treats us like children. Our hair is already turning gray, we want to *live*, and she treats us like children! We no longer have much time ahead of us—five years, ten years—and how many of them shall we still have to spend with her around?"

"I wish you wouldn't talk like that!" Helen sighed.

"I tell you it drives me mad when I think I've got to be satisfied with the pocket money she gives me, like a schoolboy! All my friends make fun of me. Every day at Capsa's they can sit and watch a real comedy, of which I'm the butt! Sometimes I'd like to hang myself."

He preferred to say nothing of those other desires which he could not satisfy.

"There are times when I could kill her," he said levelly.

His wife said nothing.

"Listen," the Colonel resumed, with a jauntier note in his voice. "It's occurred to me that we could travel for a while—do a tour of Europe with your grandmother. What do you think of it?"

"It's an idea."

"Dotty as she is, it's just the idea to appeal to her. Don't you think?"

After a moment he went on, speaking softly and smiling beneath his mustache-binder: "If you knew all the ideas I've turned over in my mind before this one occurred to me . . . But I'm certain this is the best of them—a tour of Europe. What do you think?"

Mme Vorvoreano said nothing. The Colonel turned to look at her but it was too dark to see. He felt suddenly uneasy.

"Well, say something, can't you?"

"Let's not discuss it now," Mme Vorvoreano said. "We'll consider it. It needs thinking over."

"Why? What's the use of waiting? How much longer are you going to make me go on living like a servant kept on out of pity? How much longer are we going to be at her beck and call? I tell you I can't wait any longer. If this goes on I shall clear out, I'll go off into the blue, God damn it!"

"And you choose this moment to lose patience?" Helen returned ironically. "You horrify me with your stupid talk. I'm not clear what you mean. . . ."

The Colonel growled. Mme Vorvoreano went on: "In any case, the journey couldn't possibly do Grandmama any harm. It would amuse her and make her feel better. That's why I let you go on talking. Otherwise I wouldn't even have listened."

A long silence followed. The Colonel gave a short, dry cough.

"Very well," he said, "very well. I'll take care of it. Suggest it to her and then tell me what I had better do."

"Agreed. I'll talk to her about it. Later, toward the end of the summer, when it's cooler."

"Certainly not. At once. Why wait until the end of the summer?"

"Very well, at once, if you like," Mme Vorvoreano assented.

The Colonel said no more. He had been thinking about this idea of a tour for months. They would go in a motorcar! The gasoline fumes, the shaking over bad roads, the heat: they would all be invaluable allies. . . . And if a doctor were needed they would have to have what they could find, and she might take a turn for the worse—fatal, perhaps, at her age. And then, money, gaming, the gay life! The Colonel was seized by such a surge of lust at the idea that he put out his hands to his wife, with whom he had not fulfilled his conjugal duties for a long time. And while Helen Vorvoreano was yielding with happy surprise to his impulse, the Colonel was thinking, *Why wait?* and a proverb occurred to him which might be roughly rendered as "In default of champagne, drink beer."

4

The sky was clear and its depths infinite. The acacias were coming into flower. In the garden's lilac thickets nightingales sang all night long. Mme von Bodman and the Vorvoreanos were dining in the graveled courtyard. The big wickerwork table had been cleared of all but the oil lamps surrounded by clouds of midges and the crystal carafes containing the last of the wine.

"It's bedtime, Elvira," Helen Vorvoreano said.

Elvira rose, made a little curtsy, and left them. Her mother followed her with her eyes. The child had the awkward, charming

gait of a delicate-limbed foal. *She has fine eyes, but she really is
too swarthy. I wonder how she'll turn out.*

"Grandmama," the Colonel said, "may I light a cigar?"

The old woman nodded. She was fanning herself with a white
silk fan; her face looked grave and distant. The Colonel cut the
tip off his cigar.

"What a magnificent night!" he said with decision. "Now's the
time when it would be good to be in Paris."

Mme Vorvoreano gave a start which passed unnoticed. In a
dreamy, romantic voice she said, "The spring in Paris is so beautiful."

"Rubbish!" the old lady said. "In Bucharest the spring is more
beautiful than anywhere else in the world. It's intoxicating. Even
I, in spite of my age, am disturbed by it. Only it lasts no more than
a fortnight. That's its one defect. You can't count on it. But then,
what can you count on in this country?"

"Oh, come now, Grandmama, think of May in Vienna or Paris.
Or June in London. Or July in Nice," Helen Vorvoreano said. Her
heart was beating with excitement. She realized that her husband's
calm was slightly forced. Would the old lady notice anything? Impossible. She had no reason to suspect anything whatsoever.

"Listen to me, now," the Colonel said with feigned geniality.
"The most original and amusing way of traveling for pleasure
nowadays is to make a tour of Europe in a motorcar. You get into
your car in Bucharest, drive across Hungary, make for Vienna,
cross southern Germany, linger a bit in Paris, cross the Channel,
taking the car with you, and end up in London. On the way back,
Paris, Lyons, Nice, stopping wherever and whenever you like and
for as long as you like. On the road you can have a picnic whenever you fancy it. In short—oh, well, why talk about it since it's
out of the question? It would be bad for your health, we can't run
the risk of having you fall ill abroad. . . . It can't be done and
that's that," the Colonel concluded, with a cheerfulness which emphasized the courage with which he accepted the sacrifices imposed
on him by his affection for his wife's grandmother.

Mme von Bodman was thoughtful. Suddenly she said, "Why should I fall ill? I feel very well."

The Colonel and his wife controlled their feelings simultaneously. They did not even exchange a look.

"Good for you!" the Colonel said jovially. "But you're not seriously going to suggest making a tour of Europe in a motorcar?"

The old woman gave him a challenging look. "And why not, if you please? I've traveled farther in such machines than you have, I fancy."

"It's not possible, Grandmama," Mme Vorvoreano protested. "You wouldn't be able to stand it. Don't forget that you are not well."

"I am certainly not ill! Where did you get that idea? If the machine in question has really good springs, I see absolutely nothing to be afraid of."

The Colonel feigned amused skepticism. "You're not serious, Grandmama? You mean you've made up your mind, just like that, to set out on a tour of Europe?"

The old woman turned her toadlike eyes on him. "I advise you to take me seriously, my lad. If you don't, one of these fine mornings I shall be off on my own, leaving you to come after me as best you can."

Another silence. Then Mme Vorvoreano, whose lips were quivering with excitement, managed to blurt out, "But seriously, Grandmama, you can't be intending to make a tour of Europe?"

"You're becoming thoroughly stupid, my child," her grandmother said. "A moment ago you were dying to go to Paris, and your husband was assaulting my ears with his tour of Europe. And now you can hardly believe it. I suppose you thought I was going to think it over for a week, or a month?"

"No," Mme Vorvoreano murmured, rather timidly, "but I am thinking of you, of your health, your age . . ."

"My health is excellent. How long is it since I was ill?" the old lady insisted, with childish vehemence. "As for my age—does it mean that I am never again to have any pleasure? I want to see

Vienna again, and Paris. I want to buy some pictures at Christie's.
I want to stroll on the Promenade at Nice and gamble at Monte
Carlo. I'm sick and tired of Bucharest and of——"

She was on the point of saying "and of you," but restrained
herself. She knew that at her time of life it would be very difficult
to find a pair of slaves as devoted as the Vorvoreanos. *The others
are wealthy; they don't need me. Much they care whether I live or
die—of boredom, for instance. Whereas these two, for the sake of
my money, will do whatever I ask. Besides, they want to travel
themselves. It was obvious enough from their voices how sick and
tired they are of hanging about in Bucharest with me. Oh, I know
you! Nothing you'd like better than to be having the time of your
lives by yourselves on my money! But you'll take me with you, my
lambs!*

In a hard, fierce voice which her resolution and energy made
almost masculine, she commanded, "Colonel, organize our departure. I'm bored here. I'm sick of it. In 1899 I was sick of Vienna.
Now it's Bucharest I can't put up with any longer. You won't see
me here again. If you want to come with me, I'll take you."

Husband and wife looked at each other, not, this time, involuntarily, but pretending to consult each other as if to establish a conjugal understanding. After which the Colonel smiled ruefully and,
all bogus chivalry, addressed his wife: "It's for you to decide,
Helen. You know that as far as I am concerned, there's nothing to
keep me in Bucharest. I am quite ready to leave."

Mme Vorvoreano went through the motions of hesitation and
reflection. Then, with the utmost seriousness, she said, "Of course
I agree. In the first place, traveling like that would be very enjoy-
able. And then, we're certainly not going to let you go all alone,
Grandmama."

"Oh, don't worry about that," the old woman said. "I should
manage perfectly well on my own! After Von Bodman died I lived
alone for ten years."

"That's true, Grandmama, but it's better to have some member
of the family with you," Mme Vorvoreano replied evenly. "Well

then, it's agreed, we are to go with you. But what are we going to do about poor little Elvira?"

"Send her to boarding school! At Maria-Einsiedeln, in the Tyrol. Surely I've said so already? The wonder to me is that you've waited so long. How do you expect her to make useful friends?" And, working herself into a rage, the old woman shouted, "What block-heads you are!" She promptly added, with an expression of pro-found comtempt: "Come, give me your arm, I'm going to bed. Colonel, tomorrow at lunchtime you will let me know what you've arranged."

She rose, groaning, and leaning on her granddaughter's arm, walked slowly toward the house. Concealing his laughter, the Colonel poured himself a glassful of brandy. His wife came back, but they dared not speak to each other for fear of letting slip some compromising remark in front of the servants who were clearing the table. The Colonel was too excited to remain seated. He was standing with a glass of brandy in one hand and a cigar in the other. "Let's go in. I'm cold," Mme Vorvoreano suggested.

Side by side, not touching, they walked toward the house.

Up in their room they undressed. "I hardly dared to hope it would go off so easily," the Colonel said. Mme Vorvoreano was putting her hair in curlers. The Colonel put on his nightcap and asked, "Shall we tell the others?" His wife understood that by "the others" he meant her brothers and cousins, Sophia's grand-children.

"Why should we? What business is it of theirs?" Mme Vor-voreano replied, adjusting her lace-trimmed nightcap before the looking glass. "They've never shown any interest in us or in her. If they want to find anything out, they have only to ask after us and after her. . . ."

She got into the huge double bed. They went on talking, in half-finished phrases, avoiding certain subjects. For the most part they discussed practical details requiring attention as soon as pos-sible before their journey. From time to time the Colonel's joy burst out in exclamations such as "God Almighty, whoever would have thought it! I can hardly believe it myself!" Or "I say, Helen, is it really true? We are actually going? With the old carcass? Joking apart?"

And he laughed so infectiously that his wife found herself laughing with him.

Early the next morning a gentleman with a Kaiser Wilhelm mustache, wearing a bowler hat planted solidly on his head, entered No. 14 Carol Street, whose door bore a legend announcing: "E. I. Ressel, sole representative for Rumania of De Dion-Bouton Automobiles. Garage for motorcars. Agency for sewing machines equipped with attachments for embroidering and making buttonholes. The famous Pfaff sewing machines. Peugeot cycles and motorcycles." On the following day the same gentleman came again, a little later, and in a carriage from which he helped a very old lady to alight. He accompanied her into a room unexpectedly large and full of freezing drafts and the stench of oil and gasoline as well as packing cases, cheek by jowl with motorcars, some open and others closed in, some worked by an electric motor and others, much more up to date, by a powerful gasoline engine. Some of the closed motorcars had glass windows, but the chauffeur's seat was usually open to the weather. Some of the motorcars had acetylene lamps, others oil lamps.

Herr Ressel was a German with a ginger mustache and a hard red face. He hastened forward to meet his customers, bowing several times.

"My respects, madame, good day to you, monsieur. Welcome. Welcome. Be so kind as to step inside. This is the best machine I have, and I can recommend it. Please examine it. Six doors, as you see, very elegant windows, oval, with crossbars to prevent the frames from rattling, and equipped with curtains so that the travelers can rest. One luggage compartment on top of the machine, and another at the back. Spare tires, acetylene lamps, four seats for passengers and two in front for the driver and a servant. Well-padded leather upholstery. A cupboard for provisions. The engine is very powerful, as I was explaining to the Colonel yesterday. You can do as much as forty or forty-five miles an hour. Not all the time of course! But a speed of twenty to twenty-five miles an hour can easily be reached and maintained on good roads. . . ."

The old lady examined the interior of the body, and then asked, "Tell me, my dear sir, will this carriage of yours go?"

And she transfixed the German with the same cold and critical look which she had given his motorcar. Ressel hastened to repeat the list of the motorcar's qualities.

"All right, all right. I can see for myself that you have nothing smarter than this one. But there's one thing I want you to tell me. Does it stink when it's going? *Tut sie stinken, mein lieber Herr Ressel?*"

"*Aber, gnädigste Frau Baronin*—much less than any of the others you see here!"

"Very well! Colonel, what do you say to a ride?" Mme von Bodman inquired. Although he had been a soldier and did not know the meaning of fear, the Colonel hesitated for a moment; then, with the deliberate calm of a man who is ready for anything, he agreed, declaring that he could try the machine alone, that——

"I'm the one who's going to be shaken, and I must try it for myself," the old woman said, pointing to the motorcar with the tip of her sunshade. "Start it up, Herr Ressel."

They had a trial ride as far as the fields on the far side of Calea Dorobantilor, beyond Roata Lumü, the famous pleasure gardens. The old lady, albeit only moderately satisfied, said that the motorcar would do. To his great surprise, Vorvoreano had felt violently sick owing to the stench of gasoline fumes from the engine. Twice he had been on the point of vomiting, but had managed to control himself. When they left Herr Ressel's the Colonel, green in the face, knew that the machine was as good as bought and that the grand tour would soon begin, and he was assuring himself that the old woman could not possibly survive it. Everything was going perfectly. Antofilake's visits were becoming frequent and every time he came he was closeted with his client. Then suddenly he stopped calling and the Vorvoreanos told each other, "He's finished drawing up her will." They spent the last few days before their departure in a state of nervous tension which, although un-

expressed and kept well in hand, was forever on the point of breaking out.

"I'm worried," said the Colonel in bed that night. "Everything's
going too well."

5

Colonel Vorvoreano was in such a state of nervous exhaustion that
one night he dreamed that the journey was starting. He was wearing
motoring clothes, with dark goggles, leather gaiters, and a dustcoat.
His wife was similarly dressed. The old woman, wrapped up in
skunk fur and also wearing dark goggles, seemed to be in the grip
of some strange kind of high spirits, which made the Colonel
feel afraid. The chauffeur was driving the motorcar at a wild speed,
far in excess of the forty-five miles an hour guaranteed by Ressel.
The old woman was laughing, pointing her stick at the chauffeur's
back, and saying, "Faster! Faster!"

They reached Budapest under a leaden sky. Sick, his knees shaking with weakness and anguish, the Colonel made his way into
the Hunting Horn Hotel. He went straight to bed. But he had
hardly got between the sheets when the old woman came into the
room and, poking him through the blankets with the ferrule of
her stick, said, "Well? What are we waiting for? I've seen enough
of Budapest. Come along."

And once again it was the motorcar, the wild dash over rough
roads which banged his head against the hood, Helen's disturbing
silence, and the old woman's hideous laughter. "I'm not tired. Why
stay here? I've had enough of Vienna, I spent twenty-five years
here, I want no more of it," she said in the lobby of Sacher's Hotel.
"Back into the car! *Auf wieder-schauen, Frau Sacher.*"

This will be the death of me, the Colonel thought, flung about like a ball by the motorcar's jolting. *I feel ill.*

He woke suddenly, bathed in sweat. He was panting and moaning.

"What's the matter, Michael? What's happened? What is it?" his wife asked.

"I've had a nightmare. Pass me a towel, Helen. I'm drenched in sweat! God, what a frightful dream!"

6

The newly engaged chauffeur collided with a cart while he was trying out the motorcar on the Oltenitza road. The horses had taken fright; the carter, never having seen such a contrivance in his life, lost his head. The motorcar was sent back to Ressel's garage for a week to be repaired. The old lady flew into a violent rage and bitterly reproached the Colonel and his wife, Ressel, and the chauffeur. The heat had become unbearable and seemed to affect Mme von Bodman's nerves. She was forever moving about the house from room to room, calling for the Baedeker, the road map, then throwing them down. One day she slapped Elvira's face.

One morning when he woke up the Colonel rose and went as usual to the washstand, where, before an oval mirror, he started to shave. From the street came the monotonous singsong cry of a vegetable hawker. The room was silent, so that only the scraping of the steel razor-blade was audible. Suddenly the door burst open. Colonel Vorvoreano turned toward it and saw his wife, her face distorted. She leaned against the frame of the doorway. The Colonel started; he had already realized what had happened.

"Oh, Michael——"

"Well, what is it?"

"She's dead," Mme Vorvoreano said in a whisper. The Colonel turned back to his shaving mirror, saying, "God rest her soul. At her age it was to be expected."

He resumed his toilet. His wife came into the room and sank into an armchair. Staring into vacancy she said, "Floarea found her dead in her bed. She died in her sleep."

"Fortunately, it was not necessary . . ." the Colonel began, but did not complete his thought. "The next thing is to see how we stand in the matter of her money."

"I've sent for Antofilake," Mme Vorvoreano said, rising. But she sat down again at once and put her hand to her forehead. "Oh, dear! I feel so giddy!"

The Colonel was still trying to shave. Abruptly he decided to give it up; his hand was shaking and he could not carry on. "Helen," he said, "would you pour me out some water to wash the soap off? I don't know what's wrong with me today, but I can't shave myself."

Helen went to him and mechanically poured water from the china jug into his cupped hands. Snorting and splashing, he said, "Have you let the others know?"

"No. I want to speak to Antofilake first, about the will."

"Pour me some more."

Mme Vorvoreano poured more water. "Not down my back, damn it! You've drenched my shirt."

"I can't help it, my hands are shaking too," Helen said, with a twisted smile.

Twenty-four hours later all Sophia von Bodman's descendants who happened to be in Bucharest were assembled in the Vorvoreanos' drawing room. The mirrors were draped with black crape. In the dining room the table had been transformed into a bier and covered with flowers. The old woman's favorite servants were keeping vigil over her body. There she lay, looking very strange, bloated, her hair badly dyed, her hands marked with brown spots, dressed in black and almost disappearing under the irises and lilies.

Alexander Lascari, Boniface Coziano's former *chef de cabinet,* was by now a tall, melancholy, grizzled man, beginning to go bald. His brother, Sherban Lascari, was nearly forty and as elegant as he had been at twenty, despite a paunch; he wore a light-colored suit, a monocle, and a brown beard trimmed to resemble that of King Edward VII, who had been the arbiter of elegance ever since he was Prince of Wales. Sophia, Davida's youngest daughter, was there with her husband, M. Sufana, formerly a well-to-do farmer in the Prahova region, who had made a fortune in the oil industry. Finally, there was Eleonora Smadoviceano, Helen's elder sister, a woman old before her time, with a nasal voice, a long, pointed nose, and the small round eyes of a hen. All wore mourning except Sherban, who was dressed as if for a stroll with the ladies along the Chaussée. "You're hardly dressed for the occasion," the Colonel had pointed out, to which Lascari had replied with a laugh: "Let us first see whether the occasion was worth dressing for."

Antofilake, very pale, began to read the will, of which, he said, a holograph copy had been deposited in court. After two minutes there were exclamations from every corner of the room, and as the lawyer concluded his reading everybody began shouting at once. Only Eleonora held herself apart, looking alarmed and ill at ease.

"But really, sir—" Sherban Lascari turned on the lawyer— "what has become of her money? She certainly had more than you've accounted for here. Do you take us for fools? What's she done with her fortune?"

"Alienated it," Sufana said suddenly. "Given it away. She's made fools of us, or to be exact, of you, for personally I don't care in the least."

But he was obviously furious. Colonel Vorvoreano was demanding an explanation, while his wife was looking from Antofilake to her relations and back to the lawyer.

"You knew all about it! You'll have to render an account," Sherban said, shaking his finger at the lawyer.

The latter answered coolly, "If you wish, Monsieur Sherban, you can take the matter to court. But believe me, it will get you nowhere. The deceased had a perfect right to make a personal gift of all her liquid assets. She exercised that right, and that's all there is to it."

Haggard and stunned, Alexander said, "What about her real estate?"

"Liquidated during the last months of her life," Antofilake replied phlegmatically.

Sherban struck his hands together and shouted, "In whose favor, if you please? Who profits by this infamous trick? I want to see him! I'll wring his neck! Which of you got round the old woman? Who played us this dirty trick?"

He looked at each of them in turn and demanded suddenly, sneeringly, "You? Was it you, Helen? It *was* you, wasn't it?" But Mme Vorvoreano was so pale, she seemed so shattered, that Sherban paused, embarrassed and uncertain. Then he asked, "Where's Eleonora?"

Surprised, they all looked at one another. They heard the sound of wheels. A carriage was driving out through the gateway. Sherban seized Helen by the shoulder. "Pull yourself together! Where's Eleonora?"

"She's gone," Helen said tonelessly, her voice barely issuing from between her bloodless lips. Collapsed in an armchair, the Colonel was looking at her out of bloodshot eyes. He too seemed absolutely shattered.

"It seems to me," Sufana growled, "that she's the one, all right." He laughed mirthlessly, and Sherban leapt to his feet again.

"You're right! It's her! The miserable, filthy bitch! The simpleton, mark you, the family cretin, the idiot, and that's what she was up to! She can't utter a syllable without yammering, she's in her second childhood——"

"Monsieur Sherban, please! A little decency . . ."

"——but when it comes to wangling an inheritance, she recovers her faculties! Nothing imbecile about her then! First the half-wit inherits a fortune from her husband, and now from this other half-wit——"

"Sherban!" Sophia Sufana protested.

"Sherban what? You will kindly allow me to call a fraud a fraud, alive or dead. And to have nothing whatever to do with the sort of people who let themselves be defrauded. If you agree that we should go to law, you know where to find me. Until then, I wish you a very good morning."

He slammed the door, passed through the mortuary chamber whistling, and pulled the front door so hard that he broke one of the panes. In the drawing room nobody spoke until at last Sufana rose, saying to his wife, "Your brother's right. Let's be going, madame."

Alexander remained a little while to question Antofilake and try to understand what had happened. This business of the will had upset him badly.

As for Helen Vorvoreano, pale, frozen, she sat motionless, waiting for the next disaster. She knew that something else was going to happen to her. She was afraid of her husband. She had intercepted a look from him, a look both ferocious and stupid. *He'll hold me responsible for everything,* she thought. But Vorvoreano started talking trivialities; he seemed suddenly to have been relieved of all his worries.

Helen overcame her fears in order to resume her housekeeping duties and arrange the funeral. The old woman was taken to the Bellu cemetery and there buried on a day of bright sunshine in the shade of pine trees. Mme Vorvoreano shed the requisite tears, as did her sisters and sisters-in-law, excepting Eleonora, who did not come to the funeral. Then Helen gave away the old woman's clothes to the poor and had the room where she had lived thoroughly cleaned.

The Colonel, silent and lowering, went often into town where he took his meals, returning only late at night. One morning he left the house never to return. A few days later Helen went to see Sufana, who received her in the Japanese drawing room of the mansion he had recently built himself, which the architect Mincou had embellished with coffered ceilings in gilded wood, gigantic lusters, Latin mottoes, marble facings, panels of gold-flowered brocade, and enormous carpets. There was a series of drawing rooms and a library stocked with thousands of volumes purchased *en bloc* when Boniface Coziano's books came under the hammer at his death.

"You mean you knew nothing, Helen?" Sufana said. "I thought he'd gone with your consent." Helen shook her head. "So you mean he went without warning? Bolted, in short! A pretty kettle of fish! But what I don't understand is that Sherban took him with him."

He then told Helen that Sherban had engaged the Colonel's services, appointing him a sort of secretary-valet-factotum-friend. It was the Colonel who had bought the tickets for Paris and taken charge of the luggage. He was keeping Sherban company, and uttering loud cries of admiration whenever his patron made a joke. Helen listened in silence. Then, thanking Sufana, she rose and took her leave. She went home and sat down on a chair in the deserted drawing room. Not in an armchair; in an ordinary upright chair. Elvira opened the door quietly and came in. Her mother gave her a cold glance and in a hard voice said: "Go away. Leave me in peace."

She remained alone. Elvira. The little goose. And Michael, her son. A young officer. Penniless. No income, and no capital. A few salable articles which might keep them a year or two, three at most. And then what?

She set her jaw in anger, like a man. *You made a fool of me, Grandmama. You tricked me. And you too, you miserable cretin, you made a fool of me. But I say—no! It shan't be so! You'll never beat me! I won't submit to being beaten. I shall be the winner in the end. I shall come out on top. Yes, but how? Where's my salvation, where my refuge?*

The answer came like a stab of light. *In the enemy's own camp! The very place where nobody would dream of going.*

"Elvira!" called Mme Vorvoreano. "Elvira!"

She went swiftly toward the door, but Elvira was already running to meet her.

"Go and get dressed. Tell them to bring the carriage around. We're going to the station."

"Where to, Mama?" Elvira asked her.

"To the country, child, to your Aunt Eleonora's. Stop looking at me like that. Go and get dressed. Hurry, now."

The following morning, in bright sunshine, accompanied by a dry wind which ruffled the wheatfields and bowed the screens of willow trees beside the rivers, blew through the villages and over the churches and among the cattle, Mme Vorvoreano and her daughter alighted from the train at Salcia. Helen Vorvoreano saw the carts which were waiting at the station. She went to bargain with a carter over the price of transport for herself, her daughter, and their luggage.

Half an hour later the cart was moving along the road at the trotting pace of its two little horses, rattling like a load of old iron. Large clouds, driven by the wind, sailed over the travelers' heads. In the distance, beyond a range of low hills, they caught glimpses of leafy treetops and the red-tiled roof of a manor house.

PART SIX

Family Jewels

I

Among the children of Davida's marriage with Lascar Lascari—a union cursed with issue—were two girls, who were given the names of Lascari's mother and sister, Eleonora and Helen. Eleonora, married to M. Smadoviceano, senator for a constituency in the plain and a great landowner, was widowed shortly after her marriage and left childless. She withdrew to the country, choosing the most dilapidated of her manor houses. She was a strange and solitary creature, considered simple-minded by some, by others mad. She had aged prematurely, and although only four or five years older than Helen, she looked like an old woman, whereas Helen was still in all the splendor of her fair and massive beauty, inherited from goodness knows what ancestor.

By the end of the winter of 1907, Mme Vorvoreano had been living with her sister for several months. The house was not far from Salcia railroad station. One morning a low-built railroad engine with a tall, funnel-shaped chimney, drawing six coaches across the plain, was making for Salcia. The third-class coaches were crammed with peasants, women of all ages, and soldiers who had overflowed into the first- and second-class corridors and were staring, unembarrassed, at the boyars dressed in city style, lounging on plush seats. The boyars stared back at these people, whose fur caps and jerkins were in rags; and then, with an air of embarrassment, looked the other way, out over the plain where drifts of snow still lingered here and there.

The conductor had not shaved for several days. He was a stout, greasy, red-faced man. Coming to the end of one of the third-class coaches, he stuck his head out of the window and bawled, "What are you doing there? Get off!"

The man who was riding on the step raised his head and smiled. He was small and puny and his crumpled, wrinkled face was tanned by wind and sun and emaciated by starvation. His pale-gray eyes, deep in their sockets, were lively and penetrating. He wore the black peaked cap of a high-school student, but the long peak was broken in several places, and only two or three of the gold letters that once adorned it were still visible. His old military tunic was torn, and his ragged trousers were tied around his ankles with string. His bare feet were covered with a thick layer of dried mud. He maintained himself on the step in a crouching posture, a staff under one arm, his ears hunched into the turned-up collar of his tunic, and his hands in his pockets.

Answering the conductor's rough injunction, he said, "Who? Me?"

"Yes, you! Get off there! What do you think you're doing?"

"Doing? Seeing the world by rail!"

"Get off, I say!"

"Why should I? Want me to break my neck?"

The conductor thought that one over, and then said, "Got a ticket?"

The man smiled. "No. I'm poor."

The conductor felt the blood rush to his head. He again bawled at the man to get down and again the man asked why he should do so; but little by little the smile was disappearing from his face.

"If you've no ticket, you'll have to get off. Traveling on the railroad without a ticket isn't allowed. You've got to pay."

"Well, I won't, see! Who should I pay? You? I'm certainly not going to pay you. I'm traveling by railroad and I'm not paying. That's the position."

The conductor started abusing him and was about to call the other passengers to witness the impudence of the man on the step. But he had hardly opened his mouth when he shut it again, and an expression of amazement slowly spread across his face. All the passengers in the coach had assembled behind him and were staring at him with undisguised hostility.

"Leave him alone, can't you?" a soldier said. "Can't you see how poor he is? The man probably has to use the train. . . ."

Another soldier leaned out and shouted, "I say, Marinica, where are you bound for?"

"Me? I'm off on my travels. . . ."

There was no trace of gaiety in Marinica's voice, nor in that of the man who had spoken to him. Moreover, the peasants and their women all looked lowering and sullen. A number of men began shouting, "What's all this about a ticket? You and your ticket!" They fumbled in belts and pockets for their own tickets and thrust them under the conductor's nose.

"Here's our tickets, see? We've all got tickets. You can see 'em for yourself, can't you?"

"But he hasn't got one—that fellow out there," the conductor protested.

"You leave him alone, see? We've all paid—let that be enough for you! Let him be; it won't kill you, will it? What difference can it make to you? Leave him alone, I tell you!"

"But I tell you it's not allowed! The law against it's quite definite."

"What law? You mean there's a law that allows you to kill poor people?" This from a tall fellow with bushy eyebrows, the man who had questioned Marinica.

The conductor stepped back a pace, went out onto the observation platform of the coach, leaned over its railing, and shouted roughly to Marinica, "You there! At the first stop, off you get and clear out sharp or I'll call the police. Is that clear?"

Immediately every window was crowded with angry faces. With clenched fists, the tall soldier plunged through the crowd in pursuit of the conductor. The conductor made a dash for the next coach, ran along the corridor, slamming the doors behind him, then ran from coach to coach until he reached the mail car, where he locked himself in, terrified. A few of the peasants chased him to the end of the train, then gave up and returned, cursing and swearing. A brakeman, black with soot and carrying a small red lamp, made his way through the coach and asked what was happening. He listened to the people's explanation and then grinned broadly. There was a folded newspaper sticking out of his pocket. The man who knew Marinica twitched the brakeman by the sleeve and, pointing to the newspaper, said in a voice at once hesitant and imperious, "Is this newspaper yours?"

The brakeman nodded.

"Is it today's?"

The brakeman nodded again. The man took hold of the newspaper with the tips of his horny-nailed fingers and pulled it out of the brakeman's pocket, meanwhile looking the brakeman straight in the eye and saying, "Anything new?"

"Yes, there's news," the brakeman replied seriously. "They've risen in Moldavia. . . ."

"They have, have they? In Moldavia. Sure it's true?"

The brakeman nodded by way of answer. A number of those who had protested at the conductor's behavior crowded around them.

"You don't know if they've given us land?" the young soldier asked, his voice trembling.

The brakeman looked around the ring of faces. Dozens of pairs of dark eyes, shining in lean, emaciated faces, were fixed on him. Nobody said anything. "I don't know," the railroad man stammered.

He swung himself out of the coach. Outside, a plume of white steam rose into the icy air accompanied by a sharp whistle, as the engine drew the train into the station.

This station was a small building which seemed to crouch on the plain, crushed under the immensity of the clouded, lowering sky. The platform was crowded with hundreds of men, all dressed in the same wretched rags of coarse brown or black cloth, and wearing the same fur caps. They were all talking at once. A young man, scarcely bearded as yet, was moving from group to group. He wore city clothes and a cap like Marinica's, but new. People kept stopping him as he passed among them, and questioning him. Marinica had jumped down from his perch on the step. Standing on tiptoe, he was trying to look over the peasants' shoulders and hear what they were saying. Suddenly booing and jeering broke out from somewhere and spread through the dense crowd.

Marinica's immediate neighbors gave a series of piercing whistles. The group which had formed around the young man with the cap suddenly thinned out and Marinica saw a policeman dragging the young man by the arm and forcing him into the station building through the glass door which bore the word "Stationmaster." The young man was resisting and shouting, "That is not true, monsieur. I said nothing!"

The peasants on the platform were booing and jeering more loudly than ever.

"What's the meaning of all this?" Marinica asked. The men who were hooting and whistling all around him moved away without answering and started shouting, "Let him go! Let him go!"

A switchman, passing along the platform with his ponderous hammer resting on his shoulder, said loudly, "Yes, they ought to let him go. He's done no harm. Here, take this, mate." He began distributing leaflets to everybody. Marinica took one, looked at it, folded it slowly, and put it in his pocket.

Meanwhile, like a swarm of bees, people were crowding and shouting outside the window of the stationmaster's office. Others, assembled in groups of three or four, were listening while one of their number haltingly read aloud the pamphlet distributed by the switchman, or the newspapers which had just arrived by the train. Then a clear, city voice with carefully articulated vowel sounds rose above the uproar.

"What's going on here, good people? What is it you want? What's happened? I am your Prefect. Tell me what it is all about."

The gentleman who spoke was young and handsome, with a neatly waxed mustache. He was wearing a checked suit of English cut and a collar so high that it pushed his head back and forced him to look down his nose at people.

The peasants fell silent. It was Marinica who answered.

"The student, sir. They've taken him to the station office. They've arrested him."

The people turned to look at Marinica.

"Come nearer. Who's arrested the student?"

"The policeman, sir. Tell him to let him go, otherwise there'll be trouble. . . . Is there no justice? What harm's he done? He was explaining to the men what they ought to do . . ."

Astounded, the Prefect looked all around him. Something unusual was happening. "Whom are you talking about?" he said. "The student? What was he telling the people?"

Massed in front of him like a wall, the peasants still remained silent. Then there was a rising murmur of discontent.

Under his breath Marinica said, "He did well to tell them what he did. . . ."

The Prefect flushed. He ought not to have become involved in this business, and was beginning to realize the fact. But it was too late to withdraw. Or could he still get out of it? He went into the stationmaster's office. Meanwhile the switchman who had distributed the pamphlets was reading one aloud to a group of peasants:

. . . Therefore, brother peasants, be ruthless. Cut their throats, massacre them, set fire to their houses. Think nothing of the sin, for they did not consider that you too are human beings when they put their yoke upon you and humiliated you. Hasten to do yourselves justice, for if you do not, heavy penalties will fall on you. Share out the land, burn down the manor houses, burn the registers in which your debts and obligations are recorded, drive out the boyars! I think of you constantly with a suffering and pitiful heart. This is our signature: the true friends and defenders of the Rumanian people . . .

The switchman fell silent and looked around him. His listeners stood petrified, their eyes vacant. The switchman said, "If the Army's sent against you, we'll see that they can't get there—we'll derail the troop trains or smash the brakes. We'll do something . . . Besides, the soldiers won't fire on their own brothers. They know

what they are—and what we are. All poor men and sons of peasants . . ."

He spoke very calmly, without ever raising or lowering his
voice. He went on: "If there are any army reservists among you,
lads, and the officer tells you to shoot, you shoot—but at him!"

A soldier said, "We shan't obey. We'll go home to our villages.
Considering that ours—our boyar, I mean—hasn't even fixed our
share of the crop, I'm wondering what we'll have to eat this winter. . . ."

The switchman turned to him and pulled a sad face. "You're off
home, eh? Good. And when you get there, what'll you do? Sit
down and fold your arms. That's what you all do, fold your arms.
You move about as much as the grass and the leaves. Back home
in my village at Dobrunu, we're two thousand souls. And how
many are the boyars? Five or six. And two policemen. But do you
think anyone has stirred, done anything? The men toil and moil
and sweat blood, pay the tax and the fines and the policeman's
pint of wine. That was why I ran away and took up this trade. But
those two thousand who stayed behind in the village—all they
need do is to surround the boyar in the street, and they could
crush him by pressing him between their chests, with a simple
shove. They wouldn't even have to lay a finger on him—just with
their chests, like I said. And you others, what are you doing? Going back home? Good. But once there, what will you do?"

The peasants held their tongues. It was true: none of them
knew what they would do once they were back home. In the ensuing silence Marinica's voice rose again. "All right, then, you tell
us. What should we do?"

"Listen once again to what's written on this paper," the switchman said. He pulled the sheet from his pocket and started reading
it again, emphasizing every word. He still held his hammer in the
left hand, and from time to time he swung it like a club.

The station bell sounded two clear notes. Inside the building,
the Prefect, looking bored and with his attention wandering, was
listening to the policeman's accusation.

"He's an agitator, getting the people worked up . . . telling them a lot of rubbish about sharing out the land, and how they ought to set fire to the Prince's manor house. Yes, sir, that's what he said."

The young man protested. "I didn't even understand what they wanted with me, I give you my word of honor, monsieur. In any case, I'm not a student, I'm a schoolboy in the top form, about to take my matriculation. . . . I just answered by saying whatever came into my head, I give you my word. I beg you to let me go—I'm going to miss my train."

The Prefect studied the youth's pimply face. The young man kept on giving his word of honor.

"Very well, young man, you may go." Then, turning to the policeman: "Is there a telephone here? I want to get in touch with the town."

While he was telephoning for a score of soldiers to be sent on the following day to guard the Prince's castle and park, he heard the peasants uttering shouts of joy and cheers for the high-school boy as he emerged. With burning ears and his cap askew, the youth disappeared into one of the coaches. The train started. A shout went up from the crowd of peasants. Standing on the steps of several coaches were soldiers rejoining their regiments after leave. They fired some rifle shots by way of salute.

The Prefect came out onto the platform and pushed his way through the crowd, saying, "Well, my good men, as you see, the matter was easily put right. It was simply a mistake. All you have to do is to ask for things calmly, to present your claims in an orderly manner. Come and ask me whenever you need something, and justice will be done. Why have such a crowd of you come here, to the station?"

"We're reservists . . ."

"Oh, indeed? Well, that's fine—bravo! Your king and country need you. Do your duty."

Suddenly a man hidden in the crowd cried out sharply, "But we won't open fire on our brothers!"

There was a mutter of discontent: no, they weren't going to shoot their own brothers. The Prefect's eyes went from face to face.

What had got into these people? Had they all gone mad? Been contaminated, perhaps, by the revolt which had broken out in Moldavia? Impossible! and yet . . .

"Have you been asked to, my good men? Go quietly about your business, carry out your superiors' orders, keep your faith in God, and believe me, everything will be for the best. Don't listen to the fools who go about talking thoughtless nonsense. What villages are you from?"

Some came from Hotare, others from Salcia, Vadastra, or Vladomira, all villages in the marshes. The Prefect bade them good day and made swiftly for the Prince's carriage which was waiting for him behind the station. The coachman was a gypsy. The mettlesome black horses were stamping and straining at the bit. The Prefect mopped his face with a handkerchief. The carriage set off and was soon hidden by the low houses behind the station.

When the Prefect had taken leave of the peasants only a few of them had returned his greeting, reluctantly. They were the most docile. The rest had turned their backs and formed groups around one of their number who was reading aloud from the newspapers which had come by the morning train. The papers contained news touching the rising in Moldavia. Others, talking loudly, went off along one of the muddy roads.

Marinica departed alone. He walked fast and had soon overtaken all the others who were leaving the station. Soon there were no houses in sight. Shivering with cold, Marinica moved on, carrying his staff under one arm, his shoulders hunched and his ears covered by the upturned collar of his tunic. In the dark woods the dry branches rattled against one another; here and there plowed fields were appearing beneath the last layers of snow which the March sun was beginning to melt. Clouds sailed across a smoke-colored sky. Sometimes a fine, icy rain seeped through the wet blanket of fog, pattering like small hail, and sometimes snow fell in utter silence. Numbed by cold, Marinica pushed on, hands deep in pockets, unable to grasp the thoughts that were running through his mind.

He forged ahead for some time, seeing nothing until a little yellow fox slunk across his path and stopped, ears pricked, to look at him.

"Hey!" he called.

But the fox did not move, knowing perfectly well that the man was too far away to do him any harm. Marinica laughed, shrugged his shoulders, and went on his way, watched from a distance by the little animal. He walked carefully around puddles, sometimes stepping on to the bank beside the road. From time to time he tried whistling between his teeth, but soon gave it up.

A bitter wind began to blow. It stopped snowing. Marinica sniffed the air and blinked his eyes. The earth smelled good—the wet soil the sun was beginning to warm. Marinica wiggled his toes, remembering the feel of earth under his feet when he followed the plow. The scent of plowed earth became stronger and stronger. It was coming up from the Danube, mixed with the smell of the marshes.

Marinica shivered and set off again with long strides. His mind had cleared: now he understood.

He must no longer appear timid, as hitherto. Henceforth, he must go all out, whatever happened. Marinica shut his eyes and thought of all the manor houses in the neighborhood, with their barns and byres and stables, where horses and servants slept. And suddenly he saw them drowned in blood, devoured by flames and smoke.

Squatting at the roadside, a little below the level of the road, small houses roofed with grayish thatch came in sight. Just at the entrance to the village, Marinica saw a man rise from the tree-stump on which he had been sitting beside the road, take three paces, slightly dragging one leg, and then stand waiting for him. The man was young, tall and broad-shouldered, with blue-green eyes.

"Have you come from far away?" he asked.

"Quite far . . ."

"Farther than the station?"

Marinica nodded. "From the station it's not even a day's walk."

"Then you've been several days on the road already?"

"Yes. So long that I no longer know how many," Marinica said. And he added, "But I'm tired. Also, I'm hungry—and cold. . . ."

"Then you'd better come home and have a bite and a rest," the other returned. "But we have no fire."

He said this casually, for the sake of something to say. Then he asked cautiously, "How are—things?"

"Very well, of course," Marinica said. "There are orders for the people to rise."

"Orders, eh? Are there really?"

"I have seen them with my own eyes," Marinica said.

"Come along quickly," the other said, clutching Marinica by the sleeve and dragging him toward the village. As they went he halted several times to look him over from head to foot. Suddenly suspicious, he asked, "Who sent you to us? Did you come of your own accord, just like that?"

"Never mind about that, friend," Marinica said wearily. "There's no need for you to be told everything." The man looked away, sighed deeply, and quickened his pace, still pulling Marinica along.

The village was almost deserted. Here and there a dog, its coat spiky from the rain, crossed the road. One or two men in brown homespun, with their fur caps pulled down to their eyes, turned to watch them pass. A dense group of peasants stood outside the Town Hall. One or two hailed Marinica's companion. "Hey, there, Rizea!"

But the man seemed to hear nothing; still dragging Marinica, he went on to a little footbridge which crossed the ditch beside the road and led into a yard. There Rizea seemed to hesitate for some seconds, then turned toward Marinica and asked, "So the people have revolted, have they?"

Marinica's look was candid and direct. He said, "They have. They are starting fires everywhere, killing the boyars. Yes, they are up in arms. An order is an order!"

Rizea considered this for some seconds and then, dragging one leg, he led the way into the courtyard. In front of the dilapidated cottage he stopped once more and turned to Marinica, looking him up and down suspiciously. "Who gave the order?"

"The Queen," Marinica said wearily.

Lost in thought, Rizea was silent; then he said, "That's not possible. It's the King who gives orders, not her. And he's on the boyars' side. So how can . . . ?"

"The King is dead," Marinica said.

Rizea stared at him out of his green eyes, heavy with distress. He was a handsome lad, with a broad face and arched eyebrows. He was leaning with his shoulder against the door of the house, head lowered as if listening to what was going on inside. Abruptly he made up his mind, opened the door and went in, beckoning Marinica to follow him.

"Come," he said. A number of peasants were assembled in the dim light of the tiny room. It was not possible to see their faces clearly. There was a woman among them, however, her head wrapped in a shawl. The men were talking in low voices, without haste, and quite calmly. The moment they saw Rizea and Marinica they fell silent. Marinica wished them good day; they responded with a vague murmur of greeting and closed up a little to make room for him on the bench. "Give him something to eat," Rizea said to the woman. "He has come a long way."

"What am I to give him?" the woman answered in a surly tone. "Fancy inviting company now . . ."

"Give him whatever you can find," Rizea replied.

The other men did not speak. The woman pulled her shawl more tightly around her shoulders and said, "You know perfectly well you threw it all away. You said it was bad—the *mamaliga*—and would not even taste it. You ought to have remembered that the harvest isn't in yet."

"Didn't you make another?" Rizea interrupted.

But the woman had already left the room. She came back carrying a piece of *mamaliga* and an onion. Marinica ate, dipping the onion in salt. Rizea said to him, "That's how it is with us—we've forgotten the taste of meat. For us it is *mamaliga* and onions every day."

"Don't forget the spices," one of the men said, and everybody laughed, but there was no merriment in their laughter. Another said, "The maize is spoiled because the boyar will not let us get in our share of the crop before winter. And he no longer allows us to fish in the ponds."

"My father told me that at one time the people lived quite well in these parts," Rizea said.

"I don't believe it," said the woman. The others said nothing.

"It's that swine of a Prince," Rizea muttered. "Ah, God in heaven——"

He broke off, knowing well that no oath could help him. Marinica wiped his lips with the back of his hand. Rizea gave him an odd look and said, "This man comes from far away. He brings news."

The peasants all leaned forward slightly. One of them said in a rough voice, "News? It's not news we need here, it's justice."

"Come now, father Iordake," Rizea said, "let him talk. You'll see."

"See what? I've seen it all," Iordake said. "I've no need of news. It's justice I want."

A mutter rose from the others.

"He's had troubles," Rizea said to Marinica, indicating Iordake.

Iordake leaned farther forward: he was a burly man with a florid face. His hands were gnarled and his shaven scalp almost blue. The whites of his eyes were streaked with fine red veins.

"I can see you're a stranger," he said. "Listen, I'll tell you: one day I went to see Ivancea—he's the bailiff to the rotten old hag Smadoviceano who's our landowner—and this fat pig Ivancea says to me, 'Iordake,' he says, 'I've heard that you have money.' 'Money, Master Ivancea?' I say. 'Certainly I have money. I'm full of money, what with all I inherited from my father. . . .'"

There was bitter laughter. "How was I to know what the man had at the back of his mind?" Iordake resumed. "And now only yesterday—what I've just told you happened in the autumn—yes, yesterday, the policeman comes to my house with a paper, a writ, saying I must pay my debt to Ivancea. 'What debt?' say I. 'Why,' says he, 'the debt of five hundred lei. Look at this,' he says. 'It's the decision of the judge at Salcia. You were summoned before the judge,' he says. 'You should've gone.' 'Summoned?' I say. 'When was I summoned?' He maintains I had a paper and then never went. 'Listen to me,' I say, 'about this paper and this debt; I'm ready to go before the good God if necessary, but here and now I'm going to see this judge!' The policeman was grinning under his mustache. 'The time's up,' he says, 'you can't contest it now. The case is over and done with.' "

Iordake fell silent and cast a glance around him, then went on: "I asked the advice of the people in our village. They told me, 'It's Ivancea's usual trick. He's hand in glove with the police,' they said, 'and the Mayor. He buys them drink so that the summonses don't come in time. So we don't know anything and meanwhile they judge the case.' "

Iordake sighed deeply, groaned, and putting his clenched fists on his knees, continued: "Where am I to find so much money? Who'll buy what I can still find to sell? The innkeeper and the others, the rich ones, Geambashu or Kiritza, when they see us in trouble they skin us alive. . . . Oh, God in heaven!"

Rizea said, "You could go to the Mayor; he's rich, he's got enough."

Iordake stared at him for a long time, then bowed his head.

"Hold your tongue!" the woman shouted at Rizea. "Are you mad, to make trouble for this man?"

Rizea turned calmly to Marinica and explained: "It's happened to several of them but they're ashamed to admit it; they're afraid of being the laughingstock of the village. So they'd rather pay. They sell their horses, they sell their oxen, their spades, everything. They even sell themselves. And when they've nothing left to sell, why . . ."

There was a long silence. A man broke it abruptly. "We're all in debt. I don't know how they manage it, but a man must slave all his life to pay a debt of twenty lei—and meanwhile their barns, the Prince's and old Smadoviceano's, are bursting with wheat. When we had that drought six years ago so that there were lizards

out in the very fields, we went on our knees to them to help us—
there was nothing for it—and it was 'Want a handful of flour, do
you, you good-for-nothings? Well, you can sweat for it for a
year, or two, or three . . .' "

There was another silence. This time it was Marinica who broke
it. "In Moldavia they've set fire to everything. . . . They've set
their plowshares in the boyars' land. There were estates there so
vast you couldn't reach the end of them, and all belonging to one
boyar. So you could never escape from him, because there was
nowhere to go. . . ."

"It's the same here," Rizea said. "The Prince's land runs from
Hotare to Vladomira, from Vadastra to Studine. A man can't
breathe any longer, especially now there's old Smadoviceano too."

"They've bled the farmers," Marinica said. "Yes, and they've
given them their reckoning. There was one back there who said,
'Next year it'll be you I'll harness to the yoke instead of your
oxen—you and your wives.' They killed him too. . . ."

"That Greek farmer of the Prince's at Vladomira—Alexiu, he
calls himself—he said the same thing. Here they're mostly Rumanians, but there are Greeks too . . ."

"Greek or Rumanian, what's the odds," Iordake said. "The
master's still the master."

Marinica said, "When you go through Moldavia, the smoke
from the fields is like a veil before your eyes. They've set fire to
everything. Even the wind smells of burning."

Rizea was staring, motionless, at Marinica. He wanted to join
in the conversation, but changed his mind.

"Did they set fire to the wheat as well?" one of the men asked
him.

"Those who wanted to carry it off did so, and shared it among
them. The others burned what was left. They burned everything."

Marinica spoke calmly but with manifest satisfaction of all that
had to do with the burning. The others sat and stared at him. Until
then Marinica had been in their midst as a shade among other
shades, but now they saw him clearly, as if he were lit by the
flames of the conflagrations he described. In the beginning he had

spoken in a detached, faraway voice. Now, sitting bolt upright, he looked them in the eyes and said:

"Yes, they have revolted. They are burning the manors, burning the state registers, and killing the boyars. And now they are sharing out the land. In some cases they are taking over whole estates and cultivating them in common. The rising is taking place everywhere. Wherever I went I saw them all rise. There are some who make red flags and carry them from village to village. And they ride white horses. You have heard about the students, haven't you— you've heard tell of them, surely?"

All the men were very still, with their eyes fixed on him. Even Iordake the debtor, who had not ceased to sigh and clasp his head in his hands, now looked attentively into the stranger's face. Rizea lowered his head and cast strange looks at Marinica, looks full of suspicion. The woman had drawn a corner of her shawl over her mouth and was literally devouring Marinica with her eyes. One man answered Marinica.

"We have heard of them, from time to time. . . ."

"They travel up and down the country," Marinica said. "They know a great deal and they carry sabers. They have writs which protect them, and no man has the right to do them the least harm. Even the Army must obey them. If they come to a village where the people have done nothing for themselves, the students say to them, 'Ah, so you have not shared out the boyars' lands among yourselves? Very well, you shall be punished; the land will not be given to you. But your house will be burned because you have not had faith in us,' they say. And then they kill all the people in the village."

"Have you seen this with your own eyes?" Iordake asked him.

"Yes, I have seen them," Marinica replied. "Sometimes they go to the fairs. In the train everyone was saying that they had seen them, and that there was even a student at the station who talked to them, because they're educated, these students are, and besides they know the laws. . . . This one at the station said to the re-servists who were there, 'Brothers, when the officer tells you to fire on your kinsmen, turn about and fire on your officers.' The

Prefect was at the station and he wanted to have him arrested. But when the Prefect saw that he was a student, he let him go at once. The people cried out against the Prefect, and he turned green with fright. No, nobody dares to lay a finger on the students. They are mounted on white horses and they bear letters from seven countries, and from the Queen, with orders to change the lot of the unhappy Rumanian people. For the King is dead, and that's what causes *their* misfortune. . . ."

There was no need for him to be more precise: the people knew whom he meant. In the ensuing silence all held their breath and reflected. A man gave a long sigh, then tapped Marinica on the shoulder and said to him, "Let's go and find some others."

Iordake rose also, heavily, and followed them into the yard. All three stopped a moment and breathed the strong, keen air—the air of spring which nevertheless still smelled of snow.

"Let's go to Mototolea's," Rizea said, and set out. The others followed him, slipping in the mud of the road. More and more men appeared at the doors of their cottages. A woman called something in a powerful voice from the bottom of an alley, but nobody understood what she wanted.

They crossed a deserted yard and went into a house where peasants were arguing in the dim light. Mototolea, the master of the house, was talking loudly. When the three visitors came in he paused for a moment, then went on: "Ten thousand acres. Yes, they own ten thousand acres." His listeners muttered among themselves and pressed against one another.

"What do you say to that, brothers, eh? What do you say to that? It's no longer possible. We cannot go on. Look: I lay myself down there on the earth, and let myself die. Then what? They offer us one share in three, but what they demand into the bargain, that they take care not to say. A whole acre that we must break and plow, sow with our own seed, harrow, cut, carry, and thresh. And who carries the grain to the Danube? Who loads it into the lighters? Ah, great God in heaven, if there be one among you still willing to labor for the boyar, may he rot in the open fields like Ouracou's son!"

There followed a silence; then Rizea said suddenly, "No, for since Ouracou's son was carried home it seems he will recover."

Mototolea paid no attention to him, but went on: "Nor is that all. Yet another acre of every three to sow for nothing. And five days to work with our hands for the master, carrying a hundred bushels to the Danube. When I think of all this it comes over me that I should do well to dig a trench, here in the middle of my house, and to say to my wife, 'Take this shovel and cover me with earth.'"

The men snarled. Intimidated, Mototolea's wife avoided their eyes. But, though his voice failed and beads of sweat ran down his face, Mototolea went on: "And all this does not satisfy him, brothers. Even though we take off our caps when the old hag Smadovice- ano passes in her carriage, it's no good. You go to Master Ivancea to come to terms with him. 'Ah,' says he, 'here's Mototolea. Why don't you take off your cap when you see the lady pass in her carriage?' 'Ah, but I did, to be sure I took it off, Master Ivan- cea!' 'Yes,' says he, 'but I too was in the carriage and I saw you from a distance, and you should have removed your cap the mo- ment I saw you. The fine is five lei, Mototolea!' That's how it is, brothers, that I have sweated blood since I came into this world. This slut of a wife of mine goes to the fountain to fetch water and raises her skirts to save getting them dirty. 'Mototolea! Your wife has no modesty, Mototolea!' The blood rushes to my head. What has my wife's modesty to do with him? To hell with him! But I control myself—I can't do otherwise. I say, 'What does she do, Master Ivancea?' 'She walks about like a shameless woman, lifting her skirts,' says he. 'Pay a fine of five lei and I'll call it quits.'"

Mototolea bowed very low and spread wide his arms, the image of humility and defeat.

"For my part I have had enough. Perhaps he's right. Perhaps it is written somewhere. But I'm done with living. I'm going to lie down on the earth and let myself die."

"And the business of the alignment, father Ion, how was that?" Rizea said. "Tell us the story of the alignment."

Mototolea gave a short, dry laugh; a sick laugh. "Yes. The alignment. Anyone would think you didn't know it."

"We know, we know," the others muttered.

"Tell it to this man, who is not from these parts."

"The matter of the alignment. Well then, it was like this: we were coming in from the fields, the carts full of sheaves of wheat. . . . Look: it happened to Iordake this autumn; and to me; and to Ouracou. You see, this Ivancea wants the sheaves carried straight to the threshing machine. We don't make ricks. So there are about a hundred carts loaded with all the earth's treasure, as you might say, and him not taking his eyes off it. Suddenly he says, 'What about your alignment? You're not in line with the others! Five lei fine!' And where are you to find five lei? You're in debt, like Iordake. No need to tell *him* about debts; he knows already."

Again the people laughed bitterly. Their faces were like clay. Some of them had rotten teeth. Their dark eyes were still young, but the stubble on their hollow cheeks was turning gray.

"A real master," Mototolea said, "there's no denying it. He makes himself felt. We're ready to set off for the Danube—a hundred carts at a time, when up comes Ivancea with his hog's face, and laughs and says, 'A little patience. I'm having another two hundred carts loaded.' 'But Master Ivancea,' we say, 'the weeks are passing and we have nothing to put in our bellies, and our little ones are eating moldy *mamaliga*.' 'That's all right,' he says, 'I know you. I'm not such a fool as to swallow your yarns. You're a pack of thieves.' If we're thieves, then what's he? When he offers us one in three, he always makes us work three and a half, and on top of that we have to do unpaid work on two acres."

Then Marinica spoke up. "In Moldavia the people have risen. They're burning and killing and slaughtering and destroying the registers in which the contracts are written down. . . ."

Once again he told his tale, and behind his words the clamor of the rebellious peasantry seemed audible, the thunder of falling masonry as walls collapsed in flames, the dripping of blood from the slit throats of boyars and farmers. The hatred and the hunger that had gnawed at their vitals for centuries, the accumulated humiliations, were bodied forth in their midst and bewitched them. When Marinica had finished the peasants were silent for a while. A few of them still had questions to ask. They still had their doubts. The troops might fire on them. Rizea, who had been drinking steadily, burst out laughing.

"Never!" he said. "They're under orders to do nothing. Why, don't you see, he's a student himself, he has in his pocket a letter from the seven powers of the earth and from the Queen, saying that our time is come—the time to take the fat from the lungs of the rich and lay it upon the livers of the poor."

There was a sort of cheerfulness in him which differed from that of the other peasants. Their spirit was somber and deadened, but his was vital and vibrant so that those near him were uneasy and the woman looked at him wide-eyed. Rizea said to Mototolea, "Listen, father Ion, the thing to do is to go from house to house. Come with us to Ouracou's, father Ion. Between now and nightfall we may do some good work."

Mototolea stared at Rizea. Then he jammed his fur cap hard down on his head, and in a powerful voice said, "Let's go."

He rushed out into the yard, the rest following in a crowd. Mototolea's wife held Rizea back for a moment on the threshold, and asked in a low voice, "You've made it up with my man, have you?"

Rizea did not answer her.

"Do you know what he said? That he will tie me to the tail of his cart, like a dog, and whip up the horses to teach me to run. . . . But he doesn't suspect you. Rizea, I would rather die. You heard the things he said in front of me when he was pretending to talk of other things. Don't desert me, Rizea!"

Rizea looked at her out of his troubled green eyes and said, "I am not deserting you. But now we have other things to do. The revolution has come." He looked at her again and repeated, "No, I am not deserting you; don't distress yourself."

He turned his back on her and followed the others; he dragged his leg, but he was broad and tall and walked quickly for all that.

At Ouracou's they found only the wife and son. Ouracou had gone to the Town Hall for news. Stretched on a bench, Zaharia, Ouracou's son, lay on his side, covered with a sheepskin cloak. His cheeks were hollow and his eyes bright with fever. A heavy, sickening stench hung about him, and when he spoke his voice whistled in his throat like a death rattle.

"What's happening?" he asked. "What are they all doing? It seems we are to be the laughingstock of all the world!"

"No, no," Rizea said, "it's not so."

"But it is so. We shall be shamed. At Vladomira they have already decided to burn down the Prince's house tonight."

"How do you know that?" Rizea asked suspiciously.

Zaharia moved and tossed on his couch, revived. His eyes burned in his ashen face. He looked at Marinica, raised himself on one elbow and threw back one corner of the sheepskin covering, exposing his shirt; a red stain marked it at the place where he had bled. The stench of the festering wound grew stronger and spread through the room.

Zaharia stared at Marinica and then asked Rizea, "Has he come to be your student and lead you? Is this the man?"

Rizea glanced at Marinica and said simply, "Yes."

Zaharia lowered his head and coughed slightly; his brow was damp with sweat. He said, "Ah, God in heaven," put a hand inside his shirt, felt himself, and went on, laughing: "I can feel them under the skin, against my ribs. But perhaps there is one that went deeper and is stopping me from breathing. It was the day before yesterday," he explained to Marinica. "I was going along the road in my cart, beside the Prince's private road that goes to Vadastra. And suddenly the Prince drove up in his carriage at full speed. He had been out shooting, and was lolling back against the cushions with his monocle in his eye and his dogs beside him. I had no time to protect myself. I saw him stand up, put his gun to his shoulder, and shoot at me. I don't know how I managed to jump out of the cart and make off across the fields . . ."

He paused, short of breath, and then went on, exhausted: "But he fired the other barrel . . ."

He fell back on to his side and muttered, "I felt a burning pain and fell as I ran, like a dead man. . . ."

The men standing beside him said nothing. Then Iordake spoke up. "The Prince is a greater boyar than our Ivancea. *He* doesn't amuse himself by fining you five lei. He takes your life, eh?"

Marinica looked at Ouracou's wife and at the lad who lay there under the cloak, his nostrils pinched, his nose waxen. "In Moldavia the people have risen and are cutting the boyars' throats and killing them," he said in a low voice.

Zaharia opened his eyes again. "Are they really killing the boyars? Tell me."

Smiling, he closed his eyes. He was not sleeping, he was listening. Marinica repeated his tale—the great burnings, the boyars burned alive in their manor houses. He spoke calmly, giving many details, and the others listened, filled with confidence. Twice Ouracou's neighbors came into the house, women as well as men, and little by little a crowd gathered. When Marinica had finished speaking, Rizea rose and said, "Let's get on with our round."

And they all rose, ready to depart. The wounded man called out, "Listen, Rizea, let the Prince's head be brought to me here, so that I may have it smoked and stick it upon a stake in the yard."

They began to laugh, but the rest did not laugh. Rizea and Iordake remained behind.

"How did you know?" Rizea asked Zaharia.

"Know what?" the boy replied wearily.

"About the student."

Zaharia laughed softly. "Jougoulete's son told me. He was in your house when the two of you came in. He came and told me."

Rizea understood, and prepared to leave. Ouracou's wife, a thin and withered woman, stopped him in the doorway. "He is dying," she said calmly.

Rizea nodded. Iordake stood beside him, motionless. Out in the muddy road Mototolea was shouting in the midst of Marinica's audience. In the sky above the marshes two banks of cloud floated, a streak of greenish light visible between them. A steady breeze, heavy with the smell of stagnant water, blew from the same quarter. Beyond, to the north, rose a hill bristling with trees, like a brush. That way lay old Smadoviceano's house.

Zaharia's mother sighed. "The life is draining out of him."

Iordake said hoarsely, "We shall judge them, never fear! Yes, we shall judge them!"

The woman watched, unmoving, as they went out, heads bowed and shoulders hunched. They went from house to house and the throng following Marinica, Iordake, and Mototolea swelled steadily. They talked among themselves, cursing and swearing, but without raising their voices. At each end of the village there were sheaves of blackened maize from which the boyar had not yet taken his tithe; they were covered with a thin layer of snow. The men pointed them out to one another and swore. From time to time one or two men broke away from the group to go to their own homes or to a neighbor's to spread the news. All afternoon the people assembled in the center of the village: they were waiting, and seemed uneasy and undecided. And still they came, pouring in like blood going to the head of an angry man.

Stopping outside a hovel, Rizea called out, "Hey! Pîrvou!"

He waited. After a while a man emerged and looked mutely at him. The man's lips were swollen and cracked and covered with peeling white skin. There were violet patches on his face. "What's the matter?" he asked hoarsely, and stood there with his body twisted, looking embarrassed before other men.

"Come along, Pîrvou. The people have rebelled. Come with us. Do you hear, Pîrvou?"

"I hear . . ." But he turned away, and stooping, made as if to return to his hovel. Over his shoulder, he muttered, "I can't come. I dare not show myself . . ."

Rizea caught him by the arm. "Are you out of your mind? You're not the only one who's ill!"

"Come, Pîrvou, there's no shame in it!" Iordake cried. "In the past, years ago, when I was a child, people would have pointed the finger of scorn at you. But who is there now who does not eat rotten maize flour? Do you think you're the only one in the village? Don't be such a fool, for God's sake!" He gave him a friendly blow on the back.

"If only I could eat a little fish!" Pîrvou said. "Here, look at the palms of my hands. A running sore. When shall I be able to plow the boyar's acres? And do you think he'll let me fish? Not even between Reviga and the bend in the river, where he allows all the village to fish—all the village except me. I no longer have the strength. . . . And there's Geambashu who lent me twenty lei five years ago and now makes me do five rods of hoeing and fifteen of reaping every summer. And that's only the interest; he hasn't reduced the debt. I still owe him twenty lei. I shall owe them for as long as I live. And my children will be slaves forever. One boyar was bad enough, but now we have several boyars—all the rich men of the village. But I'm not long for this world and I shall be out of it all soon. . . ."

Pîrvou's children came out onto the doorstep, sniffling. Their bellies were swollen, their eyes were sunk deep in their sockets, and their little faces were gray.

"All over the land the people have risen in revolt," Marinica said. "They are setting fire to the manor houses, tearing up the receipts, burning the registers, and cutting the boyars' throats."

Pîrvou turned back toward them; he looked at each in turn and asked, "What are they doing to the moneylenders?"

"Every man deals with them as he likes," Marinica said.

Iordake pulled at Pîrvou's sleeve to draw him after them, but the sick man still hung back. "Pîrvou," Marinica said, "you must come with us. There is much to be done in the village, many people to speak to. . . ."

And he moved off, followed by the others. But Rizea hung back, went up to Pîrvou, and gave him a friendly punch in the ribs. Pîrvou's face brightened. A sort of fever took possession of him. "Not so hard, man!" he said, almost gaily.

"Come along, Pîrvou. There's no time to lose."

"Wait!" Pîrvou said. "A moment, and I'm with you." He dived into his hovel and emerged almost at once, carrying an ax. A woman's face appeared in the doorway. Rizea and Pîrvou hastened after the others.

"What do you want to bring your ax for?" Rizea said. "Do you think we're going to chop wood?"

But Pîrvou did not answer. He walked swiftly, looking straight in front of him, and a look almost of happy expectation lit up his pellagra-disfigured face.

Between the church, the Town Hall, and one of the drink shops, a crowd had assembled; some men stood in compact groups, others were scattered about. They all seemed calm. Most of them were talking and waiting, hands in pockets. Women, their heads wrapped in shawls, stood with children in the doorways of the houses. Starved dogs, their ribs sticking through the skin, roamed about, snapping at one another.

A cart drove up at a trot, slowing down as it reached the crowd. There were three peasants and two women in it; they came from Vadastra and were known to the villagers.

"What news out your way?" someone asked.

"We're ready. You'll see what's going to happen tonight," one of the newcomers replied joyfully. The women burst out laughing and the men joined in. The assembled peasants also began to laugh, but their laughter was mirthless and as if surprised out of them. They stood watching the cart from Vadastra as it drove away.

"They're going to Dobrunu," one man said. "It seems that it's started there too. . . ."

And they went on waiting, standing, trampling the cold mud with their bare feet. In one corner Rizea was saying: "After nightfall, lads, when we ring the bells, you will all gather here to agree on what's to be done."

"I shall bring these with me, Rizea," a young man said, displaying a pair of long-barreled Turkish pistols under his jacket.

Without listening to him, Rizea went on: "Look at the Mayor! Locking himself into his house, the cur!"

The men laughed and muttered. "That's what they all do, the ones with a bit of money," Iordake said. "They go to earth and sham dead and wait to see which side comes out on top, just as

they do in politics, and believe me, Geambashu and the other rich
boys know that game all right! They share out the parts: 'You be
Liberal, I'll be Conservative.' That's politics!"

Mototolea said, "We watch them at their politics, as they call it.
And they pile up the money with a shovel!"

There was an outcry of angry voices from the drinking shop.
Shoved and hustled, the village priest and the schoolmaster came
tumbling out, ducking to avoid knocking their heads on the low
gutter. The priest was scarlet and his eyes were flashing. As he
passed through the swarm of peasants, he shouted furiously, "Just
wait and see! You shall pay for this!"

"How are we going to pay? Why should we?" the people
shouted roughly, barring his way. "What business is it of yours
what we do?" Over their heads came Rizea's voice, saying, "So
long as you get your stipend, what do you care?"

Iordake thrust his face into the priest's. "It's the boyars who
pay you, isn't it?" he cried. Someone yelled, "Listen, you pope,
we'll skin you and have you stuffed. We want your skin, and the
Mayor's! I'll flay the pair of you myself!"

The priest turned deathly pale and said in a conciliatory voice,
"Come now, come, my sons! I speak a few words in anger, not
thinking, and you round on me as if I had done God knows what."

Muttering, he tried to disappear into the crowd. With evil
glances, the peasants made way for him reluctantly. Meanwhile the
schoolmaster too had become involved. Rizea was shaking him and
saying, "Why do you hide the newspapers from us, eh? Why don't
you tell us what's happening?"

"Happening, Rizea? Why should anything be happening? What
newspapers are you talking about? I've had no newspapers any
more than you have."

Shaking with anger and impatience, Rizea let him go. "So you
don't know what's happening? Then you're soon going to find
out!"

The schoolmaster made off, head bowed. The people muttered
as he passed, ready to jeer. Iordake was saying to Pîrvou, "They're
killing you by inches too, my friend. It was the Mayor who did for

me. But patience; we shall be paying a little call on them tonight
—with a few others. We'll cure them of their craving to be moneylenders."

"They're not the only ones," Pîrvou remarked. "There's Melitaru too, and Kiritza."

"Don't worry about them! They'll all come up for trial. Not one
will get away," Iordake said.

It was already dark. Noiseless on its rubber-tired wheels, the
Prince's carriage, lamps lit, bowled into the village, drawn by two
high-stepping black horses. The Prefect was its only passenger.
"Make way! Make way for the Prefect!" the gypsy coachman
shouted to the villagers. But the crowd closed into a solid barrier
against the horses, who reared, snorting nervously.

"What's the matter here, good people? I am your Prefect. Tell
me all about it! If you have a complaint, let me hear it."

The Prefect's voice was pitched higher than usual, and his anxious eyes shifted from face to face. Not even on fair-days had he
seen such a crowd. Those nearest the carriage were all talking at
once: "Sharecropping . . . contracts . . . too harsh . . . we've
had enough . . . land! We want land!"

"The boyar has ten thousand acres!" Rizea yelled at the Prefect.
"Let him give us at least a small part of it! We'll clear virgin land
if we must. Let him sell to the Community! We'll pay him in
money or work, as he likes. We must have land! You're not going
to kill the lot of us! We need land and we need it now. It's got to
be handed over. That's our complaint."

Rizea had spoken firmly. His eyes were shining. He felt himself
arrayed against all the powers of the earth. He knew that this was
the end. But what end? The end of whom, of what? He had no
idea, but he knew that it was the end. It was that which gave him
strength to act, to speak as he had just spoken.

"I will speak to the boyar, good people. I will speak to him
myself. I will be your spokesman to the landowners and insist that
you be granted rights and better conditions. . . ."

Behind him, vibrant with excitement, the people surged and
pressed forward.

"What's he saying?"

"He says that he himself will give us land—that he will share it out."

"He's lying!" Rizea shouted. "The man's a boyar himself! It's the boyars who pay him. Boo!"

"Boo!" the crowd yelled. "Boo!" The horses took fright and bolted. The crowd scattered to make way for them. But its clamor, full of anger and heavy with hatred, roared and resounded for a long while behind them, making them gallop ever faster. From the steps of the Town Hall, Marinica cried in a strident voice, "Listen, lads!"

Once again he called on them to hear him, but the excitement persisted.

"Listen to me, lads!"

The noise died down. Marinica stood before them, erect, his arms spread wide. He began to speak.

2

The Prefect was so much upset that he felt a need to exchange a few words with the Prince's gypsy coachman. But he demeaned himself to no purpose. The carriage was being driven on the less muddy side of the road, its rubber tires splashing water from every puddle. The horses trotted briskly, slipping sometimes in the mud. There were small bushy coppices on either side of the road, and overhead black clouds were blown endlessly across the overcast sky. To restore his voice to normal, the Prefect remarked, "What's got into them today?"

He felt that he had been humiliated: fear had been manifest in his face and in the shrillness of his voice. He reviewed the scene at the station—the peasants' faces regarding him with defiance, the way they had turned their backs on him when he took leave of them. He had been called a liar and had fled at the insult. Now he had sunk so low that he was asking the gypsy coachman for his opinion.

Without turning around, the coachman mumbled indifferently, "What do you expect, sir? They have their troubles like everybody else."

The gypsy was old, fat, and surly; he was unlucky enough to see things clearly—and unemotionally. The Prefect glared murderously at his back: the fellow was too clever by half. He took out a leather case and extracted a cigarette. There was a light wind and the carriage was traveling fast. Three matches in succession went out in the Prefect's shaking fingers.

"Stop, blast your soul!" he exploded. "Stop, you unwashed pig! Can't you see I'm trying to light a cigarette? Will you stop, you vermin!"

The carriage stopped.

"Idiot!" the Prefect snarled. He lit his cigarette clumsily and growled, "All right, get on with it. What are you waiting for?" He threw himself back on the cushions, ears and cheeks flaming.

A short time later the carriage swung between the flaking stone pillars of a wide gateway. There were barns, stables, and poultry houses at the far end of the yard. Near the gates the smell of pigsties was strong. Opposite, halfway up the slope of a hill, stood Mme Smadoviceano's manor house. It was a single-story building, constructed over an enormous cellar filled with casks. A rather steep flight of steps gave access to the veranda. The house was roofed with rusty corrugated iron.

Vague figures moved about in the dusk of the yard. Several menservants were busy around a carriage. Dogs were barking in the distance.

The Prince's carriage drew up at the steps. Two young gypsy servant girls ran to help the Prefect to alight. Their faces were puffy, utterly lacking in vivacity, and they wore their mistress's castoff clothing.

Pushing the two girls out of his way, the Prefect got down and

tersely bade the coachman, who was awaiting his orders, to stay
where he was as he would be back in a moment. But he turned
away to avoid the old man's eyes, and as he went up the uneven
concrete steps cracked by frost, he was obliged to admit to himself
that he had been wanting in courage; he had not even dared to
do what should surely have been easy enough—look the coachman
in the face.

Mme Vorvoreano was sitting in a wide, deep armchair upholstered in tattered fawn. The light from the paraffin lamps was
absorbed in the old, faded tapestries which covered the walls. The
yataghans and Turkish pistols were too rusty to reflect any light,
and so was the peeling, battered surface of the huge iron stove.

Mme Vorvoreano put down a card on the embroidered table-
cloth: a ten of spades. Then she raised her eyes, shielding them
with her hand. Her green eyes were still beautiful, but her forehead was marred by lines and a double chin gave her round-
cheeked face a look of heaviness. The heavy mass of her fair hair
was drawn back from her temples into a great sleek coil on either
side of her head. The exposed temples were marked by a network
of small, swollen veins.

She turned to her sister Eleonora and said, "You're wrong to
think he's exaggerating. On the contrary, I think he's right and
that we ought to leave."

"Yes, madame," the Prefect put in, "I advise you to go. . . ."
He flushed, and his hands fidgeted nervously. "Naturally—er—I
am sure that nothing will happen . . . Madame Eleonora, please
don't look at me with that ironical expression! I assure you that in
so far as I personally am concerned I—how shall I put it?—I do
not know the meaning of fear. The peasants cannot frighten me. I
know them and they respect me."

Eleonora was wearing a dressing gown of flowered silk, completely threadbare and covered with stains, and embellished with
very dirty lace at throat and wrists. She had lost a number of her
teeth. Locks of faded, badly dyed hair hung down over her lean

cheeks. Her yellow eyes were fixed on the Prefect with an expression of mockery. From time to time she slipped a slender ivory rod tipped with a miniature carved hand like a yellowish claw inside the lace at her throat and proceeded to scratch her back. The Prefect felt intimidated. He coughed, tugged at his mustache, swallowed the coffee grounds in the bottom of his cup without realizing it, and replaced the cup on the table.

"Please don't look at me with that ironical expression. You must allow me to point out, with all due respect, that you have no right to—to—— No right at all! I risk my life for you every day——"

Eleonora uttered a sort of croaking sound and a gleam of something which might have been merriment flickered in her demented eyes.

"You risk your life? For us? My poor friend, you're mad."

Mme Vorvoreano favored the Prefect with a brief, bored smile, meant to convey that this was a joke and that he must not be offended. But the Prefect could feel the brilliant eyes of Elvira, Mme Vorvoreano's daughter, looking at him; he became angry.

"You are really too ungrateful! Your attitude is quite shocking, if you will excuse me for saying so with such brutal candor."

Mlle Vorvoreano was a very young girl who had only recently returned from abroad and was acquainted with all the gilded youth of the capital, all those nonchalant, self-satisfied young men whose fathers spent their time watching from the balcony of the Conservative Club the carriages drive along the Mogosoaïa Bridge. Tomorrow this butterfly might be dancing at the palace, might become the "good friend" of some cabinet minister or other. . . . The Prefect swung around suddenly, trying to catch the girl's expression. But Elvira had lowered her eyes and was pretending to read. Yet it seemed to the Prefect that her frail shoulders were shaking with suppressed laughter. He rose to his feet.

"I am sorry, ladies," he said bitterly, "to have come here to be insulted by persons of such distinction and whose devoted servant I am." He bowed and added with sorrowful courtesy: "My surprise is hardly less than it was this morning, when the Prince, your kinsman, did me the honor to shoot at me——"

"What! What do you mean?" Mme Vorvoreano and her daughter chorused. Eleonora appeared to be chewing something between her partially toothless gums; her hen's eyes blinked.

"It's as I said. We were out in the fields together, where we had gone to shoot snipe, when I suddenly saw the Prince take aim and shoot at me. The shot grazed my ear. The peasant who was carrying my gun said to me, 'Don't shoot any more; if you bag more than His Highness, he'll get angry and kill you.' I controlled my indignation and took his advice. But you can readily imagine how humiliating it was for me! The Prince treated me like one of his peasants, at whom he's in the habit of shooting without warning. I've received many complaints about it and I've had to hush up a lot of trouble in consequence. . . . And yet he treats me like that! Today I bitterly regretted the help I gave him before and during the elections—for the Liberals were stronger in this constituency and without any help the Prince would never have won his seat in the Senate. It goes without saying that, as a former magistrate and as Prefect, I am convinced of the need to support the landowners' authority. But it really is not fair that I should be rewarded in this fashion. I bitterly regret having supported him!"

The Prefect had turned scarlet and was pacing the room, his hands clasped behind his back. After a brief hesitation he went on: "I know that my own origins are not princely, that I am only a humble petty bourgeois. But I will not put up with being treated like one of the peasants whom His Highness is always provoking so pointlessly, while I have to try and keep them calm and force them to undertake the unpaid labor and the exhausting work required of them on your estates. And however surprised you may be, it was not I but His Highness who lost his temper. He sent me a note this afternoon announcing that urgent business compelled him to return to Bucharest, and virtually suggesting that I owed him an apology. Moreover, the Prince took his carriage, which had only just returned from the station. There was nothing for it but for me to go to the station too. It seems that His Highness does not care to have me seen riding beside him, and I have to make the trip into town by myself. The Prefect of the department is not worthy of even that much condescension. No, ladies, it's no laughing matter! God forgive me, but there is something very wrong in all this. It cannot go on like this. No, it certainly can't go on!"

Toward the end of his tirade the Prefect's tone had become declamatory and his manner theatrical; his words fell into a void; they awakened no echo.

Mme Vorvoreano said politely, "Would you like us to convey your dissatisfaction to the Prince? I feel sure that he will regret the incident and wish to apologize."

The Prefect gaped at her, wide-eyed, and stammered, "Wh-what? You're making fun of me!" And he went on solemnly: "Be so good as to excuse me, madame, and allow me to withdraw. If that is how you receive my . . . if that is how you answer a man who in all good faith is trying to be of service to you, who has come here to warn you of the great and terrible danger which is threatening you . . . I have no wish to trespass on your patience any longer. In any case, I only called in passing and I must hurry if I am not to be caught by nightfall on my way. I kiss your hands. You will hear from me before long. I promise you that. Soon."

The Prefect went out, shutting the door behind him. In a hoarse voice Eleonora said, "He's drunk."

"No," Mme Vorvoreano said; "he did not smell of drink. It's something else. The shooting incident must have shaken him."

"It's the peasants," Elvira said. "He's afraid of them. You noticed how he tried to boast when he talked about the peasants?"

"Rubbish," Eleonora said. "You're nothing but a fool."

"Mama," Elvira said abruptly, "let's leave."

"And what about me?" Eleonora said. "You ungrateful child, you haven't a thought for me!"

"You'll come with us. Aunt, let's go."

"You're a brainless idiot. If I were your mother, I'd soon teach you to hold your tongue. Some firm handling is what you need!"

"My dear Eleonora, the child is right," said Mme Vorvoreano. "You have paid no attention to them, but even the servants seem to know something. I sense a change in them. They're hiding something from us. I think it would be wiser to return to town for a while. You know perfectly well what's been happening in Moldavia."

"Rubbish! How can I possibly leave here? You can hardly expect me to entrust all my possessions to the mercy of these rustics. Anyone can see that you don't own an acre. You've a brain like a bird's, my dear Helen. You'd be capable of letting this child starve to death if it weren't for me! Though I am by no means sure that she deserves any such consideration. You heard her yourself, just now, calmly decreeing that we were to leave. And instead of slapping her face, you approve! Disgraceful!"

Mme Vorvoreano was not listening. She knew it all by heart. But she was watching Elvira with something like terror: an outburst like this could destroy in a moment the patient labors of weeks. Elvira was looking at her aunt with open hatred. Mme Vorvoreano sat down between her daughter and her sister, who was still muttering angrily. Eleonora promptly called out, "Elvira! Where are you? Where are you hiding? Come here at once!"

Obediently Elvira rose and went to her aunt, her silk dress rustling. She had contrived to master her anger. Mme Vorvoreano uttered a sigh of relief and returned to her armchair. Elvira fetched the little card table and a pack of cards and began to play écarté with her aunt, who complained constantly as she slapped her cards down on the table.

"I don't know *who* installed himself on my chest last night, while I was sleeping," she mumbled, "but I whispered my prayers and the 'thing' went away. Didn't I groan in my sleep? But how could you have heard? You sleep like a top, for all that you spend the whole day in idleness and doing absolutely nothing. You don't even help with the housekeeping. . . . These young girls, they've nothing in their heads but love and romance and young men. Did I tell you about the dream I had about women who won't have children? I dreamed I was in hell and saw them all, and each had a necklace of withered fetuses around her neck. There, you've lost again. Let's settle up—that's what you owe me. Bring the money."

"I'll go and fetch it, Elvira dear," Mme Vorvoreano said.

"No, Mama, I'll go myself," Elvira said. Together they went into the next room.

"The old beast," Elvira exclaimed. "She's rotten with money, yet she's taken some more of mine off me. She cheats. You know she cheats, the filthy old horror!"

"Be quiet! You're not to talk like that," Mme Vorvoreano whispered. "Of course she cheats. It's her only pleasure. Pretend not to have noticed."

Elvira protested with childish indignation: "But she takes my money!"

"Patience . . . Patience . . ."

"I am patient, and so are you. But she'll live to be a hundred and she's quite capable of tricking us in the end and leaving her money to a hospital or a church!"

"Be quiet," her mother murmured, and pushed her by the shoulders back into the drawing room: it was empty.

"So long as nothing happens to all three of us!" Elvira said.

"What do you mean?"

"So long as we're not . . . Suppose the peasants around here revolt, like the others? You heard what the Prefect said . . ."

Mme Vorvoreano did not answer. Aunt Eleonora came back into the drawing room and demanded acidly, "Well, child, have you got the money?"

Mme Vorvoreano looked from her sister to her daughter. The former had taken up some knitting, and the wool was sliding between her fingers; the latter was reading a novel. She pressed her lips together in dissatisfaction and rose, supple despite her height and bulk, to go to the window. Her house dress fluttered about her as she moved and a candle on the piano flickered as she passed. Elvira looked up for a moment, then resumed reading. Mme Vorvoreano pulled aside the curtains and pressed her forehead to the windowpane. Emerging out of the limbo of night, drops of water ran slowly down the glass like particles of mercury.

Aunt Eleonora put down her knitting and asked suspiciously, "What are you hoping to see?"

Mme Vorvoreano left the window and the curtains fell softly

back into place. She smiled, embarrassed, vaguely guilty. Perhaps her sister was right: perhaps the things which she expected to see out there in the dark were only the products of an imagination stimulated by fear. "Nothing," she replied. "I was just looking."

"You're lying," Eleonora cried, "but you can take it from me, *they* won't do anything. They'd never dare! It's all a lot of nonsense. I know them better than you do, for I haven't been gallivanting off to Paris, which, incidentally, is why I've been able to hold on to my lands. *I* haven't squandered everything I had on a good-for-nothing idler of a husband. I know these peasants. I've lived close to them for forty years. They don't forget what's happened to them every time they've raised their heads, and they'll stay quiet. Oh, they complain—but let them. It's all they can do. You can believe me, they'll never raise a finger. And for goodness' sake stop fidgeting. You're driving us mad. Has your game of patience come out?"

Mme Vorvoreano was standing, shuffling the cards without thinking of what she was doing. After a silence she said, "Suppose you're right. . . . Still, you saw what it said in the papers?"

"A lot of rubbish! The newspapers lie to stir up trouble. That's all I can tell you."

Mme Vorvoreano smiled feebly, and, with fear at her heart, looked questioningly at her daughter. Elvira slowly raised her head. She was dark, like her grandmother Davida Lascari, her upper lip shadowed by down. With a face devoid of expression she looked at her mother, then lowered her eyes to resume her reading. Mme Vorvoreano shrugged, took up a candlestick in one hand, and shielding it with the other to save the flame from being blown out, left the drawing room.

She passed through a series of rooms perfumed by the little sachets of tobacco and basil which were hung between the walls and the faded tapestries to keep the moths away. She left all the doors open behind her. The flickering candle flame, preceded by a hand whose fingers glowed rosily in its radiance, wandered among springless divans and rickety cupboards. In every room she came to Mme Vorvoreano looked out of the window. But the darkness was impenetrable.

At the door leading to the servants' quarters Mme Vorvoreano paused. From here the long and tortuous staircase led down to the yard, the kitchen, the servants' quarters, and the stables. Mme Vorvoreano opened the door. From below came a confused sound of male voices. Were the grooms and farm hands quarreling? Or had they been drinking? Mme Vorvoreano put out her hand to the bell cord and pulled it, the lace on her sleeve falling back to expose a plump white arm. The bell sounded feeble amid the bursts of talk in the kitchen. There was a moment's silence, then the voices rose again, a little less noisily perhaps. Mme Vorvoreano went back to the drawing room, closing all the doors behind her.

Elvira was at the piano, playing a Chopin mazurka. Eleonora was talking at the top of her voice so as to be heard above the music. "Your mother," she was saying, "is a fool to have let you have your own way, and as for you, you're another. Sending you to Paris, indeed! Paris and your father's chorus girls—they've been the ruin of you. In my day young girls only left their convent schools to be married."

Elvira stopped playing, spun around on the piano stool, and with a smile which exposed teeth as shining as her green eyes, retorted, "In your day, Aunt! A lot of water has flowed under the bridges since then!"

"More's the pity. In my time young ladies did not come home from finishing school to go straight to a doctor and arrange for an——"

Elvira turned white and stood up, saying, "Is that any business of yours? What right have you to poke your nose into——"

Mme Vorvoreano, motionless in the doorway, broke in harshly: "That will do, Elvira! Don't be insolent to your aunt!"

"I have no need whatever of Aunt Eleanora's money, Mama! I'd rather live penniless than be forced to put up with the sort of thing I have to bear here. Why did I come here? So that she could insult me day after day? We're in a desert here, surrounded by louts, and alone with this lunatic. We are going to pay dearly for it, Mama. The country's burning around us, and we sit in this tomb waiting for Aunt Eleonora to leave us her fortune. It's horrible, horrible! I can't stand any more of it. I can't!"

Elvira sobbed uncontrollably, on the brink of hysterics. She rushed out of the room. Very pale, Mme Vorvoreano said to her sister, "My dear, I wish you wouldn't upset her like that. Leave her alone. Can't you see that she's indisposed? Every time that happens, her nerves are all on edge."

"Indisposed? What of it? What's that to me? Mademoiselle has nerves, has she? A lot I care for her nerves, my dear Helen. In our day, children went in fear and trembling of their elders. And controlled themselves. Father spoiled you because he adored you, and you thought it was going to be the same story right through. You were his favorite—to your undoing. Father would have done better to spank you every morning as he did me. Your daughter would not have come home from finishing school in *that* condition. And you still allow her to have 'nerves'! If I were you, I'd give her a good whipping!"

Eleonora did not really dislike Elvira. It was simply that she got a certain satisfaction out of making her cry. Her eyes were shining now. She picked up the little ivory hand and began scratching the nape of her neck.

Mme Vorvoreano compressed her lips. Eleonora was rich, and it was absolutely essential that the children inherit her fortune. Shrugging her shoulders, she left the drawing room. She found Elvira huddled on a divan, crying in the dark. Sitting down on the edge of the divan, she murmured, "Why can't you control yourself? Follow my example. Can anyone tell what's in *my* mind? And yet, God knows, she never tires of saying poisonous things about my marriage."

In a voice broken by sobs, Elvira moaned, "They'll kill us, Mama. They'll kill us because of her. She's obstinate, the old loony, and her obstinacy will get us all murdered."

"Will you hold your tongue! You are not to say such things."

"I can't go on, Mama. I don't want to stay here any longer."

"As if you had any choice!"

"Every day she humiliates me as she did tonight. Even the servants will soon find out what's going on."

"And whose fault is that?" Mme Vorvoreano said curtly. "You've got to learn to bear the consequences of your own acts."

In the darkness Elvira sat up and cried, "You hate me too, don't you? I know it! You're mad with jealousy, aren't you?"

Mme Vorvoreano tried to strike her daughter, but succeeded only in brushing her face with the tips of her fingers. Sighing, Elvira flung herself back on the divan. Mme Vorvoreano crossed to the window, and vainly tried to make out something in the darkness; then she returned to the drawing room, tugging nervously at her long lace cuffs.

Aunt Eleonora was conferring with her cook. Mme Vorvoreano gave her sister a hard look and, for a moment, felt a surge of hatred at the sight of her distraught expression, the tangles of gray, badly dyed hair, and her wild stare. But there was nothing to be done. She could leave with Elvira, but suppose nothing happened? Eleonora would never forgive her for running away, or else she would make her pay for forgiveness by years of daily insults. Mme Vorvoreano turned her eyes, not without a certain pleasure, to the rough, bony countenance of her sister's cook, who was standing listening to the madwoman's orders. But this pleasure at once gave way to surprise. The cook had a strange, sullen expression. Mme Vorvoreano remembered the uproar she had heard from the kitchen. She ought to have gone down, demanded to know what was going on. But somehow she had not had the courage.

"What's the matter, Maria?"

"Nothing, madam, nothing at all."

"What was all that noise below stairs just now?"

"There was no noise, madam."

"Yes, there was. I heard it."

"Perhaps I was out in the yard at the time," the woman said, turning back to Eleonora to resume discussion of the menu for dinner. Mme Vorvoreano went to the window and once again looked out into the night, peering into the distance. And there, where by daylight it would have been possible to see the manor house of Vladomira, she could see the glow of a great fire—an immense ball of flame which did not even seem to flicker.

Mme Vorvoreano felt her heart stop beating, and when it resumed it thudded so violently that it made her breathless. For a moment she came near fainting. She drew the curtains quickly and pressed her hands to her breast. She thought momentarily of calling the cook, pointing out the fire, asking if she knew what was happening to Vladomira. But a glance at the woman's set face changed her mind. Maria would no doubt say that she knew nothing about it and then vanish from the house, taking all the servants with her. No. Not that. Mme Vorvoreano sat down in an armchair and put her head between her hands.

"—and try not to make the mayonnaise lumpy," Eleonora was concluding.

"Of course, madam," the cook replied smoothly as she left the room. "I know my job."

Eleonora had resumed her knitting. For several minutes she went on muttering unintelligibly. Helen tried to think. But she succeeded only in hearing the tick-tock of the clock which had not ceased for an instant, but had hitherto been devoured by the noise of conversation.

Muffled voices from the next room froze her with terror. Elvira came in, her face a mask. The dark shadows under her eyes were the only sign of her outburst of tears.

"It's Monsieur Ivancea," she said. "Can he come in?"

"What does he want?" Aunt Eleonora inquired.

"He has something to tell you," Elvira replied, with a hostility which she made no effort to conceal. She turned on the high heels of her buttoned boots and went out, to return with Ivancea. Then she sat down on her chair, picked up her book, and pretended to read.

M. Ivancea was a powerful-looking man, bull-necked, red-lipped, with an elaborate network of veins on nose and cheeks. His black hair grew low on his forehead, and hairs bristled from his ears and nostrils. His face was covered with sweat.

"I kiss your hands, ladies," he said, suiting the action to the words.

"What are you doing here at this time of night?" Eleonora demanded, much annoyed. "What do you want?"

With a distracted smile Ivancea sat down without waiting to be asked. He stared at the carpet and rubbed his hairy hands together.

"What's the matter with you, Ivancea? Are you drunk?"

The man started. "Drunk? Me? God forbid, madame! That would be the last straw. Even sober I don't know what to do. You can imagine how it would be if I were drunk!"

"You don't know what to do? Then what on earth are you talking about? What do you want?"

Nervously, Ivancea scraped his muddy boots on the carpet. Aunt Eleonora looked at the laced boots and was seized by sudden anger. "Is this the way to appear before me? You come in here as if it were a stable! You've been drinking, man! Tell me what this is all about and then spare us your presence until you are yourself again. Aren't you ashamed to come here in such a state?"

Ivancea took a sheet of thick paper out of his pocket and unfolded it. He was breathing with difficulty. "Read this, Madame Eleonora, and see for yourself."

Aunt Eleonora took the paper. While she was reading he explained: "I've just found it nailed to my gate. The paper isn't even wet. They probably put it there just now, since the rain. What do you think of it?"

With a large blue handkerchief he mopped his face, from which all trace of his original smile had vanished.

"Helen, come and look at this. See what it is. I don't understand it," Eleonora said. She had put on her glasses and was blinking behind them.

"Ask the child to read the filthy thing for you," Mme Vorvoreano said tartly.

Surprised, Eleonora turned to stare at her sister. "What's come over you, talking to me in that tone of voice?"

"Nothing's come over me. Nothing at all. Ask Elvira to read your disgusting paper."

"I'll read it to you myself," Ivancea said, and began deciphering the large, ill-formed letters:

MASTER IVANCEA: What do you intend to do about the contracts with the people, because we can see you are not able to make up your mind, it is not enough for you, all the innocent blood you have sucked and you have come to terms with old Smadoviceano so that she will let you skin us alive, so long as she gets her share to get fat on . . .

Ivancea raised his eyes and looked intently at Eleonora. She had not batted an eyelid. He went on reading:

But we all beg you to fix with the peasants the conditions they have asked for, and not to strangle us from the beginning of the spring as you have done for so many years. Because we cannot stand it any longer, and it will not be long now before you see death face to face and you can tell old Smadoviceano to go away because otherwise we shall set fire to the house, in spite of the watch kept, because our watch on you is much better, and twisting and turning will not help you, we shall get you all one after the other, because the country has risen in arms and will not put up with your kind any longer. We have nothing else to write to you, and don't waste any more time because we shall not waste ours the way we have done but shall settle your account . . .

Ivancea took a deep breath and looked about him. The three women did not seem to have understood. Elvira was studying her book, which she had closed and placed on her knees; it was a French novel with a yellow cover. Mme Vorvoreano, her chin in her hands and her white arms emerging from sleeves which had fallen back, seemed to be listening to a sound she alone could hear. Eleonora stared at Ivancea out of round yellow eyes, toying with her little ivory claw and muttering, "A lot of rubbish!"

Ivancea sighed and mopped his face again, thinking, *Let's take advantage of this comfortable easy chair to rest a little. After that, we'll see.*

In a croaking voice the old woman went on: "Is this what you disturbed me for? You may go."

Astounded, Ivancea gaped at her. "But . . . didn't you hear?"

Aunt Eleonora thought for a moment, meanwhile arranging the dirty lace around her stringy hen's neck. "Bah!" she said. "They've lost their heads. They must be drunk. Why should it worry you?"

"But they're threatening to kill you too, madame! Didn't you hear? Listen again to what they say."

He reread a part of the letter.

"What of it? What do you expect me to do about it?"

At that Ivancea, purple in the face, beside himself, jumped to his feet shouting, "What, madame! I sweat blood because of your peasants, I kill myself screwing contracts, rents, free labor out of them, everything you need, until at times I'm even ashamed of myself, bearing in mind that I've children of my own and the sin will be visited on them. And you ask me what's to be done! Who's been driving me for the last ten years to postpone renewing the contracts till the end of March, because by then the peasants are afraid of starving and beg you to sign no matter what terms? Who? Answer me! And what have I been repeating for I don't know how many springs? 'Madame,' I said, 'you'll bring them buzzing about our ears. Madame, God knows what may happen. Madame, these ruffians are capable of burning the place down.' And each time you've said the same thing: 'That's enough, Ivancea. I know them. Forty years I've lived among them and they know who's master here.' That's what you've always said, madame, and now here's disaster on our own doorstep! Not one of us will be alive tomorrow, madame! Not one! We shall share the fate of the Moldavian farmers."

Aunt Eleonora rose, trembling with rage, her skinny hands gripping the arms of her chair. On the middle finger of one dirty, wrinkled hand a great ruby set in diamonds sparkled for an instant.

"What insolence! How dare you take that tone with me? You

have the effrontery to hold me responsible for what's happening? As if I didn't know how you measure the peasants' acres at eighteen rods, instead of twenty-four! Thief! Scum! Did you not rent the glebe land in the valley at fifty centimes the acre and sublet it to the peasants at three times that rent? You thought I didn't know that, but I was living on these estates when you were still hawking *braga** in the streets of Bucharest. I let you do as you pleased. When the wretches around here came and complained to me, I showed them the door and ordered my servants to drive them away. It was you, you skulking cur, whom they came to complain of. Now get out of here, you soft-drink peddler, get out and never let me see your face again. Never again will you farm an acre of my land! I shall entrust it to Alexiu, who manages the Vladomira domain in a way you'd never learn in a thousand years. Go on, be off with you, you insolent rascal! Get out!"

Eleonora sat down again, out of breath. She took tobacco from a jar of Nuremberg china and began to roll a cigarette.

Ivancea had risen. Dumbfounded, his eyes shifting from Mme Vorvoreano to Elvira, who smiled contemptuously, he said dejectedly, "But, madame, what are we to do to prevent them from setting fire to the manor house?"

After her outburst of rage, Eleonora had relapsed into apathy. "Set fire to what?" she grunted.

The bailiff sat down again. His face had turned gray. "They'll burn the manor house tonight," he moaned. "And they'll try to kill me."

"What can I do about it?" the old woman answered.

Mme Vorvoreano had at last understood. "Monsieur Ivancea, will you come here a moment?" she murmured.

As Ivancea walked heavily across the room, his head sunk between his shoulders, she opened the curtain slightly—just enough to enable the bailiff to see Vladomira burning. The fire had taken a firmer hold and a great column of flame was now rising toward the sky. Even the surrounding trees were burning, and looked like

---

* A drink made by fermenting millet.

slender, rose-pink pillars. In a low voice Mme Vorvoreano said, "Can you harness the horses? I don't think there will be anyone left in the courtyard. And it's certain they'll come and set this house on fire next. Can you manage it? We'll take you with us, Monsieur Ivancea. . . ."

She was thinking that it might be difficult for her to drive the horses to the railroad station herself; at least this would mean they had a man with them. . . .

Ivancea narrowed his eyes and nodded. He turned toward the porcelain-shaded lamp as a new voice made itself heard, repeating like a litany: "Oh, my God, what's to become of us? Oh, my God, what's to become of us?" The words were being pronounced tonelessly, without horror or apparent fear and all in one breath, by M. Alexiu of Vladomira—a dried-up man with a lined and suntanned face. One hand lay palm upward on his knees; with the other he was tapping it gently.

"My God, what's to become of us? Oh dear, oh dear, what a disaster! What's to become of us? Oh dear, oh dear, what's to become of us?"

Alexiu had sat down opposite Eleonora in the armchair which Ivancea had vacated, and was continuing his lament. There was a long open scratch on his forehead, from which blood had flowed. The blood had clotted around one eyebrow, and a trickle had run down to the corner of his mouth.

"What a catastrophe, madame! They'll come here and cut us in pieces. Our last hour has struck, brother Ivancea, we're done for. Our wives and children will be alone in the world. You may perhaps have money banked in town, but I kept mine in the safe at the manor and now they've burned it down. Ah, my God, what's to become of me?"

"What's happening? Tell us quickly."

"God help me! Suddenly I saw them breaking down the carriage gate with axes, screaming and pouring into the courtyard. Those idiots of Turkish guards fired a few shots, but it was no use; they were overwhelmed and trampled under foot, and the peasants came rushing at me, armed with bludgeons. I hardly had time to lock the door behind me and make my escape through the window. . . . But where are you going, brother Ivancea? My dear Nelu, where are you going?"

Ivancea did not answer. Alexiu rose hastily from his chair. Terrified, ready to go down on his knees, he babbled, "What, you're leaving, brother Ivancea? You're deserting me, when I . . ."

"When you what?" Ivancea asked brutally. "Wasn't it you who had the nerve to tell them that you'd soon be harnessing them to the plow instead of their beasts? It's you who've driven them wild with rage. Devil take you!"

Alexiu moaned and grabbed Ivancea by the sleeve. "Don't abandon me! It's really not fair to say that I . . . Don't desert me, your ladyship, don't let this madman leave me! Haven't I served Madame here all my life, and the Prince too, as if I had been his slave? Madame, please!"

Falling on his knees before Mme Vorvoreano, he burst into sobs. Shuddering with disgust, she turned to Ivancea, saying, "Take him with you. He can help you."

"Get up, you worm," Ivancea said. "You ought to be ashamed of yourself."

Stumbling, sniveling, and repeating, "Where are you going? Don't leave me! They're coming to kill us!" Alexiu followed Ivancea out of the room.

Elvira, deathly pale, had fetched the ladies' furs and was feverishly pulling on her gloves. Mme Vorvoreano had taken off her house dress and was standing in her corsets, the lace of which fell to her knees. Elvira helped her into a dark-gray dress and held out her fur coat. Aunt Eleonora, still wearing her old dressing gown, was wandering about the room, wild-eyed, carrying a rosewood strongbox under her arm. She had also brought from her room a heavy document bag of soft leather, which she had put down on the floor. Strangely calm, her sister looked at her and said with a detached smile, "Come, get dressed quickly. What are you waiting for?"

Then her glance met her daughter's. Elvira's green eyes were saying clearly, coldly, *Leave her here to burn.* Mme Vorvoreano turned toward the clock. The clock too would burn tonight. Within the hour, perhaps. *And us?* Calmly Mme Vorvoreano contemplated the portraits that hung on the walls, the tapestries, the sofas, the piano with the ivory missing from some of its keys, the window curtains. She thought of the bedrooms with their great wardrobes, of the quinces laid out to ripen on old newspapers spread on the floor, of the strings of dried fruit hung between two beams. All this was going to burn. Her bed would burn too, the bed she had shared with her husband and in which, subsequently, Elvira had been born, while their house in Bucharest was being auctioned by court order to pay their creditors. Michael too had been born in that bed —on that occasion the Colonel had run away to Paris with a night-club singer and Helen had had no other recourse but to bear her son in Eleonora's house, since Alexander, Sherban, and Sophia would not take her in. They could never forgive her for having been Lascar Lascari's favorite, even as a baby. Now it would all burn. Mme Vorvoreano's gaze returned to Eleonora, who was still wandering about the room, the jewel box in her arms. Grandmama Sophia's jewels.

Mme Vorvoreano shook her head and said in a loud voice, "Get dressed! What are you walking about like that for? Elvira, child, help your aunt with her fur coat."

Elvira looked questioningly at her mother, trying to understand. Mme Vorvoreano avoided her eyes. Between them, they got Eleonora into her clothes while the old woman mumbled unintelligibly between her gums, and got her out to the porch, the jewel box clasped to her breast. They then fetched the heavy document bag so that that too could be put into the carriage.

Elvira and Mme Vorvoreano had taken hold of Eleonora's arms, preparing to help her down the steps, when suddenly she broke away from them, muttered some confused words, and went hastily back into the house, leaving the doors open behind her.

"Her colic again!" Helen said.

The air was sweet and fresh. A light breeze came up off the lake, shaking the dry branches of the trees and making them crackle. The carriage, lamps unlit, was coming toward them from the far end of the courtyard. Ivancea, who was driving, called out, "Are you ready, madame?"

"Wait," Helen said. "Just a moment!"

Elvira was looking steadily at her mother. *No, I can't do it,* Helen was thinking. *Not that. Besides—suppose nothing happened? It would be awful. I should have to see her again, face her. It would become known. She'd tell everybody. I should be ruined, and so would Elvira. All this long patience, all this nauseating kowtowing would have gone for nothing. People would despise us, point at us, turn their backs on us, shut their doors in our faces; nobody would have anything more to do with us. . . . And she'd be quite capable of making us go on living with her, simply to torture us. She could do whatever she liked with me.* Unconsciously her eyes stared into Elvira's, those deep, green, magnificent eyes. . . . Abruptly she shook off her thoughts and hurried into the house.

Doors gaped everywhere. Drawers turned out in haste had been left open, with clothing hanging over the edges. Various ornaments had been overturned. Sheets of music had fallen off the piano and one of Elvira's slippers lay on top of them. The clock was still ticking, its metallic voice muffled by the crystal globe that covered it.

On the table which stood in the middle of the drawing room, near the workbasket full of balls of wool and the little squares knitted by Aunt Eleonora, Mme Vorvoreano saw the jewel box. It was not large. The rosewood gleamed in the warm light of the lamp beside it. The drawing room was deserted. For a few seconds Mme Vorvoreano no longer heard the ticking of the clock. Eleonora was capable of staying a long time—when her colic came on, you never knew how long it would last. . . .

She rushed to the window, jerked back the curtains, and saw the red glow of the fire at Vladomira. Somewhere beyond it was the as yet feeble glow of a second fire—a granary, no doubt, or a barn, or a wine press. Mme Vorvoreano drew back a little, returned to the table, and picked up the jewel box. It seemed to her very heavy. She carried it out of the room. Seeing her mother reappear, Elvira looked hard at her face and then, lowering her eyes, saw the rosewood box.

"Won't she come?"

"She's determined to stay," Mme Vorvoreano said, her throat constricted. "I can't sacrifice you to her madness. We're leaving."

While she was speaking Elvira had taken her by the elbow to help her down the steps, for Mme Vorvoreano was unsteady on her feet.

"Quicker, madame, quicker, quicker!" shouted Ivancea.

"Madame Eleonora does not wish to come with us, Monsieur Ivancea," Mme Vorvoreano said softly. But Ivancea was not listening and made no answer.

They got into the carriage, placed Eleonora's document bag at their feet, and shoved Alexiu, who was huddled in the best seat, onto the folding seat. He was still sniveling and gazing in stupefaction at the wide-brimmed hats trimmed with ostrich feathers which the ladies were wearing. Ivancea turned the carriage, aiming to use a road that issued from the far end of the courtyard and would enable him to avoid the village. The servants' quarters were deserted. The cook stood on the threshold of her kitchen, arms folded, and watched the fugitives depart. The red glow in the sky above Vladomira was no longer visible because of the low wooded hills that masked the horizon. Several times they heard the sound of bells; each time Alexiu stopped sniveling and said, "The tocsin! It's the signal! What a disaster!"

As the carriage proceeded the sky became rosy in several places and then took on the color of red-hot iron. Alexiu craned his neck toward the box where Ivancea acted as their coachman and pronounced the names of the manor houses that were on fire. Bells were ringing everywhere simultaneously. Their sound was muffled from time to time by a gust of cold wind, or a brief shower immediately swallowed up in the darkness. The sound of voices also reached them occasionally, shouts, the roar of a mob coming from no clearly ascertainable direction. On the box, Ivancea peered through the darkness to see which way the horses pricked their sensitive ears. Then the voices fell silent, giving way to the thin whistling of the wind over the snow which still covered the furrows of deserted plowland.

At the crossroads between Vladomira and Hotare the road appeared to sink down between high banks and tall thorn hedges. Alexiu was dozing. Ivancea felt the cold of the small hours creeping into his bones and huddled into his seat. He had forgotten that he should be trying to watch the horses' ears, and did not notice them suddenly pricked forward.

Suddenly angry voices were bellowing, "Halt! Stop! Halt!"

The carriage swayed and stopped. The horses tossed their heads toward the dark sky in an effort to escape the horny hands clutching at their bridles. They neighed, jostled each other, and backed between the shafts. The voices became soft and caressing. "Gently, gently!"

Someone was patting the horses' necks. A square lantern, its glass panes dirty, appeared suddenly, revealing a group of men dressed in dark clothes. Above their heads gleamed the steel tines of the pitchforks they carried as weapons. They closed in on the carriage and surrounded it. Elvira had huddled up to her mother and was moaning in terror, her face hidden against Mme Vorvoreano's powerful bosom.

The two bailiffs, paralyzed with fear, were not even looking about them. Someone held up the lantern at arm's length; for a moment the light fell on Ivancea's terror-stricken face. The man said, "So it's you, Master Ivancea."

There was a silence. Ivancea did not answer. The young man holding the lantern pushed through the crowd to the side of the carriage and looked inside. He examined the two women coldly, almost as if he had not seen them, then directed his attention to Alexiu. From the far side of the carriage a voice exclaimed, "Hullo! Here's the other one too."

The man with the lantern straightened up and said, "They're both here."

"Knock him off the box and stick your knife in his guts!" someone in the crowd yelled.

"Don't forget, lads—Alexiu's all mine!" shouted another.

There was a general clamor. A peasant reached up to pull Ivancea off the box, but the bailiff eluded him as if he had been stung and began crying shrilly, "Wait, wait! Judge me if you must, but have some respect for justice! Respect the law, my friends. Let me get down of my own accord."

He carefully rolled the reins around the stock of the whip, which was thrust in its socket, and clambered down. The men had stopped talking.

"Where's the other one got to?" cried a voice.

They dragged Alexiu out of the carriage: the bailiff was babbling, "No, no, for the love of God! Madame, have pity on me, I have a wife and children . . ."

An irritable muttering rose from the group of peasants. Someone shouted, "Knock his teeth down his throat!" in a half-choked voice. Mme Vorvoreano said, "Let him be, good people. Judge him in the morning, not now. Remember that we are all Christians and . . ."

She fell silent, overwhelmed by her own feelings, unable to remember what she had wanted to say.

"You're bolting in the middle of the night, lady. Why shouldn't we judge him by night?"

"Good people," Mme Vorvoreano said, her voice faltering, "think of your wives and of your children! Do not commit this sin! Your punishment will be appalling. Think of your wives and children!"

"We're thinking of them all right. Our wives bear us dead children and those who live wither away from starvation."

"What punishment do you mean, lady? Who's going to punish us?" a surly voice asked.

"The Army, good people, the King," Mme Vorvoreano replied. At that the crowd roared with laughter. The man with the lantern said gravely, "The King is dead, lady, and the Queen has ordered us to burn down the manors and the big town houses."

Mme Vorvoreano had risen and was standing behind the coachman's seat. She had taken hold of the reins abandoned by Ivancea and was cautiously drawing them toward her.

"Just wait, you swine!" the peasants were snarling. "Hold him tight, Iordake, till I find something to tie him with. Just wait, you clod of manure, I'll teach you——"

"No, no!" Alexiu implored. "Forgive me, good people! I have done nothing to you. Forgive me! Don't tie me up."

He fell on his knees in the mud. The angry muttering grew louder.

"If I ever wronged you, it was not for my sake, I swear it! It was for my sons, so that I could make men of them. I swear it, good people, I swear it! Don't tie me up. Forgive me!"

He was sprawled full length, rolling about on the ground, his face in a puddle. The peasants had gathered around and were watching him. Two of them kicked him. Others were holding Ivancea by the nape of his neck and his arms, forcing him to stoop and look at the spectacle over his shoulder. Those who had stopped the horses had also pushed their way into the circle and were prodding Alexiu with their feet.

Mme Vorvoreano had gathered the reins into her left hand. She slipped them between her fingers and drew on them gently to make the horses feel the bit. Then she slackened them a little, snatched the whip from its socket, and lashed the horses savagely on their cruppers. The carriage lurched forward. At the second stroke of the whip the horses broke into a gallop. Mme Vorvoreano continued to whip them savagely. Behind the carriage as it clattered away into the darkness arose a furious clamor—shouts, boos, and a single shot.

"Boo! Boo! After the whores!" the men yelled, half amused. Some made to run after the carriage, but the young man with the lantern checked them. "Stop! Let them go."

"Why should I, you blasted fool?"

"We were bound to leave them alone anyway. We're not here to kill women. We've other fish to fry. What could we have done to them?"

The man grinned broadly, but said nothing. The young man with the lantern turned to the crowd and said, "Well, shall we bring them to trial?"

They were unanimous about that: here, at once, in the mud of the road.

"Let's make the contracts first, Rizea," someone cried.

"Yes. Take 'em to the village and let them draw up our contracts, then we can lay their necks across the Town Hall doorstep and I'll cut their heads off myself," said a mournful-looking man who was holding an ax. It was Ouracou, father of the young man who had been killed by the Prince. The eyes of both bailiffs were glassy. Sweat was running down Ivancea's face.

"Come on, then, lads," Rizea said calmly, and the whole group moved off, the two prisoners in their midst advancing at the same hurried pace as the mob, and staring straight in front of them. For a while there was still the sound of mingled voices; then silence, all sounds absorbed into the cold, raw wind which blew from the lake. Nothing was to be seen but the lantern swinging along at the head of the marching peasants. Then that too vanished into the darkness, and only the leaping flames of burning manors and granaries kept flickering watch over the sleeping plain.

3

They plodded through the sticky, half-frozen mud which covered the road to a depth of two or three inches. Beneath it, the earth was still frozen hard by winter. In places the mud was even thicker, coming up to the men's ankles and fouling the rags they used for stockings. Every step meant dragging the feet out of this deep soup of clay and water which clung to the feet and retained their imprint.

The lantern bobbed and swayed in the mist. Rizea had passed it to Alexander, Ouracou's other son, the brother of Zaharia whom the Prince had killed. The men were all talking at once and for each one of them this general, confused, and ceaseless clamor was tantamount to the silence in which each man can talk to himself, as one does in the dark.

Flakes of snow drifted down at rare intervals; then would come a gust of fine rain which ceased almost at once. Sometimes a gust of wind rose and blew in the peasants' faces, drying their wet cheeks immediately.

Ouracou walked beside Ivancea and Alexiu, small, shriveled, wrapped in a black fur cape. His grimacing face turned constantly from one to the other. He carried his ax under his arm, an ax with a short haft and a blade with a curved cutting edge on one side and a hammer on the other. It was the way axes were formerly made. From time to time Ouracou said to his son, "Raise the lantern a little." And he looked attentively at Ivancea and Alexiu, as if anxious not to forget their faces.

Those faces were now pallid and harrowed by fear, even Ivancea's, which had formerly been so pink and plump. The two bailiffs walked fast, slipping and stumbling, staring straight ahead. They were afraid of meeting the others' eyes. They were cold and were walking barefoot in the mud, for as soon as they had started out the men had stopped them and removed their shoes, saying, "Off with your shoes and be like us. You're going to see what it's like to walk as we do, you carrion!"

Ivancea had let them take off his boots without protesting, as in a dream; he had even unlaced them himself. His feet were plump and very white. Now they had been transformed into two lumps of mud. Alexiu had whimpered. From time to time he whimpered again, dragging his feet, trying to hang back. But the peasants hustled him forward with curses until he stumbled along and began to walk more quickly.

When the group arrived at the main road, where the mud was thicker than ever and scarred by deep ruts, everyone halted and watched Rizea climb a telegraph pole. He went up slowly and laboriously, raising himself chiefly by his arms, for he was not too sure of his left foot. He had a short ax stuck through his belt. When he reached the crossbar he paused for a moment, listening to the mysterious vibration of the telegraph wires; the men gathered around the pole could also hear the sound, which was like the humming of a hive of bees in winter when it is closed. Then, with his ax, Rizea cut the wires one after the other; suddenly mute, they broke away and fell gently, their ends sinking into the mud. Rizea slid down the post, wiping the sweat from his face with the palm of his hand.

"Well, come on," he said. "What are we waiting for?"

The crowd moved off again, Rizea, dragging his leg, in the rear. Mototolea walked beside him. Suddenly, out of the darkness, he said, "Listen, Rizea . . ."

Rizea was out of breath and did not answer.

"Do you hear me? I want to talk to you."

"What about, father Ion? What have you got to say to me?"

Mototolea hesitated. They were walking well behind the group. At last Mototolea made up his mind and said, "Look, I bore you a grudge, you know . . ."

"You bore me a grudge, father Ion?" Rizea said, making a poor attempt to appear surprised.

"Yes. I was angry, you see."

"But why, father Ion, why were you angry with me?" Rizea murmured, smiling in the dark. Mototolea was surprising him. He was not so stupid. It seemed that he had realized. . . .

"Come, you know why," Mototolea said. "Of course you know."

"I know nothing. Truly I know nothing. Tell me what it's all about."

"You know. Don't play the innocent. Oh, you're devilish sly, Rizea! You know well enough what I have to say to you."

Both were silent. It was true enough that Rizea knew what it was about. On the road somewhere in front of them voices were raised in anger. "What you've done to us? I'll tell you what you've done to us!" someone cried.

Mototolea walked on, deep in thought. Every now and again Rizea looked at him out of the corner of his eye. With an obvious effort Mototolea made up his mind to speak again.

"Listen, Rizea. I'm going to leave my wife. If she doesn't want . . . What can I do about her? She may be right. I'll send her back to her father. . . ."

"That's a good idea, father Ion," Rizea said.

"What do you mean, 'a good idea'? To hell with you and yours!
You pack of fools!"

Mototolea was at grips with his old torment. He was on the point
of letting himself be dominated by his rage, but he controlled it.
He was panting.

"I'd have killed you, do you realize?" he went on. "Yes, believe
me, Rizea, I would have done it. And then all this happened—this
justice we're doing. . . . And I thought . . . All day I thought.
You heard me, the rest of you, talking like an idiot from morning
till night, like a mill grinding out words. But I was thinking all the
time. If the hour of justice has come, then it is right that I be just
with my wife also. I've tormented her enough. I've beaten her.
Now let her do as she likes. And I thought of you also. Why kill
you? As if I had not troubles enough and more important ones!
The troubles we all have, with these ravening wolves of boyars!
Now tell me whether my thoughts were not right thoughts?"

"Why, yes, father Ion, it's a very good idea," Rizea murmured.

Whereupon Mototolea retorted furiously, "Ah, you think so, do
you? Devil take you, then!" He walked briskly ahead to mingle
with the crowd, and Rizea heard him yelling hoarsely: "Bash his
face in! Let me through, I'll show him!"

Alone in the darkness Rizea laughed, showing all his teeth. That
was his way of laughing. Nobody had ever heard him laugh out
loud; his laugh was silent.

One man detached himself from the mass, talking at the top of
his voice. Rizea recognized the voice: it was Iordake.

"And when his fence was shifted, what did he do then?" Iordake
was shouting. He crossed the road to a telegraph pole. Rizea waited
for him, in the dark, standing in the middle of the road. Iordake
joined him, buttoning his fly.

"What's all this about a fence?" Rizea asked.

"Listen to what that swine of a boyar did! As if he hadn't put
up this fence to steal a bit of our common land, though God knows
the whole lot doesn't amount to much, a patch of ground that isn't
nearly big enough and at that we've all to pay five lei a head and
two hens into the bargain, and eggs and a pot of clarified butter.

Goddam bloodsuckers! And when we put his fence back where it had been, what did he do to us? I ask you, what did he do?"

Rizea did not answer. Iordake breathed hard. Rizea said, "Listen, father Iordake, what do you think?"

"Me? I don't think anything."

"I mean what he says—this fellow Marinica—is it true? Do you think it's true?"

Iordake spat on the ground. "Of course it's true! Noutzou, the son of Cokina, came from the town late this afternoon. He says the same thing: in Moldavia the men have revolted, and here also. It's in the newspapers. But what's troubling you, asking such a question?"

"No, father Iordake, that's not what I meant. I know all that. But the other thing he was saying—about the Queen, the letter from the seven powers, all that stuff—— Is that true, do you think? Tell me."

"The hell it is!" Iordake said, and began to abuse the Queen with fury, spitting in rhythm with his oaths. Rizea nodded and smiled in the dark and said, "But some who are with us have come because they believe what this Marinica said."

"What they believe is their business," Iordake remarked caustically. "What matters to us is that we've made a start. Yes, made a start. We had to make a start sometime, and now it's done. We've begun. What more do you want?"

They rejoined the others and melted into the crowd. Hundreds of bare feet plodded on through the mud. Ivancea stumbled at every step. He wanted to speak, to reply, but his voice was drowned by the voices of the men and he could not order his thoughts. From time to time Ouracou struck him with his fist on the nape of the neck; and sometimes Iordake struck him likewise, imitating Ouracou. Then Ivancea stumbled as if he had caught his feet in some obstacle. Alexiu bewailed his fate in a high, broken voice, but nobody could understand a word he was saying.

They passed locked and barred houses in which the lights had been extinguished. At the Town Hall a crowd had gathered and was waiting. All the poor of the village were there, but also some of the more prosperous peasants: Geambashu, Kiritza, and Melitaru, who had been a sergeant major. The crowd poured into the Town Hall, and those who could not get in crowded the courtyard and gathered around the windows. Alexander, Ouracou's son, looking through a window, saw Iordake standing on a table, pulling Rizea by the hand to make him climb up beside him. Iordake was speaking. Alexander jabbed his elbow into the windowpane to break the glass so that he could thrust his moist-eyed, curly head into the room. There was a boil at one side of his mouth. One after another all the windowpanes were shattered, and men were looking through every window and listening.

Iordake was shouting: "Agreements? Where's the fool who would want to sign a contract with the boyar? Do you imagine he'll keep his promise? He'll arrange things so that by autumn we'll be riddled with debts again. As usual, he'll prevent us threshing the wheat in time, the cold will come, and we'll be helpless. Do you imagine he'll forgive us? Their police will be sent in, and then God help us! I tell you, we can have no more truck with the boyars. Haven't they exploited us enough? I tell you, we've got to destroy them, them and their broods. They've got to be wiped off the face of the earth, or we'll never get out of their clutches. They'll torture and starve us more than ever. Do you hear me, brothers? Like Christ on the cross, they'll torture us!"

Iordake's voice broke, and he began to weep. He stood there among all those men, big as a bear, his head shaved to a blue stubble, wiping his eyes with the tip of a thick index finger and then shaking the finger to flick off the tears. Below him, among the crowd, Ouracou bawled, "Come down off there! Come and judge them! My Zaharia's dying, do you hear? Is he to die without knowing what we've done to the boyars? Get down and let's get on with it!"

From his perch on the table Rizea responded, "We'll take the land for ourselves! We'll work it in common."

Fat Melitaru, who had the face of a doll but wore a big black mustache with waxed points, was standing in the doorway.

"No! Better to share it out!" he shouted.

"Yes, we'll share it out among us!" shouted Kiritza and several others. But Iordake looked at Melitaru and got down from the table, saying, "Make room for me, lads."

And he made for the door. Melitaru backed away from him and tried to slip outside. The crowd surged toward the door. Ouracou, Pîrvou, Mototolea, and three other men held Ivancea and Alexiu by the elbows and shoulders. Rizea cried over the heads of the people, "Let them be judged!"

A double ring of human bodies formed about the two bailiffs. The men pressed against each other, rising on their toes to see over the shoulders of those in front of them. There was a tense silence, broken only by Alexiu's sobs and low, incoherent babbling. Ouracou and Iordake pressed with all their weight on Ivancea's shoulders, forcing him to prostrate himself across the threshold of the Town Hall. Ivancea roared, "No! No! No-o-o!" and thereafter was silent.

Ouracou stooped over him, almost crouching. He held his ax in his hand. He did not raise his arm very high, only bent it at the elbow, as if he were chopping wood. In the silence the first blow was heard, sharp and short. Then two others, which resounded against the wooden threshold. The men hurriedly stepped backward as the blood spurted and flowed bubbling over the doorstep. Ivancea's knees and loins jerked strangely, obscenely, and his hands moved as if blindly groping on the ground for something. At last the headless body stiffened and was still. Alexiu's outcries changed suddenly to a shrill screaming no longer resembling a human voice. The men jostled each other. Pîrvou cried, "Not like that! Hold him tight! Lower! Careful!"

And abruptly the screaming ceased, cut short as Pîrvou's ax bit into the wood. The men stared for a moment in silence and then, one by one, moved away, regrouping farther on, out in the street. They spoke in low voices, suddenly tired out.

Ouracou sat down on the low wall around the Town Hall, put his ax down beside him, and remained there, elbows on knees and head in his hands. His son stood beside him. Without raising his head, Ouracou muttered, "Take the ax and go home. Carry the ax to your brother that he may see it."

Pîrvou stood with lowered eyes beside Alexiu's body. He could not take his eyes off the mutilated corpse and the head which had rolled into a pool of blood. Iordake also came up and stared for a long time; then he shook Pîrvou by the shoulder and said in a harsh voice, "What's the matter with you, loitering there? Come on, there's work to be done! We'll go to yours next, the usurer's. We'll pay him what's due to him. Come!"

Drawing Pîrvou after him, he led the way, followed by several other men, calling as he went, "Hey! Which of you have been sucked dry by Geambashu? Come with us! We're off to pay him his interest!"

Rizea was talking with Marinica. His body was shaken by a fearful joy, as by a fever. From a distance Marinica stared wide-eyed at the two bodies.

"Haven't you seen the like of it before?" Rizea asked.

Marinica shook his head: no, he had never seen such a thing before. Incredulous, Rizea stared at him, began to say something, then changed his mind. Pulling him toward Iordake, he said, "Wait, father Iordake. We're coming with you."

All the others followed in a crowd, spreading out across the street and filling it with black shadows and voices becoming constantly louder. Among those on the outside, a few slipped into the ditches, others hung back in twos and threes; occasionally a man made off alone, looking about him.

When they came to the little bridge across the ditch to Geambashu's house, the crowd filed over it and spread out again when they reached the yard. Pîrvou, his ax red with blood, hammered at the door. But those who were in the house would not open it.

"Open!" Rizea shouted. "Or we'll set fire to the house."

The door opened. Geambashu appeared on the threshold, his mouth gaping. "What do you want with me?" he asked with an effort.

Pîrvou raised his ax. Geambashu flung up an arm to protect

himself. Rizea checked Pîrvou and shouted, "No! Take him with us! He shall set fire to the manor house. Burn it with his own hands! And we'll watch him burn the boyar's house down! It will cure him of playing the great lord with us!"

Pîrvou would not have it so. He resisted fiercely, crying, "I want to pay him his interest! I want to pay him his interest!"

But the men made Geambashu come with them, pushing him before them, punching and jostling him. Pîrvou followed, shouting that it was unjust.

The people yelled, striking on the doors with their cudgels or their axes, to bring out the Mayor and all the rich peasants of the village. Some appeared on the threshold of their houses and asked, "Are you going to the manor?"

"Yes, to the house of the old boyar woman!"

Then the men hastily put on their fur cloaks and joined the mob.

Beyond the hill covered with dry, blackened acacias they saw the manor house. The carriage gate was still open. Through the lace curtains filtered a feeble glow of light. The crowd poured into the courtyard like an angry swarm and entered the house by all the doors at once. No part of it was closed and there was nobody there. Rizea and the others stopped when they came to the drawing room. There every object was strange and hostile. The peasants were silent. Rizea was very pale. He heard the sound of some mechanism hidden somewhere. He looked around and saw the clock, a precious thing covered with a crystal globe and embellished with winged cherubs in gilded bronze. Rizea took the bloody ax from Pîrvou's hands and struck at the clock, which stopped with a rattle of broken metal and shattered glass.

On the table Marinica saw a wand made of bone. He drew it out from beneath a crumpled shirt and held it up to the light of the porcelain-shaded lamp. At one end of the ivory stick was a claw with curved and pointed fingers, like a minute human hand, with folds at every finger joint, and nails and everything proper to a real hand, but smaller and more clenched. Marinica wondered what such an article could be for; suddenly he thought of an answer, whereupon he threw the object on the floor, spat on it, and ground it under his heel. His companions were spreading through all the other rooms. Marinica listened, for it seemed to him that he had heard Iordake's voice exclaim "Lady!"

They've found the old woman! Marinica thought, and his heart began to beat more quickly. The two who had been killed on the Town Hall doorstep were only upstarts—bailiffs, not the real masters. He thought he heard the croaking of an old woman's voice talking loudly. He ran around the table and burst into the next room. As he passed, the lamp wobbled and then fell quietly on some stockings rolled into a ball on top of a silk dressing gown. The shade broke almost noiselessly. The paraffin trickled out and caught fire, making a small crest of flames. The clothes and the tabletop began to burn at the same time. Presently the deserted drawing room rang with shouts of rage coming from the next room, and other, more distant shouts coming in through the open front door from the yard where the peasants were setting fire to the outbuildings.

4

Mme Vorvoreano had reached Salcia a little before dawn. The town was silent. She had managed to drive the carriage as far as the station. There she had skirted or passed through groups of shadows vaguely human in shape. She had climbed out of the carriage, with the jewel box under one arm and the document bag in the other hand, after having carefully attached the reins to the iron bar which ran around the coachman's box. Solicitously, forgetting her own fatigue, she had helped Elvira out. Elvira moved limply, as if she were just coming out of a faint. In the near-darkness Mme Vorvoreano could see the girl's large bright eyes fixed on her.

"Stop looking at me like that! Say what you have to say to me and then keep quiet. You look as if you'd lost your wits."

They went into the booking office and sought the stationmaster, who was in bed but soon appeared in an ecstasy of bows and compliments before this lady who was the Prince's kinswoman and Mme Eleonora Smadoviceano's sister. He confirmed that the situation among the peasantry was ugly; it was rumored that they would soon do here what they were already doing in Moldavia. Ah! If Mme Vorvoreano could have heard them talking in this very station as he himself had heard them two or three days ago! Fortunately nothing was happening in Salcia at the moment; everything was quite calm. Decent, respectable people, peaceable, all with their little bit of landed property—with small farmers of that kind, there was no danger of all this socialism, anarchy, and so forth catching on. Would the ladies be so good as to step into his office? He had nothing to offer but this old couch—alas, the leather was rather torn, but there it was. It was the times they lived in. It was all very well to be celebrating the Jubilee year, but times were hard, what with last summer's drought and a severe winter. . . . Did they want tickets for Bucharest?

"No," Mme Vorvoreano said, "we are only going as far as the town."

"Oh, forgive me! I thought it must be for Bucharest, seeing that His Highness came through here yesterday afternoon on his way to Bucharest to attend a session of the Senate. . . ."

Mme Vorvoreano merely said "I know" in her deep, musical voice, implying that the stationmaster's business was to bring the tickets, not to make conversation. The stationmaster understood, and without resentment, bowed again and prepared to leave his office, where a large fire was burning in the iron stove. Before leaving, he went to the lamp on the table with the intention of turning it up to improve the feeble glimmer it diffused.

"No need," Mme Vorvoreano said. "It's more restful as it is."

The stationmaster slipped quietly out. Mme Vorvoreano coughed. Her throat felt cold. She made to pull her shawl about her, but remembered that it was on her knees, wrapped around the heavy jewel box.

She had got rid of the stationmaster because she needed to think. Elvira snuggled up to her and squeezed her arm. Gently but firmly Mme Vorvoreano pushed her away. She needed to be alone and to think, to think fast, without being importuned by anybody. *What am I to tell the stationmaster about the carriage? Entrust it to him? That would certainly be wise, but I have done wiser things than that tonight. A carriage abandoned outside the station is bound to attract attention. People will wonder where it came from and who left it there. The stationmaster surely recognizes it; he must have seen Eleonora pass in it every time she went to Vladomira to call on that lunatic. . . . Obviously the stationmaster knows nothing as yet; the fire is invisible from here. So that if I tell him nothing he will simply imagine that I happened to be leaving unexpectedly at the last moment, like His Highness. He will see nothing odd in that. . . . But why no coachman? And why without Eleonora? I would give a great deal to know what he makes of it all. But who in fact is going to ask his opinion? Even supposing he suspects something—tomorrow, not today, tomorrow when he hears that Vladomira has been burned down—and our manor too, no doubt—no, there is no doubt: the house and everything in it will have been burned, is burning at this moment, and Eleonora with it. Yes, Eleonora too, at this very moment . . . Nothing else is possible; it would be a real miracle if she escaped. She can't escape, it's absolutely impossible. Their intentions were clear—they said, one of them said, that he would cut Ivancea's throat—— Yes, surely it is all over by now. But what am I going to do with this carriage? If anything has happened back there, or is happening at this very moment . . .*

Mme Vorvoreano smiled with trembling lips. *There will be an inquiry later, or something of the sort. And I cannot risk . . . There must be no questions for people to ask. . . . I will tell him that Eleonora's coachman drove me here . . . what's his name?*

George, I think . . . and that I ordered him to go back to the house. They will assume that George has run away. And the stationmaster will certainly take charge of Eleonora's carriage, a carriage belonging to a kinswoman of His Highness for whom trains are kept waiting in the station even after their time of departure. Yes, that's it, I came with George. He is outside, on the box. I ordered him to drive back to the house, where all was calm—to the manor which I have unexpectedly left. . . . But what if Ivancea and Alexiu manage to save themselves? The truth will be known! And if Eleonora herself manages to escape, I am lost! It would be a worse scandal than the time when Candiano-Popesco's son knifed his mistress. I shall be a marked woman, regarded as a criminal. . . .

In a low voice Elvira asked, "Mama, do you feel ill?"

"What did you say?"

"I said, do you feel ill?"

Mme Vorvoreano was thinking, *I must control myself. Now that I've put down my stake, I must play. The wine is drawn; it must be drunk.*

She turned to Elvira. "What do you want?"

"I asked if you were not feeling well."

To that Mme Vorvoreano merely replied in a stern voice, "Have you a handkerchief?" And snatching it from her daughter's hand, she added, "How can you expect me to feel well? I wear myself out for you."

The stationmaster came back with the tickets. He was much agitated. "The news is very bad, madame. It seems things have been happening at Dobrunu—on Monsieur Apostolesco's property. You know whom I mean? The stout gentleman with side whiskers. You know him, no doubt. A man of means . . . One of my men tells me they've devastated the whole place. Upon my word, the peasants have gone mad, madame. Here, look at them!"

He went to the window, wiped the condensation from the glass with his sleeve, and stared out. He had put his hands in his pockets, pushed his cap to the back of his head, and was shivering with cold. Mme Vorvoreano rose, thinking, *I shall tell him nothing. I shall*

*keep silent. Let him think what he likes and do what he pleases.
I'm at my wits' end. I must have time to think, to recover my poise.*
She went to the window and looked out onto the station platform.

Ragged men were strung out along the platform, crouching with
their backs to the station, talking more loudly than usual. Every
now and again one of them would walk out between the rails and
peer into the distance. Suddenly the muttering grew louder and the
agitation changed to tumult. A huge, dark form loomed out of
the fog, preceded by two glowing red eyes and taking shape as the
squat body and tall, funnel-shaped chimney of a switch engine
drawing an empty freight car. The crowd's excitement seemed to
subside. The men went back to their places. The locomotive was
again swallowed up by the fog and the freight car was left standing
on a siding.

Somebody opened the booking-office door and called the stationmaster in a low, hoarse voice.

"What do you want?"

"Come quickly."

The stationmaster vanished into the next room, from which came
the regular tick-tick of telegraphic instruments ceaselessly rolling
out their strips of paper. Mme Vorvoreano sat down on the couch.
She glanced at Elvira, who had fallen asleep with her mouth half
open and a lock of black hair falling over her forehead. She had an
impulse to stoop and kiss her daughter, but changed her mind.
Elvira muttered in her sleep, and whimpered as if she were about to
cry. Mme Vorvoreano shrugged her shoulders and presently fell
into a doze. Her sleep was uneasy because she was sitting bolt upright on the old leather couch. She was roused by voices. The stationmaster was talking and gesticulating to a policeman.

"Do you know who it was?"

"I recognized them, Stationmaster, I know them all. They're the
ones who came from Bucharest to repair the bridge. I spotted them
all right! Listen to them shouting. Can't you hear them?"

From outside rose cries which seemed to soar like fireworks
above even the angry muttering of the crowd. Through the window, now lit by the ashen light of dawn, the dark length of a train

in the station blocked the view of the plain. Mme Vorvoreano stood up. The place where Elvira had been sitting beside her was empty and the girl was standing by the booking-office door which opened onto the platform. Mme Vorvoreano went to join her daughter, who convulsively seized her hand and squeezed it hard. Both looked out. A railroad man, black with soot from head to foot, was standing in the middle of a group of peasants and haranguing them.

"Take their land, brothers, it's yours! We'll not finish the bridge until they've given you the land. That'll stop 'em bringing up their guns to kill your children. You'll see! And the telegraph wires must be cut. Don't let them frighten you, lads! Be your own masters. Above all, don't believe a word they tell you. They lie. They foul their souls with lies!"

Elvira opened the door a few inches and ice-cold air filtered into the room. Mme Vorvoreano put out her hand in alarm to shut the door, but Elvira whispered, "No, Mama, leave it open. We can hear better. . . ." She seemed calm, merely curious, though rather pale.

Behind them the policeman was saying, "There's the tinsmith too, the Russian, one of those who was in that Potemkin business a couple of years ago. You know the man?"

"Is it my fault?" the stationmaster demanded, ready to burst. "No, I'm not to blame. Why do they send me socialists like that from Bucharest? What can I do? It's the repair-shop management who are at fault, not me, I'm not responsible. I can't answer for them. They can do what they like to me, I still can't answer for them."

Mme Vorvoreano turned toward him. He was alone; the policeman had gone out, shrugging his shoulders.

"The railroad men have gone mad too, now, madame. You saw the policeman, Negusi? He's supposed to keep order here at the station, so naturally he tried to take the ringleaders' names. Well, when they saw him keeping an eye on them and taking notes, they went for him. Upon my soul, they were ready to kill him. They took his notebook away from him and trampled on it. Fortunately he can remember who they were, and he'll be able to issue a summons. . . ."

He thought for a moment, then added, "So now, if Negusi has a grudge against any of them, that man's name will go down on the list at once. And since he's as cunning as a fox—Negusi, I mean —you can imagine the sort of thing he'll threaten them with, to get a bit of money out of them. . . ."

The shouting on the platform was becoming more and more violent. Gliding smoothly over the rails, the empty train had left the station.

"You're well advised to leave, madame," the stationmaster said. "I really don't know what will come of all this. . . . We're waiting for a carload of soldiers from the town, you know—to guard His Highness's manor at Vladomira."

Elvira turned to him sharply. She met her mother's eyes and said nothing. Mme Vorvoreano felt as if her whole body was going to start shaking, and made an effort to take herself in hand. Her teeth almost chattering, she said, "Shut the door, Elvira dear. It's getting cold in here."

Elvira left the door ajar for a few moments longer. A voice reached them from outside: "And what are you? Haven't you homes to go to? Why are they calling you up? For a period of training? Don't you believe it! It's so they can kill your wives and children while you're away. Take it from me."

Men in gray uniforms gathered around, huddling together. They were army reservists who were being called up. One of them said, "We're not going. What do they want us in Moldavia for? There isn't a war on. Not that I've heard of."

The crowd stirred and jostled. The station bell sounded its musical note three times. Elvira shut the door, locked it carefully, and glancing furtively at the stationmaster, went to her mother, who had sat down again on the couch. Snuggling up to her, the girl said, "Mama darling, do you think they'll let us go?"

Mme Vorvoreano sighed deeply but did not answer. She was facing the fact that access to the town was cut off. These bands of rebellious peasants were occupying the station platform. It was impossible to move without being seen and perhaps attacked. Mme Vorvoreano thought of the jewel box wrapped in a shawl which she was keeping close beside her on the couch, with one hard corner sticking into her right hip; she thought also of the document bag on the floor at her feet. It had all been in vain! Why were the peasants barring her way; why had they risen in revolt? What was this sudden madness which possessed them? What reason had they for discontent? They had been bearing their lot for centuries, and now, suddenly, it seemed that they could bear it no longer. Why wouldn't they let her and her jewel box go? Couldn't they understand that she needed the jewels and the money for her daughter and her son? She put her hands to her temples and pressed hard, rocking her head from side to side. She had to make a tremendous effort to prevent herself from groaning with weariness, fear, and hatred.

5

Eleonora allowed her drowsiness to overcome her, but from time to time she started awake, recovered a measure of lucidity, and tried to put a little order into her recollections. Why was the house empty? Why had Helen and Elvira abandoned her? Eleonora wept noisily for a brief while, then dozed off again.

Suddenly there was a confused uproar, then a sound of voices and footsteps. Still only half awake, and before she had realized what was happening, Eleonora saw strangers crowd shouting into her room. Blinking, she demanded, "Who are you and what do you want?"

She began to recognize them. They were all villagers. What had come over them today? Then suddenly she remembered everything, and said in a terrified voice, "I know you. What do you want?"

The man standing directly in front of her, whose yellow eyes were mapped with fine red veins, looked at his comrades and then, moving with slow deliberation, raised a hand to his head, removed his cap, stooped, and placed it on the floor beside his feet which were covered with a thick layer of mud. Whereupon, having straightened up, he said, "Best thing you can do, lady, is to clear out."

The others muttered, "Yes, she'd better go."

"You'll have to leave because we're going to burn the house down. You're ill, you're not long for this world anyway, so we're letting you live. Besides, you're a woman, and we only settle our accounts with men. Your Ivancea—he's been judged and dealt with. And the Prince's bailiff too. So now all we have to do is to share out the land among us."

Eleonora stared at the bloodstained ax which Pîrvou held in his hand. "Why are you taking my land? It's mine. I inherited it. And besides, I've done nothing to you. It was Ivancea who persecuted you, not me. Let me keep it and I'll rent it to you."

"You hear what she says?" fat Melitaru whispered timidly. But from near the door at the far end of the room Marinica cried at the top of his voice, "Did you hear her? She knows how to talk, doesn't she? But her mug stinks of carrion. Give her one across it with a whip, that'll teach her to shut up!"

Iordake exchanged looks with Rizea, with Mototolea, with Ouracou. Rizea shook his head. So did Mototolea. Ouracou seemed too tired to care. He was thinking of his son. For his part, he would just as soon kill the old woman. It would be boyars' blood to help pay for his son's.

"We don't want to rent land, lady," Iordake said. "We haven't the money. You make us pay four times the rent we paid five years ago, which makes slaves of us, just as we were under the Turks. But we'll have no more slavery; we've had all we're going to take. If you didn't want to treat us like human beings you ought to have killed us. But it's done with now. We're going to be the masters— we, the Community. Because if every man was master of his own bit of land, we'd kill one another for a furrow more or less. But if we do as we did in the old days and hold the land and everything in common, then it will be all right. And as for you, get out of here and follow your nose wherever it leads you, but never set foot in these parts again as you value your life. Come, lads, make way! She's going."

Trembling with fear and exhaustion, Eleonora made her way out of the room. Her face was shriveled and clay-colored. In the drawing room the curtains, the clothing, the upholstery, and the photographs on the piano were all burning in eddies of smoke. Eleonora, muttering, covering her face with her arms, her elbow lifted as if to ward off a blow, passed through the flames and vanished among the deep shadows of the courtyard.

Rizea took hold of Geambashu's arm and, laughing, said to Iordake, "Come along, let's go with these gentlemen and see them set fire to the house. And hurry, for it looks as if someone has been ahead of us."

Mme Vorvoreano, holding the jewel box under her arm, put a hand on the doorknob and waited anxiously. The northbound train, coming up from the Danube, was running into the station, belching clouds of steam. Out on the platform the crowd surged around a cattle car at the rear. Frightened and questioning faces appeared at all the first- and second-class windows.

Mme Vorvoreano opened the door and swiftly crossed the platform, dragging Elvira who was carrying the document bag. She seized the bar of one of the coach doors and pulled herself up onto the step. She was going to win after all. She would be able to save the jewels.

As she was making her way into the coach, a shot made her start violently. A short, sharp sound, like the crack of a whip: an army rifle. Mme Vorvoreano went into the first compartment, which was not empty. Two gentlemen were looking out of the open window. There was a second bang, followed by a series of metallic noises: blows from a hammer. The train started.

"Did you hear? They're throwing stones!" one of the travelers said.

"I suppose the railroad men are making common cause with them," the other replied. Taking a large silver watch from the pocket of his velvet-lined shooting jacket, he added, "We have still an hour to go. . . . If all goes well for an hour, we're saved. Would you agree?"

The speaker was a handsome old man with a white mustache; he wore a massive gold ring on his little finger. "What do you think, Monsieur Hariton?" he persisted.

The other, fat and sallow, wiped the sweat off his brow with a blue handkerchief. He did not answer.

The gentleman with the white mustache turned to Mme Vorvoreano. "Did you see them attack the car in which the prisoners were being transported?"

Mme Vorvoreano looked at him in silence.

"The last car on the train, a cattle car—the ringleaders arrested in our villages, Monsieur Hariton's and mine, were in it. Allow me to introduce myself: I am Colonel Rusesco. And you are——? Ah, Madame Vorvoreano, of course. I know Vorvoreano. He was one of my cadets at the Military Academy. Delighted to make your acquaintance, madame. Even in such circumstances—terrible, terrible! An upsurge of base instincts. But the punishment must be exemplary. They must be given a lesson that will last a century at least. Ah! If I were at the head of the Ministry—as I very nearly was, by the way, in the Costake government—I'd put the whole region to fire and sword. These peasants have got to be fettered, madame. . . ."

The level, interminable plain, its monotony broken only by occasional groups of willow trees, glided past the windows. Mme Vorvoreano was thinking, *The moment I arrive people are going to start asking what I've done with Eleonora and why I left her behind. What am I going to say?*

The Colonel was still talking. "Imagine it—they even dared to threaten this gentleman, though he's one of our greatest landowners with twelve thousand acres at Izvoare; you will certainly know him by name—Monsieur Augustatos, Hariton Augustatos. My own manor, too—they tried to sack it, madame! There was a company of soldiers near by, to guard the glass factory. I went to see the captain. 'Captain,' I said, 'I beg you to do your duty.' The result was that we captured a score of them, clapped them in irons, and bundled them into a cattle car. But it looks as if these others had got wind of the thing, and are on watch at the stations to release them. . . ."

"They signal to each other at night," M. Augustatos murmured helplessly. "They have means of communication we know nothing about. . . ."

There was a silence. Mme Vorvoreano was thinking, *It isn't possible anything should go wrong now. It would be really too much, now that we're so near the end of our troubles.*

Still in a low voice, M. Augustatos resumed: "They know everything. They've found out what happened and they're on the watch for us at every station."

His hunted look, his way of wringing his hands, were not new to Mme Vorvoreano. She had already seen them the night before with Ivancea and Alexiu. Augustatos was clutching a brief case, at which he glanced from time to time.

The train went through other small stations, lost at the bottom of gullies in the clay soil or set beside roads deep in mud. At each one the peasants stared up at the windows. Voices, calling from the cattle car, drew them like a magnet. And on each occasion there were the same outbursts of fury, the same attempts at forcing open the door of the car, accompanied by an occasional shot fired over their heads by the soldiers guarding the prisoners. M. Augustatos huddled into his corner and listened in terror. When the train started again he took his large handkerchief out of his pocket and wiped his face, and then his neck under the collar.

At last the train ran into a suburb of cottages roofed with tarred paper. The station was being patrolled by a posse of city police, accompanied by a number of civilians. Clad in smoke-blackened sheepskin coats, turners and fitters from the repair shops, switchmen, and porters gathered around the cattle car at the end of the train. When the officials—the police commissioner, the prefect, and the procurator—made for the cattle car, the prisoners began shouting, while the railroad men hooted the authorities and uttered piercing whistles.

Mme Vorvoreano alighted hastily from the train and made for

the exit. She heard a few words as she hurried past. A harsh middle-class voice was shouting, "Gang of socialists! Pack of anarchists!" Mme Vorvoreano and Elvira, M. Augustatos and the Colonel, hurried out of the station, hustled by catcalls like autumn leaves by the wind. In the muddy station yard, two shabby cabs drawn by small, emaciated horses were waiting in the rain. M. Augustatos immediately commandeered the better one without a word of apology. The Colonel took off his hat and bowed to Mme Vorvoreano. In a surly voice the cab driver asked, "Where d'you want to go?"

"Saint-Spiridon Street," she said, looking at the man in surprise. Was the wind of madness blowing here too? "Why, Ghitza, don't you recognize me?"

"I kiss your hands," the man replied, still surly. "I didn't recognize you. Can you wonder, with all these troubles?"

"What troubles, Ghitza?"

The cabby did not answer. He lashed his horses and the cab lurched away over the cobbled street. It was drizzling.

"Why are the shops shut, Ghitza? Is it a holiday?" Mme Vorvoreano inquired. The cabman, huddled on the box, flicked the right-hand horse's bony back and cried, "Gee up!" Then he turned around and growled, "No, it's not a holiday, madam, it's the revolution. . . . They say the peasants are coming, and the troops quartered here have been sent to Moldavia—so the shopkeepers have got the wind up."

Mme Vorvoreano shivered. The uprising hemmed her in on all sides. She hugged the jewel box more tightly and cast a frightened glance at the statue of the Hospodar Callimachi.

The cab drove past the National Bank, where she saw in addition to the usual police guard a few soldiers in gray cloaks, with fixed bayonets, who seemed paralyzed by the cold. A score of peasants were crouching in the shelter of the Bank's wall. They looked out of place in this urban world. *Here they are not so bold,* Mme Vorvoreano reflected. *We are protected, sheltered from all danger . . .* Aloud she said, "Stop here."

The cabman pulled up. Elvira jumped out of the cab and ran to open the courtyard gate. The cab drove off, the horses' hoofs splashing dirty water from the puddles. Elvira stood aside, holding the gate for her mother to go first, and smiled. Mme Vorvoreano did not even notice her. As she crossed the threshold, she stumbled and bumped against the iron gate. She recovered her balance at once, and went on.

Elvira noticed that she was slightly unsteady in her walk. She helped her across the graveled yard. A persistent rain was driving into their faces. The hems of their skirts were trailing in the mud.

Mme Vorvoreano rang the front door bell. The door was arched, with three panels and glass panes, and the shell-shaped porch protected them from the rain. After a long delay a dormer window opened, and framed within it appeared the face of Viorica, the gypsy servant. Shortly afterward the door was opened. Without saying a word, the servant kissed their hands, then looked hard at Mme Vorvoreano, who, passing into the house, ordered her to prepare a hot bath. She walked from one room to another, all of them darkened by closed shutters, and Elvira and Viorica followed. Two or three of the chambermaids appeared in the doorways, murmuring, ". . . kiss your hands, madam," and slipped quickly away.

On the walls hung the family portraits: Sophia Coziano, plump and beautiful; the somber Alexander Coziano; Davida Lascari, withered and mysterious; Lascar Lascari, Mme Vorvoreano's father, in a white waistcoat. There were older portraits too, of men wearing the *ishlic,* the high fur hat of the boyars, and oriental-looking beards and wide silk sashes of peacock blue, in the Turkish manner. All had their velvety, expressionless eyes fixed on the worn, sumptuous rugs. Mme Vorvoreano sat down in an armchair and looked at the tall tiled stove. Elvira stood beside her.

"Draw the curtains. Put the suitcase down—here, beside me."

Viorica carried out these orders and the room became quite dark. Mme Vorvoreano remained still, the jewel box on her knees. Then she said, "You may go. What are you waiting for? Go."

Then, reluctantly, she forced herself to add a few words of justification. "Go and see to my bath. And get Mademoiselle Elvira something to eat."

The woman left them. The opening of the door allowed a strip of light to enter. Another silence followed. At last Mme Vorvoreano's voice rose in the darkness.

"Elvira!"

The girl did not answer.

"Elvira, are you there?"

"Yes, Mama."

Mme Vorvoreano seemed to hesitate for a moment, then she murmured, "You can go too. . . . Go. Go, go."

Elvira did not move, straining to make out her mother's features in the darkness. At last she sighed and went out of the room. Mme Vorvoreano rose and, knocking against the furniture, went to the door and locked it. Then she groped her way to the desk where she knew there would be a lamp and matches. She placed the jewel box in the dim light and looked at it for a long time. From the depths of the house came the vague sound of a piano.

Mme Vorvoreano opened a drawer and looked for something among the papers, sticks of sealing wax, and penholders. There should be a hammer and chisel among them. She searched for a long time, opening all the doors and drawers of the desk. At last she found the tools, and worked the edge of the chisel under the lid of the box. With all her strength she struck twice with the hammer, forcing the lock. The lid opened at once and fell back, barely retained by the delicate hinges which had half come loose. Mme Vorvoreano leaned against the back of her armchair and breathed deeply. Then she bent forward and began to remove the jewels one by one from the box's padded red silk interior. Turning up the wick, she laid them neatly in the lamplight on the table. She took each ring, each pair of earrings, and held them up at eye level, making them flash and glow. From time to time, when she realized that a ring was worth a thousand gold napoleons or even more, she examined it at greater length, but with a remote and pensive look, her face expressing a curious gravity.

There were nineteen rings. Some, set with diamonds or with large emeralds, were worth half a harvest. But there were others of no value whatever. One man's gold ring was engraved with two initials, an *S* and a *V* in Gothic letters. To whom could it have belonged? There, too, were the rings that Eleonora had given to Elvira and Michael when they were little, and then accused them of losing. Their mother had beaten them. *So Eleonora stole the children's rings . . . she actually stole them,* Mme Vorvoreano thought, astounded. She also found her husband's ring which he had mislaid on the last occasion when he stayed at the manor in the summer of 1898. Doubtless Eleonora had found the ring and hidden it. Or had she stolen that one outright too?

Mme Vorvoreano, leaning back in her chair, made an effort to control the almost hysterical laughter that was shaking her. Suddenly she felt herself turn faint. *At this very moment she has perhaps been dead for many hours. . . .* She sat motionless in her chair, trying to recover her calm. Then, pulling herself together, she began to examine the other jewels. Some were frankly ugly, others worthless. But the necklaces, especially the big one with the emeralds, the *rivière* of diamonds, the two smaller diamond necklaces, the two strings of pearls—all these had no equal in the whole country.

Mme Vorvoreano took out the lockets next, one by one. In the one ornamented with diamonds was the photograph of a gentleman with side whiskers who was perhaps the "S.V." of the gold ring. (Helen Vorvoreano had no way of knowing that the ring had been Sherban Vogoride's, and that Sophia Coziano had mislaid it in a drawer half a century ago.) A double locket contained miniatures of their parents; another, the portrait of an unknown woman; still another, a miniature of Helen herself at twenty. Mme Vorvoreano gazed at this one for a long time. Inside she found a lock of fair hair, which she had cut off before her wedding and given to Eleonora. *So she kept it . . . and my portrait, too . . . she didn't want to be parted from them. Did she look at them sometimes? Perhaps often?*

She pushed back her chair, rose, shut the locket, and threw it down on the table. Then she began to pace the room, wringing her hands. Her eyes filled with tears and she felt as if she were suffocating. She recovered her calm, however, and, still standing, examined the rest of the jewelry in the box: their father's watch and Eleonora's; some earrings set with large emeralds surrounded by diamonds; a gold brooch in the form of a spider with ruby eyes; a silver cat's head as big as an apple, also with rubies for eyes, to be attached to the belt and provided with little hooks for carrying keys to cupboards and larder. Mme Vorvoreano swept the jewelry aside in her haste to count the gold coins: there were huge Turkish pieces, pierced through the middle; Russian rubles bearing the effigy of Alexander II during whose reign her grandfather had made a fortune by selling provisions to the Russian armies which were crossing the country to fight the Turks. . . . Mme Vorvoreano scooped all this treasure into her cupped hands—rings, earrings, necklaces, gold coins. She could hardly hold it all; the jewels, cold and glittering, slipped through her fingers.

After a few minutes Mme Vorvoreano remembered the document bag. She put it on the table, opened it, and began to remove bundles of stiff, thick papers engraved at the top with symbolic figures (Commerce, Justice, Prosperity, cornucopias, sheaves of wheat, anchors, cog-wheels) and covered with seals and stamps in red, violet, or black ink. They represented shares in numerous industrial enterprises, in French, English, German, and Austro-Hungarian shipping and insurance companies. Bearer bonds. *So that's where old Sophia's money went. At last!*

Mme Vorvoreano spent a long time looking at these papers, comparing them and counting them. Then she put everything—jewel box, jewels, money, and papers—into the safe where she kept old documents concerned with legacies, sales, and marriages, as well as packets of letters and other things of no value. She locked the safe and hung the key around her neck on a ribbon. She was beginning to feel weaker and weaker. And very sleepy. Yet she still had to see to the house, and Elvira. She must also pay calls in town, try to find out what had happened at the manor house. But first she must take a bath. She put the hammer and chisel back in their drawer, gathered up a few splinters of wood which had broken off when she forced the jewel box, and threw them into a drawer. She put the now flat and empty document bag into another drawer. The desk showed no trace of what had happened. Mme Vorvoreano turned out the lamp and left the room.

6

Rizea, Iordake, and some of the others stood and looked along the road. They saw the peasants' carts coming from the manor, a long, winding procession whose end was not in sight. People had come from the neighboring villages too—from Pietri, Reviga, and Cotul Grecului. The oxen swung their heads from side to side at each step. They were small, emaciated beasts, caked with mud. The carts, as they lumbered and lurched over the ruts, gave out a mournful creaking; they were piled high with sacks of grain, and on top of each pile sat a man armed with a staff or a fork; sometimes the guard was only a boy.

One of the carts was not as heavily laden as the others; the sacks had been neatly piled side by side and a man lay on top of them, covered by his sheepskin jerkin. A boy prodded the oxen along with his staff. The man lying on the sacks was quite still, and his face was ashen, as if he had been stuffed with ashes. Rizea shouted to the boy to wait a moment, and the boy checked the oxen and brought the cart to a halt at the roadside.

"What's wrong with your father?" Rizea asked.

"He's ill," the boy answered, his eyes fixed on his team. Then he looked at his father. The man had not moved. On his face, just below the temple, was what looked like a big purple bruise.

The men standing at the roadside exchanged suspicious looks. "Why, he's dead!" Iordake said to the boy in his heavy voice.

The boy looked at his father again and said, "Oh no . . ." He put his hand on the injured man's knee and shook it gently, calling to him softly.

The man groaned and half opened his eyes, then closed them, muttering unintelligibly.

"What happened?" Iordake asked. "Who did this to him?"

"The soldier . . ."

"But why, lad? What for?"

"It was about some sacks of grain, because there weren't many left at the lady's, so there was fighting over them. . . ."

Those who were standing in the field, beyond the ditch that bordered the road, held their peace. Even Iordake asked no more questions. The boy prodded the oxen's lean flanks with his stick. The cart creaked and moved off along the muddy road. After a while Rizea muttered, "They've already started bashing each other over the head with their spades. . . . One man wants more. Another thinks his neighbor has too much. . . . Great God of madmen!"

He fell silent again. Around them people were talking quietly, sitting on clods of earth. One or two rolled cigarettes. In the distance, the last cart in the long file came into sight. A man walking alone approached slowly, carrying a sack on his back. When he drew level with the men sitting in the field he slipped the sack from his shoulder and put it down on a big stone. Rizea recognized Pîrvou.

"Why didn't you ask me to carry your sack for you, eh?" Iordake said.

Pîrvou said nothing. Then he raised his eyes to Iordake and said angrily, "Laughing at me, are you, you swine? I've carried my sack this far on my back, and a lot you care. . . . A lot of good-for-nothings . . ."

He seized the sack, lifted it, and hoisted it onto his shoulders. The men watched him: Pîrvou was a strong man, despite his illness.

"Don't be a fool. Who's laughing at you?" Iordake said.

Balancing his sack, Pîrvou looked at him out of eyes wide with anger, their whites streaked with tiny congested veins. "Laugh away!" he said. "We'll see when they come to hang us, whether you're still inclined to laugh. To hell with the lot of you!"

And he plodded on, bowed lower and lower. In the distance he looked like an ant dragging a dead insect ten times its own size.

The men kept silent. Pîrvou's troubles left them quite unmoved. They were tired. All the goods stored at the manor had been scattered now, disappearing as the carcass of an animal disappears in the forest, thousands of small active creatures each bearing off a small part until what had been the body of a hare is no more than well-picked bones and a pair of furry ears on a bare skull. Of the house itself nothing remained but a shell of charred walls. Last night's crowd had dispersed; only a few men remained, grouped around Rizea and Iordake that morning, when each man had finished what he had to do and taken his share from the boyar's granaries.

And as they sat there, waiting, they saw coming toward them across the fields Alexander, the second son of Ouracou, a thin, pale boy with a boil at the corner of his mouth. Rizea turned to him and inquired, "What news of your brother?"

"He died this morning," the boy said, lowering his eyes as if he had said something shameful.

"So he is dead," Rizea muttered.

"And your father? What of him?" Iordake demanded in a hoarse voice.

Alexander looked vaguely at Iordake's belt, simply in order to avoid raising his eyes. After a moment he said awkwardly, "He's sleeping."

"Just sleeping," Rizea said, and asked further, "What happened that your brother died? Yesterday he was on the mend, wasn't he?"

"A weakness came over him this morning," the boy replied. "We were talking to him, but he didn't know us. . . . And then he died. . . . He just came over weak and . . ."

"And why is your father sleeping, eh?" Iordake asked. "Is he made of wood or something? Is he a Turk?"

"I don't know," the lad said. "I don't know why he's sleeping. He didn't say anything. He pulled his fur jerkin over his head and went to sleep."

He studied Iordake's belt again for a moment, then looked about, still keeping his eyes lowered shyly, and added, "He told me he would go to the town. . . ."

Rizea turned sharply on the boy. "So that's what he says, is it? He wants to go to the town. What for? What will he do there in town?"

"He wants to go to the town to kill the boyars—make them pay for my brother's death. . . ."

The men fell silent, even Rizea. At last he said, "We had better go and talk to him."

"Yes, first we must talk to him," Iordake confirmed. All the others muttered that they agreed, that this must be done.

Frowning, the boy looked from one to the other. He did not understand, but when they set out he followed them without question. The place they left remained deserted. From somewhere in the distance came the cracking of whips, where impatient men had already set their plowshares in the boyar's land and were throwing down the fences. A tall, thin column of smoke was rising from a pile of wood that had been a hedge.

When Rizea and the others passed through the cart gate into the yard, they saw Ouracou standing on the porch. The house was long and narrow and edged with big stones. Inside the house the mother was keening in a singsong voice. Two or three women were standing by the open door, sobbing, the corners of their black aprons held over their mouths. Ouracou was smoking in silence; the hairs of his beard were tangled about his face like the black threads surrounding a walnut shell when the green outer shell has rotted away. The men came in and stood around him. Ouracou half closed his eyes and looked at no one. Rizea sat down beside him, elbows on knees and hands hanging down. He began to speak calmly.

"So far, so good; we've done it here. But there, what could we do? Set fire to it? The town's big. . . . And besides, not only boyars live there."

"I'll kill as many as I can," Ouracou mumbled. "What's it to you, anyway?" He turned to Rizea, but Rizea pretended not to have heard. Ouracou went on: "I'm going alone. I've an account to settle with them. And my grief. I'm going alone, I tell you."

Speaking to nobody in particular, Rizea said, "Where's Marinica got to?"

"Which Marinica? The student?" someone asked.

"He'll be at Dobrunu," Iordake growled, "or he'll have gone farther afield to Pietri or Reviga. . . . Things aren't so far along there."

"He said he would go to the town too," Rizea remarked.

"You're lying," Ouracou said coolly and without expression.

"He told me so last night," Rizea said calmly, "told me so himself."

"He is lying," Ouracou said.

"Who's lying, father Ion? Me?"

"Not you. Him."

Suddenly the sky became overcast and a cold wind began to blow. A belated cart passed along the village street on its way from the manor. The dogs barked as it went through. Inside the house Zaharia's mother, exhausted, was sobbing more and more feebly.

"Why is he lying, father Ion?"

"He is lying because he is not going to the town."

"Why is he not going there, father Ion? Why shouldn't he? Nothing's stopping him. Could he be afraid of someone? Why should he be afraid? Think it over, father Ion."

"He's afraid of the Army. The boyars will send the Army against us. They'll make the Army shoot us down. You'll see. You don't know nothing."

They all avoided one another's eyes and drew imperceptibly apart. Two or three of them rose to leave. Resolutely Rizea said, "They'll not shoot."

Iordake coughed, turned sharply toward him, and for a moment looked him straight in the eye. Then Iordake blinked as if dust had blown into his eyes and in a drawling voice asserted, "No, of course they won't shoot. Why should they fire on us? The student said they wouldn't, and he knows. They're our brothers, the soldiers are, and they couldn't fire on us. We're of the same blood."

With many blasphemies and curses Ouracou expressed his opinion of that blood-brotherhood.

Rizea turned on him furiously. "And why are you going, eh? Are you made of steel? Have you a charm to protect you, or what? Maybe you're a cleverer man than we are?"

He rose. Turning to the man beside him, he dug him in the ribs, and in the same rough tone said, "What's the matter with you, sitting there like a log? Are you waiting to drop a litter?"

"Come on, mates," Iordake said. "Come along."

They all rose and set off slowly, across the yard and out by the cart gate. Obstinately, Ouracou stood still with half-closed eyes. Suddenly he called to Alexander in an angry voice, "Hi! Go and fetch me the ax!"

Alexander started, rose, and went for the ax. Ouracou took it and ran his finger along the steel blade; he had sharpened it well and it was heavy. Ouracou addressed his son. "You are not to leave the house. If anything happens you are to stay with your mother. Take care of the little ones, understand? Don't leave the house or you'll get the worst hiding anyone ever had."

With that he set off. When he reached the gate he turned around and said, "I've gone away, so to speak . . ."

"Where to?" Alexander asked.

"To the town." And he stepped into the village street with his ax under his arm.

When Ouracou reached the Town Hall he saw that a crowd had gathered around several men who had just arrived in the courtyard. The sun was high—it must be past noon. The people were talking with a sort of joyful fury. Ouracou slipped in among them, and men made way for him. Arrived at the center of the group, he saw Rizea, who was proclaiming, "He dug pits in the ground to hide the wheat."

"Pits? What kind of pits?"

"Deep pits, to bury the grain, father Ion."

"What's all this about?"

"Deep, father Ion, twice the height of a man and round like a well. First he put in as much hay as he could, one or two armfuls, a bale, say, all he had. Then he set fire to it, so that the inside was burned and became like brick. And then he poured his grain into it and stopped the mouth with earth, because the opening was no bigger than a big basket, a man can hardly get through it. And then he stamped down the earth or put turf above it—contriving it, you see, so that the wheat couldn't be found."

"Found by whom?"

"By the boyar, of course."

"Whose wheat, Rizea? Who dug pits like that?"

"Mototolea!" shouted several voices. Then followed an avalanche of names: "Kiritza! Geambashu! Dobre! Burete!"

Rizea grinned, showing all his teeth. "They've gone into hiding so that the boyars cannot ask for the wheat back."

"What boyars?" Ouracou demanded. He raised his ax above the heads of the crowd, holding it by the end of the haft. It was heavy and wobbled a little, but Ouracou gripped it firmly in his fist and cried, "With this ax I killed the boyar! He'll never return. He won't be asking for his wheat any more. It's finished! Dig pits, will they? When I get back from the town, I'll teach them to dig pits! Yes, my lads! In a day or two I'll be back, and then I'll settle accounts with them."

There was a dull growl from the crowd. So Ouracou was going to town. All alone?

"Alone? What do you mean, alone? We're going, me and Iordake and all of them—and there'll be others."

A man standing on the Town Hall steps shouted, "Me too! But what are we going to do in the town?"

Rizea threw out his chest. "Go to the law court and burn the boyars' papers! Neither they nor their children nor their children's children will ever know where their lands lay. Come on, lads!"

He set out in the lead, dragging his leg a little. Iordake and Ouracou followed him closely. A compact column formed up in the street. Some scrambled over hedges and hid themselves in their houses, others halted by a well, pretending to stop for a drink of water so as to remain behind. But still others came out of their houses, ax or cudgel in hand, and talked with the men in the column, following slowly, then more swiftly until they ended by being absorbed into the marching column.

When they passed Ouracou's house, Alexander was standing at the door. He saw his father at the front of the mob. Ouracou passed without looking either to right or left. He was talking loudly and his eyes were bright, but nobody could hear what he was saying because of the uproar. Alexander watched him for a while and then came out into the street, where he too became a part of the column.

They came to Salcia in the evening. There was a crowd behind the station. What were all these people waiting for? What had they done, or what were they going to do? Feeling a sharp, stabbing pain in the bone of his crippled foot, Rizea went forward alone onto the station platform. He suddenly felt lost, alien, in the midst of something beyond his understanding. Why this impulsive movement toward the railroad lines? Why this disappointed return? He approached a group of men and saw, among faces grim with waiting, a gray and emaciated countenance, worn away from within by poverty and suffering. The faces of the people here were not yellow and furrowed like village people's; their skin seemed to retain in every fold a pinch of iron filings. The voices were different too; they were not drawling, but harsh and metallic. Rizea guessed that all these men were mechanics and laborers working on the new railroad. He listened to one of them and discovered with amazement that this man was saying things which he himself might have thought or done. This had the same effect on him as if he had been suddenly shown that he was twice as strong as he had thought.

"No, mates," the man was saying, "we can't let her through. If this train gets past Salcia, there's nowhere we can stop her between here and the town. And if the hostages get into the hands of the prefect and the general down there, then the villages beyond Reviga are done for. Not one of them will stir."

The switchman who had been distributing pamphlets the night before called out, "I am leaving the switches closed."

The others laughed. "Good work, Petrake. Show 'em what you can do."

"I'll keep the switches blocked, while the rest of you go for the car with the hostages and open it. I'll climb up onto the engine and tell the stoker to rake out his fire. . . ."

The crowd swarmed over the tracks and the platform. Here and there was the uniform of a reservist recalled to a regiment that was being sent to Moldavia to suppress the risings. The reservists got no farther than Salcia railroad station, where they were sucked into the whirlpool.

A bell rang four times. A shiver of anticipation ran through the crowd. The glow of the locomotive's firebox appeared in the distance. The signals flashed. A train of four coaches ran into the station, braking hard. The conductor, the men in charge of the mail car, and the engineer all leaned out to see why the train, which was not supposed to stop anywhere, had come to a halt. Rizea, on the platform, felt himself caught up and swept forward by a tide of humanity toward the coaches at the end of the train. With the rest he heaved at the sliding doors of the cattle cars in which the ringleaders had been imprisoned. There was some sporadic shooting. In the front rank of the mob the man Rizea had overheard talking and one of his companions were forcing back bolts with oiled steel instruments. Then the human wave washed back and the hostages poured out of the car onto the platform, shouting. At the front of the train Rizea saw the dark shadow of Petrake, the switchman, climbing onto the footplate. A few moments later a heap of hot coals fell out on the track between the wheels of the locomotive. The blow had been swiftly struck, and the men were intoxicated by their easy victory. Rizea, too, felt lighter-hearted. So this was how things were done. He sought Petrake in the milling crowd and twitched his sleeve. The switchman turned around and Rizea was surprised to see that he seemed deeply dejected.

"We're going to the town," Rizea said. "Come with us, friend."

The switchman gave him a keen look and said, "How many of you are there? A lot?"

"A good many," said Rizea. "There are some from Vadastra, others from Vladomira, others from our place, from Dobrunu—about two thousand of us."

"And what are you going to the town for?"

"That's easy. We're going to the law courts to burn all the boy-ars' papers—their deeds, where it's written where each man has his lands, the boundaries, and all that—their diplomas, as you might say. Come with us. If we hurry, they're done for."

The switchman studied Rizea thoughtfully. Under that inquisi-torial stare Rizea remembered the doubts which had assailed him. They stood face to face by one of the iron stanchions that held up the station roof.

"So you just set off for the city on the off-chance," the switchman said, "not even knowing yourselves where it will lead you? With or without papers, they'll be the masters just the same."

Rizea remained silent. He had long realized that he and his friends were groping blindly. He waited for what was to follow and then, since the switchman said no more, he said, "That's true. Well then, tell us what we must do. Tell us, since you know how things are done in a city. . . ."

The switchman beckoned to some of his mates. Iordake, who had seen Rizea from a distance, made his way through the crowd with several of the villagers behind him.

"Which are their strong points in a city?" the switchman asked Rizea.

Rizea thought for a moment and then said hesitantly, "The bar-racks, presumably."

"Of course," Petrake replied, "and after that the post office and telephone exchange and police headquarters. Strike there first and they'll be really done for."

Muttering, the peasants exchanged glances. What was the point of going to the barracks? It would be walking into a deathtrap and moreover it would serve no purpose, it would get them no-where. Ouracou shouted violently, "Friends, we must kill them all. There's no other way. We must break into their houses and destroy the lot of them, and their spawn! The rest doesn't matter!"

The switchman's words had displeased him. He did not feel that he could trust this man who said things which he, Ouracou, did not understand.

"Aren't we going to go to the law courts?" Iordake shouted. "Are we to let them go on persecuting us with their papers and their lawsuits? Wipe out the debts first, and then knock the boyars on the head, wherever you find them. Then we'll be our own masters. Don't listen to all this nonsense. Let's get on with it! They're at the end of their tether and their King's died on them. They've nobody left to lead them. Let's waste no more time hanging around this station. We've hours of traveling still ahead of us."

There followed a confused babel of questions and answers.

"Iordake, what's all this about the King?" Rizea cried.

Iordake's eyes were troubled and he avoided looking at Rizea, moving away from him and shouting, "Come, friends, let's go. They aren't many, and we are all the strength of the earth." Farther on, Ouracou was bawling unintelligibly and brandishing his ax above the heads of the crowd. The men surged after him. Rizea hesitated, and the switchman looked at him in silence. Rizea understood him perfectly: of course the men were right. But he could not hang back now; things were on the move and he must go on to the end. He hastened away to join the rear guard of the column, but as he went he heard Petrake call after him, "At least cut the telephone wires!"

"Right!" Rizea shouted back, and hurried on.

When he reached the station gate he collided with Alexander, Ouracou's son; recognizing him, he took the boy's arm, so as to press forward more quickly. Behind them, the railroad men and mechanics seemed to have dwindled suddenly. They fell silent. The train stood on the tracks, empty and abandoned, clouds of steam still hissing from the motionless engine. Below it, on the ballast, the cooling cinders which had charred the crossties no longer glowed. Night was beginning to fall.

All the way there Rizea chewed over his bitterness. He kept Ouracou's son at his side. He felt a need to confide in someone and talked to Alexander at random. He told him that in his opinion they ought to have followed the switchman's advice, for the men at the station knew the city well, and they too were under the boyars' heel. Was Alexander listening? Rizea desperately wanted one other at least to realize what he himself had realized.

One of the roads that led to the town went through Reviga and followed the bend in the river that was called Greek's Reach, where it joined the road which Rizea and his companions had taken. At the crossroads Rizea saw Marinica, curled up in a cart, at the head of a body of men carrying flags; among them a trumpet was sounding as in a barracks and the steel tines of pitchforks swayed above their heads. The two columns coalesced and spread out over the fields. Rizea called to Marinica, who recognized him. Rizea saw in his eyes the same glimmer of unconfessed anxiety that he thought he had seen in Iordake's. He said nothing, but he felt more wretched than ever and withdrew into himself.

They spent the night in the fields or in villages. When the sun rose there was quarreling in the air. Ouracou discovered the presence of his son and rushed at him, brandishing his ax. Swift as a lizard, Alexander melted into the crowd. Later he came back toward his father, who looked at him and said nothing, as if he had all along given him permission to be there.

They made their way into the city. The shops had their shutters up. The windows of the houses were closed. Every door was bolted. In the main square, which was paved with big round cobbles, between the Administrative Building and the Cathedral of St. Basil the Great, the mob, with its axes, cudgels, and pitchforks, came up against a geometrically straight line of soldiers in gray cloaks. Before them, several officers and a number of civilians in bowler hats were pacing up and down. In the intervals between the soldiers the peasants could see the emptiness of the square and the desertedness of the neighboring streets. The soldiers were few in number.

Ouracou raised his ax, and with all his strength and in a voice no longer his own, yelled, "Kill them!" His words sent a shudder of excitement through the crowd.

He hurled himself forward. Marinica, Iordake, Rizea, Alexander, and some others advanced into the square, the mob pressing at their heels. The officers and civilians made short, jerky motions with their arms, like puppets, before disappearing behind the cordon of soldiers.

7

Mme Vorvoreano had spent the whole of the previous day calling on friends: she was "grief-stricken, anxious, terribly worried" about Eleonora. She had repeated dozens of times that she was filled with remorse for having deserted Eleonora at a moment when "nothing had actually happened, but there was unquestionably something in the air." But who could have expected the rising to spread so quickly, or that it would break out here, in this very province? It was true that an affectionate sister who had sacrificed herself to Eleonora all her life—especially since their other brothers and sisters had broken with Eleonora over mean little questions of money—ought at least to have foreseen what would happen and either have stayed with her sister or brought her away by force if necessary. But everyone knew how obstinate Eleonora was: she seemed to have taken root in the country and for the last ten years or more had steadily refused to return to town. "And how could I persuade her?" Mme Vorvoreano appealed, in a voice which tried hard to sound tearful. "I could not convince her of the seriousness of what was happening around us, for I hardly realized it myself. When I heard the news, it was like a thunderclap out of a clear sky. It was too late to go back . . . and yet that's what I should have done. I should have gone back and died with her, for she was not only a sister to me, but a mother. Those brutes of peasants could have killed us in each other's arms. Ah! wretch that I am, why didn't I have the strength of mind to do it?" And she wept, while the ladies hugged and caressed her with their heavily beringed hands and murmured words of consolation.

Then she dabbed her handkerchief to her tearless eyes, coldly embraced Matilda or Aristitza, and went on to call on Zoë or Zenaïda to repeat the performance. This exhausting activity had lasted until evening. At nightfall Mme Vorvoreano had learned that telephone communication with the station at Salcia had been cut off and that it was no longer possible to get news from any of the villages in the direction of the Danube, which proved that the insurrection in that quarter was at its height. Helen had seemed desperate and declared that she would go at once—on foot, if necessary. The charitable ladies made as if to prevent her. "Come now, Helen, be reasonable; you're behaving like a child!" And they whispered to one another: "They were so fond of each other, you know. She's exaggerating it, of course, but she was very much attached to Eleonora, whereas the rest of them—Sherban Lascari, Sophia Sufana—well really, Helen's quite right when she says they've behaved like jackals!"

That night Mme Vorvoreano's sleep was heavy and broken by nightmares. She rang for Viorica, her chambermaid, and ordered her to raise the blinds. With her head propped up on a pillow, her eyelids heavy, and her eyes burning, she stared out at the sullen sky. She lingered in bed over her coffee. She thought of sending for an old gypsy woman she knew and having her fortune told; but, seized with fear, she changed her mind and decided instead to tell her own fortune in the coffee grounds. But she could make nothing of the murky arabesques which formed a confused pattern in the cup. In a neighboring room Elvira was playing the piano. She played well at any hour, whenever she felt bored, which was almost always. Mme Vorvoreano shut her eyes and gave herself up to drowsing. Suddenly the music stopped and she sat up with a start. Voices reached her through the window: Elvira's, Viorica's, and another, male and insolent. Mme Vorvoreano jumped out of bed, slipped on a dressing gown, and rushed out into the corridor leading to the side door of the house; the front door was bolted because of the troubles.

Out on the front steps Elvira and Viorica were arguing with a hawker. He was a squat, burly, broad-shouldered young man with a bull neck. He had pulled his fur cap down over his eyes, leaving the back of his head uncovered to reveal thick, curly, gleaming black hair. He had put his carrying yoke down on the ground. In his two baskets he was carrying lemons and oranges which he had no doubt brought from some Danubian port—perhaps by the very train that Mme Vorvoreano had caught into town. The man was angry.

"Why do you haggle, miss?" he shouted. "You won't be eating many more oranges. Why be so stingy, with the pile you've got?"

Elvira was pale with fury. "You crook! I'll show you," she said, quivering with rage.

"What will you show me, miss?" the hawker said, with a malicious smile, stooping to pick up his yoke and two baskets.

Elvira hesitated for a moment, not understanding; then she rushed into the house, running into Mme Vorvoreano on the threshold, who asked, "Where are you running to? What are you going to do?"

"I'm going to fetch my riding crop and flog him!" Elvira said, panting and trying to push past her mother. She succeeded in doing so, and meanwhile Mme Vorvoreano heard the hawker shouting as he made his way out through the big carriage gateway: "Aye, they're right to kill you and burn down your houses! You ought all to have your throats cut, to teach you manners!"

Mme Vorvoreano went to her room to dress. She was exhausted and her hands were shaking, but she told herself that she must carry this thing through to the end. She went out on foot, in an old, rather worn otterskin coat, her head wrapped in a black embroidered silk shawl.

She called on Matilda Misirliu, who lived near the Administrative Building and the Cathedral, in a big white solidly built house. It was one of the few boyars' houses whose courtyard was surrounded by a wall instead of iron railings. On each side of the massive wrought-iron carriage gates, stone seats were built into the masonry of the wall for the accommodation of the Albanian sentries who had formerly guarded such houses. These seats were now as vacant as the deserted street and the main square. With a thrill of fear Mme Vorvoreano saw a score of soldiers stamping their feet and flinging their arms about to keep warm. Their rifles were stacked near them.

Helen Vorvoreano gave a long tug at the bell wire. After a considerable delay, one of the stableboys came to open the gates. "Who is here?" Mme Vorvoreano asked him. "Is your mistress alone?"

"No, madam, there are guests, as if it were evening. They're drinking coffee and waiting for the peasants, madam."

"Indeed?" Mme Vorvoreano said in an altered voice. As she went up the steps she tried to pull herself together. With an assumed indifference she asked, "So the peasants are on their way here?"

"Yes, madam. Something like ten thousand of them, they say," the man answered, rolling his eyes to give himself an air of mystery.

Mme Vorvoreano entered the drawing room, which was in almost total darkness. Only a purplish vigil light was burning halfway up a wall whose upper part was covered with silver and gilt icons. As she kissed the ladies and bowed with sorrowful dignity to the men, Mme Vorvoreano recognized, apart from Matilda Misirliu, dressed as usual in heavy brown silk, a number of elderly women, Matilda's relations. All wore mourning, slight, stooped, shrunken old creatures, grouped in the darkest corners where they resembled heaps of black rags. Also present were Zoë Izvorano, tall, beautiful, and striking, and Aristitza Pretorian, who looked the image of a competent housewife. The men included M. Augustatos, who was sprawled in an armchair, and standing beside him, Colonel Rusesco, twisting his white mustache with the tips of his long slim fingers. There were also one or two younger men, sons or grandsons of the old ladies in mourning.

"They've all gone mad," Zoë Izvorano was saying in French, "they've been infected by the Russian anarchists. They want us to give them the lands our ancestors toiled so hard for from father to son. That land is ours, by virtue of every law in the world. By what right do they claim it, may I ask? I wish someone would explain that to me. It's a crime, an injustice! And here's your Government not raising a finger to prevent these ruffians from destroying the entire fortunes of innocent people!"

Her breath came short and fast, as if she herself had, at that very moment and by the sweat of her brow, acquired her family's wealth, which extended as far as the hill country and included ten villages.

Aristitza Pretorian sadly shook her head and whimpered, *"Parfaitement.* Zoë is right."

Echoing her friend, Mme Vorvoreano took up the refrain. "Yes, Zoë is right. The peasants are ungrateful. We have been father and mother to them, we are fond of them, they have been ours for hundreds of years. They ought to kiss our feet in gratitude for giving them work. Only the other day I was saying to Eleonora, 'My dear sister, farm your land with machinery, it's cheaper, more productive, and you'll have none of this eternal litigation with the peasantry.' But she, poor lamb, charitable as always, you know . . ."

Mme Vorvoreano's voice was drowned in tears. She fumbled in her bag with a trembling hand. The others were much moved. Zoë Izvorano ran to her, kissed and petted her, and said all in one breath, "Poor darling, don't cry, you'll see her again, never fear, and you'll be as happy together as you used to be!"

Suddenly she broke off and, looking about her with an air of surprise, said in a bright voice devoid of all emotion, "Where have you left little Elvira? Didn't you bring her?"

"She stayed at home," said Mme Vorvoreano in a faint voice.

Standing in the window embrasures, the gentlemen tactfully concealed their anxiety by pretending to look out at the street. Matilda Misirliu, the mistress of the house, smiled to herself, marveling at the artless skill with which Zoë could cut short an emotional scene. To put herself in a good light, she said, "They are poor, backward creatures. . . . We ought to improve their minds—lecture to them. . . ."

"Lecture to them? Have you too gone mad, my dear Matilda?" Zoë said, shaking her glittering earrings. And, without any particular reason, she flashed a bewitching smile at M. Augustatos, in whose eyes she had recognized a familiar gleam. Mme Vorvoreano, in her corner, sighed deeply.

There was a general silence, abruptly ended by Colonel Rusesco's polite and tranquil voice saying, "Care for a game of écarté, Augustatos?"

Augustatos mumbled an oath, which the ladies heard distinctly. Matilda Misirliu and Zoë smiled, and all the old ladies stirred in their dark corners. Colonel Rusesco quivered at the insult, but pretended to be the only one not to have heard it. Augustatos was too rich to quarrel with.

In the silence a distant murmur became audible. At first nobody paid much attention to it, although it was what they were all waiting for. Then M. Augustatos rose from his chair and walked unsteadily to the window. Clutching at the curtains with both hands, he looked out. Then he turned around, one arm still extended toward the window, and in a feeble voice said, "Well, they're here."

He sat down again. The armchair creaked. M. Augustatos buried his face in his hands and burst into tears. The others pressed toward the windows. Zoë Izvorano opened her mouth as if to cry out. The peasants were pouring down the three avenues that opened into the square, a swarm of dark, small figures who merged, scattered, and re-formed into groups. In the midst of each group flamed the scarlet splash of a flag.

The cordon of soldiers seemed taut, ready to break or disperse. The Procurator Pretorian and two officers paced up and down in front of it.

From the Administrative Building a group of officers emerged and walked toward the soldiers. Colonel Cilibia, commander of the garrison, was easily recognizable. He was advancing with his hands behind his back, his overcoat open, his enormous belly thrust out in front of him, his saber clanking against his boots. He seemed to roll like a great black ball. He exchanged a few words with the Procurator, then turned toward the soldiers. His fat, flushed face was clearly visible. The Colonel opened his mouth very wide, but the sounds issuing from this black hole were inaudible. However, it was not difficult to guess from the orator's pompous attitudes what he was saying. The file of soldiers shifted a little; probably they were giving the Colonel a cheer, but Cilibia looked dissatisfied; it was perhaps not rousing enough. He shouted something— it was easy to guess what that was: "Once again, lads!" This time the cheering was a little heartier. The soldiers were too few, however, to give a really satisfactory result. Cilibia, followed by several officers, turned toward the main gates of the Misirliu house. *They're coming here,* Matilda Misirliu thought. *All the better. We shall be defended.* But she scrutinized the too-thin line of gray uniforms with anxiety; she was almost certain that all was lost.

Cilibia could be heard coming noisily up the front steps, spurs and saber clanking. He entered the house, bellowing, "Reservists! What do you expect me to do with them? They leave me two companies of reservists and ask me to defend the city! It's crazy! My respects, madame . . ."

Mme Misirliu gave him her hand without moving from the window. The Colonel said crossly, "Can I ask for a cup of coffee myself, or will you order it?" His face had turned purple and he was sweating profusely.

"Ask for it yourself," Mme Misirliu muttered, turning back to the window. The uproar had increased. The pale faces of the peasants were distinguishable; their shouts of anger could be heard. A few of them broke away from the front rank and rushed at the soldiers, brandishing their axes and cudgels. Behind them, swarms of men ran forward, yelling. The Procurator, after waving his arms about, had retreated with the officers behind the line of soldiers. With a double, mechanical movement, the rifles swung up, bayonets flashing, and came to rest horizontally. A great cry rose from the crowd, swelled, and was suddenly rent by the sharp crackle of rifle fire. The surge forward halted abruptly. The crowd massed in front of the bayonets, then fell back step by step, leaving a clear, empty space before the soldiers.

At the sound of the shooting, Colonel Cilibia and the other officers rushed to the window, followed by M. Augustatos.

"They're shooting over their heads!" Cilibia shouted. "The swine are shooting over their heads!"

Augustatos groaned and seized Cilibia by the lapels of his gilt-buttoned gray overcoat.

"Traitor! What are you doing, drinking coffee up here? You're a soldier—defend us! That's what you're paid for. Go out into the street and order them to shoot straight into the crowd!"

Crimson in the face and uttering shrill, inarticulate cries, Cilibia struggled to break free from the landowner's short arms. The others separated them. Cilibia looked at Augustatos, who had collapsed into an armchair and was sobbing bitterly. The Colonel undid the collar of his greatcoat, saying, "Have you gone off your head?" Then he fumbled in his black tunic and drew out a large silver watch, whose case was engraved with a hunting scene. "They should be here at any moment now," he went on, "very soon. Let's keep our heads. If only those brutes of reservists hold out. . . . Radulesco! Go and tell them to fire into that mob!"

From outside a brief fusillade could be heard now and again, but no one fell on the gray cobbles. The multitude swayed and seethed in front of the line of soldiers, which was no longer as straight as it had been and was giving way in places. Cilibia ran to the French windows that opened on the balcony, wrenched them open, leaned over the rusty iron balustrade, and bawled at the top of his voice, "Shoot at them! Shoot into the thick of them!"

Suddenly a windowpane was shattered. Cilibia turned around: it was the French window. A moment later the pane of the other was starred. Cilibia retreated hastily into the drawing room. Everyone had drawn back from the windows. The Colonel took out his watch again, looked at the time, and muttered, "They ought to be here by now."

The ladies were weeping in stifled sobs. Mme Vorvoreano moved to the window, and keeping well in the shelter of the wall, glanced out. She was thinking triumphantly, *These men certainly won't have spared Eleonora's life.* At the same time she had an impulse to laugh, to laugh madly. Everything she had done had been in vain. The revolt was victorious. They were all irretrievably lost. She felt something pressing into her back: it was Cilibia's belly; he too wanted to see out, but dared do so only by peering over

Helen Vorvoreano's shoulder. He looked haggard and saliva was dribbling from the corner of his mouth. Mechanically he muttered, "They ought to be arriving now—at any moment."

"Who ought to be arriving?" Mme Vorvoreano asked.

Out on the square the soldiers were falling back in disorder, while the peasants advanced brandishing their axes and cudgels. An officer was running behind the soldiers, making for Mme Misirliu's house. He seemed to be wearing an odd headdress; it took Helen some time to realize that he was bareheaded, covered in blood, and that the blood was trickling down his face. Then she heard Cilibia's voice again. "They must come now! They can't delay any longer."

"Who can't delay any longer?"

"The Fourth Regiment of Red Hussars . . . I was informed an hour ago. They ought to be detraining in the station by now. . . ." He spoke as if in a dream.

"The Fourth Regiment of Hussars? Here? Today?"

Cilibia nodded, stunned. "This morning. But they'll be too late."

Thereupon Mme Vorvoreano began waiting impatiently. Hope revived. To herself she murmured, "Michael, my son, my little angel, come and save me, come and save your mother. . . ."

Michael, her son, was a lieutenant in this regiment, which everyone believed to be in Moldavia. But would it arrive in time to save his mother? Below the balcony Mme Vorvoreano saw a bareheaded officer in a black uniform running like an automaton. A gang of ragged youths were chasing him. Mme Vorvoreano recognized faces and clothes which she had seen before, in the gypsy quarter of the city. Yes, this was indeed the end.

It was at this moment that the Fourth Regiment of Red Hussars debouched from the station boulevard into the square. The horses advanced at walking pace, their coats gleaming, almost shoulder to shoulder. The men rode evenly in their saddles. Their gray cloaks were parted to reveal their red, befrogged tunics and white breeches. They bore their lances erect, and black and red fanions hung at the steel points. It was one of the crack regiments of the Rumanian Army, frequently admired when it rode down the Calea Victoriei in the King's presence, in the same perfect order as now.

The rebels broke and ran. The squadrons crossed the square and passed into the streets in pursuit of the fugitives, who were fleeing with cries of terror. Very soon the square was clear of all but a few officers on horseback and a score of dead and wounded, pierced by lances or trampled by the horses, who lay where they had fallen on the cobblestones. Near them, scattered on the ground, were the pitchforks and axes they had been brandishing at the moment when they had broken before the ranks of the cavalry.

8

The next day, having spent the night with the peasants of Reviga, Rizea, Marinica, Ouracou, and his son set off across the fields to Vladomira. Rizea's leg was paining him badly and he leaned with all his weight on Alexander's shoulder. Ouracou marched in silence, still carrying his ax under his heavy sheepskin-lined cloak. Marinica went forward briskly, his bare feet trampling the freshly plowed earth. The fugitives were uneasy and often looked to windward. The blue-gray shades of evening were beginning to darken the sky. Wild duck, on their way to roost on the waters of the Danube, passed overhead with a loud beat of wings.

Rizea talked on and on, at random yet always on the same subject, as if he were alone. The others listened and walked at his side without answering.

"We thought about it a great deal, brothers, but we didn't think right. That wasn't what we should have done. We should have taken the advice of those men at the station; they knew more about it than we did. We were wrong to think we were cleverer. When we saw our shadows on the wall we were surprised to see how big we were, but afterward we saw that it was not so, and now many among us will die at the boyars' hands."

"All the same, it was good," Ouracou said in his thick voice. "At least they've realized now that there's a limit to what we'll bear. And it isn't all over yet."

"No," Rizea agreed, "it isn't all over yet. In the autumn we'll try again, and this time we must talk with those who're going to be called up for their military service, so that what happened this time won't happen again. And if we don't succeed this autumn, then we'll try again next year at the same time. But sooner or later we must make an end. Do you understand, Alexander? Even though I or your father are no longer on this earth. . . . Do you understand?"

The youth nodded but said nothing. Rizea winced: his leg was very painful. "Listen carefully," he went on. "Those who go to the boyar to get money for denouncing the lads who took part in the rising, you must kill them by night and burn down their houses. And if anyone consents to work the boyars' land, you must set fire to his mills and barns."

"Good," Alexander said. "It shall be done. But why are you telling me this? Won't you be with us?"

Rizea walked on for a little while and then asked, "What about Iordake—is he still alive?"

Ouracou shook his head. "He was trampled by the horses."

"Poor Iordake," Rizea sighed, and was silent for a long time.

They were approaching the muddy and deserted main road. On their right extended a long forest. From over the horizon on all sides came the grumble of artillery, like a distant thunderstorm.

"I can't go any farther," Rizea groaned. "You go on. I'll stay here."

"I'll carry you on my back," Ouracou said.

"No, father Ion, waste no time over me. Leave me here in peace. You too, Alexander, go on your way. The more you delay, the greater your danger. You as well, Marinica."

Rizea sat down on the ground, moaned, and motioned to them to proceed. Ouracou and his son looked at him, hesitating.

"I'll stay with him," Marinica said. "You two go on home."

He squatted beside Rizea and rolled a cigarette. The others soon disappeared on the fringe of the forest.

Much later, Rizea made an effort to stand up, with Marinica helping him. Slowly they made their way toward the forest.

"The men of Dobrunu and the others who were there," Rizea said, "you led them to the city. You told them that the Queen had ordered it, didn't you? Nothing else would have done it. You told them all what you told us. . . ."

He laughed a great silent laugh, though from time to time his face was twisted by spasms of pain. "You didn't think of what might happen if the King was not dead. . . ."

"Yes, I did."

They came to the outskirts of the forest. Marinica thought he heard a sound of voices. "Be quiet—listen," he commanded. "Do you hear them?"

". . . but never fear," Rizea was saying, "a day will come when things will be righted . . ." He broke off to listen.

They lay face downward in the mud of a ditch, among the dead leaves and blackened grass of the previous autumn. They put cheek and ear close to the ground and heard the dull sound of heavy footsteps.

I wonder if Ouracou and his son have been able to escape, Rizea was thinking. *It's absolutely necessary that one of us survive to carry on. . . .* He looked at Marinica. Both listened in silence to the sound of innumerable footsteps which seemed to come simultaneously from the road, the fields, and the forest.

9

Mme Vorvoreano and her daughter took their seats in the carriage. Michael, on horseback and followed by a patrol of his Red Hussars, rode with them. It was a morning of bright sunshine.

Mme Vorvoreano did not speak on the journey. She did not even look out of the window. She was thinking, or trying to think, that her fears were ridiculous. Her sister could not possibly be alive. Elvira frequently looked hard at her mother, but she too held her tongue. As for Michael, cheerful and talkative at the outset of their journey, he also subsided rapidly into a morose silence.

When they drove through a village the children hid in the houses as soon as they saw the carriage and its cavalry escort. Doors and windows were closed. In the distance the muttering thunder of cannon could still be heard. Here, on the road, only its effects were to be seen: shelled houses and, at Vladomira, the shattered steeple of the church. On the way out of one village they passed a long file of peasants walking behind a coffin. A priest headed the procession.

Such men as were in the yards of their houses pretended to be very busy. They did not raise their heads, nor even glance at the carriage, its occupants, and the soldiers riding behind it. Michael Vorvoreano became very angry, saying, "The scum! Why don't they take off their caps?"

At Vladomira they found the charred ruins of the manor house. Such servants as had not fled had dug themselves a sort of shelter in the earth, where they could spend the summer. They had terrible tales to tell concerning the fate of M. Ivancea and M. Alexiu. Asked if they had news of Mme Eleonora, their eyes shifted uneasily and looked away, and they replied haltingly that they had heard she was dead. . . .

Mme Vorvoreano had to make a tremendous effort not to give vent to her relief. So all had come to pass just as she had foreseen! Henceforth she could be easy in her mind.

They went on to Vadastra. The land had not been plowed and all over its surface lay a sort of greenish mist: the grass was beginning to grow. At Vadastra they met another detachment of Red Hussars. Michael leaned from the saddle to question the corporal commanding the outpost. "Why aren't the people plowing?" he asked.

"At your orders, Lieutenant. They don't want to plow," the corporal said evenly, looking away. "After all, it's not their land," he added.

"What nonsense is this?" Michael said, his tone threatening. "What did you say?"

"They have nobody to make a contract with because the bailiffs around here are all dead, sir . . . and as for the lady, they can't make a contract with her either, because she's ill."

There was a moment's silence. Then a voice was heard to gasp from inside the carriage: "What lady?"

"I don't know, I haven't seen her. . . . The one who owns all this land. . . ."

Mme Vorvoreano leaned out of the window and looked hard at the corporal. "Ill, is she? You mean she's still alive?"

The man stared at her, wide-eyed with astonishment. "I can't say, lady. So I understand."

"Haven't you misunderstood? Isn't she dead?"

The corporal looked at her without answering.

"Drive on," Mme Vorvoreano said to the coachman. The carriage moved on. "But it's impossible!" Mme Vorvoreano muttered.

Elvira said not a word.

When she saw the burnt-out house, the deserted courtyard, and the charred skeletons of the barns, Mme Vorvoreano said in a low voice, "He must have misunderstood. . . . The man was a fool. . . ."

The fire had spared some rooms in the servants' quarters, but they were deserted. The two ladies got back into the carriage. Michael had gone on toward the village. They caught up with him in the deserted street outside the Town Hall. He had the village schoolmaster by the collar and was shaking the man furiously and shouting, "You're responsible for my aunt's death, you miserable wretch! Your job was to enlighten these people and keep their bad instincts in check. On your knees, you scum!" Holding the schoolmaster with one hand, he struck him in the face with the other.

The schoolmaster mumbled unintelligibly. Suddenly Michael's hand went to the holster of his revolver. He was white with rage and his fair, silky mustache quivered. The schoolmaster clasped his hands in an imploring gesture, ready to fall on his knees. Michael

Vorvoreano stepped back two paces so that he could take aim and
fire. But as he did so his saber caught in his spurs, and this gave the
schoolmaster time to cry, "It was I who saved Madame Eleonora. I
tell you I saved her life."

A patrol of cavalry passed them at the same moment. Four or
five long cords were fastened to each trooper's saddle, their other
ends lashed around the wrists of ragged peasants. The prisoners
seemed exhausted. All had several days' growth of beard and they
stumbled barefoot behind the horses, their hands swollen by the
cords. Mme Vorvoreano did not even glance at them. In a sharp,
authoritative voice she said, "What have you done? Michael, leave
the man alone. Come now, tell us what you've done."

The schoolmaster then told them that Eleonora had wandered
about the village all night long, and that, since she was ill, his wife
had taken her in and cared for her; she was still very feeble. . . .

The prisoners continued to pass along the village street, their
feet dragging in the mud. Mme Vorvoreano now looked at them
attentively. Then she turned back to the schoolmaster, studied him
for a moment, and at length asked, "She is seriously ill, isn't she?"

The schoolmaster was about to defend his honor as a nurse and
return an optimistic answer, but Mme Vorvoreano's icy look kept
him silent.

"Where is she now?"

"At home, in my house, madame. My wife is nursing her."

"Let us go there," Mme Vorvoreano said, her movements sur-
prisingly heavy and tired as she alighted from the carriage, using
both hands to hold her skirts clear of the mud.

In the hall at the entrance to his house the schoolmaster turned
to the two ladies and asked timidly, with a deep bow, "Do you
really wish to come in?"

Mme Vorvoreano pushed him aside and walked in, Elvira at
her heels. Michael remained by the door, avoiding the schoolmaster's
eyes.

The beamed ceiling of the room had not been whitewashed for
a long time. The plaster had been blackened by smoke and was
beginning to flake off. In one corner were several icons with a

bunch of basil hanging beneath them. The schoolmaster's wife, dressed in a gray skirt which reached to the ground and a blouse which exposed her thin arms, jumped up from the bed where she was sitting and stammered, "Good day, madame, good day, mademoiselle."

Eleonora was there, sitting on the bed, and the schoolmaster's wife was beside her, looking after her as one looks after a child and holding a grubby napkin in her hand which she had dropped when Mme Vorvoreano came into the room.

Eleonora was eating *mamaliga* cooked in milk. The schoolmaster's children, seated on three-legged stools, were also eating *mamaliga* with milk, their eyes fixed on the old woman, who was chumbling the porridge between her gums. The milk was trickling from the corners of her mouth in two rivulets which met under her chin and dripped back into the earthenware bowl. Eleonora was staring into vacancy. She was still wearing her dressing gown, but over it the schoolmaster's wife had put two old skirts and a threadbare velvet jacket. She had also tied a black kerchief around the old woman's head and washed her face with the corner of a towel dipped in water. Eleonora looked younger and at the same time very frail.

Mme Vorvoreano, having overcome her amazement, ran to her sister, crying loudly, "Eleonora! Dear little sister! My love!"

She hugged her and covered her with kisses, though trying as far as possible to kiss the kerchief rather than the old lady's face. Eleonora seemed so frail that she might have been made of straw, of small chicken bones, of some extremely brittle substance. Helen Vorvoreano felt as if she were going to faint; her heart missed a beat and she was seized with nausea. Holding her breath, she drew back from her sister, stood up, and stepped back. The bowl fell to the ground and broke. The old woman made as if to defend herself by raising her elbow; then, turning toward the schoolmaster's wife, she said in a grating voice, "Give me another plate. She's upset my food."

The schoolmaster's wife left the room. Mme Vorvoreano turned nervously toward the door by which she had gone out, then glanced quickly at Elvira. She was not sure whether her sister was refusing to recognize her, or was simply too far gone to do so. In a caressing voice she purred, "Little sister! Eleonora, don't you know me?"

Eleonora vouchsafed no answer. She was waiting with obvious impatience for the door to open, and when it did, and the schoolmaster's wife entered carrying a fresh bowl of *mamaliga,* her face lit up. While Eleonora was eating it greedily, Mme Vorvoreano asked the schoolmaster's wife in a low voice, "Doesn't she recognize people?"

"Oh yes, madame. She recognizes us."

Eleonora turned to look at Mme Vorvoreano and said, "I recognize you too." Then she went on eating. There was a suppressed giggle from the children. Mme Vorvoreano turned pale and requested the schoolmaster's wife to take the children away.

Distractedly, the woman shepherded her children into another room. When she made to return, Elvira barred her way, saying, "Leave us alone for a little."

Sitting beside the bed, Mme Vorvoreano addressed Eleonora. "You can have no idea what I suffered when I realized what was happening. You see, I knew nothing. I couldn't find out anything. How could I have known? Remember what you said yourself. You almost convinced us that the peasants wouldn't raise a finger. . . ."

"They respect me," Eleonora said.

"Of course they respect you. Everyone respects you. We too respect you—and we love you."

"What did you say?" Eleonora asked, gazing absently. "What was it you said?"

Mme Vorvoreano blushed and repeated, "I said that we respect and love you. Are you implying that it isn't true? Come now, you know perfectly well how much we love you."

"I know, I know," Eleonora said sleepily. "I know that very well, but I didn't understand what you were saying. Where's she gone? I want her now, at once!"

"Whom do you want, dear?" Mme Vorvoreano asked gently.

"Constantina. The woman who lives here."

"Oh, the schoolmaster's wife. I expect she's busy about the house, or out in the yard."

"She's always leaving me alone."

"But you're not alone, dear. You're with us. We shall stay with you always, just as we used to, and we'll tell you all about what's happening in town——"

"We'll play écarté," said Elvira, who was standing on the other side of the old woman. Eleonora promptly turned to face her and demanded, "Did you bring me my money?"

"What money, Aunt?" Elvira asked, suddenly stricken with fear.

"The money you owed me. You lost a great deal of money."

"Did I, Aunt? I no longer remember, but if you say so it must certainly be true."

"Exactly! I have a very good memory, you know. *I forget nothing.* I remember everything."

Mme Vorvoreano exchanged looks with her daughter and asked in a too-placid voice, "Then no doubt you remember the will?"

"What will?"

"The will you made. The will in which you wrote down to whom you were leaving your property, how you wanted it shared out among your heirs."

"I haven't the slightest idea what you're talking about. Not the slightest. Share out what? What property? I have nothing left. And if I had, whom should I give it to? You, perhaps. Why?"

Mme Vorvoreano smiled wryly. "Well, I *am* your sister. You have nobody else in the world. . . ."

Eleonora was not listening. In a hoarse voice she called, "Constantina!"

The schoolmaster's wife came in at once. "You called me, madame?"

"Yes, sit down here and tell me the end of that story, the one about your mother."

The schoolmaster's wife embarked on a long, involved story.

Eleonora listened attentively, and from time to time interrupted with a question. *A clever woman, this schoolmaster's wife,* Mme Vorvoreano was thinking. Elvira went to her mother and whispered, "Mama—do you see how this woman . . ."

Mme Vorvoreano nodded. She was thinking hard. Could Eleonora have made a will in favor of this woman who had saved her life?

"Mama—is she in her second childhood?" Elvira whispered.

Mme Vorvoreano answered under her breath, "Has it occurred to you that she may be making a fool of me?"

Eleonora was of age and mistress of her property. Nothing could be done to control her. Faced with her sister's madness—real or feigned, but probably feigned—Mme Vorvoreano felt powerless. The first thing to do was to get her away from this creature, covetous like all the lower orders, who was doing her best to win Eleonora's confidence. Mme Vorvoreano left the room and called her son. Michael entered, with a clatter of spurs and saber.

"Michael, send the soldiers to the village to see what they can find for your aunt: mattresses, straw, pillows. . . . Have them look everywhere—at the priest's, the mayor's, and the town clerk's. We want things in decent condition. And clean. We shall spend the night at the manor house. Your aunt really cannot stay in this wretched hovel any longer. If you could see the state the poor woman's in! Why are you gaping at me like an imbecile? Don't you understand? I suppose you're thinking that everything was burned down. Didn't you notice that some of the servants' rooms are intact? If they're without furniture, doors, or windows, the soldiers have only to board them up where necessary and bring whatever else is required. Tell them to start work. They're soldiers, aren't they? And don't waste any time arguing with the locals— let them give what they have. They weren't backward in helping themselves to what *they* wanted. Come now, hurry, it's getting dark."

She returned to the room, where Eleonora was shouting, "What do your children matter to me? You will kindly remain here and finish that story. Otherwise I shall be angry, and as you know, I'm not to be trifled with! You saw what happened to the wretches who tried to take my property away from me?"

The beginning of the last sentence was addressed to the schoolmaster's wife, but as she went on with it, Eleonora turned to Mme Vorvoreano. She did not look at her eyes, but at the level of her belt. "They have been properly punished," she went on. "They were bound with ropes and carried off to prison. And who knows what they have still to suffer? Did you see them? Do you know what happened to them?"

Mme Vorvoreano did not reply. She was terribly afraid that she might blush or otherwise manifest her feelings. *Oh God,* she prayed, *Oh God, do not desert me now, but give me the strength I need.* It was obviously necessary to get this madwoman away, or she would yet contrive to do her down. *If she wants to kill me by slow torture, let it at least be between ourselves.* Mme Vorvoreano made up her mind to speak.

"It is fortunate," she said, "that you fell among kind people here, who took you under their roof; but we must not inconvenience these good Samaritans longer than necessary. They have their work to do. You really cannot stay here a day longer. I shall take you into town with me, until we can put the manor house in order again. Meanwhile, as we cannot leave this evening, because it's late and the roads are dangerous—the rising has barely been put down yet—we will spend the night at the manor. I have given orders to repair whatever can be repaired, and you will sleep better there than here."

Eleonora's vacant stare seemed to imply that she had not understood a word. Perhaps she had not even been listening. Mme Vorvoreano was imprudent enough to press the matter. "Do you understand? We shall sleep at home tonight. At home. At the manor."

Eleonora blinked, and raising her voice, whimpered, "I don't want to see them, those thieving trollops. I don't want anything to do with them. They robbed me and went off without me."

Mme Vorvoreano looked at Elvira, and Elvira looked at Mme Vorvoreano. Then both of them turned to the schoolmaster's wife:

was she beginning to see daylight? Eleonora was mumbling, "Thieves! Disgusting creatures! Riffraff."

Mme Vorvoreano decided that the only thing to do was to pretend that she had not understood. In a trembling voice she asked her sister, "What thieves do you mean, dear? Have the servants stolen something?"

Motionless, her lips compressed, Eleonora seemed to hear nothing. She stared into space. Mme Vorvoreano left the room to hasten the fitting-up of the place where they were to spend the night alone with Eleonora.

Submissive as a child, Eleonora made no resistance to being taken to the manor. She had whimpered a little at leaving and cried for Constantina, but they had promised to send for her as soon as possible. In the servants' quarters at the manor the soldiers had lit a fire and nailed boards over the windows. Mattresses lay on the floor. The priest, the schoolmaster, and the well-to-do peasants, scared by the presence of the troops, had given the best they had.

Mme Vorvoreano lay on a bed of three mattresses piled on top of one another, her head sunk into pillows which were too soft. Stretched on her back in the darkness, her hands clasped under her head, she waited for sleep for several hours. Outside, an icy wind from the Danube had started to blow. The stacks of dry firewood piled near the house creaked. Lashed by the wind, the branches beat incessantly against the planks nailed over the windows. The embers in the fireplace collapsed with a faint rustle.

The red glow from the dying fire did not light the room, and although she had her eyes open Mme Vorvoreano could see nothing. However, she knew that Elvira lay on her left and Eleonora on her right, both, like herself, provided with a pile of mattresses and cushions smelling of basil and damp. Elvira's breathing was short and regular. Eleonora's was imperceptible. *She might almost be dead,* Mme Vorvoreano thought. Eleonora was much weakened and very feeble; she was a single flame, a mere flicker which could be extinguished between finger and thumb. *She might almost be dead.*

Mme Vorvoreano made three attempts to sleep, but each time she emerged from her torpor. She was bathed in sweat and felt as if she were stifling. The priest's pillows were too big and too soft. Elvira and Eleonora were sleeping deeply. How did they manage it? Elvira was young and in excellent health, and perhaps her pillow was a little harder. But Eleonora, whose breathing was imperceptible—might she not have been stifled by her own pillow? No, a person could not die like that. Not so easily. Eleonora might look frail, but she was still strong; she had eaten her *mamaliga* with an excellent appetite that afternoon. Ah, that afternoon . . . Mme Vorvoreano sighed. Was Eleonora really in her dotage? Or was she pretending? It was torture not to know where one stood. And that schoolmaster's wife, pretending to have noticed nothing, but so eagerly and greedily taking in all that happened. . . .

It was frightful, and yet there was nothing to be done about it. Even if Eleonora was out of her mind after what had happened, she was obviously recovering rapidly. Very soon she would start remembering too many things. *In that case I'm done for,* thought Mme Vorvoreano. *It will be the end. For me and for my children. Michael is an officer. What sort of officer will he be able to be once this story gets out? What will his brother officers think of him? He's capable of blowing his brains out. As for Elvira, her own conduct has already injured her quite enough; what will people say if, in addition, she is the daughter of a . . . Besides, it may well be that Eleonora has never been out of her mind at all. She's playing with me, and will keep it up for as long as it suits her, revealing what she really knows little by little, only to break me in the end, when she judges that the time has come. . . .*

Mme Vorvoreano tossed and turned on her bed. She was too hot. All these mattresses, all these blankets, all these pillows . . . The stove had been stoked too high.

"Elvira—are you asleep?" Mme Vorvoreano whispered.

No answer. Elvira's breathing was tranquil. Eleonora was very frail, despite her good appetite. Mme Vorvoreano, massive and powerful, could easily keep her still. By pressing down on her with knees and hands. In the morning it would be impossible to prove anything. Or would it be better to give the alarm in the middle of the night, to call out, wake Michael and the soldiers, say that Eleonora was ill and that they must get a doctor? No, better wait until the morning. But how pass the whole night, knowing she was there, beside her . . . ?

What time was it? Certainly very late, but there was no sign of dawn breaking. Elvira was still sleeping, her breathing deep and even.

Mme Vorvoreano rose, and standing in her bare feet, took hold of one of the priest's huge pillows. She groped, her fingers feeling gently in the darkness until at last they stopped at Eleonora's face. With a deft movement Mme Vorvoreano placed the pillow squarely over it, while with her other hand she held the head still. She pressed down with all her strength, with all her weight, controlling the jerking of the body struggling beneath the blankets until she could no longer feel the least twitch.

10

The barge, vast and vaulted, was like an enormous bell. A huge box of sheet iron, its interior was also reminiscent of a barn, a silo, even a church. High above the prisoners' heads was a small square opening. All around them, and away to the extremities of the vessel's hold, everything was pitch dark. But the sky was visible through the opening, and that morning it was a rich, deep blue. A sentry paced up and down the iron deck; his boots were hobnailed, his steps heavy, and the huge barge resounded like a bell—boom, boom, boom. . . . The sentry moved away, but the deep echo went on. Then he let the butt of his rifle strike the deck: bang. The blue of the sky quivered in the square opening. Down in the hold the light outlined in the hole was like a solid object with clear, sharp edges.

The barge was a quarter submerged. The men lay on bales of straw in the bottom of her hold; above their heads they could hear a ceaseless splashing of water. From time to time pieces of timber struck the hull, for the Danube was in spate and its tumultuous waters were uprooting trees along its banks. At other times the objects that struck against the iron plates of the hull were soft, their sound muffled and mysterious.

The straw was beginning to rot. The men were tortured by hunger. Their beards had grown. Their clothes were in rags. Their bodies were covered with bruises and sores. The faces of many among them seemed set in grimaces, with large bloodstains dried on their cheeks. Rizea, Marinica, and others from their neighborhood were there. Most of the time they said nothing, but watched the days come and go through the large square opening through which black, moldy bread was thrown to them. From time to time a jug of water was lowered by a cord.

Rizea talked more often than the others, in a completely calm voice. He was not resigned to defeat. Why had they not succeeded in accomplishing what they had hoped?

"But it's not over yet. We'll start again in the autumn."

"We shan't be there to start anything," said one of the men from Vladomira. "They've made up their minds to push us off to the next world, and you won't get them to think differently."

Rizea said nothing, but a little later he went on: "Still, we're not the only people in the world. There's no shortage of men. They may kill and kill and kill, and there'll still be plenty left, still a thousand times more than they are."

"Yes," the man from Vladomira objected, "but for one of theirs, they'll kill a thousand of ours."

Marinica wept and sighed, alone in a corner. Nobody asked him anything or said anything to him. "Brothers," he moaned, "brothers, what have I done? What a mess I've got you into. Because of me, your wrists are bound and you are dragged behind the soldiers' horses. Because of me, they are slaughtering you in the villages and on the roads. I am to blame. My folly has led you to destruction. My sin is very heavy." And he wept again.

Rizea clapped him on the shoulder. "Come, do you suppose it was your notions that made us start the revolution?"

Marinica did not answer.

"You can rest easy. You mustn't think we believed all those yarns of yours."

Marinica looked at him, glassy-eyed. He was much weakened; his face was shriveled like a monkey's. Rizea gave a short laugh. Looking at his crippled leg stretched out on the straw before him, he said, "That sort of yarn is all very well for those who need it. The whole thing was to know whether to make a start. Of course we had to make a start! So the reason, whatever it was, that set us off doesn't matter in the least. That's how it's got to begin. But this isn't how it ought to end. . . . Only this isn't the end."

Above their heads the barge resounded to heavy footsteps. It was the changing of the guard. Beside the opening a man appeared and came down the iron ladder that gave access to the hold. He could hardly stand and his lips were so swollen that what he said was unintelligible. Rizea recognized Mototolea and called to him. Mototolea sank down on the rotten straw and groaned: "Oh, my bones! . . . They've broken them. . . . I said to them, 'Kill me.' But they answered me, 'Be patient, we'll kill you later.' We were all tortured. They danced on our bodies, Rizea, as if they were floorboards, because of what Pîrvou did. . . ."

"What did Pîrvou do?"

"Hit a captain with his ax and split his head in two. He did it today and they've already shot him. Oh, my bones! Why must they go on knocking us about, since we're to be shot anyway? Savages! Damned boyars!"

All eyes were turned toward Mototolea. Somebody asked, "Who told you what they are going to do to us?"

Mototolea, exhausted, shook his head and explained: "Lower down, at Reviga, there's a barge like this one. Yesterday they emptied it."

Chins on chests, the men remained silent, except for one, who merely said, "Good."

Rizea did not seem to have heard. He asked Mototolea gently, "Do you know anything about Ouracou?"

"He escaped into the woods," Mototolea said. "He's all right."

"Ah, so he saved himself. And his son?"

"They say he was with the lads who went to burn the houses of the people who agreed to work the Prince's land, at Vladomira. . . . Nobody will work for the boyar now. The people won't go. If there are any who would be willing, they're afraid, and so they don't go either. . . ."

Rizea shook Marinica. "Do you hear?"

Marinica nodded.

"We did a good job, you see."

The sonorous clatter of the sentry's pacing stopped. The soldier, leaning on his rifle, stooped over the opening and called softly, "Hey, lads—are you down there?"

He was a redheaded youth with a likable face.

"We're here, all right!" said a voice from the depths of the hold.

"Where?" the soldier asked, peering into the darkness. When he made out the shapes, he took three packets of cigarettes from his pocket and threw them into the hold.

"Have you got matches down there?" A voice replied that they had.

"Don't worry, lads, in the autumn we'll put all this to rights. By then they won't find a single man to shoot at his brothers. In the autumn. You can rely on that. Can you hear me down there?"

"We heard," said a deep voice from the hold. "Next autumn."

The soldier straightened up and resumed pacing the deck, which rang hollowly—boom, boom, boom. Below, the prisoners began smoking. They passed the time listening to the swish of the water and the bumping of pieces of rotten wood against the hull, and looking up at the square of clear blue sky.

Then the soldiers came. With fixed bayonets they climbed down into the hold and ordered the prisoners up on deck. Passing close to them, Rizea could smell the reek of the plum brandy called *tzuica* on their breath and saw that their eyes were glittering and wild. He suddenly felt a profound sadness and a great peace. He climbed the ladder with difficulty because of his leg. A soldier struck him with the butt of his rifle and said, "Get along, there." He was drunk. The officer in charge was young and stiff and wore his black *képi* pushed to the back of his head. "Get a move on!" he shouted irritably.

Up on the deck of the barge, Rizea paused a moment to look out over the blue sweep of the Danube, the boats, the half-submerged willows as far as the eye could see, for in March the Danube rises and overflows its banks.

The prisoners went over the side into a large boat, the soldiers keeping their bayonets pointed at them. Nobody stirred or spoke. The two oarsmen were Bulgarians, who sang a slow, sad, incomprehensible chant. One of them, who had tears in his eyes, flung himself backward with a kind of fury as if he were trying to break his oars, and the veins in his neck were swollen. The officer shouted, "That will do! Shut up!" Frightened, the Bulgarians fell silent.

Rizea was impatient to see the land, to see fields again. As soon as they set foot ashore, their hands were tied behind their backs. Rizea let them tie him, his eyes seeking plowed earth. When they came to the road they had so often traveled before when the peasants' carts came in their hundreds to load the barges, Rizea looked attentively at the black earth. Between the clods of soil were tiny spearheads of bright green, and seeing them, he muttered to himself that all was well. The trees were budding. Birds were chirping in a small wood. Rizea breathed deeply, smiled, and turned to Marinica. Marinica smiled back. The corners of his lips were trembling. Behind them, the officer ordered, "Set off across the fields!"

Rizea led the way. He had some difficulty in walking over the broken ground, but he set a fair pace none the less. There were a score of them trudging after him across the fields, lifting their knees high at each step to pull their feet out of the black earth. The officer drew his pistol and made a sign to his men. The soldiers began to fire. The officer watched them, ready to empty his revolver into any man who disobeyed orders. Rizea was among the first to fall, at the same moment as Marinica, whose hand he was holding. The rifle shots were crisp and short, like nuts being cracked.

All the prisoners were down. The officer gave some orders. The soldiers fell in on the road and marched off the way they had come. One of them lingered: the fresh air had sobered him. Big drops of sweat broke out on his forehead and upper lip. He sat down on the ground. The officer turned toward him, but seeing him apparently relacing his boot, did not stop. The soldier took off the boot, and unrolled the puttee around his foot. Then he fitted his big toe to the trigger of his rifle and put the muzzle between his teeth. The officer started when he heard the shot and ducked instinctively. Then he returned, made sure that the man was dead, picked up the rifle, and hurried to resume his place at the head of the platoon moving off down the road.

I I

Following a letter from M. Hariton Augustatos to the Minister, the Prefect was relieved of his office. He was informed of his disgrace by telegram. The Prefect hastened to Bucharest to try to save his career from disaster. The *chef de cabinet* being a boyhood friend, he hoped by his intervention to recover the Minister's favor.

That evening the Prefect was deeply depressed, although his friend had invited him to the theater—with the obvious intention of excusing himself by this and similar civilities for not doing anything to help him. The play that night was *Le Marquis de Priola*, with the young Bulandra in the leading part. During the first act the audience's attention had been distracted by the arrival of latecomers. The flashing of opera glasses and an exchange of whispers greeted the arrival of politicians or famous beauties.

The lights came on in the house. The Prefect, a true provincial despite all his preoccupation, looked eagerly about him, admiring the ladies in evening dress making play with their black lace fans. Generals, all gold lace and decorations, the aides-de-camp crammed into the royal box which had been given over to them for the evening, and a sprinkling of young cavalry officers in red dolmans testified to the recently acquired importance of the Army. But evening dress predominated, frock coats, white waistcoats buttoned with difficulty over paunches swollen with political and financial importance. The people in the stalls surged like a tide toward the foyer, and the Prefect and his friend were left standing in the middle of a row of empty seats. Suddenly the *chef de cabinet* touched the Prefect's arm and said, "Look over there! Who on earth are they?"

In a box to the right of the stage were two ladies, one of them of mature years with fair hair turning gray, the other very dark and very young. The elder wore a black silk dress trimmed with lace. The girl was in dull red, her dress very discreetly *décolleté,* with black embroidery on the bodice and at the waist. The older woman was heavily bejeweled with large glittering emeralds set in rings and necklaces. The younger merely wore two splendid solitaire diamonds, one in each ear, and a third on her finger. The people in the neighboring boxes were talking to these ladies, while tail coats and uniforms crowded behind their chairs.

The Prefect recognized Mme and Mlle Vorvoreano. The former, with her thin lips and tight mouth, seemed to him much aged and faded. But Elvira had only changed for the better. Seeing his friend's admiration for the two women, the Prefect decided to recover some of his lost standing.

"Oh, I know them," he said casually. "They're the Vorvoreanos, mother and daughter. Madame Vorvoreano is a daughter of the late Lascar Lascari, the politician. I know them well; they lived in my prefecture with one of their relations who had a very large estate. They kept very much to themselves, but I was one of their intimate circle."

"They're carrying quite a packet of stones. You'd think they were a couple of jewelers' shop windows," the Prefect's friend said, with an envious glance toward the box.

"The jewels are antiques," the Prefect replied, trying to maintain his air of indifference. "Family jewels, you know."

"Would you introduce me?"

The Prefect hesitated for a moment, and then said, "Of course."

He made for the box with his heart in his mouth. He was recalling only too well the little altercation he had had at the manor not very long since. Had Mme Vorvoreano forgiven him for his outburst?

Arriving in front of the box, the Prefect bowed deeply. His friend, holding his monocle in his hand, did likewise. Mme Vorvoreano, who recognized the Prefect, gazed over his head into the auditorium, while Elvira, with a flash of diamonds, turned at the same moment to speak to one of the gentlemen in the box so that she too failed to see the two gentlemen who were bowing to her.

The Prefect, utterly disconcerted, turned in confusion to his friend, who, scarlet-faced, murmured, "They probably didn't recognize you without your uniform." And turning his back, he promptly left the theater. The Prefect remained frozen to the spot, unable to withdraw from below Mme Vorvoreano's box.

The auditorium filled up again; the visitors to the box took leave of the two ladies and returned to their seats. The lights went out. Paralyzed, his cheeks aflame, wishing the earth would open and swallow him, the Prefect heard Elvira's musical laugh ring out in the darkness.

"Why are you laughing?" Mme Vorvoreano asked her.

The curtain rose on the second act of *Le Marquis de Priola*. The noise in the house died down.

"I was remembering that night when you drove the horses to the station, Mama," Elvira said softly. "I had the jewel box on the seat beside me. Do you realize that I very nearly threw it out?"

Mme Vorvoreano did not answer. She was watching Bulandra through her opera glasses.

"I thought of throwing it out as we were crossing the bridge," Elvira whispered. "I very nearly threw it into the water, you know. And then, little mother, that night at the manor . . ."

"Yes?"

"I was not asleep."

A moment passed. On the stage Bulandra was speaking, romantic and appealing. In a low voice Mme Vorvoreano said, "Be quiet. Pay attention to the play. . . ."

The Prefect had listened to their conversation without understanding a word. He turned to take one more look at the two women whose jewels gleamed in the shadows of the box. Under his breath and between clenched teeth he cursed them roundly in good, sound Rumanian. Then he made his way to the exit, quite unremarked.

5701 Grove Ave

12 . 18
12 - 28
1 - 4
1- 18
2 - 1
2 - 19